THE
BURDEN
OF
TRUTH

BOOKS BY NEAL GRIFFIN

Benefit of the Doubt

A Voice from the Field

By His Own Hand

The Burden of Truth

THE
BURDEN
OF
TRUTH

NEAL GRIFFIN

A TOM DOHERTY ASSOCIATES BOOK
NEW YORK

For Eli

THE BURDEN OF TRUTH

Copyright © 2020 by Neal Griffin

A Forge Book
Published by Tom Doherty Associates
120 Broadway
New York, NY 10271

www.tor-forge.com

Forge® is a registered trademark of Macmillan Publishing Group, LLC.

The Library of Congress Cataloging-in-Publication Data is available upon request.

ISBN 978-0-7653-9562-7 (hardcover)
ISBN 978-0-7653-9563-4 (ebook)

Our books may be purchased in bulk for promotional, educational, or business use. Please contact your local bookseller or the Macmillan Corporate and Premium Sales Department at 1-800-221-7945, extension 5442, or by email at MacmillanSpecialMarkets@macmillan.com.

First Edition: May 2020

Printed in the United States of America

0 9 8 7 6 5 4 3 2 1

Violence is the most elemental truth of life.

JAMES CARLOS BLAKE

PROLOGUE

SATURDAY, 7:00 A.M.; VISTA, CALIFORNIA

He woke to a timid knock on the bathroom door, followed by Sofia's whispered voice.

"Omar? You still in there?"

Lying balled up on the cold tile floor, his head throbbed, but nowhere near as bad as his ankle, where the pain went bone deep. Muddled images flashed across his mind in a terrifying haze. Leftovers from a nightmare? Had to be. It couldn't be real. He didn't want to believe it, but when he ran his fingers across his scalp, his dread was confirmed by the moistness of blood.

Oh God, no. Please no.

She knocked again, her voice quicker in its urgency.

"Omar? Answer me. Are you okay?"

He struggled to his feet, keeping most of his weight on his one good foot. He leaned against the door, eyes closed. With the back of his hand, he wiped at the thick spit that had pooled on his chin. He rolled out the stiffness in his neck and shoulders, grabbed the door handle, and pulled. His younger sister, still in her nightgown, stood in the doorway, and he sensed her uncertain relief at the sight of him.

"Omar, I heard noises outside. I—"

An explosion of splintering wood and shattering glass came from the living room. The entire apartment shifted and the floor shook with the intensity of a California tremor worth paying attention to. Sofia screamed and dropped to her knees, hands over her ears. Enraged voices of angry men filled the air along with clouds of dust and smoke.

"Sheriff's department! Get on the ground! Sheriff's department! Get on the ground!"

From just inside the bathroom, Omar watched a helmeted green swarm descend on Sofia as she cowered on the floor. Omar stepped in front of her and faced the leader, whose armor-clad body clogged the narrow hallway, his wide-open eyes shielded behind protective goggles. More men followed, all of them yelling.

"Get on the ground! Get on the ground!"

Omar put his open hands in the air as a sign of surrender, keeping his gaze fixed on the lead man's finger as it squeezed against the trigger of a strange-looking gun with a bore the size of a gaping mouth. A sledgehammer blow to the center of Omar's chest sent the teenager reeling backward. Dazed and flat on his back, Omar attempted to stand, but before he could even begin to gather himself, another man took up a position straddling his body. From directly above, this man pointed yet another gun at Omar—a bright yellow pistol that looked like a toy. A *snap* and a *pop*, like a cheap firecracker, was followed by a strong piercing sensation in his chest and stomach. A crackling current seized his body, and every molecule of his flesh convulsed uncontrollably. Minutes seemed to pass before the shuddering eased. He went limp.

"Omar!" Sofia screamed, as men dragged her prone body down the hall. "What's happening? Omar, help me!"

"Let her go!" he tried to shout, but his voice was weak. Again, he tried to push off the floor, but his strength was gone. "She didn't do nothing."

What felt like a dozen gloved hands flipped him over onto his stomach. The heavy weight of a man's knee came down on the back of his neck, pinning his face against the carpet. Omar's arms were jerked behind his back and cold metal slapped against both wrists.

Trapped facedown and surrounded, Omar felt panic take hold as he struggled to breathe. With a desperate effort, he turned his face sideways and sucked in a breath of musty air that smelled of the sweat of the cops and the metal of their guns. From ground level, he watched men in green armor funnel into the bedroom. Seconds later, they re-emerged with Hector in tow, underwear low on the boy's hips and a T-shirt twisted awkwardly around his neck. With a man pulling on each arm, his brother stumbled past, his face contorted in confusion and terror. Their mother followed behind, looking tiny in the shadow of the man guiding her by one arm. Omar, still sprawled in the hallway, heard her crying and chanting to God.

The weight lifted from his neck. An instant later, a pair of cops grabbed Omar by his handcuffed arms and yanked him to his feet. His injured ankle exploded in pain and he screamed as his leg gave way. The men let him fall, then hauled him up again, rougher than before. This time, Omar willed himself to stay on his feet.

"Whatta ya say, Seso?" Detective Murphy stood in front of Omar, in the same black uniform he'd been wearing the day before.

Murphy looked around at the SWAT cops and pointed to the black, two-inch-square box mounted on his own chest. "We good?"

One of the green crew gave a thumbs-up and spoke, his voice muffled behind a black mask. "Runnin' silent, Murph."

Murphy raised his pistol, pushing the barrel hard against Omar's chest. He leaned in close and practically snarled in Omar's ear, "Man up, boy. Give me a reason to end this shit right now."

Omar ignored the threat. "Just leave my family alone. They haven't done anything."

"They haven't, huh?" Murphy said, staying in close. "Sounds kinda like admitting you have."

Holstering his gun, the detective keyed his radio mic. "Station A, show us code four on suspect location. S-1 in custody. Family detained. You can have your air back." He grabbed Omar's arm. "Come on, Seso. Time to get famous."

Omar winced. The skin around his ankle felt hot and stretched. His foot was like a chunk of wood.

"I can't walk."

"The hell you say. You're walking the gauntlet, homie." Murphy motioned to another cop. "Stevens, grab his other arm. Let's get him over to the front door."

The men shoved Omar down the hall and into the living room, where his mother, brother, and sister clung to one another on the couch. All three were crying. Two more masked men, both with machine guns slung around their necks, stood behind them.

Staring wide-eyed at Omar, his mother sobbed out, "Hijo, que—"

One of the men leaned over the couch and shouted, "Whatta I just tell you? No ha-blo!"

His head was barely two inches from hers; the words struck with the force of a blow. Her shoulders hunched and she covered her face with her hands.

Furious at the way the cops were treating his mother, Omar yelled, "You don't need to be like that." Spit flew from his mouth. His eyes blazed with hate. "I told you, she hasn't done anything."

Murphy lifted the cuffs, pulling Omar's arms into a painful position and pinning him against the wall. At the tearing sound of Velcro, Omar turned his head in time to see Murphy pull a phone from a pouch on his vest.

"Okay. We're walking him out. Down the stairs, out to the sidewalk, to the patrol car. Make sure they get plenty of video. And I want some good stills."

The detective jerked Omar off the wall and stood him up straight. "Here we go, Seso. Do your best badass for me, alright?"

With another cop's help, Murphy half pushed, half dragged Omar through the hanging shreds of particleboard and splintered two-by-fours that, minutes earlier, had been the apartment's front door. Omar drew a breath—the moist air was cool on his skin and a momentary relief from the smoke inside. As Omar hobbled down the three flights of stairs, the cops doing little to help him, he heard a commotion building below. When he stepped off the last stair, an eruption of both steady and flashing lights hit him like yet another electric shock. Large cameras mounted on tripods lined both edges of the sidewalk. Several microphones were thrust in Omar's direction, and what seemed like a dozen voices fired questions at him.

"Tell us why you did it."

"Why did you kill him?"

Omar stumbled forward. The pain that racked his body, the pounding in his skull, and the slow realization of his circumstances converged in a tight ball of nausea. His stomach heaved, his throat burned, and his mouth filled with bile. Pressing his lips together, he tried to swallow, but rancid liquid escaped his mouth and ran down his shirt. He lowered his face in shame, but Murphy yanked his head back. The flash of the cameras fired faster. Again, anger and rage boiled over; Omar shouted and tried to pull away.

"Let me go, Murphy!"

The reporters moved in closer. Basking in the attention, the two cops seemed to slow down, prolonging their time in the bright lights of the cameras. At the curb, a sheriff's black and white idled with the rear door open. Murphy pushed Omar into the caged backseat. Without bothering with the seat belt, he shouted to the driver through the thick wire mesh.

"Omar Ortega. He's eighteen, so no kiddie-jail bullshit. His ass goes to adult lockup. Straight to the station. Strip his property. An evidence tech is coming up from Ridgehaven to process him. After that, stick him in a cell. No visitors. No phone calls. No contact. You got all that?"

"Yeah. Got it."

The door slammed shut and the car pulled away. Omar watched a few of the younger cameramen run alongside for a few moments, then fall behind and out of view. Turning to look ahead, Omar stared into the rear-view mirror and, for a moment, locked eyes with the driver.

White. Blond. Blue-eyed.

"Hey." The haze cleared. "You're that cop. The one from yesterday."

The man's voice was as corrosive as acid, his hatred cutting through the metal mesh.

"Yeah, I am. And you're that *cop killer* from last night."

The words hung in the air, like a noose ready to be slipped over Omar's head.

The patrol car sped up. Omar looked through the caged window, the familiar streets of the barrio passing by in a blur. Captured. Defeated. He lost himself in thoughts of what had brought him to this moment, as well as the nightmare that still lay ahead.

PART ONE

BEFORE

1

Run.

His eyes blinked open and went to work like two rescue searchlights, scanning for threats. Just as it had been every morning for going on four years now, his first waking thought was to get away. Get gone before it was too late. *The hell with everyone else*, he thought. *Just run.*

No. Not ever. Omar Ortega was never going to be that guy.

The stifling heat of the previous day still lingered, transforming the eight-by-eight room into a cocoon, incubating the three damp adolescent bodies. Omar's little brother, Hector, was pressed against him on the twin mattress, snoring lightly, his mouth hanging open like a flytrap. Omar grabbed the metal bar just above his head and vaulted over the thirteen-year-old boy with ease. He landed in the middle of the room, which was cluttered with a mishmash of cheap furniture he and his mother had saved from the roadside, dumped there by a prick of a landlord after his most recent eviction.

He looked to the corner of the room, not surprised by what he saw: small cot neatly made, crucifix and rosary beads left on the pillow. He hadn't heard her leave, but he knew she was already on the bus headed to Rancho Santa Fe. There, she'd make breakfast, pack lunches. Hustle her employers and their children off to work and school, then spend the day cleaning their home and scrubbing their toilets. He fought against jealousy and bitterness, knowing it damn sure wasn't her fault.

Omar hoisted himself up to look at the top bunk, where his sixteen-year-old sister, Sofia, still slept. He gently brushed the long strands of damp black hair from her cheeks, then kissed her lightly on the forehead. He was filled with his usual combination of love, fear, and dread, but, more than anything, he felt a determination to keep her safe from the almost daily threats of the California barrio.

"Buenos dias, mija." Her eyes fluttered open as he whispered in her ear. She hunched her shoulders and settled farther into her pillow, smiling at the sound of his voice. "Time to get up."

Dropping back to the floor, Omar looked out the pane of dull glass to the low-slung rooftops, a dark tapestry woven in a hundred shades of black and gray. Tar-covered power poles jutted out from the ground, staring back at him like an army of defiant middle fingers. Dozens of cables crisscrossed the air in the haphazard pattern of a botched afterthought. Off in the distance, barely visible dots of pink stucco shimmered on the hills of San Marcos. Seven miles, he thought. Might as well be seven hundred. Seven light-years. Like faraway planets at the end of a telescope.

Omar allowed himself a grim smile of satisfaction. *Not so far anymore.*

He turned away from the window and checked himself out in the mirror. His skin, deep brown from months of outdoor labor, stood in contrast to the white boxer shorts he slept in. He flexed, proud of the ten pounds of muscle he'd gained in the past six months. His body lean and toned. Stomach flat and well-defined, arms sculpted—to his own eyes, he looked like a welterweight. Pushing aside a pile of his brother's dirty clothes with his foot, Omar dropped to the threadbare carpet and began his morning routine of a hundred push-ups. The first thirty took less than thirty seconds and his chest bounced off the floor with each repetition.

Thirty-one, thirty-two, thirty-three . . .

His excitement for the coming days fueled him. The past three years had been tough, but now it was official. Come next week, he'd be the first Ortega to ever graduate high school. And he wasn't just dragging himself across the finish line. Hell no. Straight A's since ninth grade and top of the honor roll.

Forty-one, forty-two, forty-three . . .

He glanced at his preenlistment certificate, tacked to the dingy, yellowed paint near the bed. The army recruiter had made it clear: turn eighteen, finish high school, and you're in. To celebrate his birthday last month, his mom had made him a cake decorated with toy soldiers. He locked his elbows in the up position, feeling strong. A moment of rest, then he kept going.

Sixty-one, sixty-two, sixty-three . . .

Omar pictured himself graduating from basic training. His mother would want to be there, but how? A cross-country trip to Fort Sill, Oklahoma, meant money for a bus ticket, food, hotels. All sorts of things that multiplied the possibility of a run-in with a state trooper or some other inquiring asshole of a cop. Or worst of all, a Border Patrol checkpoint tossed up across some random highway. No. The expense and risks were too high. She couldn't come. But there would be a day when Omar returned to her in his dress green uniform, an army insignia on his shoulder.

Seventy-six, seventy-seven, seventy-eight . . .

The soldier with the close-cropped hair and chiseled face hadn't just walked through the galleria. He strutted, like he owned it, everyone stepping aside, reaching out to clap him on the back. Like his brown skin didn't matter a bit. All that baggage just washed away. All people saw was that he was dressed in green. Omar had only been five years old that day, but he knew. Even then, he *knew* he'd be that man. He'd wear that uniform. People would step aside and let him pass. That night, he'd told his father, and the man's face had lit up. The voice, still so clear it rang out in Omar's memory.

"Un soldado? Aye, hijo. That would be a very proud thing."

Ninety-eight, ninety-nine, one hundred.

Omar went low one last time, pushed off the floor, and jumped back to his feet. He shook out his arms and shadowboxed like Ruben Olivares, whom his dad had always said was, pound for pound, the best fighter to ever come out of Mexico.

He lifted his pillow and picked up his one pair of Levi's, carefully folded and placed there the night before. He slipped them on, then slid his hand into the pocket, unable to resist the desire to have a look. Two neatly folded, hard-earned hundred-dollar bills. His off-the-books pay from a week of heavy lifting at a construction site. Today, after school, he'd go to the bank and deposit the cash and that would do it. Two thousand seven hundred fifty bucks. Hundreds of hours of backbreaking labor. Months of saving. But finally he could cover the security deposit and first month's rent. A three-bedroom house in a safe San Marcos neighborhood, a world away from the Vista barrio. They could put the last three years behind them like some kind of bad dream.

Shaking off the dark thoughts, Omar told himself he had it all worked out. The army would provide a roof over his head and plenty to eat, which was all he needed. His paycheck would go directly to his mother. It wouldn't be much, not even two grand a month, but it would cover the rent and take the edge off groceries. Once he finished basic training, he'd find part-time work near his army base. He'd clerk at a convenience store or work the counter at a fast-food place. He heard lots of soldiers did that. In the meantime, his family would be safe.

He pulled his number 84 Dodgers jersey from the closet. Seventy-eight bucks. A crazy extravagance, but he'd been caught up in the moment during a field trip to Chavez Ravine. From a seat in the bleachers, he'd watched twenty-three-year-old Mexican phenom Julio Urias four-hit the Astros. A poor kid from Mexico, just a few years older than Omar, Urias could throw a baseball ninety-eight miles an hour into a ten-inch square. Urias had used his skills to bust out, and Omar couldn't help but feel a sense of kinship. He might not have the ballplayer's arm, but he was no less determined.

Bending down, he scooped up a pair of dirty chonies and threw them at his brother's head. "Get up, Hector. Get out so your sister can get dressed."

Once his brother was moving, Omar poked his head out the bedroom door. The coast was clear. He'd made a game out of avoiding contact, like a Special Forces fighter trapped in enemy territory. He moved down the short hallway without a sound and locked himself in the bathroom.

After splashing cold water on his face, he rubbed wet hands across the stubble of hair, liking the low maintenance of his new look. He'd shaved his head a week ago, getting rid of his thick, collar-length black mane. When his mom had walked in and seen his shorn head and the clumps of hair on the floor, she'd crossed herself and brought her hand to her mouth. "Porque, hijo? Tu no eres chollo."

He had laughed in agreement. "You're right, Ma. I'm not a chollo."

He told her the army cut off everyone's hair, so he was just planning ahead. She raised her hands in the air with relief and took hold of his face, pulling him down to kiss each cheek.

The drone of a Mexican telenovela came from the living room. He peered into the room, dimly lit by the glow of the television. The back of the man's massive head, clouded in cigarette smoke, poked up over the blue Naugahyde couch that dominated the small room. A nearly empty bottle of Fireball tequila sat on a crusty wooden end table next to an over-flowing ashtray and half a bag of pork rinds. Omar had walked in on his mom cleaning the room a few days after they had moved in. He'd been angry about it, telling her the man's filth was his own problem.

Omar slipped into the kitchen and poured himself a small bowl of corn-flakes, careful to leave enough for his brother and sister. He opened the refrigerator. Plenty of beer. A soggy 7-Eleven Big Gulp, half full of some-thing, on top of a pizza box. He bent down to look all the way to the back.

"Shit." He stood up and slammed the door.

"What's your problem, pendejo?"

The man stood swaying in the doorway, holding a coffee cup that no doubt came with a little pick-me-up way beyond caffeine. His thick, gray-ing mustache was damp with drink and peppered with crumbs from last night's dinner. The gap between his stained boxers and his wife-beater T-shirt left the six roundest inches of his hairy stomach exposed. He wore a dirty robe that hung open in the front, giving him the look of a wandering mental patient.

A fortysomething unemployable alcoholic, Edgar Renteria was a day laborer who had worked off and on for Omar's dad before all the trou-ble started. A few months ago, when he'd heard about the Ortegas falling on hard times, Renteria came along, passing himself off as some sort of guardian angel and wannabe father figure. He'd offered the Ortega family a room—in exchange for half the rent on the whole apartment. At first, Omar's mother had said no thanks. But eventually, out of desperation, they moved in.

Of course, the man was a fraud. A drunk. A goddamn desviado. Omar loved his mother, but he wished she understood. They could make it on their own. They sure as hell didn't need another man around. That was Omar's role now.

Omar stared at Renteria, his eyes and voice full of contempt. "There's no milk."

"So tell your mother to go shopping." Renteria worked to set his feet at a forty-five-degree angle, doing his best to post up. He used two fingers to pull his cigarette from his mouth and extended it toward Omar with a gangster's tilt. "Don't be slamming shit around in my house."

"It ain't a house. It's a shithole apartment. And how can she go shopping? You spend all her money on booze and beer."

The man moved closer but gave a quick look of reluctance when Omar took a step in as well.

"I let your ma move in here 'cuz she was getting thrown out in the street. What's your punk ass ever done to keep a roof over her head?"

Omar considered telling the old man of his well-laid plans. Renteria knew all about Omar's upcoming departure for basic training; that was common knowledge. But he didn't know about the escape plan; that was a jealously guarded secret known only to Omar and his mother. If Renteria or any of the homies from the neighborhood knew of it, there'd be trouble. To Renteria, it would be a loss of income. To others, an act of disloyalty. Omar needed to keep it quiet for a few more days, but he couldn't resist a chance to say what he knew to be true.

"She works three jobs while you sit around and get drunk all day. We'd be better off on our own."

"Watch your mouth, flaco. Mommy ain't here to protect you."

Unimpressed, Omar turned his back on a man he saw as no physical threat. He poured the cereal back in the box and pulled an overripe banana from a blackened bunch on the counter. He took a bite and stared out the window. Maybe when they walked out for the last time, he'd drive his fist into Renteria's bulbous nose. He imagined the release of all that anger. He could practically feel the spongy flesh collapsing under the force of his punch. See the spray of blood and the red smeared on the man's bloated face as he crumpled to the floor. A little going-away present from the Ortega family. Omar was pretty sure his father would have approved.

Renteria's voice got his attention. "I'll give your sister a ride to school. You and your brother get going."

"Ah, hell no. She's taking the bus with me."

"I said I'd take her. Now mind your business and get moving."

Omar closed the distance to less than a foot. He and Renteria were the same height, so he could look him straight in the eye. The man was a hundred pounds heavier, but all of it hair, grease, and fat.

"She is my business and you're not taking her anywhere. She'll ride the bus with me."

Renteria stared back, glassy-eyed. Omar knew the man would fold. When it came to protecting his sister, there was no question how far Omar would go.

"I'm thinking it'll be good when you're gone, soldier boy." The words were slurred by the booze, along with the heavy accent of the barrio. "Two roosters, one henhouse. Ain't working out, eh? One too many *cocks*."

Before Omar could respond, his brother and sister walked in. In these last days of the school year, neither carried books or even a backpack. Hector, slouching, hands buried in his pockets, wore a blue Easton baseball cap with a board-stiff bill on top of his greased-back hair. His untucked but crisp white T-shirt was three sizes too big, and his khaki Dickies sagged low on his hips. Omar looked down at the boy's knockoff Vans with bright blue laces and shook his head. He knew Hector was just playing the part of fool wannabe, but it still aggravated the shit out of him.

Sofia wore jeans and the pink blouse he had bought for her at Macy's at the beginning of the school year. It was the only item of clothing she had left that didn't come from a secondhand store. Her eyes searched Omar's, as always looking for direction.

Omar pushed past Renteria, taking another bite out of the soft banana before he dropped it in the trash. "Both of you come on. We'll stop by Mickey D's. We can catch the bus from there."

"You got money?" the old man said, his voice louder and anxious.

"Yeah. My money."

"Then you buy the fucking milk."

Omar steered his brother and sister out of the kitchen as the man yelled behind them, stepping out into the stairwell to continue his drunken rant.

"Go on, soldier boy. I want you *out*. One too many cocks."

On the sidewalk, Omar nudged his brother to walk ahead and threw a casual arm around his sister's shoulder. He pulled her close, feeling a quiver like that of a tiny bird. It pained him that, these days, Sofia lived in a constant state of fear and uncertainty. And Hector was so desperate for acceptance he'd do near anything just to feel a sense of belonging. Then there was his mother. Sixty hours a week at three jobs so they could rent a room and eat. And all of it had been completely, one hundred percent avoidable.

What was it the homies say? *Mi vida loca.* Man, they got no idea.

Omar shook it off, knowing all that self-pity bullshit didn't change a thing. Yeah, no doubt. The last few years had been hard on all of them, but things were about to change. Everything was set. The time had come. The Ortegas were getting the hell out.

2

0715 HOURS

The intruding sounds trespassed into the haze of his exhaustion, like the slow and steady *tap, tap, tap* of a ball-peen hammer inside his skull.

"I didn't wear it yesterday." Always with the belligerence. When had that started? "I wore it two days ago."

"Then you took it out of the hamper and that's why it stinks." The woman made little effort to disguise her barely controlled tension. "Wear something else."

"I'll be late," the boy said.

"Well, you won't stink," she replied.

"I can't believe you said I stink!" the boy screamed back.

"I don't mean *you* stink, Tyler. Your shirt stinks. Now change it." Her new tone indicated the argument was over, and the slam of a door confirmed it. The sudden silence was deafening but the damage was done. Travis Jackson was wide awake.

A couple of guys from work had been telling him to set up a sleep room. Dark. Cool. No windows. Some kind of white noise. A walk-in closet with a cot works great. It was the only way to survive night watch. Late radio calls, impounding evidence, downloading the body cam, and printing out reports almost always turned a ten-hour shift into something closer to twelve. On top of that was his forty-five-minute commute to Riverside County.

Yeah, right. Wall myself off in a closet. She'd love that.

Travis stared up at the popcorn ceiling. After four hours of restless sleep, he lay sprawled across the bed, his legs twisted in sheets that felt straight out of the dryer. His T-shirt was soaked with sweat, mostly because he hadn't changed after last night's shift. Why bother? Seven fifteen in the morning and the temperature was already pushing ninety degrees. The oscillating fan blew hot air across the small room and kicked up an arid red dust, a not-so-subtle reminder of something that all the strip malls, golf courses, and thousands of houses with postage stamp yards couldn't refute: he'd moved his family to live in a desert.

After graduating from the San Diego Sheriff's Academy, Travis got lucky and pulled an assignment to the city of Vista. It was the closest sheriff's substation to the home he and Molly, along with their four children, rented in the Riverside County community of Temecula—using "community" in the loosest sense of the word. It was more like a sprawling contagion of stucco and red tile, infested almost entirely by San Diego– and Los Angeles–area commuters. During the week the place emptied out like an Old West ghost town, only to be refilled on weekends with mostly conservative, white, middle-age residents who constantly grumbled about California's progressive politics, sky-high gas prices, and, most passionately, the long lines at the Claim Jumper restaurant. And of course, Travis thought, everybody complains about the heat. Because who would've ever thought it could get so hot in a desert?

"All right, that's it." Molly was practically yelling now, and the slam of the refrigerator door told Travis the stakes had somehow been raised. "If you need me to find you some proper school clothes, Tyler Henry Jackson, I will do it."

"You told me to change." The boy sounded damn near possessed. "*Well, I changed!*"

There was no more ignoring it. Travis threw back the sheets and pulled himself out of bed. He made his way to the kitchen, where Molly stood with her fists on her hips, blocking the path to the door. Tyler, their teenage son, wore a pair of baggy athletic shorts that went down past his knees, topped with an oversize Milwaukee Bucks tank top. On his feet were tennis shoes with the laces pulled out. No socks.

"Damn, Mom. What's your problem? It's gonna be like a thousand degrees today."

Molly ignored her son and keyed in on Travis. "Did you hear that? 'Damn, Mom'? I've had it. You deal with him."

Tyler spun around, shoulders slouched, his long dark bangs hanging over his eyes. "Dad, would you talk to her? It's fricking high school. It's the last week. Believe me, nobody cares what I wear."

Molly stared back at her husband, signaling he'd better choose carefully. His next words would come with consequences.

"You heard your mother, Tyler. Go change."

"Ah, screw that." The boy managed to squeeze past his mom. "If I've got to go to this effed-up school, I can pick my own clothes."

As Tyler headed for the door, his mother grabbed him by the arm. "You wait just one minute, young man. You are not—"

"Let me go!"

Tyler shook loose, shooting his dad a parting glance over one shoulder. Travis saw the anger. The look of rebellion, like he was daring his father to say something. Then he was gone, slamming the door behind him.

"Are you kidding me?" She threw out one arm and pointed dramatically in the direction of their escaping son. Travis recognized that her disdain for him was a definite step up from what she had directed at the back-talking teenager. "That's it? You're just going to let him go?"

"Come on, Molly. His clothes? Really? He's right. They're down to the last couple of days, not to mention the kid is practically eighteen years old. Don't you think we ought to . . . I don't know. Pick our battles?"

Molly blew out a long, shaky breath and closed her eyes. She leaned her head back and called out in a voice that was gentle and kind. Obviously, she wasn't talking to him. "All right, you two. Turn off the TV. Let's get going."

Nicole and Hannah walked obediently into the kitchen. Hannah, the oblivious preschooler, wore a checkered dress, white tights, and black patent leather shoes. She ran to Travis, her heels clicking lightly against the tile, and hugged his legs.

"Daddy! Did you wake up to kiss me good-bye?"

Travis lifted the four-year-old high in the air and said, "That's exactly why I woke up."

He kissed his daughter on the neck until she giggled and squirmed and told him to stop. He turned to Nicole, a seventh grader, who was much more serious and had no doubt heard the argument between her parents and brother. Nicole had always been close to Tyler, but lately that relationship was being tested.

"Hey, Nicki. All set for the last week of school?"

"Hi, Daddy."

Travis didn't miss the fact that she avoided the question. As a middle schooler, Nicole's experience of being the new kid had been every bit as difficult as Tyler's in high school. It had surprised Travis and Molly that Nicole had been much more capable than her older brother in dealing with the stressful transition.

"Where's Brandon?" Travis asked, realizing the living room was empty.

"I'm letting him sleep in," Molly said, and Travis picked up on her lingering anger, even a bit of disgust. "He's got a molar coming in. Had a rough night. I'll be back in a half hour."

"I've got court. What if you get stuck in traffic?"

"You *cannot* be serious." If Molly were anything other than a well-mannered Midwestern girl, he knew her choice of words would have been much more colorful.

Travis pointed to the calendar of Wisconsin landscapes hanging by the fridge. "I wrote it down, Molly. I've got court at nine o'clock. I need to get on the road by eight. You know how southbound traffic is in the morning."

Molly stared back, her face nearly expressionless and her voice void of emotion. "Nicki, get your brother for me, okay? Try not to wake him."

Travis recognized his tactical error. "Wait. That's okay. I'll—"

Molly answered even as she managed to completely ignore him. She aimed the palm of her hand at Travis while smiling at her daughter. "Get your brother, sweetie. Put him in his car seat."

Molly looked back his way, her mouth a straight line. "Are you coming home at all? After court, I mean?"

"My shift starts at three-thirty. Probably won't be able to make it back up."

"So, what then? We'll see you tomorrow? Or should I check the calendar?"

She was way beyond pissed off, and Travis didn't blame her or attempt a comeback.

Four days a week, Travis worked swing shift as a patrol deputy for the

San Diego County Sheriff's Department. During that time, he typically slept until after the kids went to school, left for work before they got home, and came back long after the whole family had gone to bed. Add in the round-trip commute of eighty miles a day and Travis was pretty much a ghost for half the week. On the days he was home, he was like some drop-in visitor, always anxious to leave. A relative who used to be close but, because of a long absence, now just didn't fit in.

Not for the first time, Travis considered the reality of their circumstances. A three-bedroom rented house sandwiched between two identical houses on an eight-thousand-square-foot lot, a twelve-lane interstate within rock-throwing distance, and a family that was as cracked and broken as the hard dirt of the desert floor. Looking now at his wife's careworn expression, he could only wonder, *What the hell was I thinking? More like* traumatic *impact*, he thought.

It had been almost two years since they'd moved from small-town Wisconsin to Southern California. To allow even quiet acknowledgment that things hadn't gone according to his well-laid plans was to start down a path of personal self-loathing and ridicule. The truth was, when Travis agreed to take the job with the sheriff's department, he'd failed to take into account the dramatic impact the move would have on his family.

"Today's day three," he said, speaking to his wife's back. "I should be able to get off on time. Then just one more workday and I've got no subpoenas until next week. We'll have some time together. I promise."

Her shoulders dropped and her spiteful tone was replaced with one of intense sadness—and that hurt all the more. "We're losing him, Travis. You know we are. He's not going to graduate with his class, and if he doesn't pass his summer school courses, he won't graduate at all. And with what happened last month? I'm really scared for him. He could throw his whole life away."

"Come on, Molly." He moved in closer and gently turned her to face him. "That's not going to happen. We won't let it happen."

There was no denying it. The boy was drifting. He was angry. Resentful. Acting out. All the typical ways that Travis had heard kids described in a courtroom during a sentencing hearing or probation report. But not his son. Not Tyler.

"He's a good kid, Molly. It's just that the move has been hard on him.

But you know I'm right. He's got a good heart. And on top of that, he's smart. He'll come around."

"Shoplifting, Travis?" She looked up with glistening eyes. "You don't think that's some huge red flag?"

"I took care of all that, Molly. We'll handle it as a family."

"Took care of it? Is that what you call it? Getting your cop buddies to let it slide?"

"You want him to go to court?" he asked. "Juvenile hall? Probation? Is that what you want?"

When Tyler had gotten snagged by a mall cop for shoplifting video games, the responding deputy from the Riverside sheriff's office had given Travis a courtesy call. It had made for a lousy week at home, but Travis was glad to keep his son out of the system. He knew Molly didn't agree, and the argument over that had been one of their worst in almost eighteen years of marriage. The way she saw it, she was the one sticking up for Tyler. She was the one looking out for their son.

"I want him to face some consequences," she said, pulling away. "And so far? He hasn't. Now he's out the door dressed like some . . . some trashy, wannabe rapper. Defying me. Defying *you*, Travis. You're his father. Act like it."

Travis had started to smile at her colorful description of Tyler, but his anger surged at the insult. Trying to show as little emotion as possible, he couldn't help but be terse. "I said I'll talk to him, Molly. We're not losing him. I won't let that happen."

A scream of frustration from their two-year-old ended the conversation. Nicole walked into the kitchen carrying her little brother, still in his pajamas, his cheeks bright red, his curly yellow hair matted and damp with sweat. The boy was crying and banging his small fists against his sister's chest.

"Sorry, Mom," Nicole said. "He woke up."

Molly forced a smile. "I can see that. Get him in his car seat and sit with him. I'll be right out."

"Yes, ma'am." With Hannah trailing her closely, Nicole walked to the door leading to the garage, doing her best to console her brother. Travis thought again of his older daughter's amazing maturity.

"Sorry we woke you," Molly said, the anger replaced by something close to surrender. "Be safe tonight. Text me later, okay?"

She moved to the door and Travis called out to her. "It's supposed to get up to a hundred and ten. I'll shut the house up before I leave and turn on the AC."

Not bothering to look back, Molly shook her head. "The electric bill was over four hundred dollars last month. Better we tough it out."

"I love you, Molly."

"I know you do, Travis," she said, her voice hollow. "I know you do."

The door shut behind her. The house went quiet and he was alone.

3

7:30 A.M.

Omar zigzagged through the morning crowd, getting hung up behind an old white dude in an electric fatman cart. The man was dressed in orange sweatpants and a tent-size canary-colored T-shirt, and Omar figured the fella went 350, maybe 400 pounds. Steering past tables, the man showed some mad driving skills, with one hand on the controls and the other balancing a tray of food, high up, like a waiter in some fancy restaurant. Omar spied a plastic CVS bag in the basket under the seat. The twelver of Pabst and the bottle of Dewar's White Label meant old boy had big plans after breakfast.

A table of day laborers sat grabbing a bite before heading out in search of work—any work. Omar nodded at two of the men he recognized from a construction job a few weeks back. Most of the restaurant crowd was made up of old white folks from the mobile home park across the street. Seniors got coffee for a dime and free refills. For that, they'd hang out all morning and beat the heat with free air-conditioning.

Ducking around the old man's cart, Omar passed a woman whose three small children were sharing a Happy Meal while she used her thumbnail to scratch at a half-dozen lotto tickets. As he headed for his brother and sister, Omar picked up a snatch of conversation between two white men bemoaning the "hordes of illegals invading the whole damn town."

Reaching the table where Hector and Sofia sat waiting, Omar put down the plastic tray, loaded with two breakfast meals. He slid into a seat and took another look at his brother.

"Sit up, Hector. And damn it, boy, what I say about wearing that chollo shit?"

Hector pulled himself from his slumped position, busted open the Styrofoam clamshell, and got to work on his pancakes. He shoveled in a bite, syrup running down his chin. His answer was hard to make out around the food. "Chill, homes. Why you trippin'? You sittin' right there all done up in blue."

"Don't call me *homes*." Omar reached out, grabbed the hat off his brother's head, and threw it at his chest. "And blue's got nothing to do with it. You know I just—"

A familiar voice called out from nearby. "Yo, what up, peewee?"

Omar swiveled in his chair as Carlos Lopez sauntered up from behind and gave Hector a light smack on the arm. Omar watched as his little brother's face came alive with enthusiastic respect. As if Carlos was a guy worth looking up to. A player.

"Yo, Boo." Hector sat up straight, using Carlos's street name. "What up?"

Ignoring the younger boy, Carlos looked at Omar. With his blue Easton cap at a forty-five-degree angle, Carlos bent back at the waist and posted up with his usual swagger. Carlos was small for seventeen, but the nature of his life had taught him to pull off big. His fists stayed buried in the front pocket of his generic navy blue hoodie in a way intended to make anyone think twice about what might be concealed inside.

Carlos spoke in a tone brimming with a confidence that implied the conversation was barely worth his time. "So what up, Seso? You buying everybody breakfast?"

Omar threw out his chin and nodded, acknowledging his own street name. Omar had met Carlos when they'd started their freshman year at James Madison. They had the same first period English class, but it turned out that Carlos wasn't much of a morning person. At some point that year, Carlos stopped showing up for school at all, and Omar lost track of him. A few months later, when the Ortegas first moved into the barrio, Omar ran into Carlos—it turned out they were practically neighbors. By then, Carlos was all in for Eastside, but he didn't bust Omar's balls about jumping in. Omar liked Carlos. Didn't have any problem with him at all. But he sure as hell didn't plan on buying him breakfast.

"Yo, Boo. What up?"

"Nada. Chillin'. 'Bout to make some cash today, but I'm light now. What ya say you spot me some nuggets?"

"Nah, man. I just had enough for these two." Omar told himself it really wasn't a lie. He'd used his last ten-dollar bill to cover the breakfast. The two hundreds still in his pocket were spoken for. He gestured to the empty table in front of him. "See? I ain't eating nothing."

Carlos waved a hand in the air. "Shit, I know how you be. Your uppity ass? You be thinking you too good for Mickey D's. Like army food gonna be all healthy. Come on, Seso. You's always holding. Hook me up with a five-piece."

Seso was the name one of the Eastsiders had tagged Omar with when they'd moved into the barrio and, whether he liked it or not, he was stuck with it. It fit, though. Omar had always been that guy. Even way back in grade school, during what Sofia called "los buenos años," he was known as the kid who could just figure stuff out, who could excel in just about any subject thrown at him. This wasn't limited to the classroom, either. Sitting here now, he was smart enough to know how to handle Carlos. He talked to the other boy honestly, and in a way he'd understand, but didn't make him feel disrespected.

"Man, they don't even sell nuggets till eleven. And for reals . . ." He tapped his pockets to sell the lie. "I got no money."

Carlos looked dejected, but just as Omar figured, he was unwilling to beg. With a shrug, Carlos backed off on the hit-up and took a seat next to Hector. He looked across the table at Sofia. His voice was respectful, and Omar knew the boy would be careful how he talked to his sister.

"Hey, Sofia."

"Hey, Carlos." Sofia never lifted her eyes from the powdered eggs on her plate. She took a last, small bite, then said, in a voice barely above a whisper, "We're going to miss the bus."

"Yeah, all right. You finished?"

Sofia nodded and pushed the tray away. Omar picked up the Styrofoam plate, still nearly full with eggs and something in the shape of sausage links, and set it down in front of Carlos.

"Here you go. She's done."

Carlos clicked his tongue and waved off the food. He looked away and did his best to sound offended. "Forget that. I ain't eatin' nobody's damn leftovers."

Omar shrugged and stood. He left the food. He knew better, and was happy to help out. "Let's go, you two."

The three stood up and Carlos stayed at the table, already eyeing the eggs. "Yo, Seso. Come find me after you get done wasting your time at school. I'll be kicking it at the wall."

Hector jumped at the offer. "I can come by, Boo."

Omar smacked his brother across the chest. "He wasn't talking to you." Omar looked to Carlos and avoided the topic of the wall. "What? You don't have to go to that continuation shit or whatever?"

"Hell, no. I'm on home study." Carlos sounded like a man who had counted the cards at blackjack and cashed in. "I don't spend no time with stupid-ass teachers or nothing. You be leaving pretty soon, right?"

"Next week." He herded his siblings toward the door and saw the sadness in Sofia's eyes.

"All right, then, like I said. You be at the wall after school, yo?" Carlos called out. "Chunks'll be there. You need to see him before you take off. Pay your respects and shit."

"What?" Omar stopped, stunned, but forced himself to recover quickly. He did his best to sound casual. Maybe even upbeat. "Chunks is out? I thought he was doing four years?"

Carlos puffed up in his role as dispenser of valuable insider information. The details of who was going in and out of jail or prison, on what charges and for how long, this was his area of expertise. "Big man did five months in county before he got his plea worked out. Now'days, they be countin' that time as double. Then sixteen months in Soledad, hangin' with homies from all over SoCal. He took some bullshit classes and got a deal where every good day counts for two. So, yeah. He be out."

Carlos went on, his tone serious, "For reals, you need to come by. This shit up around here? It ain't like where you be living before. You gonna want Chunks to be havin' somebody watch out for your family, know what I'm sayin'?"

Carlos was right about the neighborhood. The Ortegas' forced relocation, three years before, had been a distance of less than three miles, but the change had flipped life upside down. Still, he sure as hell didn't need any help from Chunks Gutierrez.

"Yeah, yeah. For sure." Once again, just like with Renteria, Omar took care not to tip his hand. He'd managed to go all this time without pissing off Chunks or ending up in the back of a cop car. He just needed to walk this damn tightrope a few more days, then his family would have relocated and he'd be off to basic training. Omar knew that Chunks would consider the move a show of disrespect to the neighborhood. Well, the hell with him, he thought. *It ain't my neighborhood and never will be.* Making sure his face was unreadable, he answered with confidence. "I'll definitely come find him before I take off. Later, Carlos."

"Be sure you do." Carlos stuck his hand out and fist-bumped Omar, then tapped three fingers flat against his chest in the rough shape of a capital *E.*

"Yeah, Carlos. Later, man." Hector put out his own fist, but Carlos left him hanging. Omar saw the embarrassment on his brother's face as he pulled him by the collar toward the door. He glanced back and saw Carlos, already with a mouthful of Sofia's eggs, dumping the last bites of Hector's pancakes onto the plate. Carlos was a good guy. Loyal and, in his own way, trustworthy as hell. Omar would even miss him, but it couldn't be helped.

On the sidewalk, the Ortegas headed for the public bus stop. Omar wasted no time. "Don't be going to the wall after school, Hector. Do it and I'll tell Ma *and* beat your ass."

Hector answered, looking away in frustration, "Man, what up with you? Everybody kicks it at the wall. At least everybody who knows the score and shit. I ain't the one runnin' off to join the army. I gotta live here, fool."

Omar let the comment go. His plan was to sit down with Hector and Sofia this weekend and tell them about their upcoming relocation. He figured Sofia would be thrilled, but he wasn't sure about Hector. He'd use the opportunity to remind his brother how their lives used to be and to tell him that it could be like that again.

At the corner, Omar pulled out the bus passes he bought for all three of them each month. There was no school bus service where they lived, and Omar didn't want either Hector or Sofia walking through the crime-ridden neighborhoods, although sometimes the city bus didn't seem much safer.

Hector moved off to stand alone, his expression somewhere between anger and tears. Omar walked over and took hold of his little brother by the back of the neck. His affection for the boy was complicated, but undeniable.

"Think about it, Hector. Boo? He ain't a bad dude, but he ain't got nothing you want. He's in there eating leftover Mickey D's, nowhere to be all day. Not a dime in his pocket. He just talks game, man. Think about that. See it for what it really be."

The bus came into view and Hector yanked at the sleeve of his T-shirt to swipe his eyes. Omar looked past the clothing and saw an angry thirteen-year-old. And yeah, no doubt, he had plenty to be angry about. Omar was about to say more, but Hector snatched the pass from his hand and stepped away.

"Oh no." Sofia's voice was panicked.

"What?" Omar said, as the bus pulled to the curb.

"My library book. I left it on the desk in our room and today's the last day to turn it in. Mr. Zewalt, he'll give me a white slip. I have to go back."

Omar pictured Renteria's face if Sofia walked in. "No, I'll go get it. Get on the bus."

"But Omar, you'll be late. You—"

"Your first class is algebra, right? Watch for me outside the door."

"You don't have to. It's my fault."

"Get on the bus, Sofia. I'll be right behind you." Omar turned to Hector. He told himself to be reasonable but firm. "Meet us by the flagpole after school. Right after school. I got somewhere I gotta be. You need to hang out with Sofia at the apartment until I can get back. You hear me?"

Hector shoved his hands into the pockets of his Dickies shorts and let his shoulders drop. The bus door opened and Omar herded both of them up the steps. His sister looked back and he saw gratitude, along with what he'd like to think was admiration.

"Thanks, Omar. Sorry, I—"

He winked. "Time me. I'll be right behind you."

Looking up through the bus window, he saw Sofia take a seat up front. Hector walked down the aisle. For a moment, Omar and the boy exchanged a look through the glass and Omar felt the brotherly connection. Hector quickly looked away.

As Omar turned to head back to the apartment, his mind began to re-hash the past few years. He knew this was a waste of time; he couldn't change what had already happened. Omar forced himself to think ahead—not just to the weekend, or even a month or two down the road. Not even a year. No. He imagined Hector as a grown man, with a family, with a home of his own.

He remembered how his father's strong hand would grip him by the shoulder and pull him close. He heard his voice, brimming with the cock-sure confidence of a man who had blazed the way. *"That's what me and your mama want for all of you, hijo. And you'll have it. Good lives. Families. You're Americans. You'll have it all."*

Omar passed businesses that were starting to open up. Homeless men were emerging from alleyways, stepping into the sunlight to warm them-selves after a long night on the street. Omar fell into a steady jog that, for most anyone else, would be a full sprint. He felt powerful. Unstoppable. He wondered where the strength came from, and then he realized what it was.

Hope.

4

Hector grabbed the handrail and climbed the two steep steps, a short list of internal commands running through his head. *The main thing is attitude. Be confident and shit. Come off like you be part of the game.* With a lingering twinge of self-doubt, he glanced out the window and caught Omar's eye. He felt the pull of his big brother's affection but rejected it, forcing himself to get in character.

A dozen different conversations, punctuated with Spanglish shouts and curses, came at him all at once. The bus was almost filled to capacity with students from the nearby middle school and a few from the high school. The only adult on board was the driver, who hid under headphones, his distrustful eyes flickering back and forth between the road and the oversize rearview mirror above his head. Hector barely glanced at the girls who occupied the first four rows of seats, or the few white kids that hung toward the middle. He scanned the far back of the bus, searching for allies but mindful of enemies.

Standing there in the aisle of the crowded bus, loneliness filled him, pushing all the air out of his body, no different than if he'd been punched in the chest. Through the window he saw Omar a hundred yards down the sidewalk, running like a track star, and fought the urge to get off the bus and chase after him. To call out, *Wait for me*. As Omar disappeared down the road, Hector felt like a part of him was running too—the best part. Running as hard as he could, trying to keep up with his big brother but falling farther and farther behind.

Damn it, man up already. You don't need him hanging around.

When Omar was along, they'd wind up in seats that didn't let Hector fit in anywhere. Omar liked it that way. He said it was like sitting in Switzerland, but Hector didn't have a clue what the hell that even meant.

Sofia had already found a seat right behind the driver, next to her friend from the old neighborhood, Gabriella. Hector was still eyeing the crowd when a familiar voice called out, "Yo, Ortega. You trying to hide up there 'mongst them bitches or what? Come see me."

The bus gained speed as Hector walked toward the chorus of jeers and insults, using his own smirk and laughter to mask his fear. He moved down the aisle, easily balancing as the vehicle lumbered along, his hands high overhead, flashing three fingers on each side.

"Ease up with that shit, ese," the voice called out. "You ain't Eastside."

Manuel "Little Beast" Montoya was a twelve-year-old seventh grader, small for his age but fearless. He was the youngest homie allowed to claim full membership in the Eastside gang, a status he made clear by relentlessly screwing with guys like Hector: teenagers who might be older, bigger, and maybe even stronger but who lacked the pedigree and street cred of Little Beast.

The original Beast was old-school Eastside. Sixteen years back, he'd shot and killed a rival gangster, and he'd been locked up ever since. Hector had heard that Manuel came from one of those prison things called a "conjugal." Because of all the shit his old man had done back in the day, the boy had been adopted by Eastside from the time he was born, kicking it in the street with the homies since he was eight years old.

They called him Little Beast from the first, but he was just some kind of mascot until right about the time he turned eleven. That's when he'd tripped with some Eastsiders to the beach in Oceanside, where he made his bones by jacking an iPhone off some streetwalking he-she. Word had come down to jump the boy in, but Chunks had given orders to go easy on him out of respect for his old man. Hector knew he'd never get that sort of special treatment when his time came.

Hector made his way to the back of the bus. Montoya sat in the far corner of the last seat. Jaqueline Alarza sat next to him, her body leaning in to his. Her hand rested high on Montoya's thigh, her long fingernails spread out even higher. She looked up at Hector, her eyes smoky behind a heavy coat of eyeliner and what Hector figured to be a couple of early-morning bong hits.

Her lashes were gone, plucked and replaced by thin pencil lines that extended well past the corner of each eye. She wore a low-cut halter top that not only left her belly bare but also showed off about half of the biggest tetas in all of Chavez Middle School. She didn't smile, but she wasn't frowning. Hector made sure not to get caught staring and forced himself to look away. Another half-dozen boys sat in the seats around Montoya, all of them dressed in khaki and blue. A few of them had girlfriends, near carbon copies of Jaqueline.

"So what you got for me?" Montoya said, his eyes doing a last quick check of the aisle. With Omar not around, Hector knew the daily hit-up was coming earlier than usual.

He reached into his pocket and pulled out a five-dollar bill. As if the humiliation of being taxed by a twelve-year-old wasn't enough, the guilt was almost more than he could stand. He'd taken the money from his mother's purse the night before, when everyone else had been asleep. Stealing from his own ma was some seriously low-life shit, but what choice did he have?

Montoya snatched the bill, then shoved it into Jaqueline's shirt. He dug in deep and groped pretty much all around, keeping his eyes on Hector. Jaqueline stared at him too, her expression never changing. When Montoya finally pulled back his hand, the money was gone.

"I don't like taxin' you this way, homes, like you be some bitch. I mean, you a friendly and all, but unless you gonna step up, you gotta pay to ride, hear what I'm sayin'? But so you know, I'm looking out for you. I be charging the white boys ten."

"I know what up, LB. You gotta do what you do to represent." Hector tried to come off like none of it bothered him. Like five dollars was nothing. He didn't mention that none of them ever tried to pull this sort of bullshit when Omar was around. And Hector damn well knew Montoya wasn't hitting up everybody on the bus. Only the ones he knew would cave. But, for now, Hector was one of the marks, and it was up to him to build some cred.

"Maybe I can trip with you guys next week somewhere," Hector said.

"You know, bang or some shit. You gotta know, LB, I be down for East-side."

"That right? You ready?"

Hector shrugged, thinking that, in a few days, Omar would be gone. The cop in his life would be out the door. Then again, so would his guardian.

"Hell yeah, LB. Been ready." Hector wasn't lying. He knew it was time to jump in. All things considered, he figured it was a smart move. Omar just didn't get it, and besides, he was leaving. And this time, Hector knew, he'd really be on his own.

Ever since their dad got rolled up, things had been different. Hector had never resented following his dad's rules. He loved his father. Missed him. Missed riding to school in the pickup truck. Coming out at the end of the day and finding his dad waiting for him. Having him coach Hector's soccer team. But the old man was gone and he wasn't coming back.

"I'll get with Chunks," Little Beast said. "But till then? Go on and get up there with them faggotty-ass white boys. Back up in here . . . ?" With one arm draped around Jaqueline's shoulder, Montoya used the other to gesture to the rest of his entourage. "Eastside only, ese."

Hector walked halfway back up the aisle, the profane chorus of jeers and comments stinging with each step. Knowing he was still being watched and judged, he stopped alongside a slightly built white kid who looked to be in high school. Hector didn't recognize him as a regular rider. With a couple of Coke bottles perched on the end of his nose, the kid sat with his face planted in some Harry Potter bullshit, mouth hanging open. The way Hector saw it, the kid was begging for it.

Hector palm-slapped the boy hard on the back of his dome, emboldened when the kid squealed and raised his hands to cover his head. "Get ya ass up, culo. I'm sitting here."

The boy fumbled a bit, adjusting his glasses, which had been nearly knocked off by Hector's blow. He picked his book up off the floor, stood, and made his way fast up the aisle, to a row behind Sofia. Hector saw his sister staring at him with disappointment, maybe even sadness. He dropped into the now vacant seat, not bothering to turn around, hearing a low hum of approval from the back. Still filled with satisfaction, he looked across the aisle to another high schooler, who met his gaze with contempt and not a hint of fear. The guy probably had six inches on him, not to mention fifty pounds. Unable to help himself, Hector stood back up and took a stance in the aisle.

"What's with the hard look, white boy?" he shouted, throwing his hands out to both sides like some cornered animal trying to appear bigger than it was. He made sure to make plenty of noise. "You got something to say?"

"Back off, wetback." The kid started to get up and Hector felt the onset of panic, not sure what he'd do next.

"Hey, you two," the driver called out. "Cut the shit or I'll stop this bus right now. You'll both be kickin' rocks."

The bigger kid gave him a halfhearted smirk, but Hector saw him swallow hard and lick his lips. This time, Hector allowed himself to look toward the back of the bus. Montoya nodded in satisfaction and waved an arm his way.

"Get on back here, fool. That shit was tight."

Hector moved to the rear, doing his best to be cool about it. He took a seat in the crowd, returning the victory shoves and fist bumps. Heart still pounding, he felt stronger and more alive than he had in months. And damn, it felt good. Who knows. Maybe Omar leaving town wouldn't be such a bad thing after all.

5

The bell signaling first period chimed loud and shrill. Omar put his head
down and sprinted the last hundred yards to James Madison High School.
He took the steps three at a time and ran past the sign reminding everyone
that drugs and weapons were not allowed on school grounds. He pulled
on the heavy door, knowing what he'd find.

Locked.

Omar cupped his hands up against the thick glass and peered through
the wire mesh. Just inside the door was the reception desk. Maybe Omar
had caught a lucky break. Then again, maybe not.

Randy Cabrera sat at the counter, responsible for checking in parents
or other legitimate school visitors. The job was a privilege reserved for seniors on the honor roll, and one Omar had enjoyed more than a few times.
Best thing was, it gave him a rare opportunity to check in on the latest Real
Madrid soccer highlights using the school's high-speed internet. Randy,
his eyes fixed on the computer screen, looked to be doing the same.

Omar gave a light rap on the glass and Randy looked up quick. Omar,
still less than hopeful, made eye contact and did his best to clown it up
a bit. A joke between friends. He grinned and pointed down to the door

handle. Randy shot a glance up and down the hall, then looked back at Omar, shaking his head. No surprise, Omar thought.

Damn gringo wannabe.

Through most of grade school and all of middle school, Randy and his family had lived just three doors down from the Ortegas. Their dads were good friends, so the families got together on a regular basis. Omar and Randy got along because they had to, but the reality was they could barely stand each other. Omar was willing to admit he was probably a little jealous, but he also knew Randy had his own problem: shame and embarrassment about who he really was.

Randy's parents were from Honduras. Omar didn't know the details, but somehow they'd walked into the country and had both gotten legal status. A few years back, Randy's dad, who worked as a mechanic, had even gotten citizenship. His mom worked at a local tortilleria. Like a lot of Latino parents, the Cabreras wanted to do everything they could to help their American-born son blend in. They gave the boy a gringo name and felt blessed when he grew up light-skinned. He even had what most Latinos saw as a priceless gift from God: green eyes.

Omar knew that Randy did everything he could to pass as white. Despite growing up in a Spanish-speaking house, Randy had gone dumb in his native language. He'd even taken to signing his name as "Ran-D," but Omar was pretty sure that when he filled out his college apps he put his real name on the dotted line. Randall Gustavo Cabrera was headed for UCLA in the fall, on a full scholarship.

What really pissed Omar off was Randy's status as starting forward for James Madison's varsity soccer team. When they'd both been on the freshman squad, Omar had run circles around Randy. Omar was ten times the player the other boy was, but with the way things had unfolded since then, there was no way he could commit to the practice schedule, not to mention the cost of equipment.

The hell with all the history. What Omar needed right now was for Ran-D to open the damn door. When Randy just stared back, Omar took a deep breath, cocked his head, and pointed harder. He spoke pleadingly, though he knew he couldn't be heard through the thick glass. "Come on, man."

Randy pulled himself to his feet, pointed to the door of the admin office behind him, and once again shook his head. Omar raised his fist. Careful to strike the glass lightly, he gave his best menacing scowl.

He jammed his pointer finger toward the handle and whispered, "Get over here, damn it."

Randy took one last look over his shoulder then came around the desk. He reached down and pushed the door open a crack.

"You're late, Ortega," Randy said, stepping back as Omar yanked the door open and strode in. "You have to go around to the assistant principal's door and check in there."

"Don't worry about it," Omar said. He'd gotten what he needed and was already walking away.

Randy whispered, loud enough for Omar to hear, "You're just going to have to come back here to get a white slip. You'd better not tell anybody I let you in."

Omar didn't bother to look back. His heart was still beating hard from the nearly two-mile run that he'd made in less than fifteen minutes. He'd slipped in and out of the apartment undetected—the old man was passed out in his chair.

He jogged down the concrete hallway lined with lockers that didn't lock and shut doorways, each with a thin strip of thick glass for a window. When he reached his sister's classroom, he heard near pandemonium inside, with a lone adult voice calling for everyone to be quiet and take a seat. Omar looked through the glass and saw Sofia staring nervously toward the door.

When she saw her brother, she slipped from her desk and pushed the door open just enough to take the book. Pressing her face to the opening, she said softly, "Thanks, Omar. Sorry I made you late. Now you're going to get the white slip."

"Don't worry about it. How was the bus ride?"

She hesitated half a beat. "It was okay."

"What? Did something happen? Did someone bother you?"

"No, Omar. It was fine."

"Hector?"

"It was nothing."

"What, Sofia? Tell me."

"I think some of the boys are giving him a hard time. He just doesn't act the same when you're not around. I think they . . . I don't know. They make him do things."

"Ms. Ortega?" The teacher sounded exasperated but was doing her best to establish control. "Are you going to be joining us?"

"Go sit down," Omar said. "I'll see you out front after school."

"Thanks, Omar."

Omar watched as she made her way through the chaos of forty wandering students, the teacher now calling out names, trying to take attendance. Sofia got to her desk, took a seat, and did all she could to be invisible. Next year, he thought, she'll be in a school where the teachers are in control.

Back when Omar was going to Chavez Middle School, his father dropped him off in front of the main entrance every morning. And every afternoon, Omar walked out of the building to find the burnt-orange Ford pickup parked right at the curb. He'd jump into the back and bang on the roof as a hello, then sit down behind the plywood siding, among the half-dozen trash cans filled with lawn clippings. His father would pull away while Omar listened to Sofia and Hector in the cab, jabbering about their days.

Back then, none of them could have gotten into any trouble even if they'd wanted to. School nights were all about homework and getting to bed on time. Weekends were busy with soccer practices, family outings, and neighborhood get-togethers. But yeah. That was then.

He checked his phone and saw he was a full three minutes late for Latin American History. Sofia was right—that meant a formal white slip. He flew up the steps to the third floor. If he did end up in the assistant principal's office, he'd rat out Cabrera quick as shit. Hell, it might be worth the demerit.

As he expected, the classroom door was locked. When he peeked in, he was not surprised to see Ms. Hillman in full control. Ms. Hillman didn't believe in letting any school day go to waste, and Omar could hear she was already engaged in a lecture on Simón Bolivar.

Omar tapped lightly on the glass. Ms. Hillman turned to look. Her gaze went to the clock, then back to Omar. She stood, unmoving, for several seconds that felt like minutes. With what looked to be reluctance, she finally walked to the door, unlocked it, and pushed it open. Instead of letting him in, she stepped into the hallway.

"I started class already, Omar. Where's your white slip?"

Omar didn't bother trying to pull any kind of game. Not on Ms. Hillman. He knew the woman was married to a cop and was highly skilled at picking up on a con. "Sorry, Ms. H. I didn't get one. It's just my sister, she forgot her library book. I had to run back home and get it for her."

Omar saw a glint of respect in his teacher's eyes, but the woman was nobody's pushover.

"Sorry, Omar. You know Mr. Thompson's rule. Any student arriving after the doors are locked needs to get a white slip from the assistant principal. No exceptions."

"Ma'am, please." Ms. Hillman was one of the few adults Omar felt he could trust. She'd gone to bat for him before, and the last thing he wanted was to put her in a bad spot. But damn. A white slip? Now? "It's my fault, I know. But, well . . . graduation is next week. I've never had a white slip in four years. Not one."

The woman shook her head, feigning frustration, then stepped aside.

"Get in there." She shut the door behind them both and gave him a soft shove toward his seat. "Now, as I was saying, Bolivar was a leading figure in the fight against the Spanish Empire."

Omar took his seat and, for the first time since he woke up, allowed himself to relax. Ms. Hillman's voice drifted away as he thought of what the next few days would bring. A new home for his family. A new life and career for himself. A whole new world for all of them. Then again, not exactly new. Really, it was just getting things back to the way they should be.

His ma liked to say that God tests his children, and maybe that was true. But Omar smiled, thinking about his dad's slightly different philosophy. According to his father, every once in a while in life, you come to a locked door. First thing you do is knock, politely. Be patient. Talk your way in. Kind of like this morning. *"But if that don't work,"* the old man said, *"kick the damn thing open."*

Maybe they were both right. God had locked a few doors, and Omar had been more than patient. He'd played by the rules and things were finally starting to look up. But, yeah, no doubt. If Randy Cabrera, Edgar Renteria, or anybody else thought they were going to keep him or his family locked out, they had another thing coming.

6

0850 HOURS

The dozen fenced-in parking spaces reserved for law enforcement were all taken by unmarked detective cars, and Travis couldn't help but silently curse the privileged class of cops. Then again, it hadn't been so long since he'd enjoyed the perks of plainclothes work. As in most departments, sheriff's detectives were authorized a take-home ride. That paid off in a lot of ways—the savings in gas money alone could add up to a few hundred bucks a month. Then there were the more subtle advantages, like getting an early jump for prime parking at the Vista courthouse.

As a lowly patrol dep, Travis had driven his own truck down from Temecula, then swung by the substation to put on a uniform and check out a squad car. Now he drove up and down the rows of the public parking lot without success, finally gave up, and headed for the overflow lot. He found a spot in the dirt field, pulled in, and started the long trek back to the main courthouse. It would've been quicker to just walk from the locker room. It shouldn't be so complicated for a deputy to go to court. But around here? It was.

Looking down at his black boots, which were already brown with dust, Travis remembered one of his first court appearances as a San Diego sheriff's deputy. To save time, he'd gotten dressed in his uniform at home and had driven his own pickup truck to the courthouse. Of course, he'd worn a cover shirt for the drive down the I-15, then took it off before going inside. Two hours later, when he returned to his truck, he had found a deep tag gouged in the paint, right down to the metal, courtesy of a gang out of Oceanside. One tire was slashed and both taillights were busted out. Worst of all was the lousy attitude of the senior patrol deputy, who made it clear just how annoyed he was about having to take the vandalism report. Travis barely knew the day shift deputy's name, but the man knew Travis was the new guy from somewhere it snowed a lot.

"You drove your own vehicle for a court appearance? *In uniform?* You ain't in Kansas no more, Jackson. Best adjust your way of thinking."

Travis didn't try to correct the man's geography or argue with his logic. Wisconsin or Kansas, it didn't much matter. The days of comfortably traveling in uniform and driving his own truck to the courthouse were gone.

Ignoring the long line of defendants and family court combatants who were required to pass through the metal detector, Travis stepped up to the turnstile marked "Officers and Attorneys Only." The court services deputy, a heavyset man with fleshy, hooded eyes and gray hair that matched his skin, motioned him through without a greeting. Another stark difference in working for a department with more than two thousand sworn personnel.

Travis made his way to Issuing, a small, dingy courtroom where all trial procedures began. If a quick resolution wasn't reached, the case would be assigned to a judge in a more glamorous setting. As usual, the cramped confines of Issuing were filled with lawyers and cops, along with a wide range of citizens who had somehow gotten themselves caught up in the justice system.

Not interested in wedging himself into one of the theater-style seats, Travis found a spot along the back wall, between a uniformed cop from Oceanside he'd never met before and a high-dollar private defense lawyer he'd sparred with on the stand a time or two. He tossed the cop a friendly nod but ignored the attorney completely, other than to give him a casual elbow in the ribs to create a little extra space. He made small talk with the cop until the doorway that led to the long corridor connecting the courthouse and the county jail swung open. Travis rolled his eyes at the number of shackled men in jumpsuits that shuffled in. Looked like it could be a long morning. He leaned back against the wall as the well-established and repetitious legal proceeding known as the last-minute plea bargain got under way.

The clerk of courts called out names one by one. A beleaguered defendant would stand in front of the crude speaking hole cut into the Plexiglas enclosure that corralled the in-custody defendants like zoo animals. After the charges were read, a slickly dressed member of the district attorney's crew would confer briefly with the court-appointed defense attorney, who would then whisper the state's final ultimatum to the client. Almost inevitably, a deal would be struck.

After doing their best to raise a shackled hand to be sworn in, the accused would spit out the only words the power brokers wanted to hear. For some, it had just been a few days and the phrase came easily, often laced with a minor sense of resentment. Others cried, having held out for months—in some cases, even years. For them, it was as if they'd finally succumbed to torture. But in the end, they all gave in. One by one, they surrendered to the relentless power of the state, with three simple words: "Guilty, Your Honor."

The herd thinned pretty quickly and the clerk moved on to calling the names of defendants who were not in custody. Two cases were settled with pleas and another was continued. Travis felt lucky when the next case read off by the clerk was the one he'd been waiting for.

"The People versus Albert James Schofield."

Travis straightened up from where he'd been leaning against the wall and moved into the aisle. Let the games begin.

Albert Schofield was a transient well known to the deputies who patrolled the city of Vista. Travis had cited Schofield for urinating on the sidewalk in front of a private residence; the woman homeowner had insisted on making an "enough is enough" citizen's arrest. For all the folklore that surrounded being a cop in Southern California, Travis found that he spent a good bit of his time settling squabbles between the homeless and regular folk, like some never-ending domestic dispute.

In less time than it took a California native to grow from pimply-faced teenager to middle age, San Diego County had devolved from a virtual seaside paradise to a slightly less smoggy but equally overcrowded, traffic-clogged version of her rich cousin to the north. In one generation, sleepy suburban towns like Vista went from Beach Boys ballad material to poorly planned collections of strip malls, tract housing, high-density apartment complexes, and overburdened public facilities. In less than a decade, towns throughout San Diego County had doubled and tripled in population.

It often seemed to many of the locals that the greatest area of population growth was from the nation's seemingly endless supply of sun-loving, homeless vagabonds. It didn't help that there was no shortage of hard-working but undocumented foreign nationals streaming into California from south of the nearby border. Well-meaning white people called them "illegals"; the haters called them "wetbacks."

The people of Vista responded by electing local officials who promised to get a handle on things. An aggressive law enforcement strategy, championed by cops, prosecutors, and politicians, took hold. The power brokers made no effort to disguise their mission. Target certain populations, specifically the homeless and migrant workers, and pull up the welcome mat.

"Elizabeth Stanton for the people, Your Honor." Travis recognized the deputy district attorney. When their eyes met, she nodded to acknowledge his presence. She leaned against the railing that separated the spectators from the players, dressed in high-end designer wear that Travis figured was, from head to toe, equal to a month of his take-home pay. An affluent and athletic member of the twentysomething set, she exuded the confidence of a youthful woman backed up by the ultimate power of the State of California. A player in a game rigged for her to win. "I have the arresting deputy and the victim in court. We're ready to proceed."

"Andrew Reed, public defender's office, for Mr. Schofield, Your Honor." The man stood from the audience. He was squat and round, with a full head of wiry hair that Travis figured was a pain to comb. His rumpled, double-knit blue suit shimmered in the flurescent light. He entered the well of the courtroom with an unpracticed, nervous gait, several case files trapped under one arm and another awkwardly open in his hands. Travis figured the guy was in his midtwenties and probably a newcomer to the industry of prisoner production.

"If I may, Your Honor." His voice cracked, earning scoffs from the dozen or so cops in the room. "Mr. Schofield is present and in the courtroom. I have discussed the circumstances of his case and he has elected to enter a plea of no contest to the charge of urinating in public, a violation of penal code section three fourteen."

Without missing a beat, the deputy district attorney said, "The people do not object, Your Honor, and we would agree to a suspended sentence with a period of summary probation."

The judge looked out over the audience. "Mr. Schofield? Please approach the bench."

Travis was impressed with how Schofield had managed to clean up, figuring he must've squeezed in an early morning Starbucks sink-bath. His jeans were soiled, but not to the level of filth typically associated with street living. He wore a snappy Western-style shirt that looked like it had come from the "Free for Court" rack at the AmVets thrift store. For a thirty-year-old who could easily pass for fifty, Schofield looked pretty good. Of course, even from a distance that Travis figured had to be at least thirty feet, the man's stench was nearly as bad as it had been the night Travis had put him in the back of his patrol car. While Schofield took a position next to his attorney, the people closest to him moved away, most with watery eyes and a hand to their mouth. Schofield, either oblivious or apathetic, ignored them. Wise to the ways of courthouse deal making, he stood up straight and kept his mouth shut.

"Mr. Schofield, you've agreed to plead to a violation of public indecency, a misdemeanor for which I could send you to jail. However, the district attorney has agreed to a suspended sentence and summary probation. Do you agree to this arrangement?"

"Yes, sir."

"Fine. So ordered. Next time keep it in your pants and find a restroom." The judge softened his tone and looked out to the crowd. "And the victim in this case . . . Mrs. Reinhart? Could you stand, please?"

Judith Reinhart, who had been seated in the audience, got to her feet, a look of confused disbelief on her face.

The victim might be confused, but Travis recognized exactly what was going on. When a petty, nothingburger case refused to go away, an unspoken agreement between the prosecutor and defense counsel kicked in, with the judge as a coconspirator. A little reality check to the Mrs. Reinharts of the world, citizens who seemed to think something as petty as a man's habit of relieving himself wherever he damn well pleased rose to the concern of the Superior Court of the State of California. It was as if both attorneys grabbed an arm so the judge could reach down from on high, slap Mrs. Reinhart across the face, and say, *Bitch, get over yourself.*

"Thank you for coming in today, Mrs. Reinhart," the judge said, and

Travis was impressed with his tone of sincerity. "As you no doubt heard, we've reached a settlement in this case. We won't be needing your testimony after all. Sorry for any inconvenience."

A trim, well-dressed woman, Judith Reinhart wore her gray hair short, in an almost military cut, and Travis hadn't been surprised to learn she'd been an army nurse who had served with a MASH unit during Operation Desert Storm. When she had found Schofield relieving himself on her flower bed, she'd expertly applied an arm bar takedown and held him until Travis arrived.

Like many of the longtime residents of Vista, she'd taken twenty minutes to lecture Travis on the slow and steady decline of her neighborhood. Travis had listened, keeping an expression on his face that would leave her with the illusion that he really gave a shit. When she'd finished, he'd done his best to convince Mrs. Reinhart to forego what he told her would likely be a useless paper drill. He'd even promised to drive Schofield all the way to El Cajon before pushing him out of the car, but Mrs. Reinhart would have none of it. She wanted her day in court.

Well, here you go, Mrs. R. Have at it.

Mrs. Reinhart stared up at the judge, her five-and-a-half-foot frame braced, with her hands on her hips as if she were dressing down a misbehaving private. "What are you saying? That I came down here for nothing?"

Of course you did, Travis thought. But he knew the judge would do his best to sell it.

"Not at all, ma'am. Because of your diligence in reporting this crime, the case has been resolved. Mr. Schofield has pled guilty and will be held accountable, with a record of a misdemeanor conviction."

"That's it?" Mrs. Reinhart was incensed. "What about me? Don't I get a say?"

"Is there something you wanted to add, Mrs. Reinhart?" The judge sounded conciliatory, but Travis knew right away that the man was asking for trouble.

"You're darn right, I have something to add."

Here goes. Travis had already sat through the lecture once.

"I've lived in this town for over twenty years. Scrimped and saved and bought my house in 1999, just after I discharged from active duty. It was a quiet, beautiful neighborhood, filled with families. The *right kind* of families, I might add. Now? People just come and go. All the houses have gone to heck. Dirt yards. Ten cars in every driveway." Mrs. Reinhart pointed a bony finger at her nemesis. "On top of that, every night I've got these animals sleeping in my front yard, urinating on my perennials, defecating in my potted plants. I did not go off and fight overseas just to come back and live in a third world country. I'm absolutely fed up. If the courts aren't going to do something about this situation, then I most certainly will."

"That is never wise, ma'am. I would ask that if you have any future problems, you again notify the sheriff's department. Or perhaps you should reach out to your local elected official." The judge looked down and literally turned the page. "Clerk, please call the next case."

Travis headed for the door. Once in the hall, he walked a little faster. The last thing he needed was to give Mrs. Reinhart another target.

He looked at his watch and saw he'd been in court less than thirty minutes. That, plus the fifty-minute drive. He'd get his automatic four hours of court overtime for some lost sleep and a little less than ninety minutes of inconvenience. If he could manage that three times a pay period, it would give Molly a little cushion to work with when the first of the month rolled around.

Molly. He'd known her since third grade and loved her since fourth. He'd never so much as held another woman's hand in his entire life. The last eighteen months had been the most difficult of all their time together. He'd asked a lot of her. He'd be lying to himself if he said she'd never complained, but she sure didn't complain as much as she was entitled to.

He had planned to head over to the substation to get in a good workout, then maybe sneak off somewhere for a quiet bite before briefing started at three o'clock. But now, given his quick exit from the courthouse, he had another idea.

If he dropped the squad car off at the substation, he could keep it logged out so it would be ready for his afternoon shift. He could stow his uniform shirt and gun belt in the trunk. Factoring in midday traffic, he could probably get back to the house in time to spend an hour with Molly and Brandon while the older kids were in school. Maybe the boy would even go down for a nap.

Twenty minutes later he was headed north on the I-15, thinking his wife might get a kick out of the story of Mrs. Reinhart and her pissed-on perennials.

7

3:30 P.M.

Omar rushed through the hallways, dodging students pinballing off the walls, down to their last hours of high school. He felt the same sense of exhilaration, but for a totally different reason. He'd thought it over for most of the day and his mind was made up. He'd take Sofia and Hector with him to the bank. He'd make the final two-hundred–dollar deposit and get the cashier's check. After that, they'd ride the bus into San Marcos to deliver the security deposit and he'd show them their new home.

Omar figured Sofia would cry with happiness and relief. He could only hope that even Hector would be excited—and, oh man, had it been a long time since anyone in his family had been excited about anything. Especially Hector. In two days they'd be moving. Away from Renteria. Away from the craziness of the neighborhood.

Stepping out into the afternoon heat was like opening an oven door. The intensity and brightness of the cloudless sky turned the blue almost white. Squinting, he stood still for a moment, waiting for his vision to adjust to the harsh light, then shaded his eyes with one hand and scanned the crowd of several hundred lingering students. Sofia was waiting by the flagpole. Omar jogged over and took a quick look around.

"Where's Hector?" The middle school where Hector attended eighth

THE BURDEN OF TRUTH

grade was three blocks away and had let out twenty minutes earlier. He should've walked over already.

"He didn't show. Maybe he walked home by himself."

"Nah," Omar said, his good mood melting away in the heat. "He's going to the wall. Damn it. I knew he'd do that. He never listens."

Omar took out his flip phone and saw it was already after three. The property management office closed at four o'clock. He'd promised the manager he would drop off the bank check today so they could move in on Sunday. If he went to fetch his brother, he'd be cutting it close, but he could still make it.

What about Sofia? He sure wasn't taking her to the wall, and there was no way he could send her home alone, not with Renteria on the prowl. With his plan for a celebration scorched, he gave in to a moment of self-pity for having to deal with the logistics of all their lives.

"Still got your bus pass?" he asked his sister.

"Yeah, but—"

"Take the bus with Gabrielle," he said, nodding toward the curb, where a few dozen kids were already filing onto the city bus. "Go to her house. Stay there. I'll come get you before dinner, okay?"

"All right." Sofia started to walk away, then stopped, looking back. "Thanks again for this morning. Did you get a white slip?"

Omar winked at his sister. "Nah. I talked my way out of it."

Sofia smiled, and Omar knew she was proud of his ability to navigate the system.

"I'll wait for you at Gabby's."

"Make sure you do. Don't go back to the apartment without me."

Omar watched as Sofia walked to the bus. Through the window, he saw her friend Gabrielle Hernandez. Gabby smiled at Omar and waved. Omar nodded back as nonchalantly as he could manage. Gabby's family owned their own home, right next door to the house the Ortegas had rented in the old neighborhood. Gabby was second generation; both her parents had been born and raised in California. Mr. Hernandez was a foreman for one of the largest construction companies in all of San Diego County. Before the Ortegas had moved, Gabby and Sofia ran back and forth between the two families' houses with such frequency that everyone came to see the girls as sisters.

Omar was pretty sure Gabby had a crush on him, and there was no denying he felt something for her. He'd always figured there'd come a day when the two years between them wouldn't seem like such a big deal. But not now. Not given what had happened to the Ortegas. Omar knew it wasn't his fault, but the humiliation was more than he could bear.

When I come back from basic, he thought. Maybe we'll go to a movie. Get a burger or something. Both their mothers would no doubt insist that Sofia tag along as chaperone. Once again he pictured himself in uniform. He was still daydreaming when Gabby looked his way again, catching him staring. For a second time she flashed a smile, but this time Omar was quick to look away. Embarrassed, he turned and headed down the road leading to downtown Vista, the roughest part of the barrio.

If Omar found Hector at the wall, he decided, he'd humiliate the hell out of the boy. Make him think twice about blowing him off. Then he remembered what Hector had said earlier, about Omar running off to join the army. It was true: in just a few days, Hector would be on his own. But he'd be in a new neighborhood, the kind of place where he could make friends with whoever he wanted, with no worries about getting dragged into some gangster bullshit. Omar was already deciding he'd go easy on his brother when he heard a familiar voice call his name.

"Omar. Wait up for a minute."

The principal, Mr. Thompson, with Omar's teacher, Ms. Hillman, was heading straight for him across the schoolyard. Thompson was waving a white envelope over his head.

Damn it, Omar thought, sensing his perfect discipline record drifting away. If Cabrera had given him up, he would sure as hell figure out some payback.

"Yes, sir?" Omar waited for the boom to be lowered.

"I've got big news for you, Omar." Mr. Thompson, a short but very large man, was out of breath. His nearly bald head glistened with sweat, his peach-colored skin already pink. Omar waited while the man tried to settle himself.

"The final GPAs are in. Congratulations. You're the class valedictorian."

Omar was sure he hadn't heard right. "Valedictorian? No shit? I mean, really, sir?"

Both adults managed to smile and frown at the same time. "Not exactly the quote I want for the school paper. But yes. *No shit.*"

Omar's head rang with excitement. He'd known it was close, between him and Julie Stetson, but he couldn't believe it. After four years of scratching and clawing for every point on every test, Omar had won.

"Sorry about that, sir," Omar said, embarrassed. "But for reals? You're sure?"

"It was so close, we had to wait for the final grades." Mr. Thompson said. "It's official. Congratulations, son."

Mr. Thompson offered him the envelope with the school logo and the typed words, "To the parents of Omar Ortega."

Ms. Hillman smiled as Omar took the envelope. Student and teacher had become close over the past few years. She knew what the Ortega family had been through. She'd once come to the apartment to talk with Omar's mother about some of the after-school programs available for Sofia—and even for Hector, at the middle school. Renteria had been drunk, of course, and ranting in Spanish, making racist comments about Ms. Hillman, who was African American. When the teacher began to speak with Omar's mother in nearly perfect Spanish, Renteria had left the room, still muttering obscenities.

During that visit, Omar had told Ms. Hillman the exact details of his father's disappearance and about his plans to join the army. Omar trusted Ms. Hillman completely. She was the only person, other than his mother, who knew about the upcoming relocation.

Omar opened the envelope and saw that the letter of congratulations was written in English on one side of the paper and in Spanish on the other. The words "Dear Mr. and Mrs. Ortega" created a stab of loss, but Omar forced himself to enjoy the moment.

"Now, if I could only get you to reconsider," Mr. Thompson said, pushing up his round glasses, which had slipped down because of the sweat on his face.

Omar looked up from the letter. "Reconsider?"

"Omar, the army is a wonderful career. An honorable profession." Mr. Thompson reached out and squeezed his shoulder. "But you can do so much more.

"Look, it's too late to get into a four-year school for fall semester, but you could still go to the community college. Just for now. We'll help you complete the transfer paperwork so next year you can go to a university. Any school would be glad to have you. I'm sure you could earn scholarships that would cover most of the cost."

Omar knew "most" meant "not all," and that meant "no way." He'd already investigated the possibility of college. Even with the tuition at the community college being covered by the state, the incidental costs added up to more than he and his mother could afford.

Ms. Hillman spoke up. "Ed, I think Omar has a fine plan for his future. You just watch. In a few years he'll be coming back here as an officer, and he'll have that college degree, too."

The principal nodded, his face still glowing with respect. "You're absolutely right, Carol. I certainly don't mean to diminish any of Omar's accomplishments or his potential. I know you will be a success in whatever path you choose. We're all very proud of you, son."

Son. The word alone created a lump in his throat, and he swallowed hard.

"Thanks, Mr. Thompson," Omar said, carefully refolding the letter. "This means a lot."

The man put his hand on Omar's shoulder and began to steer him back toward the school. "Before you go, I need to get your picture for the graduation program. Plus, I'd like to call your parents and congratulate them personally. Invite them to the ceremony. And your speech—let's talk about that."

"It'll just be my mom, and she only speaks Spanish," Omar said. "But what speech?"

"For the commencement, of course."

"I gotta give a speech?"

"You'll do fine," Mr. Thompson said. "Five or six minutes is all. Nothing controversial, please. Your mother will have a seat reserved in the front row. Any other family, too. Come on in the office. We can talk there."

Omar looked down the road. The speech, the photo, and whatever else would have to wait. "My brother's waiting for me. I'll tell my mom about it tonight and I'll work on the speech. But I need to go, sir."

"All right, Omar," Mr. Thompson said. "Come see me in my office first thing Monday. Graduation is Wednesday, after all."

Omar nodded. "Yes, sir. I'll be there."

"And be sure to tell your mother I said felicidades."

The man's effort—his pronunciation wasn't too bad—made Omar smile. He saw tears glistening in Ms. Hillman's eyes as she pulled him in for a long hug. She spoke directly into his ear.

"I am very proud of you, Omar. You've worked so hard. Congratulations."

Omar returned the hug and felt a bit of emotion stirring, but shook it off. The celebrating and self-congratulatory stuff would have to wait. Returning the letter to its envelope, he folded it in half and put it in his back pocket. Right now, the thing he needed to do was track down his knucklehead brother.

"Thanks, Ms. H." He nodded to them both. "You too, Mr. Thompson. Thanks for everything, and I'll see you both on Monday."

A moment later, for the second time since waking up in the morning, he was running.

8

1530 HOURS

Travis grabbed a seat toward the middle of the briefing room, surrounded by other uniformed patrol deputies. When he'd been a probie, he'd been required to sit in the front row, and he was glad to be done with that. As with most any Friday afternoon briefing, the room was crowded. The bosses liked to beef up the numbers on the weekends, when calls for service and the deputies' self-initiated activity was bound to be high.

Scanning the room, Travis checked out the "drop-in" deputies, who had specialized assignments. The patrol deputies were neatly attired in their official uniforms, groomed according to regulation. But when assigned to a specialized unit, deputies were allowed a bit more leeway. When cops got to pick what they wore, how they looked wasn't so much about comfort, professionalism, or even safety. Hell, no. It was about attitude. Even a little personality.

The motorcycle deputies took up the back row, sitting in something akin to a military formation, their sleek aerodynamic spaceman helmets lined up on the desks in front of them. Their usual leather bomber jackets had been replaced by long-sleeve shirts with extra padding on the elbows. Considering the potential hazards of their job, it was the lightest a motor dep would ever ride, no matter what the thermostat read.

Deputies from the Community Oriented Policing unit had decided to pay a visit. Always ready to make a quick getaway to a neighborhood watch meeting or to grab up some free chow at a MADD luncheon, they sat clustered near the exit, looking nervous and out of place. Known officially as the COP unit, at the troop level, the politically required soft underbelly of the department was dubbed the DINO squad: Deputies in Name Only.

Their days were spent placating business owners and civic leaders on hot-button topics like addressing the transient population and rampant graffiti. They wore dress trousers, neatly pressed, dark green cotton polo shirts with embroidered badges, and no vest. Attire built for comfort in restaurants and office spaces, with zero use in the field. The only actual police equipment on their smooth leather dress belts was a sidearm in a high-rise pancake holster. Travis figured the gun served as a reminder to everyone, maybe even themselves, that the *D* in DINO still stood for "deputy."

Along the back wall, the four-man Gang Suppression unit, known as GSU, looked a hell of a lot like a gang. They wore black, military-style cotton trousers with large cargo pockets tailor-made to stow their field interview book, which was pretty much the bible of gang enforcement. An external, load-bearing vest covered a short-sleeve black T-shirt that usually sported the logo of a favorite gun manufacturer or some off-color social commentary. While they wore different T-shirts, the four men wore identical tactical nylon gun belts with a low-slung holster strapped to the thigh. The belts also held pouches for extra clips of ammunition and handcuffs. Each of them wore their hair long, way past their collars. None of their faces had seen a razor in over a week.

GSU deputies were allowed to ignore department grooming regulations, just in case any one of them suddenly needed to dress down and go under cover. Travis had never actually seen that happen, but he sure wanted to. The idea of one of the thirtysomething white boys throwing on a flannel and some Dickies to mix with the homies? Oh, man, that'd be fun to watch.

The GSU team leader, Sean Murphy, stood tall in the middle of his crew. Sean was yoked in a way that screamed of hard-core daily workouts, if not some sort of performance enhancer that went way beyond the over-the-counter variety. One muscular arm was completely sleeved with tattoos; the other was still a work in progress. He wore a faded Yankees ball cap over his thick, rust-colored hair, further evidence that GSU detectives pretty much did whatever the hell they wanted.

From his spot near the middle of the room, Travis watched Sean scan the pack with the look of an alpha male getting ready to mark his territory. Chewing hard and fast on a wad of gum, Sean elbowed the man standing next to him and nodded toward the DINOs, signaling that he'd selected a target.

"Hey, Wally." Sean's voice was friendly. Too friendly, Travis thought. "Later tonight, we plan to hard knock a gangster crib over on Smilax. That's your whatever the fuck you call it, right? Your community zone or some such shit?"

Walter Lowenstein, the senior member of the DINO squad, nodded with a forced smile that signaled he was pretty sure he was being set up for something. "Yeah, Sean. That's my assigned outreach area."

"Yeah, yeah, that's it. Outreach area." The detective winked at his teammates. "We're gonna do a hasty brief in the parking lot right around seven, then go blow it up. Why don't you and your guys gear up and come along?"

"Sorry, man. Wish we could, but we've got to—"

The whole GSU yelled in unison, finishing his sentence: "Go to a meeting!"

Most of the deputies in the room, instinctively carnivorous themselves, but still anxious to not be anyone's next meal, joined in with a round of harsh laughter.

"No sweat, Wally." Sean's snide tone left no doubt of the low regard he had for the deskbound DINO squad. "I'll be sure to drop off any intel. You still got that corner desk in the admin wing? The one by the window? With all the certificates and shit?"

Lowenstein looked away, red-faced, as the laughter went on.

"Hey, fellas, check this out."

Ted "Teddy" Rosado, one of the senior patrol deputies assigned to the substation and self-designated night watch clown, sat at the main computer terminal in the back of the room. Rosado had almost nine years on the job and could easily have rotated off the night weekend shift, but he stuck around. When Travis graduated from the academy, Ted had been his first field training officer. They spent three weeks riding together and, because of Travis's years of prior experience, their time together was more like a partnership than a training phase. Ted bragged it around that the money he made while "training" Jackson was the easiest FTO pay he ever got. Travis had spent enough time with the hardworking deputy to know that he thrived on the high-speed, low-drag nature of night watch.

Ted queued up the computer and yelled, "Somebody kill the lights."

The room went dark. The theater-size screen at the front of the room lit up with an image of the world-famous burly white cop from Texas kneeling on a crying black girl in a bathing suit. His knee was buried against her neck and his gun was pointed at the gathering crowd. The images were accompanied by the infamous NWA rap "Fuck the Police." The song rolled on as more graphic video of cops gone wild appeared, mixed in with still images of gangbangers with their cars and women. The music was cranked high, and the outlandish lyrics got both jeers and cheers from the audience. An L.A. cop captured on camera taking a baseball-like swing with his baton and laying out a suspect armed with a knife got a round of enthusiastic applause.

"Rosado, turn that shit off!" Sergeant Orlando Peña strode into the room like the marine he had been for twenty years before he became a cop, twenty-five years ago. The music stopped immediately but the pictures stayed up, and for a few seconds an image of full-on convict sex spilled onto the sergeant as he passed the screen.

"Goddamn it, all of it. Turn it off. And turn my lights back on."

Sergeant Peña took his position behind the podium. He was a compact, leathery man with skin the color and texture of coarse desert sand. He was rumored to be somewhere north of sixty, but that had never been confirmed because no one had the balls to ask. As always, his gray crew cut was tight and his uniform tailored to perfection. His well-earned reputation was that of a no-nonsense, patrol-oriented supervisor who had earned his stripes after spending two decades in a beat car. He refused transfer orders to the detective bureau on three occasions before admin finally gave up.

The images clicked off and the lights came on. Whenever Sergeant Peña addressed a crowd, the words started deep in his diaphragm, a skill he'd learned as a Parris Island drill instructor. The man could yell harder, longer, and louder than most anyone Travis had ever met.

"What do you say, Rosado? You finished with your little motivational presentation? Okay with you if I start briefing?"

"Yeah, Sarge. I'm done." Ted was senior enough to get away with being a little more salty than most of the deputies. "Some Crip set out of San Diego posted that shit on YouTube. I just figured it'd be good for everyone to know how that particular segment of the public holds us in such high regard."

Sergeant Peña ignored the comment. The room was silent. Travis knew that when Sergeant Peña ran a briefing, there was no confusion about who was in charge. This was night watch patrol, and if the sheriff himself walked in, he'd abide by the rules of Peña.

Scanning his audience, the sergeant said, "Murphy, what the hell do you think you're doing? Take that raggedy shit off your head."

GSU might be assigned to the detective bureau, but Peña's right to discipline was not hampered by such technicalities. Sean removed his ball cap, no questions asked.

"And if your team wants to attend my briefing, you best square your shit away. Or else just stay on the second floor. And get rid of the damn gum."

Sean gave a mock but respectful salute and swallowed hard.

Sergeant Peña panned the crowd, searching for any other infractions or offenses that might rate a quick Peña-colitis of an ass chewing. Finally satisfied, he got down to business.

"All right, listen up. All you sons of bitches complaining you don't have enough deps on the street? Well, here you go. We got us a major deployment tonight and we're going to take advantage of it. We're going to do some got'damn crime fighting."

Sergeant Peña began filling out the watch log, the document he would provide to the communications center, listing all patrol units and specialty assignments.

"GSU." Peña acknowledged the team once again, this time dep to dep. His voice sincere, he said, "Appreciate you detectives coming out on the weekend. We can use the help."

Peña's gaze settled on the smartly dressed crew by the door. "Is the COP unit hitting the field?"

Walter Lowenstein spoke for the group, and Travis heard the faint quiver in his voice. "Ah, no, Sergeant. We just came down to get up to speed on what's happening on the street. But if—"

"We appreciate your visiting." Dismissive, Sergeant Peña didn't need to hear any more. He was well aware of the political reality of the DINO squad.

Peña looked at the back row. "I want to thank the traffic unit for coming out to work a special detail tonight. Seeing that there are six of you and you're all making the big bucks on grant-funded OT, I'm assuming you'll take any and all crashes?"

A hoot of support went up in the room. Everyone knew that if you wanted to get out of taking the dreaded collision report, the best thing to do was to join the traffic division and become a motor cop. Left to their own devices, a good motor deputy could fill two ticket books in a ten-hour shift. The ability to generate that kind of revenue made them far too valuable a commodity to waste on something as trivial as collision reports. But Peña had a way of making even the motor cops feel conciliatory.

One of the men responded, "Sure, Sarge. We got you covered."

A lone voice called, "That includes complaint-of-pain crashes, right?"

The motor cop smiled and put his hand up in the air with his middle finger extended, stabbing it in the direction of the voice. The gesture was accepted without offense. Even Sergeant Peña almost smiled. For all their quirks, idiosyncrasies, and general prima donna attitudes, motorcycle deputies were highly respected for their skills on the road. Not to mention their willingness to haul ass to a cover call, no matter who put it out.

Sergeant Peña kept things moving. "Like I said, we got a lot of bodies tonight, so let's do some police work. I want to put out a two-dep X-ray unit. Any takers?"

X-ray was the designator for "extra unit." A two-deputy car not limited to a specific beat and not required to take report calls. The car would roam the city, looking for trouble. X-ray units were allowed to pick and choose the calls they would respond to, but being taken off regular work was expected to translate into felony arrests and bad guys in the jail. It was considered a good assignment for cops who liked to do police work. Especially on a Friday night.

"I'm in, Sarge," Ellie Peralta said, sucking the oxygen out of the room. Other than two deputies on the DINO squad, Peralta was the only female in briefing. She'd been on the night watch since Travis had come to the shift three months ago. In the few dealings he'd had with her—two deputy calls and occasional run-ins in the report room—he'd liked her. Travis raised his hand as well and nodded toward the podium.

"All right." The sergeant looked down, scribbling their names onto the list of beat units. "Peralta and Jackson. You got Thirty-One Paul X. Your job is to fill my jail, got it?"

"No problem, sir." Ellie looked at Travis from across the room. They'd never ridden together. She gave a quick nod and Travis nodded back.

Still a bit of a newcomer, Travis had been with the two thousand–member department long enough to learn about an ugly organizational norm. Like most any badge-carrying, gun-toting cop shop, the sheriff's department was dominated by men who weren't really big on hope and change. To them, conservative traditions were the greatest of values, and even those required a particular anatomical appendage. Women who joined the ranks paid a price. To Travis, it seemed like a high price.

Just about every female deputy in the department was tagged with her own personalized collection of unflattering rumors. No one was safe, from the newest rookie to the most senior member of the command. And from what Travis had gathered, no one's reputation was more sullied than Ellie Peralta's.

It was pretty typical stuff. The story went that, a few years back, Peralta had bedded down with her patrol watch commander. Eventually things had soured. The details were sketchy but the results were obvious. Peralta was still around. The lieutenant was not. Word on the street was she'd even filed a civil suit, alleging a hostile work environment, and had gotten a nice payday out of it. But that was just the base layer of innuendo.

Ellie Peralta was known first and foremost as the wife of Commander Roberto Peralta, the number three man on the organizational chart, just below the sheriff and assistant sheriff. That was all most deputies needed to hear before making up their minds about what kind of partner she might make. Travis had heard all the unflattering rumors about how Peralta had hooked up with the commander, but he paid little attention. Any cop or deputy, male or female, who was married to a high-ranking member of a command staff could walk over even the most qualified applicants to claim their choice of assignment. The way Travis had it figured, if Ellie Peralta stuck around to push a patrol sled on nights and weekends, she must be all right.

Sergeant Peña called out the rest of the beat assignments, covered a few wanted suspects sent down from the detective bureau, and read a memorandum from human resources about new, respectful workplace regulations. Peña held the paper aloft, then crumpled it in his hand.

"Rosado, I'll put this shit in your mailbox. You can train everybody on it next week. Feel free to use your visual aids."

A round of applause went through the room. Teddy, being Teddy, didn't just stand but climbed up on his chair to take a bow.

"All right, let's get out there." Peña's voice again filled the room, and the cops immediately started to move. "And remember: whatever it takes, everybody goes home tonight."

Travis stood and looked around the briefing room but didn't see his partner.

"Yo, Jackson." Ellie Peralta was outside the open doorway, already in the hall. "You ready to go or what?"

Travis walked over, towering over the female cop by a good six inches. Her dark hair, which was streaked with gray, had been put up in a tight bun on the back of her head. Her uniform was tailored to fit neatly over her thick frame, which he guessed was probably earned more at the dinner table than at the gym. Her skin was olive and smooth. Her brown eyes were bright, with just the beginning signs of crow's-feet at the outer corners.

"How's it going, Ellie?" Travis was forced in close as deputies pushed their way through the hallway. He stood with one hand on his gun belt and the other on the back strap of his Glock. She nodded a hello and started to speak but was interrupted by someone calling Travis's name.

"Hey, Jackson." Sean Murphy walked up. The gang detective glanced at Ellie before settling his attention on Travis.

"I got a call on my cell just before briefing. Clerk at the liquor store over on Santa Fe."

"Chito's?" Travis was familiar with the location. One of way too many liquor outlets located in the business district just outside the Vista barrio. "The new Eastside hangout?"

"So you're up on that place, huh?" Sean nodded in approval. "I gave the clerk my number. She gives me a heads-up when the gangsters start acting up. Little bastards have really dug in. It's gotten to the point they're pretty much claiming it Eastside territory. Apparently they figured out it's not included in the injunction."

Travis nodded, knowing that Sean was referring to the court-ordered injunction the sheriff's department had served against the Eastside street gang. Right after graduating from the academy, Travis had been assigned to the tedious paper drill, getting statements from residents and business owners whose lives were adversely impacted by the antics and criminal activity of the members of Eastside. He'd also helped to document dozens of teenagers, and even a few adults, as court-recognized gang members.

Armed with all this criminal intelligence, the district attorney's office filed a civil suit that declared specific gang members a public nuisance. The order prevented anyone named in the injunction from engaging in certain types of behavior or from associating with other gang members in specific locations.

Chiefs and sheriffs loved gang injunctions. It gave them a chance to pepper their public speeches with talk of creative crime fighting and community partnerships. Cops hated the early paperwork, but there was no denying the satisfaction of arresting a gangster for nothing more than wearing the wrong belt buckle or kicking it on certain street corners. Civil libertarians went nuts filing countersuits, claiming the Constitution was under assault. The gang members had shrugged it off and said fuck it. They moved their hangout a few blocks outside the designated safety zone and had been raising hell at Chito's ever since.

"So you rolling over there?" Travis asked.

"Yeah. The clerk wants to stay anonymous, but she says a bunch of the little pumpkin heads are hanging out behind the store. They already came in and ripped her for some beer and a bunch of pork rinds."

And there's the problem, Travis thought. Store clerks get ripped off by gang members but are too scared to fill out a theft report. Any contact the deps had with the group would have to be established independent of the complaint.

"They've been hanging out for over an hour, in the rear parking lot by that cement block wall. She wants us to run 'em off." Travis noticed that Sean was completely ignoring Ellie, not even glancing at her. "I'm thinking maybe we can rustle up something more than that. Try to get a hook or two out of it. You up for taking the cover?"

"Absolutely," Travis said, shooting a look at his partner, who was staring at Murphy with no apparent interest in weighing in. "You want us to head over now?"

"Yeah, but stay out of sight. I want you to set up on the street in front of the store. I'll bring my boys in from the other side, by the vacant lot. When we crash in, we'll spook them your way, so they don't head up the hill."

"Sounds good." Travis was familiar with the area and had a good visual of the plan. He looked at Ellie. "You good with that?"

"Oh sure. Whatever you guys say." She seemed to be doing her best doe-eyed-rookie impression.

Travis nodded, not sure what to make of her. Sean was already walking away. Travis called after him, "We'll be there in five."

Turning back to Ellie, Travis said, "I guess we'd better get going. I had court this morning, so I already checked out a squad. Loaded up an eight seventy and an AR. We should be all set."

Gazing up at him, Ellie batted her eyes and put a hand to her chest. "Oh, I just love a man who takes charge."

"Uh, yeah. Okay." Travis was already uncomfortable with this woman, who seemed to be communicating in riddles. "I'm parked out in the lot. Who's driving?"

She tilted her face up and batted her eyes again. "Well, you of course."

Travis was beginning to wonder what he'd gotten himself into when she shook her head as if it was her turn to be dismissive and her expression hardened. She shoved past him with enough force to actually move him out of her way. "Let's go. I'll powder my nose and change my pad later."

Travis watched as she headed out the door, thinking to himself that the ten-hour shift had just gotten a whole lot longer.

9

Omar stood at the top of a steep dirt embankment, peering through an opening in the chain-link fence. At the bottom of the hill, a dozen or so dark-skinned, brazen young men were gathered, pack-like, in the out-of-the-way parking lot behind Chito's Liquor. Dressed in mostly khaki, white, and blue, they clustered together, forcing Omar to search among them for his brother. He spotted Carlos Lopez, who was strictly known as Boo in this crowd. Off to one side was Little Beast. Omar didn't know the kid's real name. Snoop sat on the cement block wall with his usual, dull-witted look plastered on his misshapen face. Omar recognized a few others but didn't know all their names. Most noticeably, standing in the middle of the group as if holding court, was a man Omar regarded with equal parts loathing and fear: Chunks Gutierrez.

It wasn't long after their first eviction, which had landed the Ortegas in a rough part of the barrio, that he and Hector, walking home from school, got hit up by a group of Eastsiders. Omar had already decided on a survival strategy. Friendly but not too friendly. Respectful but not fearful. He told Hector to hold back and let him do the talking.

There had been three of them, all pissed off about legal papers the deputies had been dropping on homies all over the east side.

"The deps wanna be makin' it so we can't even kick it and shit." That was Snoop, a twentysomething Eastsider who spoke with a bad lisp. His head was lopsided, and one of his eyes wandered aimlessly around in its socket. Later, Omar had been told this was the result of a blow from a baseball bat, delivered by a Deep Valley King out of Oceanside.

That day, Snoop looked at the typed pages like he was trying to decipher Greek. "Says here they gonna get all up in our ass just for flyin' colors. Hangin' out on the corners. Says we can't even be whistlin' and shit. How they tell us who we can kick it with? What the hell we wear?"

It had been Omar who actually read the documents. After a quick scan, Omar explained the papers were what was called a restraining order. He looked back into Snoop's one good eye and told him the papers didn't have any power outside a few blocks.

"For reals, boy?" Snoop was already pulling out his phone. "You need to talk to the man about this shit."

The Eastsiders had escorted Omar and Hector to an alley a few blocks away; there, Omar had his first face-to-face meeting with Alonzo "Chunks" Gutierrez. Tucked away in a detached one-car garage, surrounded by his lieutenants, the twenty-five-year-old undisputed leader of Eastside puffed on a Faro and listened as Omar filled him in. Chunks sat in an overstuffed upholstered chair that Omar was pretty sure he'd seen on a street corner the previous day, with a scrawled sign that read "Free" perched on the seat.

When explaining the particulars of the paperwork to Chunks, Omar mentioned that not everyone in the gang was listed. Omar remembered how the big man wanted to be sure that his name appeared.

"Yeah, for sure," Omar said, already knowing what Chunks wanted to hear. "Right up at the top."

Chunks snatched away the documents and began to read the list of names, which immediately became a badge of honor in the minds of the gangsters. Being listed alongside their leader was good for their rep. Finished, Chunks looked Omar over long and hard before speaking.

"Who you be?"

"Ortega. Omar Ortega. This is my brother, Hector."

Chunks ignored the younger boy, who was barely eleven at the time, and pointed his cigarette at Omar.

"So you be like a smart-ass paisa, huh?" Even now, Omar could still hear the resentment in the man's voice, like Omar had somehow showed him up. "Some kinda brainy motherfucker, eh? Like a walkin' seso or some shit?"

The others laughed, shoving at Omar and calling out his new name. But when Omar looked back at Chunks, he didn't get a good vibe. Not at all. That had been almost three years ago. They'd been dancing the same dance ever since, Omar trying to stay out of the shot caller's reach while remaining in his comfort zone.

There. The small one in the center, like a yearling among dominant males. Anger flashed through him again and settled in his jaw. He wanted to grab Hector by the scruff of his neck and drag him home.

Omar thought about just calling out from the top of the hill, but he knew better. A punk-ass move like that? There'd be consequences. His only choice was to get down there and front the boy out. Aggravation still building, Omar stepped up on a plastic crate and easily vaulted the fence, dropping to the ground on the other side.

The chain link shook and rattled under Omar's weight. Every head turned his way, and each body cocked in anticipation of a possible attack by rivals or cops. In seconds, the startled looks disappeared, giving way to a chorus of familiar catcalls. Omar jogged down the embankment, deftly navigating the minefield of junk and trash. He reached the bottom, jumped from the five-foot cinder-block retaining wall to the pavement, then gathered himself up. Time to pay his respects. Kiss the damn ring.

Chunks Gutierrez stood dressed in khaki Dickies shorts that went down below his knees and a loose-fitting, crisp white T-shirt that had to be at least a 5X to cover his three hundred–pound body. His white socks were pulled up to his knees; his black slip-on loafers were no doubt a trophy from his recent stint in prison. He wore a blue Easton hat, new and stiff as a board, pulled down over blacked-out Locs sunglasses. The man's skin was a washed-out, sickly beige, evidence that being locked up took its toll in a lot of ways. Of all the personalities Omar had to handle with care, Chunks Gutierrez was far and away the toughest.

After their initial meeting, it didn't take long for Chunks to start focusing on the new kid: *Seso.* At sixteen, Omar was the prime age for gang recruitment, and Chunks had definitely taken a personal interest. Omar did everything he could to avoid any contact with the man and his entourage, but it soon became clear: either jump in with Eastside and take a ceremonial beating or refuse and earn himself frequent beatings that would have nothing to do with ceremony. Hell of a choice. Just when it seemed hopeless, all his mother's prayers were answered. It was as if God himself stepped in. Omar would have preferred that a lightning bolt rained down on the fat man's shaved head, but a K-9 cop from Oceanside worked out just as well.

Chunks had stolen a car down by Oceanside Harbor, probably planning to bop his way back to Vista and dump it. Before he even got out of town, an Oceanside cop lit him up for no front plate. A fifteen-mile car chase down the 78 ended on the outskirts of Vista, when Chunks couldn't make a tight corner and crashed into some paisa's living room. The cop sent his dog in through the hole in the wall and the animal sank its teeth into a meaty portion of the gangster's ample ass.

Shaking the dog loose, Chunks got in a few hard knocks of his own. That led to a righteous beat-down by ten or twelve cops from the half-dozen agencies that had joined in the pursuit. In the end, Chunks got rolled up for auto theft, felony evading, destruction of property, and assault on a police dog. Chunks spent the first three days in custody in Tri-City hospital, then got transferred to the county jail infirmary. Omar heard talk that the cops and the prosecutor had gotten a little worried about the use of force that left Chunks with two broken ribs, two black eyes, and wearing a neck brace. To keep the case out of a courtroom and out of the papers, they gifted Chunks a four-year deal. That had been just two years ago. Now, somehow, the Eastside shot caller was back, complicating Omar's exit plans.

Omar walked closer, smoothing his shirt with the palms of his hands, playing the part. From the corner of his eye, he saw a look of dread on Hector's face, but Omar would deal with him later. First order of business had to be acknowledging the triumphant return of the leader of the Eastside gang.

Chunks called out, a not-so-subtle challenge in his voice.

"Damn, if it ain't my boy Seso." Chunks held a forty of Modelo in one hand and used the other to lift his shirt, revealing the black grip of a semi-auto handgun. "Y'ought not be droppin' in like that, fool. Damn near put a cap in your ass."

Seeing the gun and the crowd, Omar felt a familiar premonition of trouble brewing. His gut told him to grab Hector, get back to the apartment, and lock the door. The hell with offending these guys. Just hunker down. In a few days, he and his family would be gone.

He knew better. The habits and skills he'd honed for this world ran deep. He showed no concern at the sight of the gun. Stepping closer, he went through the routine of loosely brushing palms with Chunks, followed by a fist bump. When he spoke, his voice was smooth and conveyed a confident respect.

"Come on, Chunks, you know better. Just wanted to come by. Pay my respects. Welcome ya home. I thought you was kickin' it with the state. How'd you scam your way out already?"

Chunks posted up, his feet at a perfect seventy-degree angle, long arms dangling, his head cocked to the side. As he spoke, Omar couldn't help but stare at the sizable gap between the man's two upper front teeth. Wide apart at the gum, they grew closer as they went down, until the bottoms of the teeth nearly touched.

"Ain't no scam to it. I was good with the arrangement. Eatin' three a day and chillin'. Hanging with gangsters from all over SoCal, dawg. Didn't need to be worrying about none of this street drama, who's throwing down with who. Then one morning? CO shows up, talking all this Prop Fifty-Seven bullshit. Tells me to pack my shit. Says my time's up."

"No shit?"

"For real, homes. They threw my ass *outta* jail."

Omar nodded, feigning interest. He needed to get moving, but it was clear Chunks wasn't done.

"What's this I hear, you still ain't jumped in? The fuck, Seso?" Chunks spoke with his arms as well as his mouth, but his feet stayed planted to the ground so that Omar would know he was representing Eastside. "You oughta be steppin' up by now. Puttin' in the work."

"I just kick it, Chunks. You know how it is."

"That how you see it? Kick it but don't risk it?" Omar picked up on the edge in the man's voice. "Now I hear you be runnin' off to join the army or some shit?"

Omar nodded again. "Leave next week."

"So the Brain is headed for Bagdad. Gonna ice a couple of sheiks? Maybe get your junk sucked by one of them genies all covered up in black 'n' shit?"

The boys around them yukked it up in a show of respect for their leader's sense of humor. Chunks took it all in.

Omar saw an opening.

"Yo, Hector. You were supposed to meet me after school. We need to get home."

Chunks looked at the younger boy. "What up, peewee? You dissin' your big bro?"

Hector shook his head but looked guilty as hell.

"Sorry about that, Seso," Chunks said, sounding anything but sorry. "I didn't figure you'd have any problem if the boy kicked it with the homies for a while."

"Yeah, no worries, man." Omar did his best to play it down. "Just, you know . . . Ma's house rules and shit."

Chunks walked up to Hector and gave him a shove hard enough to knock him back a few feet. "Get your punk ass outta here and don't be coming back till your brother tells me it's okay. You feel me?"

"Yeah, all right, Chunks." Hector shot his brother a look. Omar knew Hector would be hot about the put-down. Serves him right, Omar thought. Maybe he'll listen next time.

"Go on, boy," Chunks said. When Omar made to leave with his brother, the leader called out, "Seso. Stick around."

"I can't, man. I got to—"

"What?" Chunks cut him off. "I put in two years for the barrio and you ain't got five minutes to hang with me? You gotta live by Ma's house rules too?"

Every head turned to Omar, and the sudden tension was lost on no one. A misstep could be costly. Omar looked at his brother. "Go home, Hector. I'm gonna kick it."

"I can stick around and wait for you."

"Get home." Omar stared at his brother, making it clear this bullshit predicament was on him. When Hector still didn't move, Omar feigned a step in his direction and shouted, "Go, goddamn it."

Hector flinched, then ran, scaling the embankment like a mountain goat, pursued by catcalls and laughter. Total humiliation. At least, Omar thought, that'll keep him from coming back anytime soon.

"So tell me, Seso, how much the army gonna pay you to go out and cap ragheads?"

"Around eighteen hundred a month."

"Eighteen hundred?" Chunks cocked his head, looking disgusted. "Homes, I wouldn't ask you to kill nobody for less than—hell, at least two Gs. And that's just one hit. Government got some cheap-ass ways."

The crowd nodded in agreement and Omar felt himself being moved into a position of outsider. Chunks went on.

"And for what? Camp you out in some A-rab desert?"

"I probably won't even go overseas, Chunks. All that stuff is pretty much over."

Chunks waved Omar off. "Shit, army be sendin' you wherever the hell they want. You can have that shit. I'm going to make a thousand bucks in the next two hours and I ain't gotta sleep in some hot-ass tent to do it. Come watch this shit."

Omar knew he couldn't bolt just yet, but first chance he got, he was down the road.

"Toon. Get ya ass over here."

Miguel "Toon" Fuentes posted up in front of his leader. Miguel's short, fireplug build was topped off by a face that bore an uncanny resemblance to the cartoon character Bart Simpson, so he'd picked up the name Bart. He'd objected, saying that was some weak-ass shit for Eastside. Somehow he'd come to be known as Cartoon, which eventually got cut down to Toon. He wore it well and the name had stuck.

Omar and Toon had been in the same kindergarten class at Carson Elementary. Back then, he had been "Migs," and both he and Omar had been big fans of *Captain Underpants*. Through most of grade school they were forwards on the same soccer team. Omar's dad was the coach. The year they won the city parks and rec tournament, in fifth grade, the whole team had come to the Ortegas' house to celebrate.

Migs had dropped out after eighth grade and Omar had lost track of him until his family moved to the barrio. Soon after that, Migs stopped by the first apartment the Ortegas had managed to rent.

"Sorry about your dad." They were sitting on the front stoop, and Migs spoke from the heart. "I use to pretend that he was, like, my dad too, ya know? Hope that's okay, that I say that."

"Yeah, Migs," Omar had managed to answer. He knew Migs's father had been in and out of jail the boy's whole life. "It's fine. He liked you a lot."

Now Toon gave Omar a nod and half smile—for old times' sake—then looked at the boss. "Yo, Chunks."

"You good to go, boy?"

"Yeah, I'm packed up." There was clear reluctance in Toon's voice.

Chunks took a long hit off his beer, then grabbed the younger boy by the back of the neck and pulled him in tight against his much larger body. "You do like I said? Just one knuckle deep?"

"Yeah, Chunks."

"I mean, you go two knuckles, homes, I'm thinking maybe you be likin' it."

Omar wasn't following, but whatever Chunks was talking about, it got a good laugh from the crowd.

It was less funny to Toon, and his eyes blazed at the onlookers. His voice was flat and humorless. "I just went one knuckle in, Chunks. That's all."

"Good. And you wrapped it up nice and tight? 'Cuz you know Mexican brown don't mean *that* Mexican brown."

More laughs from the crowd. This time, even Toon smiled.

"It's all good, Chunks."

"All right, then. Let's get at it." Chunks looked at Omar. "Come on, army boy. I'm going to show you how to make some serious cash."

The entire entourage moved to a spot behind the building, where they could see up the alley and out to the street. Aware that time was slipping by, Omar listened while Chunks explained the latest scam.

"You hear about my man Psycho?"

"Yeah. I saw it on the news."

"The news?" Omar heard disgust in the shot caller's voice. "Boy, you need to get the word off the street. Not sittin' at home listening to some bullshit on television."

Omar had walked right into that one, so he didn't bother trying to defend himself. Chunks went on.

"Gotta call while I be locked up, telling me Psycho got his ass rolled up for a robbery at the Kwik Stop. He jacked some slant-eyed player. I had the homies pay Ho Chi a visit. Got 'im to see the wisdom of staying quiet. Problem is, Five-O's got Psycho on video, comin' and goin' out the store. Homes may as well be holdin' one of them bags with a big old dollar sign on it, looking up to say fuckin' 'Cheese.'"

Chunks stopped and shook his head, as if contemplating the cruel nature of technology. "I mean, Asians, right? Bitches be invested in all that surveillance shit. Psycho's already got a strike. He's lookin' at fifteen years."

"That's rough, Chunks."

"For twenty-two lousy dollars? *Word.*" Chunks spoke with certainty. "Hear me on this, ese. Even when they don't say shit? Asians got weight. Psycho? Gonna have to do the time, is all."

Omar had heard the official version on the local Univision newscast. The press had been all over the story: an armed robbery of a Korean store owner who tried to hold on to his money but was pistol-whipped into submission. The crook made off with twenty-two dollars and a case of Modelo. The victim ended up in the hospital with a fractured skull.

It happened on a slow news day, so the press rolled a camera crew out to the barrio. That led to the mayor of Vista calling for justice and the sheriff putting a couple of downtown detectives on the case. The dicks quickly made Luis "Psycho" Valdez off the video. To leave a lasting impression on the entire Eastside gang, the sheriff's SWAT team hit the door of Psycho's house at daybreak on a Sunday morning. The evening news showed Psycho being dragged out in chonies and handcuffs, his pregnant girlfriend, with a seven-month bump, screaming in the background.

Chunks pulled a fresh spray can from the side pocket of his Dickies and tossed it to Toon. "You up, vato. Be sure you get all the way out there by the street. Plant the flag, homes."

Toon caught the can and jogged awkwardly toward the end of the alley. Chunks called out, "And remember. Throw that shit at 'em, then haul ass for a bit, bro. Make it good enough for a booking."

From their vantage point behind the liquor store, Omar watched as Toon gave the can a good shake and went to work on a smooth cement wall.

"Psycho's old lady got hold of me," Chunks continued. "Said Psycho's gonna be kickin' it in county for a while before they ship his ass out. Wants to set up a little action. Put up as the big dog and be representin' Eastside."

With long, looping sprays, Toon threw up the Eastside tag and started to blow out a roster of names, with Chunks right at the top of the list.

"I got my boy Toon keistered up with a big old chunk'a H."

Omar wondered if he was supposed to already know what that was. "'H,' Chunks?"

"Heroin, Seso. Toon's gonna make a house call to Psycho. Home delivery, if you hear what I'm sayin'. That shit oughta bring in two Gs." Chunks puffed up a bit and went on, "I'm in for half and I don't even have to touch it."

Chunks tilted his head back, looking at Omar out of the corner of one eye. "You see how it is, soldier boy? That's smart money."

"For reals, Chunks." Omar again resisted the temptation to check his phone. The minutes were slipping by. He couldn't help but wonder, Did this fat-ass even think maybe Psycho's pregnant girlfriend could use a few bucks? He did his best to sound respectful. "You be all hooked up."

"When you get settled somewhere, reach out to me. We'll start dealing to all the junkie soldiers. I'll cut you in for a piece. Say, fifteen percent?"

"I don't know, Chunks. The army is pretty careful who gets in. Not much in the way of dope fiends these days."

"Is that right? Soldiers never be hittin' the pipe or nothing? Sounds like a pussified outfit to me."

There was real anger in the gang leader's voice. Why hadn't Omar just gone along? *Sure, Chunks. You bet. Fifteen percent sounds great.* Too late. Now he had to scramble.

"Nah, Chunks, it ain't that. It's just, in the army, if you get caught just blazin' up a joint they lock you up."

"Well then, that's a fucked-up situation to walk into, ain't it?"

"Just trying to take care of my family, you know? I mean, it's work." Omar shrugged, trying to maneuver his way out of this self-made jam, realizing too late that he was just making it worse.

Chunks leaned in close enough that Omar was looking at the black hair follicles on his chin and the funny little gap in his teeth. A cloud of stale beer washed over Omar as Chunks said, "And hitting the street to represent Eastside? That ain't *work*, Seso?"

"I ain't saying that, Chunks. I'm just looking to, you know, make some steady money. I ain't all hooked up like you."

Omar and Chunks stood face-to-face. The hiss of Toon's spray can filled the air from fifty feet away. The crowd was silent, waiting for Chunks to decide whether or not he'd been disrespected.

10

1552 HOURS

Weaving through afternoon traffic, Travis took surface streets to avoid the jam on the 78. He drove through the small but upscale downtown district of shops and restaurants and headed for the east side. From the substation to Chito's was less than five minutes, but with the windows down, that was enough time for the interior of the car to reach the temperature of a sauna. Travis's vest was already moist with sweat and his T-shirt clung to his skin, but none of that mattered. The sounds of the street were too critical to give up for a little personal comfort.

A half mile from the liquor store, Ellie still hadn't spoken, so Travis tried to kick things off.

"Can you believe this heat?" he said, not bothering to look in her direction. "It's like patrolling the surface of the sun. And it's barely June."

"Oh, for shit's sake." Her tone was droll and labored, like talking to him was heavy lifting. "Seriously? The weather?"

Travis kept his eyes on the road, cocked his head to one side, and raised his hand partway off the steering wheel in a gesture of confusion. They rode on in silence, sitting through a long red light, and Travis began to have serious regrets about raising his hand during briefing. His partner of one day went back to staring out the window. Finally, the faded, hand-painted billboard that read "Chito's Liquor" came into view. He slowed and pulled to the curb across the street.

"Nah, not here," Ellie said. "You're going to want to hug the other side of the street. We don't want to get caught in cross traffic when GSU calls us to move in." She pointed across the lane, busy with cars headed in the other direction. "Get over there, in the bike lane."

Travis inched back into traffic, turn signal on, waiting for an opening.

"Damn, man, it's a police car. Quit driving like a pussy. Just flip on the red-and-blues and get over there." Her voice held a new note of command. "Pull up closer to the alley."

Travis repositioned the car and Ellie grabbed the microphone. "Thirty-One Paul X, ten ninety-seven front of Chito's. GSU, we're in position and standing by."

With the mouth of the alley about ten feet in front of the car, Travis crept a bit closer. As he nosed up to the corner of the building, a familiar hissing sound came through the open windows. When he glanced at the passenger seat, Ellie gave a tight nod. She heard it too.

They sat and waited for the order from GSU. The hissing stopped, replaced by the tumble of the marble. A guy Travis figured to be around eighteen, wearing a white crewneck T-shirt that fit him like a dress, sauntered out of the alley, shaking a can of spray paint. Spotting the black and white idling three feet in front of him, he froze, then let out a loud whistle.

"Shit. We're burned," Ellie said. Grabbing the mic, she spoke in rapid staccato. "Thirty-One Paul X out on a five nine-four in progress, Chito's Liquor, alley side. GSU, they made us. Move in."

In the background, Travis heard the immediate rev of several engines as the GSU cars stormed the rear of the store. He shoved the gearshift into park and burst out of the car, but even before he got clear of the doorway, the kid reared back and launched the spray can directly at his head. Travis ducked, almost losing his balance. By the time he stood back up, Ellie was in front of the car in a fighting stance, toe to toe with the suspect.

The guy took a wild swing at Ellie, who made a *Matrix*-like move, leaning back at the waist and avoiding the punch by an easy six inches. He came around with another haymaker and she ducked, once again completely avoiding the blow. This time, when she stood up, Ellie buried the short end of her baton in her attacker's stomach. He doubled over and she grabbed him around the head and threw him onto the hood of the patrol car.

Ellie pressed herself over his body and used a forearm to hold him down against the metal hood, which Travis figured had to be a good 120 degrees. The suspect screamed as his cheek cooked on the hot surface. Ellie used her free hand to pull out her cuffs. Travis moved to assist, but before he even came around the front of the car, Ellie had the guy hooked up and standing. Travis used his portable radio to notify GSU.

"Thirty-One Paul X, in the alley. One in custody for five nine-four and assault on a deputy."

"*Great. Good for you.*"

Travis recognized the voice of Sean Murphy and knew the unorthodox radio transmission probably meant he was pissed about their early move. Sean continued, "Station A, GSU is to the rear of Chito's Liquor. We've got several fleeing up the hill onto Palm Drive. Send a unit to do a drive-through."

The handcuffed suspect was still gasping for breath from the gut punch, and the left side of his face was bright red and blistered. Ellie pushed him up against the back fender and gave him a quick but thorough pat down. Still leaning against her prisoner, she looked at Travis.

"Little help, partner?" She nodded toward the closed car door.

Snapping out of his role of observer, Travis came around and opened the rear passenger door. Ellie put her hand gently on top of her prisoner's head and guided him into the tight space that barely qualified as a back-seat. She buckled him in, lowered the window a couple of inches, and shut the door. She spoke through the thick mesh, sounding to Travis like a mother addressing a misbehaving child.

"Sorry about your face, but you know you can't be fighting back like that. We'll get some water on it at the station."

Travis kept an eye on the prisoner while Ellie went into the alley and used her phone to snap a few pictures of the graffiti and collect the paint can as evidence. She came back just as the radio squawked. Sean's voice had a no-nonsense, pissed-off quality. "GSU, out on two to the rear of the store. Everybody else is in the wind. Thirty-One Paul X, get back here *now*."

Travis looked down the alleyway; he could see the GSU detectives standing over two men who were seated on the ground, legs out and ankles crossed, hands behind their heads. Ellie, calmly smoothing her uniform and adjusting her gear, seemed to read his mind.

"Forget about him. He can be as shitty as he wants. We had to improvise." She climbed into the passenger seat. "But we'd better get back there. See what they got."

Travis stood with his hand on the frame of the open door, looking down at her.

"What?" she said.

"Nothing. I mean . . ." He shook his head. "Damn, Ellie. Nice job. You looked like Cat Zingano back in the day gettin' after it."

"Just get in the car." She pulled the door shut and Travis walked around to the driver's side. Maybe it wouldn't be such a bad shift after all.

11

3:58 P.M.

Chunks stayed in close, and Omar knew the leader of Eastside was contemplating whether or not he needed to dole out some punishment. He looked ready to rule. Omar decided he wouldn't just stand there and take a beating. Hell, no. Strike first and strike quick, then bolt back up the embankment. He'd have the element of surprise, not to mention superior speed to nearly everyone in the group. He widened his stance and balled his fists, telling himself the throw-down was long overdue. A piercing whistle split the air, a well-known warning to anyone associated with the barrio.

Nearly every voice called out, "La chota!"

Like an animal reacting to a sudden threat, Chunks swiveled his head, looking for the source of danger as well as an escape route. Omar looked up the alley in time to see Toon heave his paint can at one uniformed deputy before taking a swing at a second.

Engines revved and vehicles could be heard approaching from the vacant lot.

"Oh, shit. Slow day for Five-O." Chunks walked quickly to a nearby dumpster. He lifted the lid, tossed his gun inside, and shouted, "All right, Eastside. Haul ass."

A black and white SUV accelerated around the corner; to Omar, it seemed the car was coming straight at him. Another vehicle came in right behind it. Chunks bolted, calling over his shoulder, "Later, Seso."

Deputies jumped from the cars and ran full tilt toward the scattering group. Most of the Eastsiders were up the embankment and over the fence before the deputies got anywhere near them. Even Chunks displayed a rare burst of energy before one of the deputies vectored in at an intersect- ing angle. A hard shove caught Chunks midstride, and for the briefest moment, he looked almost graceful in flight. Gravity took over and the big man hit the ground hard, bounced, then rolled to a humiliating stop.

Omar looked back toward the street. A female deputy had Toon sprawled across the hood of the cop car that still blocked the alley. Omar turned, ready to scale the hillside, but some of the deputies had formed a skirmish line at the bottom of the embankment, so that was out of the question.

Pissed at himself for hesitating, he saw no other option. Cornered, and no stranger to interactions with deputies who patrolled the barrio, he stood still, put his hands in the air, and waited for instructions. He didn't have to wait long, and he knew exactly who he was dealing with.

Murphy.

The muscular white cop, tatted out like some kind of biker convict, walked directly toward Omar. His eyes were hidden behind Oakley wrap- arounds, but Omar could tell from the bounce of the man's step that he was daring him to run. Murphy wore his usual black uniform with the vest on the outside, just like the soldiers Omar had seen on TV, patrolling Afghanistan. The well-known tag of GSU was emblazoned above the cloth badge sewn onto his vest; his name was stenciled on the opposite side. With a quick flick of his wrist, the short metal baton Murphy carried in his right hand snapped out to full length. He pointed the steel rod directly at Omar and spoke with more than his usual hatefulness.

"On your ass, Seso. Sit down and shut up."

Omar dropped straight to the ground, resisting the natural inclination to put his hands down so he could ease himself to the pavement. That could get him lit up with a stun gun or a few well-placed whacks with that baton. In some cases, shot. He knew the police report would record any such gesture as a "furtive movement," so the deputies would have cover for their actions. So Omar had learned how to drop to the pavement with- out the assistance of his hands. Sure, it was hard on the ass, but a sore ass wouldn't land you in the hospital or get you buried in the ground.

Two other deputies, also dressed in GSU colors, walked up with Chunks Gutierrez in tow. The shot caller's shirt was smeared with dirt and grass stains. His sunglasses sat cockeyed on his face. The deputies gave Chunks another good shove to the ground. Murphy shouted commands at the other deputies and yelled into his radio, making it obvious he was in charge.

"Sit down, fat-ass. Hands on top of your head. Pull up next to your homie."

I got your "homie" right here, asshole, Omar thought, but when he looked up at Murphy and the rest of the deps, he made sure to mask his anger and disrespect. In his time in the barrio, Omar had come to know Detective Murphy, known to most Eastside gangsters as "Moho" because of his thick, rust-colored hair. The man held a contemptuous view of the public in general and gangsters in particular.

Murphy had a rep of always pushing things to the limit. He cut no slack. More than a few times, Omar had seen Murphy turn jaywalking into a full-on stop, frisk, search, and haul-away. Omar had been stopped and frisked by Murphy three different times; he knew the drill all too well. Their last go-around had been a few months ago. Omar had been walking home from school.

"One of these days, Seso, I'm gonna catch you holding," Murphy had said, frustration obvious in his voice and stance. Omar had been reassembling his backpack after Murphy dumped it out across the hood of his SUV and searched through every book and folder. "I'll hang some paper on your ass and you can bet, from then on, I'll be all up in your shit."

Omar never argued, but he always wondered why Murphy was after him. What had he ever done? Then again, Omar knew damn well the deputies who worked gang enforcement didn't need a reason to get *all up in your shit*. It was like some kind of contest, a sport where cops were the hunters and everyone else was prey.

Murphy stared down through his Oakleys. "Damn, Gutierrez. You ain't been out a week. Already out here starting shit?"

"Ease up, boss." Chunks straightened his shades and brushed off his shirt, doing his best imitation of an innocent bystander. "We just hanging out, conversin' and catching up on old times. What's got you deps so riled? Must be the heat, am I right?"

Four deputies formed a semicircle around Omar and Chunks. The rapid rise and fall of each man's chest signaled the deputies were pretty jacked up. Omar was glad to see that all pistols were holstered, but Murphy was still gripping his baton, tapping it against his leg. Things could still get ugly.

Murphy spoke without taking his eyes off either of them. "Donnie, do the honors. Pat these homies down."

One of the deputies pulled out a pair of short, black leather gloves that fit tightly and came just to his wrist. He moved behind the seated men and, as Omar could see in his peripheral vision, began to search Chunks. He ran his hands rough over the man's body, spending a lot of time on his waistband.

Finished with Chunks, the deputy stepped over to Omar and pulled his hands together behind his head. With one hand, the deputy squeezed Omar's fingers into a bunched-up knot and held on tight. The deputy then ran his other hand, palm down, roughly over Omar's back, chest, and stomach, then down both trouser legs. Just like with Chunks, the deputy spent a good bit of time searching Omar's waistband. Finally, he backed off and stood. Omar knew enough to keep his hands up.

"They're clean, Murph," the deputy said.

"Just hanging out, huh?" Murphy tossed his head in the direction of the alley. He looked at Chunks. "Which little soldier did you send out to tag up the wall?"

Chunks gave Omar a bored look. Murphy kept talking, pointing his baton down the alley. "Blowing out a roster. Let everybody know the big man's back."

"Uh-uh, homes," Chunks said. "I wasn't nowhere near the scene of that crime, you feel me?"

Murphy sneered in anger and moved a step closer, then reared back and sliced the air with his baton. Unsure who was the intended target, Omar lowered his arms around his head. The baton stopped an inch from the gangster's ear, and Murphy's voice was nothing short of venomous. "Call me *homes* again, and I will crack that pumpkin-ass head of yours till you bleed in the street. *Feel me?*"

Omar was amazed by the big man's calm demeanor. Though his hands were still laced behind his head and his legs were straight out in front of him, Chunks appeared almost serene. He showed no reaction other than to look up at the deputy and give him his best gap-toothed smile.

"Come on, Officer Murphy. If you're gonna keep chillin' with us down here in the barrio, you need to relax. Otherwise, maybe you should be like one of them DARE cops. Maybe work community relations or some shit."

"Shut your mouth, Gutierrez." Murphy pulled back his baton. "And it's 'detective' or 'deputy.' *Don't* call me 'officer.'"

"Oh yeah, I forgot." Chunks feigned confusion. "You deps get all hung up on that shit, huh? My apologies, *Deputy*."

Murphy's scare tactic and tough talk hadn't fazed the Eastside leader. Frustrated and now even more pissed off, Murphy turned to Omar.

"It's about time, Seso. Looks like you're all in now, huh?"

"Excuse me, sir?" Omar looked at his own reflection in the cop's glasses. His heart pounded harder in his chest. His hands, which had drifted down a bit, went higher in the air.

"*Excuse me, sir*," Murphy said mockingly, then reached out with his baton to flick the sleeve of Omar's jersey. "Flying the flag. You finally throwing down for Eastside?"

"Uh, I just like the Dodgers is all."

"Oh yeah?" Murphy said, doubtful. "Who starts at short?"

"Corey Seager. Hit three hundred last season."

"Third?"

"Justin Turner. Three twenty-seven."

"Best pitcher?"

Omar smirked a bit and nodded to the number on his jersey. "Julio Urias, but I know you'll say Kershaw."

Obviously unsatisfied, Murphy wouldn't let it go. "So you know the names of a few ballplayers. Big deal. When did you jump in? You're claiming now, right?"

Omar could feel Chunks glaring at him, demanding that he step up for Eastside. Before Omar had to answer, another deputy spoke up.

"Yo, Murph. Check this out."

Everyone, including Omar and Chunks, turned to the voice. The deputy who'd done the pat-downs stood next to the dumpster, holding up the handgun like a trophy. With a wide grin, he pulled back the slide, ejecting a round. "Forty cal, and the damn thing's loaded."

"Shit, Donnie." Murphy didn't sound happy. "Maybe you coulda left that for prints? Photograph it in place?"

"Oh." The deputy's enthusiasm vanished. "Sorry, man. You want I should put it back?"

Murphy shook his head. "Just quit finger-fucking it and collect the damn thing." As the deputy walked to his car with the firearm, Murphy lowered his gaze to the two men sitting in front of him and snarled, "Whose gat?"

Chunks spoke up, his voice firm but unconvincing. "We got no idea, Deputy."

Murphy looked to Omar. "He speak for you, sports fan?"

"That isn't mine," Omar said, shaking his head.

"Then whose is it?"

Omar had no intention of getting drawn into this bullshit. If Murphy was going to hook Chunks for a gun charge, he'd have to do it on his own. "How would I know? People come through here a lot."

"I guess it's a mystery then, huh, Seso? Well, hell then. Let's investigate." Murphy stared at Chunks with a look of snide satisfaction. "Simmons. Transport Gutierrez. Get hold of his PO."

"What up, Murphy?" Chunks shouted as two deps moved to take him into custody. "Why you gotta be draggin' parole into this? You got nothing. I was kicking it, yo."

"Save it, Gutierrez. You're a newly minted parolee, standing four feet away from a loaded firearm. You're going to the station. What happens after that is up to your parole officer."

The deputies bent down and pulled Chunks's arms behind his back. Between his wide girth and lack of flexibility, as much as the deputies tried, they couldn't get him cuffed. Chunks shouted and moaned in protest while making the deputies' task as difficult as possible without displaying any overt resistance.

Arms crossed, Murphy tapped his baton against his shoulder. "Jesus, you two. Just string up some flexicuffs. Get him outta here."

The deputies laced together two pairs of plastic handcuffs that looked like a couple of zip ties from Home Depot. They managed to get Chunks cuffed up, but it took both men and all their strength to get the man on his feet.

"Later, Seso," Chunks said, looking straight at Omar over his shoulder. He gave a single, deliberate nod. "Represent, ese."

Still on the ground, Omar watched the deputies escort Chunks to a nearby cop car. After a good bit of maneuvering and no shortage of shoving, the deputies eventually shoehorned the man into the backseat and closed the door. The car pulled out.

Murphy used both hands to retract his baton, then slipped it into a black nylon pouch on his vest. "Put your hands down."

Omar lowered his arms and rolled out the stiffness in his shoulders. He put his hands in his lap and looked up, making eye contact with Murphy, who had raised his Oakleys up on his forehead.

"All right, quit bullshitting around. Gutierrez dumped the piece, didn't he?" It was more statement than question, but Omar knew the man needed confirmation. Not gonna happen.

"I told you. I just—"

"Yeah, yeah, I know. You just barely got here." The cop squatted so he was on the same level as Omar. "What's it been now? Two, three years you been bangin' with Eastside?"

"I've told you before, I don't bang and I don't claim." Omar shook his head almost defiantly. "I *live* on the east side. That's all."

"Yeah. That's what you always tell me when we're alone. But here you are. Hanging at the wall. Kicking it with Chunks. Flyin' the blue. Going by your street name. Sure sounds like you're part of the set. Even went and got yourself a pumpkin head. I think it's about time we get you in the system."

Omar dropped his head in frustration. That was the last thing he needed. Being officially named a gang member, what the deps called "getting documented," was a big deal. Omar had read somewhere that it was a special legal classification that made it easier for cops to arrest someone and charge them with a crime. If he got documented, Omar knew, his name would be listed in a nationwide database—and the army would take that very seriously.

Maybe he should tell Murphy he'd enlisted? Maybe that would make him back off. But then again, what if, just to be an asshole, Murphy called Omar's recruiter? Said some shit just to try and screw him over? Omar knew, when it came to dealing with cops, especially this one, the less he volunteered, the better. But it was time to push back a little.

"Look, Detective, my little brother was hanging out and I came to get him. I was about to head home when you all came pulling up.

"This?" He plucked at his jersey with two fingers and looked Murphy straight in the eye. "I told you, I like the Dodgers is all. I don't bang, I'm not in a gang, and I don't know anything about that gun. Now, if we're finished here, I'd like to go home."

"Listen to Seso." Murphy stood up and his voice again took on a mocking tone. "Always been a smart homie, huh?"

"Yes sir, I have. Now can I leave?" It was probably too late for him to get to the bank; he couldn't risk pulling out his phone to check the time.

Murphy dropped his sunglasses back over his eyes and Omar picked up on the special disdain cops reserved for those who didn't know their role in the whole "law comes to the barrio" drama. When gangsters hurled insults and started name-calling, that was to be expected, on account of their vile and criminal nature. Someone who tried to push back on an equal level, who knew their rights and how to articulate them—that was a threat.

"You're not going anywhere just yet," Murphy said, looking squarely at Omar as he pulled the familiar field interview book from the cargo pocket of his trousers. "Let's go through the drill, Seso."

"Again? Come on, Detective Murphy."

"Give me your date of birth. You turn eighteen yet?"

"Last month."

Murphy nodded as though the answer provided him with some kind of satisfaction. "Well then, the stakes have gone up."

Omar answered all Murphy's usual questions about address, height, and weight. He pushed back his sleeves, held out his arms, and lifted his shirt to prove he still didn't have any tattoos. He and Murphy had been through this before.

"Remind me. When was the last time you were arrested?"

"You know I've never been arrested."

"And how is that, Seso?" Murphy said. "I need to start paying more attention to you, huh? I mean, hell, maybe that's *your* gun. I'm thinking I oughta take you in with Chunks. Sweat you both for a couple of hours."

The black and white from the alley pulled up, with Migs sitting slumped in the backseat. The car stopped a good twenty feet away, but Omar was pretty sure he could see Migs crying. Good thing Chunks had already been hauled off. Tears would not have gone over well with the gang leader, and Migs would have caught some hell. Omar tried to give Migs a look of reassurance. Migs smiled back but it was weak.

"You stay right there," Murphy said, pointing at Omar with four fingers. "You are not free to go, so don't move."

"Whatever." Omar waved him off, pretty sure at this point his schedule was blown.

Murphy walked over to the black and white. The passenger window of the car was down, but Murphy walked around the car to speak to the driver.

The female cop got out of the front passenger seat, ignoring Murphy. She pulled a blue rubber glove onto one hand and opened the back door. She squatted down like a baseball catcher to talk to Migs. With her gloved hand, she pulled a paper towel from her back pocket and wiped sweat from his forehead. She dabbed at his eyes and held the towel up so he could blow his nose. When she took off the glove, the sweaty, snotty towel ended up inside it. She dropped the wadded-up, inside-out glove onto the floor of the car, patted Migs on the shoulder, and shut the door. As she got back into the front seat, she made eye contact with Omar. She smiled, winked, and nodded in a way that seemed almost friendly. Omar surprised himself by nodding back.

The driver of the patrol car, a tall, blond, white dude, had gotten out of the car and was standing face-to-face with Murphy. Omar couldn't hear most of what they were saying, but the two cops, who were about the same size, were definitely arguing, and it was getting serious. Murphy said something like "You blew the call" and the other cop came back with "No choice." After a few more exchanges, the blond cop got back in the car and drove out through the parking lot and Murphy walked back to Omar.

"All right, Seso." Omar could hear the anger simmering in his voice. "Get your ass outta here. And this is the last time I'm telling you. I find you kicking it with these vatos again, I'm damn sure going to document your ass as Eastside and you can just deal with the sheet. You hear me?"

Omar stood up and answered with a determination he was sure this cop could never understand. "Believe me, you won't be seeing me anywhere."

Murphy stared at him for a few more seconds, then tossed his head in the direction of the street. "Go. Get the hell out of here."

Omar offered up his hand, not so much out of respect as to demonstrate that, in his mind, he and Murphy were equals and their business was concluded. He made sure to let the sarcasm come through. Kind of a hard knock at a locked door. "Good seeing you again, Deputy."

Murphy looked at Omar's hand, incredulous. After a few seconds he walked away, mumbling under his breath.

Omar waited until Murphy's car pulled away. Totally alone, he looked around the space that, minutes ago, had been filled with such intense drama that the sudden emptiness was unsettling. He pulled out his phone and saw it was six minutes past four o'clock. The property management office was closed and he still hadn't made the deposit. Frustrated, he headed for home.

He knew he should be feeling anger. Anger at Hector. Anger at Chunks. And he sure as hell should be angry with the never-ending bullshit he got from Murphy. But he felt nothing like that. He'd done it again—squirmed through the tiniest opening, the gangsters coming at him from one side and the cops from the other. And here he was, walking away unscathed. Maybe, just maybe, this would be the last time he'd have to walk this particular knife's edge in his life.

He'd leave a note at the management office with his phone number. He'd print out a copy of his account balance and convince the man he was good for the money. He'd get things taken care of one way or another. Then, come Sunday? They were gone.

He hit the street, pumped his fist in the air, and broke into a run. Murphy was right, he thought to himself.

Seso is one smart homie.

12

1610 HOURS

"Can you believe that bullshit? Calling me out like that? Saying we screwed up his call, right in front of that punk-ass kid. Then he tops it all off by stealing our stat."

Travis looked over to Ellie, who had gone back to the silent treatment, staring out the window. They'd dropped off their prisoner at the substation holding cell, after Murphy said GSU would be taking credit for the arrest.

"Like I'm some damn probie. I mean, I know I'm new around here, but I got some years behind me."

"Yeah, I heard. How many? Like, in Iowa, right?" Clearly Ellie wanted to change the subject.

"Ten, and it was in Wisconsin."

"Oh yeah. I forgot." He could practically hear her eyes rolling in her head. "Wisconsin."

"How about you? How many years you got on?"

"Almost thirteen. All of it with the SO."

"No shit?" Travis was shocked. "So why are you working night watch patrol?"

"What's that supposed to mean?" She looked at him, expression and voice defensive.

"Nothing." He stared through the windshield. "Just seems like you could've moved on to something better, I guess."

"Yeah, right," she said, letting it go.

"And by the way," Travis said, "nice job scrappin' back there. That was badass." He looked at her closely, for the first time seeing the nearly right angle of her jaw and the strength she carried in her neck and shoulders. He'd missed it before. More honestly, he'd just plain underestimated her.

"So what was all that bullshit in the hallway?" he asked, with a bit of challenge in his voice.

"What bullshit?"

Travis raised his voice a couple of octaves and singsonged, "Oh, I just love a man who takes charge." He went back to his normal voice. "That bullshit."

That earned Travis a short laugh, but Ellie reset immediately and went back to giving the street a hard look. Her voice held an edge. "How long you been here, Jackson? With the SO, I mean? A year? Two?"

"Coming up on two. Why?"

"Like I said, I've been here for more than a decade. But after briefing? You and that Neanderthal, Murphy, didn't so much as acknowledge that I was standing right there." She shook her head and puffed up a little bit. "You're pissed about the way he spoke at you? You give any thought to the crap I put up with every day?"

Travis hadn't anticipated her anger, but she had a point.

"So yeah, I was just getting in character for you. Figured that's what you're comfortable with." Even sitting down, she managed to wiggle her ass a bit, messing with him. "Little old female deputy working with a big strong man like you."

He laughed, but she didn't. Her voice took on more of a bite. "Admit it, you bought right into it."

Travis rolled his eyes, but he knew she was right. It hadn't been hard for her to convince him that she was deadweight that he'd be dragging around for the whole shift.

"But I tell you what," she said. "I'm glad you were with me on the call. Even if you did stand there with your thumb up your ass."

Travis let the insult go. "And why's that? You didn't look like you needed any help."

"Damn right, I didn't. But when things don't go exactly according to plan?" The snide quality came back to her voice. "It's good for *us girls* to have a cop around who has a swinging dick. That way the fallout isn't so bad."

"I still don't follow."

"You don't, huh?" She sounded worn down. "Then maybe it's not just your thumb that's up your ass. Maybe it's your whole head."

"Then why don't you explain it to me?"

Once again she showed remarkable agility, whipping off her seat belt and leaning across the computer console. All the playacting was gone. She narrowed her eyes and spoke in a tone so raw he felt like he was talking to his wife on her worst day.

"You want me to explain it to you, Jackson? Fine. Here's the thing. You and Murphy had your little spat in the parking lot. Coupla guys just going at it. That'll probably be the end of it. No doubt you bros will drink a beer together, smooth it all over."

"Yeah? So what?"

She shook her head as if too disgusted to even answer his idiotic question, then drew in a deep breath through her nose.

"If I, or any other female cop, handled that call alone and it got jacked up like that? Believe me, there wouldn't be some macho, mano a mano face-off in the alley. I don't care how reasonable the explanation, that shit would be legend. A story for the ages. My tactical incompetency would be known to all.

"And none of it would go on face-to-face. Hell, no. It'd all be backstabbing locker room bullshit."

She looked straight out the windshield. "By the time you fellas were done with all the colorful embellishment? Years from now, rookies would *still* be told about the day Deputy Peralta pissed her panties and jumped the gun on a gang call."

After several seconds of silence, Travis started to laugh. "Man, do you ever remind me of someone."

"Oh yeah?" He could hear the steam in her voice; her patience was definitely at an end. "Who's that?"

"A cop I use to work with. Female."

"In Iowa?"

"I told you, Wisconsin."

She turned to face him again and Travis realized he had not fully appreciated just how angry she was. "Let me guess. Nice Swedish type? Blonde with a big rack, no doubt. What was her name? Helga? No, wait. Heidi?"

"Her name was Suarez. Mexican American, if that matters to you."

"Oh, I get it. We're both a little on the brown side."

"It ain't about that. I'm just saying you're both pretty damn good cops."

She blew off his attempt at a compliment. "So I'm as good as some meter maid back in cow country? I'm sure you got a bunch of hard knockers back there. Thanks for the compliment."

"Actually, yeah, we do. Especially that one."

"How so?" She yanked hard on her seat belt, then rebuckled it. Travis figured she was pretty much done listening to him, but he went on anyway.

"Did some years in the marines, saw combat. And as a cop? She's been involved in two shootings. One where she took two in the gut and fought her way back to full duty. Another where she put a forty-cal round in a crook's eye socket from twenty-five feet away in a rainstorm. Deboned him on the spot."

"Deboned him?"

"Yeah. You know . . . when you put a guy's lights out so fast, they fall like you took all the bones out of their skin." Now Travis did his own little shimmy in his seat. "Deboned him."

Ellie stared out the windshield, sounding embarrassed, maybe regretting that she'd jumped to a conclusion. "Yeah, all right. I guess I don't mind that so much."

"She's like you in one other way." When Ellie said nothing, Travis went on. "You both like to walk around with this boulder-size chip on your shoulder. That must get old."

"Yeah?" He thought he might have heard the slightest crack in her voice. "So what's your friend's name? This Mexican supercop out in cheese land?"

"I told you. Suarez."

Ellie pulled her sunglasses out of the pocket on the passenger door. She cleared her throat and her tone softened, though her words were still intense.

"I can guarantee you this: I haven't even met her, but if this Suarez is walking around with a chip on her shoulder half the size of the one I strap on every day before I walk into that frat house you boys call a substation? Then yeah. I'll bet she's a hell of a good cop. Because that is some heavy shit to tote around. But trust me, Jackson. It's not something a white, blond, blue-eyed male cop is ever going to be able to get his big—or little—head around. So what do you say we just drop it?"

He blurted out, "Oh my god."

"What?"

"Nothing. I'm just . . ." He looked at her, smiling. "That's *exactly* the kind of bullshit she would've said."

"Fine." She gave up a faint smile. "And I'm Italian, by the way."

"Got it." He nodded, being intentionally officious. "Good to know."

"I don't know a word of Spanish that's not on a menu." She looked out her window, but Travis knew she was smiling even more.

"Roger that."

"And that dismissive bullshit after briefing? I'm not letting you off the hook. Fuck you very much for that." He couldn't see her face but he knew she was enjoying herself.

"Oh yeah?" He tried not to laugh. "You know that part where you called me a pussy? Fuck you, too."

"I didn't *call* you a pussy. I said you *drive* like a pussy."

Travis waved her off. "Same difference, you goombah bitch."

"Eat shit, you hayseed prick."

They kept at it, exchanging insults and laughing, until the radio fired up with a fight call a few blocks away.

"Should we take that?" Travis said, already accelerating toward the call.

"Sure." Ellie picked up the mic. "And this time, *I* get to watch. I want to see what you got under that sexy little hood of yours."

13

2230 HOURS

Travis hit Print and waited for the report to churn out. Three hours left in the shift and, no doubt, it had been a good one. The fight call turned out to be none other than Mrs. Reinhart, from the courtroom. True to her word, Mrs. Reinhart had gone home and taken matters into her own hands. When she found Albert Schofield stretched out inside a refrigerator box in the alley behind her home, she decided to light things up by torching the man's cardboard condo. Fortunately for everyone involved, Schofield crawled out of his makeshift domicile as soon as Mrs. Reinhart had begun dousing it in lighter fluid. That way, when she struck the match, the only crime she committed was a nonpermitted burn and not the aggravated arson it might have been. That left room for negotiation.

As they drove toward the location, Travis filled Ellie in on the two in-volved parties. They arrived to find Mrs. Reinhart calmly hosing down the sidewalk, sending blackened chunks of cardboard down the gutter. Scho-field was livid and demanded some sort of compensation for the loss of all his worldly possessions. Mrs. Reinhart, showing zero remorse, shot water at him every time he opened his mouth. After separating the combatants, Travis dealt with the retired army officer and Ellie handled the transient.

In the end, Mrs. Reinhart agreed to fork over twenty dollars in damages and to never strike a match in anger again.

They cleared the call by giving Schofield a ride to the pier in Oceanside, where he'd decided to take his windfall and enjoy dinner at Ruby's Diner. With any luck, he'd take a liking to the beach and make O'side his permanent home. All in all, Travis saw it as an excellent piece of problem-solving police work. Economical and effective, with a potential long-term solution built in. The little bit of mirth value was a nice bonus.

"Yo, Jackson." Sean Murphy walked into the patrol report room. "Hey, man, sorry if I came off as kind of a dick out in the field. It's just I was hoping we'd get a couple of good hooks over at Chito's. Ended up we pretty much just showed our ass to Eastside, but hey, not your fault. So, like I said, sorry."

Travis accepted Sean's offered hand, thinking back on his conversation with Ellie. "Hey, you got a nice vandalism for the tagging. Assault on an officer. But I appreciate your saying something. Bygones?"

"Ancient history," Sean said.

"What about Gutierrez?"

"Yeah," Sean said. "I need to talk to you about that. Hoping you can help us out."

"How's that?"

"We still got a chance to send a message. Chunks is on ice in a holding cell. I talked to his PO. Said if we can put that gun on him, he'll violate him tonight. We can write up the case as a felon in possession of a firearm. That, plus the gang enhancement, he'll be looking at three to five, state. And we can start that clock tonight."

"Sounds great. Whatta you need from me?"

"You know how it is. We won't get the lab work back for a couple of weeks. And even then, dipshit Donny, he fingered the hell out of the weapon. I'm sure the prints are screwed, but hopefully we can pull some of Gutierrez's DNA off it."

"Why won't parole violate him now?"

"Are you kidding? In this fricking commie-ass state? Prop Fifty-Seven practically put a revolving door on the prisons. They'd sooner lock up one of us than infringe on the rights of that fat bastard."

Sean was probably right. Twenty-five years of "three strikes and you're out" had been a hundred-billion-dollar binge that had made the prison–industrial complex the fastest-growing job market in the state. Dozens of new prisons were built and filled to capacity before the construction crews even got done putting the finishing touches on the geriatric ward. But a recent voter initiative had swung the pendulum, and nowadays getting anyone locked up for real time usually required a few gallons of spilled blood and a body count.

Travis shrugged it off. "So we'll just keep a close eye on him until you get the lab results."

"Better idea." Sean perched on the corner of the table where Travis sat. "I figure, with you being at the end of the alley when they all scattered, you probably saw Gutierrez dump the gun."

"How's that?"

"I mean, you had a clear angle. You must've seen Chunks toss the piece." Sean nodded toward the paper Travis was holding. "Put that in your report and we can book him tonight. Hell, I'll give you the collar. Parolee gangster with a gun? That'll look good on you."

"Oh, I got ya." Travis nodded, realizing the true nature of Sean's apology and the reason for this little heart-to-heart. "No, Sean. I can't say as I did see that. We pretty much had our hands full."

"Well, damn, dude, you must have at least seen him near the dumpster. We can make that work."

"If I'd seen him near the dumpster, I would've already told you."

Travis heard the man's frustration building. "Well, what about that other little prick? Seso. Maybe you saw him. You'll be busting the kid's cherry. I guarantee you, he'll plead out before prelim. It'll never get near a courtroom."

Travis pushed back. "If you're that spun up about it, why don't *you* write it? Maybe *you* saw one of them dump the gun."

"We came around the corner too late. The homies will know we couldn't have seen it. They could take it to a motion hearing and then it gets complicated. Too many eyeballs involved. But you? You had a clear view and you can remember whatever the fuck you want and nobody's gonna tell you any different."

Travis didn't appreciate being worked like some rook and he was done talking about it. "Sorry, man. Can't help you."

"All right. Let me spell it out for you, Jackson. This ain't . . . wherever the hell it is you came from. This is SoCal. We got dangerous crooks walking the streets, and every once in a while we get a chance to take one of them down. Sometimes it takes a little creative writing. You hear what I'm saying?"

When Travis said nothing, Sean kept talking.

"That call went to shit today. If we'd played it right, if you'd held off like I told you, my guys could've swooped in and caught those fuckers flat-footed. We'd have seen whoever dumped the gun and we'd have a whole jail full of those pumpkin heads. But they're not in our jail, are they? Instead, you know where they are? Sitting around their shitty little crib, blazin' up a joint, laughing their asses off, *at us*."

Dealing with cops like this was nothing new for Travis. Back in Newberg, before he had been promoted to sergeant, he'd gone through the same sort of bullshit. Travis knew that if he made himself clear, he and Sean would only have this conversation one time. Then the bar would be set.

"Sounds like you take this stuff pretty personally, Sean." Travis spoke plainly so there would be no mistaking his message. "But like I said, I can't help you. I can't write what I didn't see."

"What didn't you see?" Ellie Peralta asked as she walked into the report room.

Sean kept staring at Travis. "I was thinking your partner here might've been able to do two things at once. Hook up a prisoner while he kept obs on the alleyway like he was told to."

"He didn't hook the prisoner," Ellie said, "I did. And you didn't ask us to take a position of observation. You asked us to wait out of sight. But that didn't matter, because the tagger forced our hand. Anyway, what is it you were hoping we saw?"

"Never mind, Peralta. It doesn't concern you."

"If it happened in the last seven hours and it involved him, it concerns me."

"Okay, Peralta." Sean spoke like he was throwing out a challenge. "How about it? You want to get in the game? Did you happen to see either Gutierrez or Ortega chuck the gun in the dumpster?"

"Ah." Ellie nodded. "That's it, huh? You want us to put the gun on somebody. Sorry. I guess I'm with Jackson. I didn't see anything like that."

Travis tried to offer another solution. "You know, Sean, if you talk with the PO and tell him what we got, you could probably at least get Gutierrez an ankle bracelet. We can keep track of him. Then you could put a rush on the lab work."

"Jesus, you just don't get it, do you?" Travis heard the contempt in Sean's voice. "It ain't about the lab work or putting a bracelet on him or even the damn law. It's about the message. It's about us keeping our boot right up against their throat. We let Chunks or even this little shit, Seso, walk around free after what happened today? You know how much street cred they get from that? They get to walk on a gun?"

"Hey, Murph." Don Travers, another GSU member, walked in. "I'm finished up with the evidence impound. We charging Chunks? Felon in possession?"

Sean stared back at Travis. After several seconds, he stood. "No, Donny. Apparently not. Cut him loose."

"What's that now?" Don was never the smartest guy in the room.

"I said, cut him loose. Put him out the back door. I'll meet you guys back upstairs and tell you what's up."

"Yeah, all right." Don started to leave, then paused. "So you want I should let him go, then?"

Sean stared at him, not saying a word. The dim bulb got the message and walked away.

"You know, Jackson," Sean said, "you might be more comfortable working day shift. Or maybe even a special assignment down at Ridgehaven. I'm sure your partner could, I don't know . . . pull a few strings? Or whatever."

Travis got the reference to the sheriff's headquarters building located off the I-15 on Ridgehaven Court. It was the last place any actual police work ever got done.

"Or whatever?" Ellie smiled as if she was looking for a fight. "What's that supposed to mean, Murphy?"

"This conversation is over." Sergeant Peña stood in the doorway leading to the watch commander's office, a coffee mug in one hand and a copy of *Guns Magazine* in the other. "There's a bunch of empty cells back there. So wrap it up and get back out in the field."

Travis started gathering his reports as Ellie headed for the exit.

Peña took two steps through the door and looked at Murphy. "And you. Next time you want to have a conversation about doctoring a police report, do me a favor and make sure I'm not in the next room."

"It ain't like that, Sarge. Just wanted to make sure all our bases were covered."

"Get your ass upstairs, Murphy. I don't want you on the first floor for the rest of the night. You hear me?"

"No problem, sir." Murphy gave a mock salute and headed to the hallway. "Me and my team are headed back out. Something tells me the gangsters are going to be acting up. But no worries. GSU is rolling four deep."

14

Omar had never given a speech. Sure, mandatory stuff in class—group presentations and book reports—but he'd never stood in front of a crowd and given a real speech. He'd been working on the assignment since he'd gotten home and things had settled down. He'd had a hard talk with Hector, filled him in on everything that had gone down after he left.

"All that? Coulda been you, little bro," Omar said. "Then what? Court? Maybe some time in juvie?"

Hector seemed to take it to heart, so, in the end, maybe the whole experience had been a good thing.

Omar sat on the lower bunk, back resting against the wall, pen poised over a yellow pad of paper. He recalled Mr. Thompson's instructions: five or six minutes, nothing controversial. Omar figured that probably meant he shouldn't give the speech in Spanish first, followed by the English translation. Too bad, because he was doing it anyway. He'd keep the subject upbeat, all about family, hard work, and achievement, but if he was going to give a speech in front of five hundred people, his mother was damn sure going to understand every word.

This speech, Omar thought, is for her. No one else.

Only thirty-five years old, Isadora Ortega had spent the first half of her life living on a farm in the mountains of Coahuila, Mexico. She remembered her childhood fondly, telling her children stories of herding goats in the summer and playing in snow in the winter. A bride at sixteen, she was three months pregnant by her seventeenth birthday. Her husband, Mateo, was two years older and full of love for her as well as pride in the baby boy he was certain she was carrying. Isadora found his enthusiastic dreams infectious, and when he talked about a better life in America, she followed him willingly. With less than a hundred dollars and their scant possessions tucked into a schoolgirl's mochila, they crossed the border together. Covertly, but easily. Omar was born four months later.

The family's first years in America were difficult. The three of them shared a small apartment in Escondido with two other families. Every morning, Mateo, a skilled mason by trade, got up before sunrise and joined dozens of other men on street corners and in parking lots, hoping for a day of work. For years, he cut grass, trimmed trees, hauled junk. He washed dishes. His first break came when he managed to get hired on at a housing construction job site. The foreman took notice of his skills with a floating trowel and offered him a steady job on the crew.

Before long, Mateo was working fifty hours a week, pouring slabs and finishing driveways, building a reputation as one of the best concrete artists in San Diego County. Eventually he had his own crew, and he could barely keep up with the demand for his skills.

By then, the Ortegas had an apartment of their own. When Sofia came along, they were able to afford a new dress for her baptism. By the time Hector was born, they were renting a four-bedroom house in a working-class neighborhood near downtown Vista. Most of their neighbors were recent arrivals from Mexico, some from farther south, and the bonds among the families grew strong. Every week brought another celebration: a new birth, a first Communion, and, later, the occasional quinceañera. Omar remembered that every house seemed to be full of children; his mother started a home day care business that grew steadily.

The life Mateo and Isadora built was tenuous, but it allowed them to feel a cautious optimism about the future opportunities for all three of their American-born children.

Omar remembered that, even in the best of times, his parents always spoke well of their early years of farm life, where kinship and hard work were linked through labor and sweat. For his father, life's greatest reward was to work with his hands and put food on his family's table—this kept him working as a landscaper one or two days a week even as his concrete business grew. His mother wanted to care for her children and felt that being able to do so was a blessing from God.

But now his father was gone and his mother had been forced into a life of menial service to others. People who rarely showed much in the way of appreciation.

Even now, nearly eleven o'clock at night, she was cleaning a two-story office building that had six bathrooms. She wouldn't finish until after midnight. Renteria had driven her to the building, and while nothing prevented him from helping, Omar knew he'd drink and sleep in the car until she was done.

It seemed to Omar that Isadora's greatest happiness, since Mateo had disappeared, came through the lives of her children. This speech was his best chance, maybe his only chance, to show her that all her—and Mateo's—hard work and sacrifice had paid off.

"Are you really going to give a speech, Omar?" Sofia, who sat next to him, reading, lowered her book and slid up close to see what he was writing. The almost constant worry was gone from her voice, and he knew it was because she felt safe and content. With Renteria gone, it was just the three Ortega children at home, and, better yet, with Hector watching TV in the living room, she had Omar all to herself.

"Sure am, but that's nothing." Omar had looked forward to telling her about the move, and he didn't want to wait any longer.

A rap on the door got him up quick. Late-night knocks were never good. Omar considered himself the gatekeeper, but by the time he got to the living room, Hector was already looking through the peephole. Before Omar could stop him, Hector opened the door.

"Yo, peewee . . . how you doin'? Still on lockdown after your little fuckup today?"

Omar came to stand alongside his brother as Chunks Gutierrez walked through the doorway. "There he is. What up, Warden?"

Omar smiled, trying to go along with the joke. "Yo, Chunks. They cut you loose, huh?" He did his best to hide the sudden flood of whatever it was that caused his heart to pound and his skin to go clammy.

"Hell yeah, bro." Chunks put up a fist for a bump and Omar accepted.

Chunks pulled him close and gave him a long hug. "You did good today, homes. I thought maybe after I got hauled off you'd get all talkative and shit. I read you wrong, my brother."

Omar relaxed a bit. "'Course, Chunks. It's all good."

"They sweat me for 'bout five hours. Telling me you gave me up. I knew it was all bullshit. Told 'em, too. Told Murphy I knew my boy Seso didn't say shit. I knew the homes was down for Eastside."

Even though Chunks was out from under the cops and standing in front of him, Omar sensed the man was still testing him. Still working to confirm that Omar had kept his mouth shut about the gun.

"I'd never rat you out, Chunks. You know that."

"Never, Seso?" Chunks nodded in approval. "That's a bold statement, vato."

Omar saw a shadow just outside the still-open door, marked only by the glow of a cigarette.

"Yo, Seso. This here be E-Boy. We met in the joint. He got out a couple months back, so I hooked up with him. We was blazing up and I got to thinking, what with you running off to join the damn army and all, shit. I said to E-Boy, We gotta go pick up my homeboy Seso. He's leaving and he might not ever come back."

Before he went off to prison, Omar had seen Chunks under nearly every circumstance. Looking at the big man now, he could tell that Chunks was in his favorite altered state, baked on marijuana crusted off with a bit of crank. This version of Chunks was the most dangerous of all.

"Let's go, Seso. We gonna party a bit."

Omar worked to sound convincing. "Ah man, I wish I could, but my ma's at work. Told me to keep an eye on these two fools." Omar hooked a thumb over his shoulder toward Hector, who still stood behind him, and Sofia, who was standing in the doorway of the bedroom, listening.

"What you worried about? Ain't nobody gonna mess with your people. Everybody knows you be tight with Eastside. Let's go."

"Maybe tomorrow. Right now, I gotta write a speech for—"

"A speech?" Chunks shouted. He leaned in and his voice went low. "What the fuck, Seso?" Omar heard the tone of embarrassment and he knew he'd messed up. Chunks was feeling disrespected—and in front of another con, at that.

"I just . . . man . . ." Omar was scrambling. "Serious. Tomorrow night for sure."

"What up, Chunks?" The shadow moved into the light. E-Boy looked Omar over, sizing him up. The man's scalp was freshly Bic'ed, and his cheekbones protruded from a gaunt face that was tinted gray. He wore a long-sleeve checkered flannel that hung loose, open except for the top button. Under that, a white T-shirt clung to his rail-thin torso. Omar guessed him to be around twenty-five, maybe a few years older. "I thought you said your boy was a player, ese. Sounds like a punk to me."

Chunks shook his head, disgusted. Omar sensed that Chunks was ready to give in, but there would be conditions.

"Fine, Ortega." Gone was the term of brotherhood. "Stay home like a bitch, but give me some beer money."

Omar's heart, already thumping, almost came out of his chest. He entered a state of awareness so intense that he could sense the slight pressure on his thigh from the two hundred-dollar bills nestled there.

He patted his pockets and lied as smoothly as he could.

"Sorry, man. I'm tapped out."

"Bullshit. You always got money. Gimme twenty bucks."

E-Boy took another step inside. "Forty be better."

"Hell yeah." Chunks was heating up. "Make it forty."

Omar knew he'd pushed the situation to the brink. He again thought of the cash in his pocket, but if he pulled out even one of the Franklins, Chunks was not about to make change.

E-Boy eyeballed the apartment interior like he was casing it. He drew on his cigarette and focused on Sofia, who still stood in the doorway to the bedroom. "Well hey, baby. Maybe you wanna come out?"

Sofia quickly retreated and Omar heard the bedroom door shut. He looked into the pinned-out eyes of the stranger in his house. E-Boy stared back, exhaling a billow of smoke.

"What say, Ortega?" Chunks was no longer an ally. "You coming, or should we just take your sister for a ride?"

"All right, Chunks. Ease up. Let me grab my ATM card. You guys wait in the car. I'll be right down."

"Nah, man, we'll wait here." Chunks didn't trust Omar. That much was obvious.

Omar headed for the bedroom, making eye contact with Hector, who started to follow him. Chunks called out, "Hang with me, peewee."

Seeing the fear in his brother's eyes, Omar tried to speak with some assurance. "Hang out, Hector. I'm just going to get my wallet."

In the bedroom, he found Sofia standing with her hands over her mouth, crying quietly. Omar went to her, and put his arm around her.

"Stop," he said as comfortingly as possible. "You're okay. I'll take care of it."

"How, Omar?" Her voice shook. "Why did they come here?"

"Don't worry. I'm going to handle it." Omar pulled the cash from his pocket and slipped the two bills into the pillowcase on his bed. He went to the bookshelf, where he kept his wallet. "I'll get them their beer money, then come right back home."

"No," Sofia pleaded, pointing at the pillowcase. "Don't leave. Give them that money."

Omar shook his head. "No way. I'm not giving those guys a hundred bucks. Now, just stay in here. When I'm gone, come out and lock the door. Don't open it for anybody. You understand?"

"How long will you be gone?"

"Twenty minutes. Half hour, tops." He hugged her close. "Don't be afraid, okay? Just do your schoolwork and I'll be home before you know it."

"But I *am* afraid." She hugged him tighter. "I don't want you to go with them."

Omar sat his sister down on the bed and took a seat beside her. Resting his palm lightly on her cheek, he used a thumb to smudge away a tear. "Remember how I fixed things this morning, at school?"

She nodded.

"You didn't think I could do it, did you?" He smiled and winked at her. "You thought I'd get a white slip. But I didn't, did I?"

A faint smile appeared on her face.

"Same thing here. Sit tight. I'm going to fix it so these guys don't come back. Then I'll be home."

"Can I wait up for you?"

"You better."

"Don't you drink any beer, Omar." She sounded like she was in charge.

"Okay, Mom." He smiled, but she didn't. He got up and headed for the door. "Stay in here until we leave. Then what are you going to do?"

"Lock the door."

"And?"

"Stay inside and wait for you to come home."

He gave her a thumbs-up. "Perfect. I'll be right back."

Omar hurried to the living room, where Hector sat on the couch, staring at the two gangsters, who had moved into the kitchen and were whispering to each other.

"I'm ready, Chunks. Let's go."

"I'm thinking you oughta bring your peewee brother along. He's probably ready for a night out," Chunks said. "What about it, ese? You ready to step up?"

Hector began to speak but Omar cut him off. "He's thirteen years old. He's not going anywhere."

"How about your sister?" E-Boy said.

"No." Omar faced both men directly, giving them a hard stare. "They're both staying home. Now, you want beer money or not?"

Chunks smiled and looked past Omar, at Hector. "Don't sweat it, little man. Next time, when the warden here is off chasing A-rabs, we'll party, and oh hell yeah, we'll bring your sister along."

"Let's go." Omar held the door open and Chunks walked out first. E-Boy took his time, still puffing on his cigarette and looking around like he was memorizing the details. Now wasn't the time to worry about that. Just get them their money. That would settle things down for the weekend and that was all the time they would need.

Omar took a last look back as he left, trailing the two ex-cons. Sofia had crept out of the bedroom and was peeking down the hall. Hector was still rooted to the couch, looking nervous. Omar stood in the doorway as if his feet were nailed to the floor.

What the hell is happening? Minutes before, he'd been working on his speech, trying to describe his place in the world. The love he felt for his mother, for his brother and sister. The empty space that was once filled by his father. All that wasn't something he could write down on a sheet of paper or talk about to a crowd of people. It was a connection that ran between all of them but never beyond them. Now it felt as if that connection was being cut, but what choice did he really have?

Omar smiled at Sofia and Hector with as much assurance as he could muster, pulled the door firmly shut, and stepped into the night. He went down the steps three at a time and walked to the waiting car, eager to get this over with, pushing back hard against an overwhelming sense of dread.

15

2312 HOURS

Travis and Ellie had planned to take their food to go, but the light crowd inside La Gordita Mexican Restaurant meant there was plenty of room to sit. That, along with the aroma of carne asada mixed with peppers and spices, led Ellie to key up the radio and put them out at the restaurant for code 7. They ordered at the counter and, as usual, the owner, a forty-something Mexican woman who was as wide as she was tall, refused their offered money with a good-natured wave of her hand. Travis tried twice but didn't want to make a scene. He leaned in so she could hear him over the music and butchered a few words of thanks in Spanish.

The deputies carried their food to a corner table, where Travis deferred to Ellie's seniority. He let her settle in and relax while he positioned himself to take the long eye on the door. He scanned the restaurant's other patrons, noting three ankle bracelets, two teardrop tattoos, and no shortage of sleeved-out arms covered in drab green ink. He saw no reason for major concern. Cons, parolees, and cops all had the same passion for good Mexican.

He devoted some attention to his meal, a half portion of taco salad, while Ellie bellied up to the specialty of the house: a spicy lobster burrito that was damn near the size of Travis's forearm. When she put her tray down, he was pretty sure the table shook. She started in on the foil like a kid unwrapping a Christmas present, not looking up when she spoke.

"So Murphy definitely has your number tonight. Dresses you down in the field, right in front of a couple of homies, then tries to work you over in the report room. Gotta say, he's pretty much treating you like his *bitch*."

From the emphasis on the last word, he knew she was screwing with him, trying to get a reaction. He didn't bite. "Yeah. Whatever. I don't know him very well, but I'm starting to think he's kind of a prick."

"Kind of?"

He shrugged. "I like giving people the benefit of the doubt, but yeah. I'm pretty confident at this point. He's a prick."

"Astute of you." Ellie used both hands to heft the burrito.

"You work much with him?"

She was ready to take a bite, mouth open to the point it was like she had a double-jointed jaw. She hesitated long enough to answer Travis's question. "Murphy? No way. He'd never go for that. He's got enough juice that he can steer clear of me. Which I'm okay with. I don't need any of his condescending bullshit."

Ellie hesitated, still holding off on her food. Her voice had a quality that made it feel like her words were a test. "Thing is, though, about the gun. Really doesn't matter who, somebody should be getting hooked for it."

He picked at the limp, wilted greens in front of him, thinking there must be a reason the restaurant name translated to "Chubby Girl"—but this salad wasn't it. Glancing up, he spotted three young men come through the door, dressed down in blue and khaki, hats kicked backward, white socks pulled up high. He kept an eye on them while he replied to Ellie.

"I thought we already had this discussion."

She finally sank her teeth into the burrito. Travis was shocked by the size of her magnum bite. She held up a finger to apologize for her bad timing and he waited. Her eyes rolled back in her head like the taste had a sexual quality.

"Good stuff?"

She gave a thumbs-up and nodded. When she could manage, she mumbled out an answer. "I wouldn't exactly say we discussed it."

She worked to chew and swallowed a bit more and her message cleared up. "I'm just saying, my feeling on it? You can recall seeing whatever you want. They're your eyeballs, and I won't make any judgments about what you say you saw. But if you go that way, when you write it, make sure you leave me out of it, and make damn sure nobody can piss backwards on you.

"And by the way, Murphy was right about one thing. Putting that gun on somebody? It'd look good, and it's not a bad way to get along around here. I mean, if that's important to you."

"Do you think the gun was his? Gutierrez's, I mean?"

"Oh shit, are you serious?" She gave him a look of bemused disbelief over the top of her burrito. "Of course it's his gun. I mean, damn, hayseed. Did you take the turnip truck all the way from Iowa before you fell off?"

Travis pushed back. "Then why don't *you* write it? Say you saw him dump it?"

"I don't need gun stats," she said, taking another, only slightly smaller bite and talking while she chewed. "Besides, I already told you. I didn't see anybody dump a gun."

Pissed at the whole conversation, he stabbed at his lettuce. "Neither did I. So what do you say we just drop it?"

"Fine by me." She nodded her head toward his food. "That looks pathetic. Maybe you oughta go with the fruit bowl next time."

Travis changed the subject. "Why does Murphy steer clear of you? You got history with him?"

"I got history with everybody." She shoved the burrito back into her mouth. Travis couldn't believe the thing was damn near half gone.

"What's that supposed to mean?"

"Knock it off." Even with her mouth practically overflowing, he could hear the cynicism in her voice. "Like you don't know."

"Know what?"

She freed up one hand to make air quotes. "My 'lawsuit'?"

"Well, yeah. I mean, that's pretty common knowledge. But—"

"Is it, now?" She swallowed hard, nodding like she was enjoying a joke that never got old.

"Yeah. Something about you and a lieutenant?"

"Well, here's a news flash for you." Her eyes glared with a new intensity that set him back on his chair. "I've never sued anyone."

"But . . . I mean . . . I heard you—"

She put the burrito down, took a long slurp of her drink, and leaned toward him over the table. "You *heard* that I had an affair with my watch commander. You heard that he tried to break it off so I sued the department for sexual harassment. You heard I got him fired and a big chunk of cash, because, you know, women always come out ahead in those things. Is that about right?"

She picked up her burrito and took an angry bite.

"Ellie, I don't know anything about all that." Of course he knew the story. It was department folklore. But now, with one of the involved parties sitting in front of him, he discovered he had no interest in hearing the sordid details. He backpedaled as best he could. "I mean, it's your business."

Recognizing his response as bullshit, she laughed out loud, showering him with debris.

"Oops, sorry." She used a napkin to wipe flakes of lobster and a few grains of rice off his arm. She gestured to her own face, embarrassed. "And you got a little bit right there."

Travis used his napkin to wipe his cheek. "Like I said, I don't know what you're talking about."

"Don't lie. You've heard it all."

"Maybe I have, but I don't know the specifics and you don't have to explain anything to me."

"Dude, I love talking about it. I love pushing back on all you knuckle-draggers."

"Me?" His offense was genuine. "What did I do?"

She ignored him and started in.

"I was on my first shift out of training, still on probation. I had a lieutenant—who shall remain nameless—who, for the life of him, couldn't keep his hands off my ass. But, in his defense, I was smoking hot back then. My ass was *fine*."

She paused, apparently to let that image sink in, then went on. "Every time I walked through his office, he'd brush up against me or give me the once-over with his eyes while he sat at his desk with his feet up, grabbing his crotch.

"I let it go. Tried to be polite. Thanks, but not interested, I said. Gotta boyfriend, I told him, even though I didn't. Then he started in with the shit assignments. The lousy comments to other bosses. So yeah, you could say I took matters into my own hands."

Travis took a bite of salad, nodding in support. "I would've sued him, too."

"What did I say, hayseed? I told you, I didn't sue anybody." She winked. "Got his ass on tape, though."

"How's that?"

"I went into his office, closed the door, and took a seat on his desk. Microcassette running in my pocket. Gave him a chance to tell me how we could make things right. Poor bastard just followed his little head right down the rabbit hole.

"Next morning, first thing, I walked into the sheriff's office, played the tape for him. Told him it had been going on for months. I said, 'Either he goes or I go.'"

"What happened?"

"Sheriff thought it over. For like ten seconds. Then he said, 'Do I have to fire him or would you be satisfied if he just resigned?'"

Travis's fork stopped halfway to his mouth. "No shit?"

"Next day I came to work and the lieutenant's office looked like they were getting ready to paint. Nothing left but a few empty hooks on his 'I love me' wall, empty desk drawers all half pulled out. I'm telling you, you could stand in that office and feel how *pissed* he'd been while he was cleaning his shit out."

"That's it? No lawsuit? No cash?"

Ellie wedged the last of the burrito into her mouth. When she spoke this time, she made sure to point her mouth up toward the ceiling so he wouldn't have to deal with the fallout. "That's a bingo."

Travis smiled. "*Inglourious Basterds.* I love that movie."

She laughed until she inhaled some food and started choking.

"Why don't you tell everyone what really happened? Set them straight?"

Another hit off her soda. "And lose the reputation of being the vengeful woman who can take down a lieutenant? That's my hole card, dude. That's why the Murphys of the department stay clear of me. Anytime somebody starts messing with me, I just recirculate that story and they back right off."

"Who's going to give you any shit? I mean, the other part's true, isn't it?"

"What other part?" He knew she was toying with him again.

"Your husband?"

"Oh. You mean Commander Peralta?" She leaned back from the table until her chair balanced on two legs. "You heard about that, too?"

"I heard you're married to someone on the command staff."

"Yeah. But that happened way after I slept with the lieutenant."

"Wait. I thought you said you didn't—"

"Jesus, Travis. I'm joking. Keep up." Her eyes were sparkling.

He smiled. "Okay. Got it. So, after you slept with the lieutenant that you really didn't sleep with, that's when you—"

She cut him off. "Tell me how it goes again? I got caught on my knees under the commander's desk?"

Travis smiled and lied again, making no effort to hide it. "Nah, I've never heard that one."

"Well, you're the only one who hasn't." She stuck a chip into the guacamole. "That one's true, by the way."

Travis laughed, sure he was being played, but he had started to enjoy the whole exchange. "Stop it."

"For reals," she said, and went on eating chips. "At least it's partly true. Rob—that's my husband—he and I met in college. Got married in our senior year, when we didn't have ten bucks between us. After graduation, he hired on with San Diego PD. I got a job teaching middle school. A few years into that gig, I decided his work stories sounded a hell of a lot more interesting than mine. So I went to work for the SO."

"Why not work with him? At San Diego PD?"

"What? Work together and sleep together? No thanks."

"Okay, but now . . . ?"

"Yeah, I know. It's confusing. He made lieutenant over at the PD. Then, just a couple of years ago, he got involved in the sheriff's reelection campaign. Pretty heavily involved, actually. He's got a knack for all that political bullshit. When the sheriff won, Rob's reward was to transfer to the SO and get promoted to commander. I still give him shit about it. Damn politician." She was smiling as she said it.

Travis nodded. "Okay. And the rumors?"

"Listen to you." She put a chip to her lip and touched it to her tongue. With her chin buried against her chest, she looked at him, batting her eyes, doing her best imitation of coy. "Looking for all the sexy details, huh?"

He laughed, and after a moment she went on, with a casual shrug of one shoulder. "It was late; we thought the building was empty. We'd been married over ten years by then. Two kids at home. Just trying to spice things up a bit, you know what I'm saying?"

Her eyes unfocused for a moment as if she was picturing the details. "And, I mean . . . it's not like I was actually *under* the desk."

Travis stared at her, not sure if she was done. Ellie popped the last chip into her mouth. She sounded more annoyed than embarrassed about getting caught. "Janitor walked in. Clicked on the lights. Damn blabbermouth."

She pushed away her plate. "But how a little fun with my husband of ten years turns into me trying to marry my way to the top beats the hell out me. To say you guys gossip like a bunch of old women is an insult to old women."

Travis was trying to think of a comeback when he saw a familiar figure enter the restaurant.

Ted Rosado crossed to their table. "You two gonna sit in here all night? X-ray car means extra bodies in the jail. Not extra chow."

"Hey, Teddy," Ellie said, looking up with a relaxed smile. "How's your night going?"

"Easy money." Ted helped himself to a chip, dipped it deep into the bowl of guacamole, then shoved the loaded chip into his mouth. Bits of food sprayed from his lips as he spoke. "Only caught two paper calls. The rest have all been advisements. Chance to work on my listening skills."

Ted nudged Travis on the shoulder. "You believe this one? She's like a secret weapon, am I right? I was gonna partner up with her, but you beat me to the punch."

Ellie's voice was friendly when she said, "Teddy and I have a thing. We ride together once in a while, and what happens in the car, stays in the car."

"Yeah." He grabbed another chip. "I keep telling her she should let me start some new rumors. Her rep's getting weak."

Travis motioned to the empty chair. "Take a load off."

"Nah. I called in an order. Gonna pull in behind the Lucky Star, eat off the top of my computer. Hope to get a deuce coming out of the bar. If I time it right, it'll get me a couple hours of overtime."

"Sounds like you," Ellie said, trying to shame the man. "Trolling for drunk drivers."

"Hey, moneybags, we can't all be married to commanders. Am I right, Jackson?"

"Damn straight."

Ted looked at his watch, then grabbed another chip. "So whatta' we got? Couple hours left in the shift, right? I get a stop, say, in the next twenty minutes, get the arrest. Stick around for the tow truck which you know is gonna take at least forty minutes on a Friday night. Do my own booking paperwork, write the report—*very thorough*, of course. Boom. Three hours OT. With any luck, the twins will still be asleep and my wife will be waking up about the time I get home. Maybe she'll even be feeling a little grateful for all my hard work, bringing home the extra cash. And you know what they say, 'Happy wife . . .'"

Both Travis and Ellie finished for him, "'Happy life.'"

"Nah," Ted said. "Happy wife means morning sex. Then I get a solid four hours' sleep before heading back down here for another night of fun and games."

"Sounds like a great plan, Teddy." Ellie picked at a last remnant of lobster, then changed her mind and dropped it back on the plate. "We'd better go. I still have to write my use-of-force paper for that bullshit in the alley."

"Yeah. I heard the guys talking about that," Ted said. "Call kinda went to shit, huh?"

"Exactly," Ellie said, smiling at Travis. "Good thing GSU was there to bail us out."

"Yeah, right." Ted laughed out loud. "Like you need bailing out, Peralta. Later, you two."

Ted walked to the counter, where Travis saw the owner once again refuse to take money from a deputy. Smiling and shaking his head, Rosado put a ten and a five in the tip jar on the counter. He waved at Ellie and Travis as he left.

"Good guy," Ellie said, watching Ted go. "Always the cutup. A real smart-ass, but never mean, you know?"

"Yeah," Travis said, digging into his pocket. He laid a twenty-dollar bill on the table. "I got the tip."

"Let me get it."

"Nah, that's all right. Next time." Commander husband or not, Travis wasn't going to let her pay his way.

"Damn it, Travis," she said, standing up and pawing at her uniform shirt to adjust her vest. "Why did you make me eat that?"

"*Make* you?"

When they got to the parking lot, Ellie took out her phone and checked the time. "Let's go hide somewhere. Write our paper in the field. We can head in afterwards and call it a night."

Travis opened his car door. The air had finally reached a tolerable temperature, and spending the last hour outdoors but hidden from public view sounded way better than the report room. "You got a favorite spot?"

"I usually dole out the nightly blowjobs behind the 7-Eleven. We could head over there."

Travis laughed. "Would you just stop already?"

She stood on her side of the car. "Probably ought to run through Chito's one more time. Make sure the bangers aren't congregating. Murphy's right about that. They're going to be full of themselves for a few days. I know a nice corner we can back into, take the long eye from across the parking lot. Don't have to worry about our six. Hang out there till it's time to go in."

"Sounds like a plan."

She opened her door and stopped to look over the top of the car. Her voice serious but friendly, she said, "Good shift, Travis. What do you say we do it again sometime?"

"Absolutely, Ellie. Any time."

16

Omar sat in the backseat of the '65 Impala. When he'd gotten into the car, Chunks had said it belonged to his uncle, then corrected himself. Maybe it was a cousin. Either way, he said, it didn't matter. They wouldn't mind if he took it out for a few hours.

A few hours. What with all the drama that had gone down with E-Boy and Chunks, Omar had walked out without his phone. He was sure it had been around eleven o'clock when Chunks came calling. By now, he figured, it had to be way past midnight.

Chunks had driven straight to an ATM, where Omar had withdrawn forty dollars. He made sure to hit the button for no transaction receipt. The last thing he needed was for either Chunks or this E-Boy to see his account balance.

Back at the car, Omar offered the cash to Chunks, but E-Boy snatched the bills from his hand. They made a quick stop at Chito's; E-Boy came out with a case of Modelo, a jumbo bag of pork rinds, and two packs of Faros. As expected, E-Boy didn't offer Omar any change, and Omar didn't ask. His duty complete, he told Chunks to drop him at his apartment.

"Chill, solider boy." Chunks had reached back over the seat and shoved a bottle of beer against Omar's chest. "Like I said, we're gonna party. Besides, gotta keep you around. Might be we need some more money."

E-Boy lit a cigarette and blew smoke toward the backseat. "Always good to have a workin' paisa along on Friday night."

Omar sat alone in a backseat that could hold four grown men. Chunks drove and E-Boy rode shotgun. After refusing a cigarette, Omar nursed the beer, only taking sips when Chunks glared at him in the rearview and demanded he drink up. Omar sensed an unavoidable confrontation looming and recognized that part of him welcomed it. He had no intention of giving these fools any more money. He sized up the two men. If the time came, he'd drop E-Boy first—he was the bigger threat. After that, he'd deal with the fat-ass behind the wheel. He found himself looking forward to it.

The interior of the car was trashed; it smelled like it had spent fifty years under a plastic tarp in the sun. The cutout suspension left the car so low that the undercarriage sparked against the asphalt on even the slightest bump in the road. The shit-magnet of a lowrider attracted all the wrong kind of attention—it was just the type of car cops loved to pull over.

They'd left the barrio and were passing through the newly built mixed-use commercial district, heavy with pedestrians, upscale bars, and even a few suburban-chic restaurants. Chunks drove slowly, windows down and speakers cranked high, blaring out a música norteña ballad that had something to do with lost love and a fondness for horses. The accordion riffs and grita screams of the Mexican polka music had the intended effect, causing people to stare, their expressions showing irritation and, in some cases, intimidation.

Chunks bobbed his head in time with the music. "Look at all these gringo fools. We oughta hang here awhile. Find one of 'em all liquored up and shit. Jack 'em. Get an iPhone out of it. Some cash. Nice piece of ass, maybe."

He locked his eyes on Omar in the rearview. "How 'bout it, Seso? You finally ready to make your bones? Throw down for Eastside?"

Omar looked at the busy sidewalk. The time had come. If Chunks stopped the car, he'd bail. If they came at him on the street, so be it.

You want me to make my bones, Chunks? Omar felt his heartbeat pick up, powered by unspoken anger. *How about I beat down your ass?*

But what if the two of them drove back to the apartment once he was out of the car? What if he got home to find Sofia gone? Hector beat to shit?

The possibilities kept Omar in the Impala. Chunks took an on-ramp and merged onto Highway 78, heading out of town. Both Chunks and E-Boy rolled up their windows and Chunks blazed a joint, filling the interior of the car with a thick, acrid smoke that made Omar think of dead skunk. E-Boy pulled a short vial of dark glass from his pocket, screwed off the top, and spilled chunky, brownish-white powder onto the back of his hand. He snorted it and finished off with a vigorous shake of his head.

A few exits later, Chunks left the highway.

"Damn, Chunks?" Omar said, trying to sound casual. "What up, man? You got your beer. Drop me off somewhere. I need to get home."

Chunks looked at E-Boy. "You believe this? *I need to get home.* Sounds like some punk-ass guero."

E-Boy leaned across the bench seat and spoke to Chunks in a low whisper. Both men laughed with a giddiness brought on by booze and dope. Neither so much as glanced at Omar, who went back to staring out the window.

They drove down residential streets that eventually led to a neighborhood of massive two-story homes set far back from the road, with manicured lawns and wide driveways. Most were dark, but a few were warmly lit. Seeing the expensive homes, Omar fought against a familiar sense of resentment, an old jealousy.

When Omar was just six or seven years old, his dad would take on landscaping jobs for extra money. In the summer, Omar would tag along to the homes of his dad's clients—houses a lot like these. Omar would help with some of the light work, and at the end of the day they'd hit the Tastee Freez, where his dad let him order anything on the menu. Back then, Omar figured a big enough ice cream cone pretty much made you king for a day.

Years went by and eventually the fun started to feel a lot like work. One day, right around the time Omar entered middle school, he was pushing a mower across a half acre of thick, green carpet. It was one of those hot September Saturdays that served as a reminder that they actually lived in a desert.

Eager to finish, Omar came around the back of the near-million-dollar home, his arms, face, and neck covered in dirt, sweat, and errant blades of grass. Too late, he noticed a dozen schoolmates sitting by the pool, kicked back in lawn chairs or stretched out on beach towels. The guys were in bathing suits, the girls wore bikinis. Their tanned bodies glistened with oil, and they looked as if they were part of a casting call for one of those TV shows about how rich white folks live.

Omar pushed the mower past them, his gaze locked straight ahead, hoping the heat of the day hid the flush of his embarrassment. What had always been a shared adventure with his dad became a moment of humiliation. Soon after that, his father was able to put his masonry skills to use full-time and give up landscaping once and for all. When he told Omar they wouldn't be able to work together anymore, the teenager had done his best to come off as disappointed.

The Impala entered an area of new construction: block after block of cement slabs and half-framed structures. When they came to a street of houses where the framing was finished and the drywall hung, Chunks pulled the car into a new driveway of smoothly poured stamped concrete.

Omar thought this would have been his dad's job. Mateo Ortega's skills weren't wasted on foundation slabs. No way. Mateo poured the cement of the driveway and the sidewalk that would lead to the new home. The backyard patios, where families would throw parties and entertain their friends. Nobody, *nobody* could get down on their knees and finish off a cement job like his dad. Stamped, colored, terra-cotta, it didn't matter. From mixing to framing to finishing, his father would pour cement smooth as glass, that even a 5.0 tremor wouldn't crack. He was an artist with a flooring trowel. The king of the hand float. His dad was the man.

"Nice crib, eh? Let's check it out," Chunks said. "Maybe I'll buy it, eh?"

E-Boy and Chunks stumbled out of the car. Chunks opened the back door and pulled Omar out by the arm. "Come on, soldier boy."

They walked through the framed doorway into part of the structure that looked to be near completion. E-Boy took a running start and kicked hard at the drywall, creating a boot-shaped hole. Chunks laughed and did the same. Finding a set of stairs, they both ran up. Guessing he was a good eight or ten miles from home, Omar had no choice but to follow them.

"Shit, man." Chunks stopped to spin slowly and take in what Omar figured was going to be a master bedroom. "This is, like, bigger than my whole crib. Player who buy this place be rolling in it."

"Check it out," E-Boy said, unzipping his pants. "This here is where the shitter will go."

E-Boy stood in the small room boarded off with studs and pissed against the unfinished wall. With one hand to his mouth, Chunks pointed and laughed, staggering toward his pal. Omar figured it was best to just keep out of it. He crossed the floor to what looked like the wood framing hung for a large window. He stood staring down toward the street, until the gunfire caused his heart to jump and he wheeled around.

Pistol in hand, E-Boy stood grinning. He again aimed at the drywall and pulled the trigger. Omar resisted the temptation to cover his ears.

"Let me cap a couple, man." Chunks took the pistol from E-Boy, aimed and fired, sending shot after shot into the wall. The brass casings landed with a dull *clink* on the plywood floor.

"Damn, fellas," Omar said. "You want to bring the cops down on us? Be cool with that shit."

E-Boy grabbed the gun back from Chunks. Omar watched E-Boy fumble with the gun, removing a thin metal case from inside the handle and shoving an identical case back inside. E-Boy pushed a button with his thumb and it sounded like a small metal door slammed shut. With the piece at his side, E-Boy stalked over.

"Let's see what you got, Seso. " He pushed the gun against Omar's chest. It was small and compact. "Three eighty semiauto, homes. Easy to shoot. Easy to kill with, too."

"No, man." Omar took a step back. "Let's just bounce outta here before somebody calls the cops."

"Nah, nah, nah." E-Boy shifted closer, until he and Omar stood forehead to forehead. Omar could smell the combination of alcohol and drugs on E-Boy's breath when he spoke. "I wanna see you shoot the gun, vato."

Without thinking, Omar shoved the man away. E-Boy stumbled and nearly fell, then recovered quickly. Jumping forward, he pressed the barrel of the gun into Omar's forehead, right above his eye.

"Either you shoot it, bitch, or I will."

"Damn, Seso," Chunks said, sounding almost indifferent. "You best get on with it."

Omar's hands had instinctively gone out to his sides, with his palms up. He locked eyes with E-Boy and saw the pinpoint pupils that seemed to buzz in the man's head. Omar didn't doubt that the wrong answer would get him shot.

"Fine. Give it to me."

E-Boy eased back just far enough to once again press the gun against Omar's chest.

Omar took the weapon, surprised by the heft of it, like a good-size rock being dropped in his hand. Even under these shit circumstances, he couldn't help but feel some excitement, holding a firearm for the first time in his life. For a brief moment, Omar gave some thought to turning the gun on these assholes and pulling the trigger. It would be that easy. Shoot them both. Ditch the piece. Dump the car. Go home.

And, he thought, go to jail for the rest of my life.

He pointed at the ceiling and fired twice. He felt the recoil all the way up his arm to his shoulder. The gun jumped in his hand and he nearly dropped it. "There. Now can we go?"

"Fuck that," Chunks said. "Shoot like a gangster, ese."

Omar faced the wall, seething with anger and frustration. Squeezing tighter this time, he pulled the trigger and kept pulling until the gun stopped firing.

"Now," Omar said. "Let's get out of here before we all go to jail."

E-Boy stepped forward, taking his time. Omar knew the ex-con wanted it to be clear, he didn't sweat the cops or anything else. He took the gun from Omar and, without looking, once again ejected the empty clip into his hand. He pulled a fresh one from his pocket, jammed it home, and released the slide. He tucked the gun back under his shirt. "You scared of a little jail time? No worries, man. I got some players to look out for you."

"Homeboy's right," Chunks said, already moving toward the steps. "We best sky outta here."

"Finally," Omar said, pushing his way past E-Boy. "And the last thing I need is you or any of your *players* looking out for me."

17

The radio still crackled, cops putting out car stops and dispatchers force-feeding deputies calls for service, but most of the activity now belonged to the graveyard shift. The deputies who would work through the night were in-service, initiating contacts and handling calls. It was after midnight, and end of watch was at 0130 hours. Thirty more minutes and they could head in to the station. Turn in reports, book evidence, download body cams, and call it a night.

It had been a good shift, Travis thought. He looked at Ellie in the passenger seat, her face bathed in green light from the screen of the computer mounted on a swivel. She was banging out the report from the call at Chito's, way back at the beginning of their shift. Even though GSU had stolen the arrest stat, Ellie still had to cover her use of force and the suspect's assault on her.

On top of all that, Ellie had gotten a phone call from the intake deputy. The suspect, a kid who went by "Toon," had tried to keister a good-size chunk of heroin into the jail. He'd gotten caught by the X-ray security. That meant they'd tack on another felony. What started as simple vandalism was going to send the boy to state prison, probably for somewhere north of five years.

Well deserved, Travis thought. He couldn't understand how Murphy didn't see that as a pretty strong message sent to the Eastsiders. Sure, it would've been even better if somebody went down for the gun recovered from the dumpster, but at least this one would be hitting the pit pretty hard. Popping a gangster for assault on a deputy and smuggling a controlled substance into a correctional facility was a good night's work.

After they'd eaten, Ellie had directed Travis to a back-in spot half a block up the street from the liquor store. The building provided cover on two sides, and a thick row of thorny bougainvillea bushes covered the third. The only way to approach the car was head-on. Perfect writing spot. A midnight Santa Ana blew hot but was still a welcome relief from the day's stifling heat. Travis had seen a few customers leave the liquor store, carrying suitcases of beer; others gripped brown paper bags. A couple of lowriders went by, but nothing out of the ordinary.

Travis kept an eye on the street, providing cover while Ellie finished her work. He took a few seconds to text Molly the good news that he'd be getting home on time.

Ellie spoke without looking up. "You're like my teenage daughter over there. You bang on that phone faster than I type on a computer."

"Texting the wife. Trying to talk her into waiting up."

"You gotta convince her that's a good idea?"

"Chasing after four kids all day, she's pretty beat by sundown."

"Jesus, four? What are you? Mormon?"

Uncanny, he thought, laughing and thinking about the grief his former partner had given him about the size of his family. "Are you sure you've never been to Wisconsin? Maybe you got some long-lost family there?"

"Again with that?" Ellie finally looked at him. "If you loved the place so much, what made you walk away?"

The mood had been light, but Travis decided that question deserved a serious response. "Not an easy call. I just figured . . . I mean, Molly and I, we struggled with it. But, thing is, I just wanted to do . . . I wanted to do *this*."

"Yeah?" Ellie's voice was weighted with doubt. "*You* wanted to, huh? So tell me, what is *this*?"

Travis decided to start at the beginning. "You remember that cop a few years back, up in Oakland? Guy named Ben Sawyer? He got thrown under the bus for jamming his gun down the gullet of some skell parolee."

"Oh, hell yeah. That boy got way more than his fifteen minutes. CNN, Fox, MSN. To be honest, I love that video. You know him?"

"More than know him. I worked for him."

"Come again?"

"After he got shitcanned in Oakland, he ended up in Newberg, of all places. That's where I worked for ten years. He came on as a sergeant but worked his way up to chief."

"No shit?" Ellie said. "Score one for the good guys."

"Oh man, believe me, that's the truth. Great chief. Great place to work." Travis smiled, thinking back. "He and I, we got pretty close. And the more he talked about big-city policing—and not just any big city but *California* big city—the more I realized that was what I wanted to do."

She seemed to be really listening, so Travis went on, "I mean, I grew up in Newberg. Love that town, but I wanted to come out here and . . . I don't know. Play with the big dogs, I guess."

"And how did your wife and mother of four feel about that?"

"Good at first. Not so much since. But we're doing okay."

Ellie went from cop-jovial to something more serious. "You realize how much you were asking? For her to follow your dream?"

"Yeah, yeah. I absolutely do. Molly gave up a lot. Her family goes back like three generations in Newburg. But I guess she's old-fashioned that way."

"Old-fashioned? Dude, a woman who picks up her life and moves cross-country with four kids in tow? That's like covered wagon old-fashioned. You're a lucky man."

Travis shrugged. He didn't expect Ellie to understand, but he tried anyway. "We grew up together. Known each other since grade school. Started dating in junior high. Got married right after high school."

"And the first kid came along when?"

Maybe she did get him. He smiled. "About six months later."

"Yeah." She looked back at the computer screen. "Keep texting. I can see now why she might take some convincing."

The radio gave three quick beeps, meaning the next transmission was significant. Both deputies stared at the radio speaker and waited.

"Station A to all North County units, attention San Marcos, several reports of eleven sixes in the vicinity of Triumph Lane and Santa Barbara Drive. Heard only. No further information. Station A, clear."

The call didn't come as a surprise. The sound of gunfire on a Friday night wasn't unusual. The fact the reporting parties were calling from the typically quiet town of San Marcos was a twist.

"San Marcos stepping up," Ellie said. "Guess they got some boys that, how did you say it? Want to play with the big dogs?"

Amused, Travis nodded toward the computer screen. "How much you got left?"

"Sending it to the printer right now." Ellie tapped the keyboard. "Let's get going. I don't want you to keep the little missus waiting. She's probably lighting candles, putting on your favorite shitkicker love song. That's a thing, right? In Iowa, I mean?"

He cranked the ignition. "You ready?"

"Oh man, so ready." Ellie shut the computer and pushed the console back to the center of the dash. She strapped on her seat belt. "Let's head in."

18

Omar's head buzzed as a consequence of two force-fed beers. The billowing pot smoke trapped in the closed space of the car only made it worse. He'd heard a person could get high just from being around burning marijuana. Would the army drug test him when he reported for basic? Would he fail? Kicked out before he even started? He rolled the window down half an inch and shimmied across the seat to lean against the door. He drew deeply of the cool night air.

"Roll it up, Seso," Chunks said from the front seat. "I like hotboxin' it."

Omar had reached his limit. It was time to start pushing back. "I can't even breathe, Chunks. I need some air."

This time it was Chunks who leaned across the seat, but instead of laughter, Omar heard Chunks mumble to E-Boy, "Damn ese, he's like an embarrassment, eh?"

"You gotta deal with it," E-Boy said. "Shit reflects on you, know what I'm sayin'?"

They exited the 78 at Civic Center, less than a mile from Omar's apartment, but Omar was now reluctant to ask Chunks to take him home or even drop him somewhere. Every time he mentioned going home, Chunks drove in the opposite direction.

The sudden gift from E-Boy was unexpected.

"I'm wiped, man. Drop me at my cousin's crib."

Omar saw the opening. "Yeah, me too, Chunks. Just let me out. I can walk from here."

Chunks still wasn't ready to give in, but at least now Omar had an ally. When Chunks pushed back, his words lacked real commitment. "What are you guys? Couple pussies? It's still early."

"Nah." E-Boy leaned back against the headrest and closed his eyes. "I'm tired of you fools. Take me home."

"All right, dawg. Let me drop off soldier boy, then we can trip to your place. Okay if I crash there for a few hours?"

"Whatever." E-Boy kept his eyes shut, turned his head slightly, and raised his voice enough so Omar would know he was talking to him. "So, for reals. You need to hook me up with your sister."

"She's only sixteen."

"Perfect."

Chunks gave a low laugh. "Careful, homes. Seso gets all weird and shit about his family. 'Specially his sister. I think he's gonna turn her into a nun or some shit."

"That'd be a waste." E-Boy opened his eyes and stared into the backseat. Omar didn't look away.

"Seso, I'll take you home first. We'll see if your sister still be awake, huh?"

"Hell, that don't matter," E-Boy said, grabbing at his crotch. "I got just the thing to like . . . shock her into consciousness and shit."

Both men laughed, and E-Boy put his fist up to Chunks, looking for acknowledgment. Before Chunks could respond, Omar grabbed E-Boy by the wrist. He squeezed hard and pulled him in, getting as close to E-Boy's face as he could from the backseat.

"That ain't gonna happen, dude." There was no fear in his voice. "Not ever."

Chunks made a sharp turn. "See? I told you, man. He gets all fired up about that little piece of puta."

"Ain't a problem." E-Boy pulled free and looked away. "When you leaving, ese? Coupla days? I can wait."

Omar felt his face grow hot. This shit was over. No more lying down for it. He'd do what was needed. No limits. Then, come Sunday, the Ortegas would be gone without a trace.

Red and blue lights lit up the interior of the car and the short chirp of a siren made all three men sit up. Omar started to turn around but stopped himself.

"Oh, shit." Chunks groaned. "Dude, I'm baked and drunk as hell. I'm gonna jam. You guys ready?"

"Fuck that," E-Boy said, looking into the side mirror and shifting in his seat. "Pull over. Just play it cool."

"Dude, I'm on parole. I already got busted once today. They'll violate my ass for sure. I ain't goin' back to prison."

"Well, you ain't gonna outrun a cop car in this pile of shit," E-Boy shouted. "Now, *pull over.*"

Chunks put on his signal and steered the car to the side of the road. Omar slumped lower in the backseat.

Shit. He could not be found in this car with two gangster parolees. He'd been drinking. They were drunk, too, and high on marijuana. If he got caught with them, there was no way he didn't end up officially documented as a gang member, and probably in handcuffs. His army career would be over before it started.

Ten blocks. If he got a jump, if he got off with a good first step and just kept his head down, he figured he could outpace anyone who might give chase. Then again, night shift deputies were typically young, and some of them were straight-up studs when it came to running down gangsters.

The hell with it. He had no options. Problem was, Chunks wouldn't be outrunning anybody, and they'd been seen together earlier in the day. Omar could only hope Chunks would return the favor and keep his mouth shut.

Rage—at himself—filled his head. He'd let this happen. He'd gotten himself into this jam. Now his only choice was to run.

He'd go home and lock the door. Wake up his mom. They'd light a candle and pray Hail Marys until the sun came up.

Omar sat up straight, gripped the door handle, and bounced his feet on the floor mat, getting loose. Getting ready. He took a couple of deep breaths and waited for the car to roll to a stop.

19

0052 HOURS

Travis drove down South Santa Fe, headed toward the substation, staying ten miles below the speed limit. The road was clear and the breeze through the open window was like a natural balm against his skin. Ellie leaned back against the headrest, her eyes closed.

"Twelve hundred calories in twenty minutes will do it to you every time," he said.

She flipped him off without opening her eyes. He looked back to the road just in time to see a lowrider pull in front of him. He mashed the brakes and Ellie sat up.

Travis whipped a U-turn and fell in behind the vehicle. He clicked on the high beams and did a quick scan of the inside of the car, making out the silhouette of three shaved heads. He also saw that the rear license plate lamp was out. That, plus the failure to yield, was more than enough probable cause for a traffic stop. But that was all pretextual bullshit. Three pumpkin heads in a lowrider was the real PC.

"What the hell, Travis?" Ellie adjusted in her seat after the lurching turn. "I thought we were headed in."

"I'm going to pull this guy over."

"Seriously?" Ellie sounded annoyed. "We're thirty minutes from end of watch. Let's just get to the barn. I want to go home."

"Come on. It's a good stop. If we get anything, I'll handle it."

"I swear, you and Teddy. Couple of overtime whores. Just tell your wife to get a job, why don't you?"

Travis laughed as he reached for the overheads. "Call it out. I'll take contact. You cover. Like I said, I'll buy any paper."

"Damn right you will." As she leaned forward to grab the microphone, she tilted slightly in her seat. Even with the windows down, the air went foul.

"Damn, Ellie. Seriously?"

"Oh, come on, man. Did you see what I ate?" She held the mic to her lips. "Just get 'em stopped and get on with it."

Travis clicked the toggle for the overhead lights. Ellie called out their location along with the make, model, and license plate of the target car. A red and blue halo glowed over the patrol car and Travis's predatory instincts kicked in, topped off by an anticipatory dump of adrenaline. His hands tightened on the wheel and his boot hovered over the accelerator, certain the driver was about to bolt. Instead, the turn signal came on and the car moved toward the curb. Part of Travis was surprised. Another part disappointed. The bald head in the back sat up a little higher.

He spoke without taking his eyes off the car. "So, did you shit your pants or can you cover?"

"I'm good, but be quick," she said. "My colon's about to go into self-cleansing mode. Trust me, you don't want to be around for that."

"Keep obs on the one in the rear and the front passenger. I got the driver."

Travis stopped the squad and dialed back the overheads to just the yellow arrow stick. He activated the emergency takedowns along with both side spots, creating a curtain of blinding white light that he knew rendered them virtually invisible to the three occupants of the lowrider.

"Thirty-One Paul X," Ellie said into the mic. "Vehicle yielded. Final stop, eleven hundred block of South Santa Fe."

Travis got out on his side, careful to stay behind the light shield. Ellie stood and took a position in the V of the open passenger door. The lowrider was lit up like a bug specimen under a microscope. The occupants' heads bobbled around a bit, looking back and forth among each other.

The one in the back leaned forward like he was talking to the front seat passenger. Ellie saw it as well and called him on it.

"Here you go, hayseed," Ellie said in an "I told you so" sort of tone. "Looks like they're getting their story straight for you. This oughta be fun. Time consuming, too."

He pressed on his earpiece, listening to the chatter of the other patrol units. Travis knew he should wait for a return on the license plate, but with this amount of radio traffic, that could take a while. Ellie was right. The longer they waited, the more time the little homies had to put a story together to cover up whatever bullshit they'd been up to. A car drove by slowly, rubbernecking the stop, then continued on.

Without taking his eyes off the lowrider, Travis called to Ellie, "You ready?"

"Get on with it, already."

Travis took two steps out and away from the patrol car to avoid being silhouetted. With his flashlight held high and away from his body, one hand hovering near his gun, and all his attention dialed in, he moved up to make contact with the driver.

20

A brilliant white light flooded the interior of the Impala as a car passed, slowing as if to have a look at what was going on. Omar told himself again that he had no choice in the matter. He gripped the door handle and pulled up a street map in his head.

Then everything changed.

"Oh shit." Chunks spoke in a voice that was nothing more than a wheeze of air. He stared toward E-Boy's crotch. "Don't be fucking around. Put that shit away, homie."

Omar leaned forward and looked into the front seat. The dull metal handgun was an ominous shape in E-Boy's lap. A kaleidoscope of random images tumbled through Omar's mind: working with his father; imagining his mother as a girl in Mexico; signing his recruitment papers. This was potentially the end of everything. All because, three hours ago, he'd gotten in a car and been taken for a ride.

He heard a voice from outside the car and knew it had to be a cop. Talking to another cop? Talking on the radio? Omar couldn't be sure, but a moment later a shape moved past his window: beige shirt, black leather belt loaded with gear, fingers dancing lightly on the handle of a holstered handgun. The man bent down, flashlight in hand, and looked through the window at Omar. His eyes were kind, his smile easy. He moved on until he stood just outside the driver's door. Omar saw the deputy rap his knuckles against the window.

Options gone, there was only one thing to do. Omar barely recognized his own voice as he shrieked, "Look out! He's got a gun! He's got a gun!"

Omar banged his fist against the window and the man outside lurched in response. A series of explosions blasted through the interior of the car, sending stabbing pains through both of Omar's ears. His own screams from inside the car were followed by more explosions, all of it now muffled like he was being held underwater. With each flash of the gun, the figure outside the window lit up and tumbled back. Omar caught strobing, snapshot images of pale skin, black leather, and gleaming metal.

The cop stumbled back, arms flailing like broken wings, legs crumpling beneath him. The explosions finally stopped, but the ringing inside his head nearly drowned out the roar of the engine. The car pitched forward and Omar threw all his weight against the door, yanking up on the handle. He tumbled out, smacking his head hard against the asphalt. His leg got caught in the door and the car dragged him painfully for a few seconds until he twisted free. He rolled into the street and the car sped away.

21

0053 HOURS

Travis used his flashlight to illuminate the interior of the car; Ellie did the same on the passenger side. Satisfied with his position, he moved forward to contact the driver. He got as far as the rear passenger door.

The shots came in quick succession, and he instinctively began to draw his gun, then stopped. He counted.

One, two, three. Pause. *Four, five.*

Ellie had already turned her back to the lowrider. Her weapon was out and pointed toward the sound of gunfire.

"*Jesus*, those were close," she said. Travis heard the quiver in her voice as she spoke into the mic attached to her uniform shirt. Her words flowed through his earpiece. "Station A, Thirty-One Paul X. We've got multiple eleven sixes, heard only, immediately north of our location."

The dispatcher repeated the information, his voice calm and dispassionate. "Ten four, Thirty-One Paul X. Attention to all Vista units, shots fired, heard only, north of the eleven hundred block of South Santa Fe. Station A clear."

Travis knew every deputy in Vista and beyond was listening, waiting. This info wasn't from some mope citizen. It wasn't some panicked 911 caller who didn't know a firecracker from a shotgun. This was coming from a deputy, and that meant shit just got real. The radio went quiet, waiting for another deputy who might have more information or might need to call out an emergency transmission. Several seconds went by and Travis felt his tension begin to ease. Just more random gunfire, but when it was that close, it was enough to shake up even the most hardened street cop. Hand still gripping his holstered gun, Travis blew out a deep, choppy breath.

Ellie slowly lowered her weapon. "Okay, that did it. I'm pretty sure I shit myself."

"Somebody just capping rounds, I guess," Travis said, still staring in the direction of the gunfire. "Let's cut these guys loose and we'll go roll through the—"

The radio keyed up with several seconds of a muffled scraping sound. It was that unintelligible shuffling that any cop would associate with another cop under duress or in a fight. A deputy fumbling with the radio mic, unable to get out a clear transmission. Travis stood still, waiting.

Another sound came across the radio and, from the moment he heard it, Travis knew he'd never be able to unhear it. That sound would stay with him for the remainder of his life. Even if he never heard it again in the waking world, it would surface in his dreams, his nightmares. In unguarded moments, the sound would fill any quiet space. Like all the cops listening that night, Travis knew he'd be taking that sound with him to his grave.

It was a choking sound mixed with a gurgle of desperation. Someone was trying to speak. To call for help.

It was a cop.

A cop who was dying.

The transmission cut off, freeing up the frequency, and the commanding voice of Sergeant Peña immediately took over. "Station A, this is Sam Unit One. Whose portable was that, and their last location?"

The dispatcher's tone was an octave higher than usual and his words came quickly. "Deputy Rosado, he was on a traffic stop at Civic Center and Pala."

Peña came back, "Give him code three cover and roll paramedics."

Ellie beat Travis to the car, already pulling the AR-15 out of the gun rack as Travis threw the transmission in reverse, did a 180-degree power turn, and shifted into drive. Ten seconds later he was doing ninety miles an hour before he even thought about the forward overhead lights and siren. He didn't bother with the radio but shouted out loud.

"We're eight blocks out. *Hang on!*"

In that moment he wasn't sure whether he was talking to his partner or to Deputy Teddy Rosado.

22

Lying on the bed, Hector nudged at the springs of the top bunk with one foot. "Hey, sis. You asleep?"

"No." Her answer was immediate and her voice clear. It was just a few minutes before one in the morning but, like him, Sofia was wide awake. The mattress over his head shifted and squeaked until her long hair spilled down and her face appeared over the edge. She was looking at him upside down.

"We should call the police," she said. "Tell them what happened."

Sometimes Hector wondered what planet his sister lived on. "Are you crazy, girl? We can't call the police. What are we gonna say? Our brother left to go hang out with a couple of homies? Went out to drink beer and raise hell?"

Sofia disappeared for a moment and then her legs swung over, dangling briefly before she dropped down and landed catlike on the floor. She sat on the edge of Hector's bed, her concern and worry making her look much older than her sixteen years. Hector felt bad for how he'd talked to her.

"He's not out drinking beer," Sofia said. "Those boys made him go. They threatened him. The police could find him and bring him home."

Hector rolled on his side and leaned on one elbow. "We can't do that,

Sofia. Omar would just get in trouble. The deps aren't going to listen to some story like that."

"But it's the truth. He's been gone for hours. He said he'd be home in twenty minutes."

She was right about that. Omar had been gone for almost two hours. That wasn't like him. He'd never left them home alone this late. Something had definitely gone wrong.

"How about Mom? We could call her."

"And what could she do?" He tried to be more patient. "She's working. And besides, the last thing we need is that crusty old bastard Renteria to come back here. Getting in our business. You know that would just make Omar mad."

Sofia's eyes went wistfully to the bedroom doorway, like she was trying to will Omar to walk through it. "We need to do something. I don't know what, but I know he's in trouble. He wouldn't leave us like this."

Hector got out of bed and walked to the window. He'd carefully locked the front door, but the bedroom window, three stories above the street, was wide open to allow the breeze to come through. The barrio was strangely quiet—no sounds other than the occasional barking dog or passing car. Right now, the only noises Hector wanted to hear were the sounds of his brother coming up the stairs, slipping his key into the lock. Hector imagined Omar walking inside. He'd hug Sofia and, at the same time, he'd lay into Hector, blaming him for the whole mess.

And I'd take it.

Hector knew that if anything had gone wrong, it was all his fault. If only he had listened to his brother in the first place. If only he hadn't gone to the wall. A tightness grew in his throat and he began a silent bargaining session with God. A God his mother swore was looking out for them but one he'd grown to believe didn't give a holy shit about the Ortega family. Now, he promised to turn all that around. Stop with the lousy attitude. Stay clear of the bangers. He'd clean up his act. *Swear to God I will. Just let him walk through the door.*

Sofia spoke from where she sat on the bed. "Maybe if we—"

The gunfire cut her off and sounded so close that Hector instinctively ducked. He counted the shots.

One, two, three. Pause. *Four, five.*

"Oh my god!" Sofia screamed and dropped to the floor.

Hector assessed. No shattering of glass. No sounds of impact. He stood up and looked down onto the empty street. He'd come to understand the nature of gunfire. It was always hard to know which direction shots had come from or how close they'd really been. But he was sure those shots had been damn close. He thought maybe he heard an engine revving, but he couldn't be sure.

"That's it, Hector." Sofia stood and headed for the door. "I don't care what you say. I'm calling the police."

The air filled with what sounded like a hundred screaming sirens. On the street below, a sheriff's car sped by. Seconds later, two more followed.

"Don't bother," Hector said, overwhelmed with a premonition of disaster. "They already know."

Sofia came and stood with him by the window. Her hand shook as she reached for his. In the distance, Hector could see a pulsing cloud of blue and red light that hovered just above the street. He was sure Sofia saw it too, and she began to cry.

"Oh, Omar," she whispered. "Please come home."

23

"I don't get it, Joaquin. Three hours sitting around with our thumbs up our asses, and for what? To get some footage of a couple of ambulance jockeys loading up a blanket-covered gurney and driving away. You know how many times I've shot that scene? How much B-roll I've got of that same shit? Three fricking hours for that? Makes no sense."

Coming up on 1:00 A.M., Joaquin Fonseca leaned back in the passenger seat of the panel van, eyes closed, listening to the latest rant of Manuel Rodriguez, his cameraman of fifteen years. Twice as long as both of Joaquin's marriages combined. The only thing in Joaquin's life that had lasted longer was his relationship with his twenty-six-year-old daughter, but since they hadn't been on speaking terms in three years, he wasn't sure that counted.

"We don't use B-roll on an event-specific news story," Joaquin said. "You know that. It'd be no different than staging."

"And what's wrong with that? You've never seen a thirty-foot section of yellow tape slapped up as the backdrop of some make-believe crime scene?"

Joaquin wondered why he even tried anymore. Mannie would argue about anything. Not bothering to open his eyes, Joaquin replied, "Sure. I've seen it. But never done it. Never will, either. This ain't TMZ. People gotta be able to believe the news."

"Right." Mannie laughed. "Because they do now."

"Maybe not, but they *can*."

Joaquin had been partnered with Mannie since he'd left a cushy job as a network sports anchor and hired on with Univision as a field reporter. On his first day of work, Joaquin's new boss met him in the parking lot, handed him a generic press credential, and told him to head out to the remote East County town of Ramona to cover a "little brush fire" that had kicked up in the Cleveland National Forest.

"Get up there and let Mannie shoot some footage for the five o'clock," the executive producer said. "You do the voice-over. Families fleeing with pets always makes good copy. If you get some colorful stuff, I mean like roaring flames, we'll lead with it. That'd make for a pretty good first day, wouldn't you say?"

Joaquin hesitated, saying he'd never done an actual on-location news broadcast before. The exec shoved him toward the van, saying, "Chat up some firefighters. They're just like football players. Mannie's a great cameraman. He can school you on the way."

By the time they made their way up the mountain, the fire had burned two thousand acres and dozens of fire crews from throughout San Diego County had been deployed. That was just in the first four hours. Then they closed the mountain and the inferno began.

Joaquin and Mannie spent the next two weeks reporting on and filming one of the deadliest and most devastating natural disasters in California history. The Cedar Fire burned a quarter-million acres and destroyed more than two thousand homes. Fifteen people were killed, including a firefighter.

Between broadcasts, the duo from Univision assisted families in hosing down houses and barns, directed traffic, delivered water and meals to first responders, and even evacuated a few pets. When they finally returned to the studios, Joaquin learned that, in thirteen days, he had become a household name for the Spanish-speaking population of Southern California. He was the trusted face of Univision before he ever stepped into the studio. He and Mannie had been joined at the hip ever since.

Still bitching, Mannie said, "You're the one who should be pissed. Since when do you get detailed to ambulance chasing? You should be covering the border story. You're Univision's lead field reporter. You're Joaquin Molina-Fonseca, damn it."

Driving east on the 78, they were headed back to the Kearney Mesa studios after covering a triple-fatality traffic accident on the I-5, just south of the old San Clemente nuclear power plant. They'd broadcast live from the collision scene but got buried pretty deep behind the lead: day four of demonstrations touched off by a recent Border Patrol shooting.

Mannie was right—that was the story Joaquin should have been covering. Instead, the new thirty-one-year-old executive producer of the news division had brought in a half-dozen stringers—nowadays they were called "citizen journalists"—to infiltrate the crowd and interview demonstrators with their iPhones. The footage was cobbled together at the station and presented by a Barbie-doll wannabe news anchor who broadcast while sitting on a couch.

Joaquin lowered his window a few inches; the rush of air blended with the occasional transmission from the handheld police scanner balanced on the dashboard. For all his bitching, Mannie was right about one thing: Joaquin needed to sit down with the new EP. If the plan was to ease him out, keep him driving all over the damn county chasing down the latest wreck on the highway, well then, adios.

Pushing sixty, Joaquin knew that, in today's media reality, he was a journalistic dinosaur. But he also knew he had the skills, credibility, and connection to the community that generated a quality of reporting that no one else at Univision could equal. Joaquin Fonseca had been a first-rate field reporter for going on twenty years and had the Emmys to prove it.

He sat up straight. Gunshots. Close. He counted at least four, maybe five.

"Did you hear that?"

Mannie must have, because he'd eased up on the accelerator and lowered his window, thrusting his head out into the open air. The traffic was light enough that he was able to slow down to a crawl and listen. Nothing. He shrugged and hit the gas.

"Vista on a Friday night," he said. "No big—"

The scanner squawked with the voice of a female deputy who put out the code for gunshots, heard only. Joaquin grabbed the scanner off the dashboard and locked in the frequency before it could trip to a call from another agency. The transmission had come over the channel assigned to the Vista sheriff substation.

Joaquin stared at the scanner and waited. The next sound made the skin on his arms crawl in a way so disturbing he almost heaved the scanner out the window.

"What the—" Mannie had heard it too. "Damn. Sounded like somebody getting choked or something."

Voices came over the air.

"*Station A, this is Sam Unit One. Whose portable was that, and their last location?*"

"*Deputy Rosado, he was on a traffic stop at Civic Center and Pala.*"

"*Give him code three cover and roll paramedics.*"

The wail of sirens came from every direction. A sheriff's black and white sped past them from behind, doing a hundred-plus. Joaquin looked at the road sign overhead.

"That's the next exit, Mannie. Get us there."

24

12:54 A.M.

Lying on his back in the road, Omar touched one hand to the dull thud rocking through his head. He flinched against the pain and his fingers came back covered with blood. His entire body throbbed and he wondered if he'd be able to move. A current hummed inside his skull, alternating between surging power and a flickering spark. He struggled to orient himself; his thoughts jumbled.

He'd been in a car. Had there been a wreck? No, not a wreck. An explosion.

He'd fallen. He'd jumped. Why had he jumped?

Flashing blue and red lights drew his attention. He heard frantic chatter on a police radio and, closer, a thick, choking cough. He blinked his eyes in quick succession, overwhelmed by a moment of terrifying clarity.

A gun. The shadow of a man. A shouted warning.

His ears still rang, though the sound now resembled the warning bell at a train crossing. Memories flooded back and horror propelled him to a standing position. Pain shot up his leg, dropping him back hard onto the ground. He got up again and staggered toward the light, scanning the street. Searching.

There. Along the curb. A crumpled figure. Omar stumbled toward it, but fell again, landing so close that the deputy's contorted face took up his entire field of vision. The man's eyes were wild with fear, his mouth opened and closed as if stuck on a silent scream.

One hand was pressed to his neck in what Omar knew at a glance was a hopeless effort to stop the bubbling flow of blood. Red spilled over his fingers and down his throat, soaking his tan shirt. The deputy's other arm was stiff at his side. His legs kicked spastically against the road as if somewhere in his mind he was still in the fight.

A vicious wound had laid open the deputy's throat and Omar could see a wet, pulsing patch of flesh. The man's eyes fluttered, went still, and all movement ceased. Blood stopped pumping even as the crimson pool beneath the body continued to spread.

Omar crawled closer on his hands and knees. He looked down at the deputy, whose eyes were still open but the life had run out. For a solitary and silent moment, it was as if the entire planet and even the heavens above joined in the horrifying realization of the tragedy that had just occurred. There'd been no grand design to it or even any real sense of life-or-death desperation. It had been completely avoidable, brought about by foolishness, depravity, and happenstance.

It was a tragedy that could never be undone. And it was a tragedy that would demand retribution. But none of that mattered to Omar. Sirens erupted from every direction, like someone had hit a switch. Deputies were coming. Lots of them.

For an instant, Omar thought about resigning himself to the inevitable. Let them kill me, he thought. Just let it be.

As always in his most desperate moments, Omar's family filled his mind. His mother. Sofia and Hector. Even his father, whom he hadn't seen in years. He wasn't going to let them down. Wasn't going to give up.

Sobbing, he struggled to a kneeling position over the lifeless man. Overwhelmed with grief and fear, Omar spoke the only words that came to mind.

"I'm sorry. God, I'm so sorry."

He pulled himself to his feet and staggered away into the darkness.

25

0300 HOURS

Travis leaned back against the horizontal cast iron bar of the push bumper, the idling engine blowing hot air against the backs of his legs. Two deputies stood nearby at parade rest, one on each side of the dark green sheet in the roadway. It occurred to Travis that a sheet over a body was never allowed at a crime scene, dignity of the dead being considered secondary to evidence integrity. Never, that is, unless the body was that of a fallen deputy. Then nothing came before dignity.

Ted's body. Ted's dead body. The same Ted who had been dicking around in the briefing room at the start of shift. The same guy who helped himself to Ellie's chips and guac just over three hours ago. Teddy Rosado. He was dead and his corpse was under that sheet.

What if I just drove away?

The idea had merit. Just drive, as far as the patrol car that had brought him to this miserable moment would take him. Load up his family and drive nonstop to their life back in Newburg. Drive until the events of the last two hours were so far removed from his reality that he might be able to convince himself that none of it had happened. But looking at the scene around him, he knew better. He wasn't leaving this place anytime soon.

The patrol car Travis and Ellie had arrived in a little over two hours ago was now hemmed in by dozens of police cars from every jurisdiction in San Diego County, and more than a few from beyond. Cars fanned out in a blurred sea of blue and red, all jammed together in a haphazard pattern that signified their frenzied arrival. It would be a long time before the car at the very center of it all went anywhere.

He and Ellie had been first to arrive, first to find Ted's crumpled, lifeless body. Ellie maintained her composure long enough to put out a transmission heard around the county, then rebroadcast around the entire state. City by city, station by station.

"Eleven ninety-nine. Deputy down. Civic Center and Pala."

After that, she kneeled next to her friend, bowed her head, and sobbed. Travis forced himself to compartmentalize those first minutes. He locked them away, knowing full well that he would eventually have to confront the memory. But not now.

Within two minutes every on-duty patrol car in Vista had arrived on the scene, engines pinging, melted brake pads churning out hot, white smoke. Cops from Oceanside, Carlsbad, and Escondido arrived next, jumping out of still-rocking police cars. The deputy from Valley Center barely avoided a head-on collision with a black and white coming down from Riverside County. So it continued, until police cars from as far south as National City and as far north as Los Angeles surrounded the body of Ted Rosado, as if the fury of their response would somehow bring him back from the dead.

A squad of downtown detectives showed up on scene within thirty minutes. The sheriff and the undersheriff shortly after that. Travis watched as one of the detectives, dressed in a jacket and tie, gloved up and lifted the blanket to view Ted's body. When the blanket dropped from his hand, the detective remained kneeling; he bowed his head in what Travis took to be a moment of prayer.

Two of the detectives walked toward the designated command center, where Sergeant Peña was coordinating the block-by-block, building-by-building, and house-to-house search of the area. One of the detectives, who looked to be nearly as old as Peña, shook hands with the senior patrol sergeant. They leaned into each other for an embrace that lasted several seconds.

When Peña tried to pull back, the detective grasped him by the back of the neck and spoke directly into his ear. Peña stared at the ground and, even from a good distance, Travis could see the agony that deepened the lines of the sergeant's face. At last Peña lifted his head and pointed at Travis. The detective shook Peña's hand a second time, then walked toward Travis.

"Deputy Jackson?"

"Yeah." Travis straightened up—he'd still been leaning against the patrol car—as the man grew closer.

"I don't think we've ever met. I'm Enrique Soledad. Homicide. You doing all right?"

Now that Soledad was closer, Travis recognized him from frequent appearances on local news broadcasts. As the homicide sergeant, Enrique Soledad had one of the most high-profile assignments in the department. Nothing got the media's attention like a killing. And that was never truer than for a cop killing. Sergeant Soledad was tall, taller than Travis even, and lean. His salt-and-pepper hair was thick, giving him what Molly would probably call rugged good looks.

Molly. The last she'd heard from him had been a text asking her to wait up. He hoped she'd given up and gone to bed. He wondered, was Ted's wife waiting up?

"Travis?" the sergeant tried again.

Travis shook his head. "Sorry. Yeah. I guess I'm doing all right."

"Orlando, I mean Sergeant Peña, says you and your partner were first on scene?"

"Yes, we were." Travis looked back to where Ellie sat in the passenger side of their patrol car, her expression a complete blank.

After the initial burst of insanity had subsided, he'd tried to speak with her, but she'd retreated to the car. Understanding, he'd left her alone for a while. But when he knocked on her window twenty minutes later, she shook her head and said, "Not now."

"I'd like to get you both back to the station," Soledad continued, as Travis refocused on him. "We need to get your statements. Are you ready to do that?"

"Sure." He glanced at his car again.

"Don't worry about your squad. We're going to leave it right where it is, along with Deputy Rosado's car. You didn't move it for any reason, did you?"

"What?" His mind was working in slow motion. The sergeant's words came at him like they were in a foreign language. "You mean Ted's car? Did I move it? Is that what you're asking me?"

"Right." The voice was patient. Understanding. Even kind. "Did you, for any reason, feel the need to move his car?"

"No. I didn't."

"And what about Deputy Rosado? Ted? Did you touch him?" Soledad asked, as if he already knew the answer. He looked at Travis's bloodied hands and uniform shirt.

"Yeah. Yeah, I did."

Ellie had been kneeling next to Ted when Travis shoved her aside. He'd dropped to his knees, tilted back Ted's head, and blew two breaths into his mouth, then began chest compressions, just as he'd been trained. What the academy training never included was what to do if every breath of air wheezed out of an open throat and every compression resulted in a violent spray of blood.

Ellie yelled at him to stop, shouting that Ted was already gone. When she tried to pull him away, Travis flung out an arm and knocked her back. He kept at it, one hand covering the wound and the other pumping Ted's chest. When the paramedics arrived, it took both of them, plus Ellie, to pull Travis away. The lead paramedic took one look at Ted and called it at the scene.

"I tried to help him," Travis said, staring at the green sheet. "But I guess he was already dead."

"I get it, Travis. I know what you were trying to do. And I just want to confirm, you never saw a vehicle? A suspect vehicle, that is?"

"No. No car."

"And no suspects either? I mean, nobody fleeing on foot?"

"Right." Travis thought back to their arrival, feeling like it had occurred years before. "I put that out, didn't I? On the radio?"

"Yes. You did." Soledad paused, and Travis looked up to find the sergeant staring, his expression softer. "My understanding is, your initial response was excellent. You and your partner did everything you could."

Travis nodded absently, looking overhead at the circling news helicopters, the drone of their engines adding to the white noise already in his head. Within a minute or two of his arrival on scene, a two-person media crew had showed up. Travis was pretty sure he recognized the reporter as the guy from Univision. He'd dealt with him a time or two. They'd filmed for several minutes, until one of the other responding units finally shoved them back. By this point, yellow tape was set up a half mile out in every direction; close-ups would be impossible, except for the damn helicopters.

How does the saying go? "If it bleeds, it leads."

Sergeant Soledad looked up as well. "We'll clear the airspace pretty soon. But now, I really want to get you and your partner out of here. Get you over to the substation. Let you clean up. Change into some civvies. We're probably going to collect that shirt. Are you okay with that?"

"Whatever you need, Sergeant. I just . . ." Travis wasn't sure what he was trying to say. "Just tell me what you need me to do."

Soledad waved at a nearby cluster of investigators. "Yo, Bennett."

A burly white detective hustled over. "Travis," Soledad said, "this is Detective Mike Bennett. He's going to drive you back to the substation. We'll get you processed for evidence, then decompress as best you can. You and I will talk later."

Travis looked again at Ellie, who finally met his eyes. "Can I talk to her before we go?"

"That's not a good idea right now."

"Just let me make sure she's okay."

"All right," Soledad said. "I know this sounds stupid, but I need to be there."

"Yeah, yeah. I get it."

When he got close, Ellie opened the patrol car door and stepped out, nearly falling into his arms. She hugged him, and Travis once again realized just how physically strong she was. He remembered her fight earlier that day, just two blocks from where they now stood, how easily she'd dealt with that confrontation.

"I'm sorry, Travis." He could feel the wetness of her mouth against his ear. "I was no help to you. I was a mess. I blew it. I'm sorry."

"You didn't blow anything." Travis returned the hug just as tight, then pulled back. He stood awkwardly, his hands on her shoulders. "What could we do? He was gone when we got here. Now we just need to catch whoever did this."

Soledad stepped closer. "Deputy Peralta, I was just telling Deputy Jackson I want to get you both back to the substation. Out of the craziness. We're going to have people here all night, but you two don't need to be."

Ellie nodded. "I'm ready. I can go now." She turned toward Detective Bennett, who was jiggling his keys nervously in one hand.

"Actually," Soledad said, waving over another detective, "someone else will take you."

This was a murder investigation now, Travis realized. At this point, he and Ellie would be separated. They'd give their statements alone, without consulting each other. Standard procedure for any police shooting. Both of them had been through it before, but never when it involved losing one of their own.

"Yeah, of course," Ellie said. Even in the dark he could see moisture glistening in her eyes. "We'll talk later."

Detective Bennett patted Travis lightly on the back. "I'm parked over this way."

Travis trailed Bennett to his car, still thinking of Ellie's tears. Then it came to him, another image he'd be stuck with for the rest of his life: the lifeless, sorrow-filled eyes of Teddy Rosado.

Teddy had been crying too.

26

Omar stood in the narrow gap between buildings and looked across the two-lane street that felt like the I-5 border crossing. It had never seemed wider or bathed in a brighter light. A half-dozen black and white police cars had driven by in the past few minutes—two from Escondido, another from Chula Vista. Some sped. Some crawled. Some had bright spotlights, sweeping the street; others rolled dark. He didn't know if they were just prowling the area or if somehow they were already looking for him.

He'd hobbled ten blocks from where the deputy had been killed, staying in the shadows as sirens shrieked all around him. Patrol cars from all over San Diego County flooded the area as if it were a war zone. At one point he'd been out in the open when two patrol cars approached, and his only option had been to dive into a dumpster. The cops had stayed in the area for what felt like hours, until excited voices came over the police radio and the cars had sped off. Wincing, Omar had pulled himself from his hiding spot. He kept moving.

Now he stood across the street from where his family slept. The staircase led to the door, imposing and impossibly tall. With a last look in both directions, he limped and hopped across the road, getting the most out of one foot and dragging the other like a bag of cement. He waited for a shot to ring out. Would he even feel the bullet smash through his skull? With each step, the curb seemed to move farther away, but at last he was stumbling across the hard dirt of the yard.

He crawled up the steps to the breezeway and collapsed outside the door. Chest heaving, he dug his key from his pocket and reached over his head. Without looking, he finessed the key into the lock, turned it, and pushed. He fell inside and, without standing, low crawled on his back into the kitchen. He kicked the door shut with his good foot.

He lay there, lungs desperately pulling in air and heart pumping with such intensity it felt as if his body were bouncing against the cracked and crusted linoleum. He'd made it, but there was no sense of relief. His mother walked in from the living room, small Bible in one hand and rosary beads in the other. Omar pulled himself into a sitting position. She dropped onto her knees and fell against him, hugging his neck. She was crying softly.

"Gracias, Dios mio. Gracias."

"Let go, Mama. Please. Let me go."

Omar pried her hands loose from his neck, struggled to his feet, then headed down the hall, using the wall for support. She followed him, still crying.

"Que esta pasando, mijo? Que?"

"Mama, no digas nada, por favor," he whispered, grasping her tightly by the shoulders. He knew he was only scaring her more, but he couldn't help it. "I'm okay. Go to bed, please."

Sofia emerged from the bedroom, in her nightgown. The alertness in her voice told him that she, too, had been wide awake. "Omar, what's going on? Where have you been? Why are there so many sirens?"

She got a good look at him and gasped. "Omar, you're bleeding! What happened? Are you okay?"

His own emotional overload mixed with theirs and it was more than he could take. He pushed past them and into the bathroom, where he locked the door.

Sofia knocked. "Omar, you're hurt. Open the door and let me help you."

"Sofia, please." He knew he sounded desperate and worked to calm his voice. "I just don't feel well, that's all. Take Mom. Both of you go to bed."

She whispered through the door, "Have you been drinking?"

He closed his eyes and wished that was all it was. "Yes, yes, I have. Please, Sofia, leave me alone. I'll be fine."

Through the door, Omar heard his sister lead his mother back to the room they all shared. He listened through the door as Sofia spoke patiently to her mother in Spanish, explaining that Omar was sick. No need to worry. Isadora kept chanting her prayers, but Omar could hear the relief in her words.

"Omar. What happened out there? Those gunshots—they sounded close."

Omar fought back tears at the sound of his brother's worried voice. "Nothing. Nothing happened. Go to bed. I'll be in there in a little while."

"I'm sorry, Omar. I know I made a lot of trouble for you."

Flooded with fear, anger, and love, he wanted to scream but managed an almost reasonable tone. "We'll talk about it later. Go to bed."

As Hector retreated down the hallway, Omar sank to the floor. He saw the deputy's wide open eyes, the blood spilling from his throat. He heard the man's desperation, trying to speak as he moved toward death. Omar's body began to shake. He lay on the tile and curled into a fetal position, arms and legs quaking. He fought against the need to cry, to sob out his grief and pain. He bit hard against his fist, fighting to keep the screams inside.

He'd never known dread like this, never really been afraid before now. He'd thought he understood the depths of human misery, but now he realized he'd only scratched the surface. Compared to this moment, even the worst circumstances of his life had been nothing more than tragic but manageable inconveniences. He'd known sadness, but until now, he'd never really known hopelessness.

What could I have done differently?

Had breakfast at McDonald's led him here? What if he hadn't gone to the wall? Was he supposed to leave his brother around a guy like Chunks Gutierrez?

That damn gun. Why didn't he just tell the cops Chunks had tossed it? And, *Christ.*

Of course he'd gotten in the car. What choice did he have? What would they have done to his family if he'd refused?

If there had been milk in the refrigerator, they wouldn't have gone to McDonald's. If they hadn't gone to McDonald's, Hector wouldn't have gone to the wall. If Hector hadn't—

"Ah, stop it already!" He cursed himself out loud. He cursed his life.

Each decision he'd made was to help and protect his family. And each decision had led him to this place.

In the morning, he'd go to the police, tell them everything. He'd tell them how Chunks had showed up at the apartment. How he saw E-Boy murder the deputy sheriff. He'd tell them all of it, and he'd insist that his family be protected. What the cops or the gangsters did to him after that didn't matter. None of it mattered. The truth was, none of it had ever mattered. None of it was up to him.

Omar understood now. Whatever dreams he'd had, whatever plans he'd made, life had led him here. *Generations* had led to this moment. Why had he ever expected anything different? Anything more? He drifted toward a fitful sleep, accepting a difficult but plain truth.

I'm a pobrecito from the barrio. And that's all I'm ever gonna be.

PART TWO

AFTER

27

"You *cannot* air this, Philip. Not any of it."

The wall clock read 3:16 A.M., less than two hours to airtime. Joaquin sat in the production room with Mannie and Philip Cordova, the recently hired and bombastic executive producer of the Univision San Diego news broadcast.

Born and raised in West Los Angeles, Philip was the great-grandson of wealthy Argentinean immigrants. He'd traveled to the land of his ancestors and attended college at the University of Buenos Aires, then returned to his native California, to the Berkeley Graduate School of Journalism. After college, he used his father's wealth and influence to cobble together a dozen venture capitalists. With their money and his marketing savvy, he started his own online media outlet, viewed exclusively on Facebook.

In less than six months, *L.A. Unfiltered* had expanded to include YouTube, Hulu, and Amazon Prime. At the one-year mark, *L.A. Unfiltered* "news segments" were logging a million hits a month across a dozen media platforms. With Univision ratings at a ten-year low, the network board of directors aggressively recruited Philip to come on as the executive producer of the news division. Philip accepted, although he publicly referred to his new job as a demotion. In his first week at the network, Philip booked himself as a guest on the A.M. broadcast of *Al Punto*, where he guaranteed the audience he would transform Univision into an online powerhouse. That had been less than one year ago, and viewership in the under thirty demographic was now up over forty percent and still climbing.

"See? That's what I've been trying to get you to understand." Philip leaned back in his chair, with his low-cut Berluti boots resting on the table. He was dressed in creased designer jeans and a cream-colored linen shirt that he'd barely bothered to button.

He pointed at the frozen image on the computer. "This? This is the best footage of an officer-involved shooting I've ever seen. And I worked L.A. for ten years. You think it's unairable? I say it goes out as is."

"If you worked L.A., then you should understand this isn't an OIS," Joaquin said. "This is a deputy down call. A *fatal* deputy down. Those are two very different things."

"Maybe in your yesteryear world, but not anymore. We're airing it. And you should know, we've offered to share it with the other networks so long as they give us full credit. Several have already jumped on board, so I'll need you to do the voice-over in both English and Spanish."

Joaquin couldn't believe what he was hearing. When he and Mannie had arrived on the scene, a deputy was on the ground, clearly dead. Two other deputies were present, one attempting CPR and the other trying to stop him. Both deputies had been screaming. Shrieking, really. At each other, at the downed deputy. It was chaotic, macabre. It was as surreal and gut-wrenching a scene as Joaquin had ever experienced.

Of course Mannie had been recording. He did it instinctively. That was his job. But as was often the case at death scenes, what he'd captured could never be shared. Not with anyone. The digital footage needed to be deleted, permanently. Destroyed without a trace or burned onto a computer drive and never played again.

Joaquin's new boss, almost twenty-five years his junior, saw things differently. Joaquin dug his heels into the carpet and rolled his chair closer.

"Philip, it's raw footage we took on the fly. When Mannie shot the scene, he never expected it would be aired. At least not without some heavy editing. But this?" Now it was Joaquin who gestured to the image, surprised to find his hand was shaking. "This can't be saved. You need to bury it."

Philip pulled his feet down and swiveled in his chair. "What do you say,

Mannie? You ready to get famous? Have your work broadcast around the planet? CNN? Fox? All the major networks?"

"I think the FCC might have an opinion." Mannie, who most often worked in flip-flops and board shorts, didn't try to hide his true feelings for his Rico Suave of a boss. "But if I get famous off this stuff? It'll be because I go public saying you aired it against the wishes of the crew who documented it."

Philip threw up his hands in disgust but still laughed out loud. "Jesus, you two are something else."

Joaquin suspected Philip considered the discussion a waste of his time. His mind was made up. His next words proved it.

"It's airing on the five A.M. morning show. Right after that, we'll post it online. We'll lead in with a warning that it depicts graphic images and may not be suitable for all viewers. People always sit up and pay attention to that kind of thing. They love that shit. Besides, Jack. Don't you think we owe this to our audience?"

Joaquin let the English version of his name pass. Now wasn't the time. "What are you talking about? What do we owe them?"

"Honesty. Reality."

"And what about the man's family? His wife? Kids, maybe? How about all the other cops he works with? What do we owe them? Don't you see? There are lives involved here. People's lives, Philip."

"Now you're talking, Jack." Philip pumped his fist. "That's great. That's the kind of emotion I want you to have on camera. Talk about the tragedy. The loss. This is going to be awesome."

Shaking his head, Joaquin said, "I'm not going on camera with this. Like I told you before, the yellow tape is still up. I'm sure it'll still be there at five o'clock. I'll go live from the scene, but I'm not doing any voice-over for this footage."

"So what, then? We sit on this and go hang out at the tape line with every field reporter from Tijuana to L.A.? You call that journalism?" Philip looked back and forth at both men. "And what's up with that perimeter, anyway? Where do the cops get off closing a mile of access? You ever see them do that for a dead gangster? Or what about a domestic violence victim? You ever see that kind of deference for anyone other than a cop?"

Joaquin ignored him. "I'll cover our arrival. I'll paint a picture so colorful it'll be just like being there. I'll be as eloquent as the Psalms. As tragic as Job. I promise there won't be a dry eye watching when I get done. But I'm not going to break every known ethical standard of journalism just so you can boost your advertising revenue. I'm sorry, Philip, but it's just wrong."

"Then I guess you can go home, Jack," Philip said. "I know it's been a long night. I'm pretty sure I can find someone willing to do the voice-over. And by the way, don't bother coming back."

"You're going to fire me over this?"

"The way I see it, you're firing yourself." Philip went on, and Joaquin could feel the arrogance dripping off the man and practically pooling on the glass-top table. "Dude, I can walk down the hallway right now and get some of these young bucks to fistfight for a chance to do the lead-in for this shit.

"No way this story doesn't go national. I'm betting we get a million hits on our YouTube channel in the first week. This is the breakthrough we've been waiting for. If you can't see that, then yeah." Philip stood abruptly, both hands flat against the glass. "You're done."

Heading to the door that led to the studio, Philip paused, ready to push through. "You know, it's weird. I want to say, Great job. To both of you. Really. You have incredible instincts. There's still a place around here for that sort of thing. But it's a new world out there. So it's time to decide. Get on board or get run over."

He waited, but when he got no response, he shook his head and walked out.

After a minute or so, Mannie said, "He's right, you know. I hate the smug bastard, but he's right."

"No, he's not, Mannie."

"Think about it, man. Remember that woman? The one up in Minneapolis or wherever? Dude, she livestreamed her boyfriend dying after he got shot by a cop. I mean, *we watched him die.* That's what people want. Times have changed, brother."

"So that's our new standard? A Facebook video?"

"Yeah, it is," Mannie said. "Facebook. YouTube. Instagram. Twitter. That's where people get their news, and they don't want it packaged up and sanitized. That paternalistic bullshit is over."

"It's not sanitizing and it's not paternalistic," Joaquin said, looking at the monitor. A frozen image of the deputy sheriff stared back, sorrowful eyes wide open but lifeless. His mouth agape and spilling blood. The sheriff's department hadn't even released his name yet, but in less than two hours his death mask would be viewed by the world. "It's human decency."

"Well then, I guess they don't want that, either."

Mannie got up and left without another word. After a minute, Joaquin clicked off the monitor and followed him out.

28

The steady pound of gunfire was unrelenting. Travis stood by the patrol car, spinning in helpless circles, desperate to figure out where the shots were coming from. He pulled at his sidearm with both hands, but somehow the metal of the gun had become fused to the leather holster. None of the incoming bullets struck him; each one smacked against the flesh of Teddy Rosado, who lay at Travis's feet, twitching and thrashing, struggling to speak. His shredded throat pulsed dark red. He reached up with a bloody hand, grabbing for Travis. His crazed eyes begged for help.

The gunfire gave way to a steady, hard knocking. Sitting up on the narrow cot, Travis flipped the light switch. His hand came up automatically to shield his eyes from the harsh fluorescent glare. Still sitting on the bed, which pretty much took up the whole room, Travis swiped his palm across his face, then reached out and opened the door.

"Sorry, Travis." Sergeant Soledad backed away from the entrance to the rest and recovery room, or what the deputies called the "crash cave," tucked away in the basement of the substation. "We're ready when you are. We're using the captain's office for interviews. You mind coming up?"

"Sure. No problem," Travis said, though he still felt foggy. "What time is it?"

Soledad checked his phone. "Almost five thirty."

Less than three hours' sleep and he felt like he could use ten more. At least he'd been able to change out of his uniform and shower before sacking out.

"Is it okay if I call my wife? It'll just take a few minutes. I haven't checked in with her yet."

"Of course. Take your time." Soledad walked away, giving him some privacy.

Molly answered on the third ring. Her voice was filled with sleep and he realized that, since it was Saturday, she wouldn't have been up for at least another three hours. Too late.

"Hey, hon. Sorry to wake you. I got mixed up in some stuff. I'll be home in a few hours."

"Yeah, okay. I tried to wait up, but I guess I dropped off." He could tell she was barely awake; if he kept it short, she might be able to go back to sleep. "What kind of stuff?"

"I'll tell you when I get home." Travis heard the television in the bedroom click on.

"*Deputy killed?*" In an instant, she'd come wide awake. "Travis, are you okay? What happened? Who was killed?"

Her voice, already loud, became panicked. "Oh my god, Travis. Is that you? Is that blood? Where are you?"

"I'm at the station. I'm fine. Yes, a deputy was shot and killed last night. You remember Ted? My first-phase FTO?" His voice nearly broke, then he went on, "I've got to give a statement. After that, I—"

"Are you sure you're okay? I'm looking right at you on television. You . . . Travis. Baby . . . you're covered in blood. Jesus, what's happening?"

Travis remembered the first news crew on the scene; they'd been close. Too close. He could only imagine what she might be watching. "I'm fine, Molly. I'm talking to you, aren't I?"

"Come home, Travis. Come home to me right now."

"I can't leave yet, but I'll be home as soon as I can."

It took several minutes to calm Molly down. He was still trying to say good-bye as he walked into the admin wing, where the station captain kept his office. Ellie was walking out. He hadn't seen her since they'd been driven from the shooting scene in separate cars.

When he'd arrived at the substation, hours earlier, Travis had been photographed and his uniform shirt was collected. His firearm had been seized, but once it had been confirmed the gun had not been fired, it was returned to him. After the evidence techs released him, Travis took a hot shower, the water running red down the drain. He'd put on a pair of jeans and a clean T-shirt, then passed out in the crash cave.

Looking at Ellie now, he saw that she had dressed down a little, too. She still wore her uniform trousers, but with an oversize flannel cover shirt, untucked. She stood in the open doorway, talking with Sergeant Soledad. Spotting a man standing next to Ellie, dressed in slacks and a uniform polo, Travis figured she had opted for a union rep. Then he recognized the man as Ellie's husband, Commander Roberto Peralta. Travis had seen him in some department photographs.

Grim-faced, Ellie listened as Soledad spoke. Commander Peralta asked questions. Noticing Travis, Soledad wrapped things up and shook hands with both Ellie and her husband. He waved Travis over.

"You all set?" Soledad asked. "How's your wife?"

"Pretty freaked out, actually. Did you know they're broadcasting pictures taken from the scene? It sounds pretty intense."

"I heard," Soledad said. "Apparently a crew from Univision got some ground zero stuff, shared it with all the networks. The sheriff is mad as hell. The public information office is dealing with it. Sorry. I should've warned you."

"It's all right." But it wasn't. Molly had sounded terrified. And what about Ted's wife? He did his best to push those thoughts aside. "Ready when you are."

"Can you give me just a couple of minutes?"

Travis nodded and Soledad retreated into his office, closing the door.

"Hey, Ellie," Travis said.

"You're Deputy Jackson?" Roberto Peralta said.

"Yes, sir," Travis said, offering his hand.

"Nice to meet you, Travis. Of course, not under these circumstances. You doing okay?"

Before he could answer, Ellie jumped in. "Let's go, Rob. They probably shouldn't see us talking."

The commander's tone softened. "Don't worry, Els. I just want to say hello."

"Don't worry?" Travis was shocked by the emotion in her voice. "Did you hear that . . . bullshit just now? As if somehow we—" Ellie cut herself off as the door opened.

Giving the little group a nod, Soledad addressed Commander Peralta, deference in his voice. "Sorry to interrupt, sir, but we're ready for Deputy Jackson now."

"No interruption, Sergeant." The commander nodded and turned back to Travis. "I know this is difficult, Travis. Be strong. I'm sure we'll talk again soon."

Travis looked at Ellie, who stared back at him, her eyes projecting a warning mixed with sadness. Or was it anger? She walked away without another word.

"Come on, Travis." They walked toward the office and the sergeant put a hand on his shoulder. "So seriously. You doing okay? You ready to do this?"

"Yes, sir," Travis said, tense at the thought of the interview.

"Relax, Travis," Soledad said. "And please. It's Enrique. I know this is tough, but we'll get through it together, okay?"

Travis nodded. "Thanks, Enrique."

Travis walked into the office, surprised to find Sean Murphy and a woman already seated inside. Once the door closed, Enrique didn't waste any time on small talk.

"I understand you and Sean know each other?"

"Yeah, we do. Hey, Sean."

Sean Murphy glared back, stone-faced.

"If you don't have any objections," Enrique went on, "Sean will be sitting in on the interview."

"Can I ask why?"

"Early indications are that the murder of Deputy Rosado might very well be gang-related. As the homicide sergeant, I'll be supervising the overall investigation, but I've appointed Detective Murphy as lead investigator."

Travis nodded. "No problem, Sarge."

"And do you know Ms. Gaines?" Enrique said, gesturing at the woman sitting in the corner of the office. "She'll be personally handling vertical prosecution."

Travis hadn't recognized Danielle Gaines, chief prosecutor for the North County branch of the district attorney's office. All their dealings had been in courtrooms, where she always looked the part of a big-time legal shot caller. This morning, her gray hair was down, loose around her shoulders, and she was wearing blue jeans and a gray Georgetown Law hoodie.

"Hey, Dannie," Travis said. They had crossed paths several times in the past two years. The woman was popular among the deputies because of her aggressive reputation.

It didn't surprise Travis to learn Dannie Gaines would be handling the murder of Ted Rosado vertically. That meant she'd be in charge from round one. There'd be no procedural shuffling among DAs from one court appearance to the next. If a suspect came to trial, he or she would be up against a top-shelf, ball-busting prosecutor from the opening gavel of the arraignment until the needle went into their arm in the San Quentin death chamber.

Dannie gave Travis a pained smile.

"Hey, Travis. Sorry you're going through this."

Enrique moved things along. "I know you've barely slept and you're scheduled to work tonight, so if you don't mind, we'll get started. Get you out of here as quick as we can. You good with that?"

Travis nodded. "Ready when you are, Sarge."

Enrique turned on a digital audio recorder and placed it on the desk. He called out the time, date, and case number and directed everyone in the room to identify themselves by name and assignment. Travis went last.

"Deputy Jackson." For the first time since they'd met at the crime scene, the sergeant sounded officious and dispassionate. "Start at what you consider to be the beginning of your response to the emergency call for assistance by Deputy Rosado. Take us through all your observations and actions. Please be as detailed as possible."

Travis went through the events, step by step. He told them of hearing the gunshots while out on their own traffic stop. He recalled the radio transmissions and their code 3 response from eight blocks away. He related his futile attempts to provide first aid.

Along the way, he answered tactical and investigative questions from Enrique. A few potential evidentiary and legal issues were raised by Dannie Gaines. Sean said nothing and Travis wondered if he intended to carry on with the bullshit from the report room.

"So again, just to be clear," Enrique asked, "you didn't pass any vehicles? No peds, either?"

"No one," Travis said.

Enrique jotted notes as he spoke. "Based on the position of Deputy Rosado's patrol car, it's likely the suspect vehicle had been eastbound on Pala. From what you're telling us, they probably banged a U-turn in the parking lot across the street. Headed for the Seventy-Eight. That would explain why they didn't pass you. Does that sound accurate?"

Travis nodded in agreement, recalling the narrow section of roadway with no sidewalks, lined with parked cars. "Yeah. That makes sense."

Enrique went on, still sounding robotic, "Deputy Jackson, is there anything else you'd like to add?"

Travis glanced at Sean Murphy but spoke to the sergeant. "You're already thinking there's a gang connection?"

Enrique ignored the question. He held up his hand and leaned toward the recorder. "This will conclude the recorded interview of Deputy Travis Jackson. The time is now zero six eleven hours."

Enrique turned off the recorder and Travis asked, a bit surprised, "That's it? We're done?"

"Not quite," Enrique said. "I want you to view some video footage." He shook his head. "I tell you, I've seen it half a dozen times. It doesn't get any easier to watch. Dannie and I agree that it would be inappropriate and unnecessary to record this portion of your interview."

Travis looked at all three faces staring back at him. Mystified, he asked, "What video? What is it?"

Enrique turned the desktop computer screen to face Travis. The screen showed what looked to be the glare of light on glass. Leaning in for a closer look, Travis saw the metal trim of a car door around a window. Frozen on the screen was the reflected image of Deputy Ted Rosado, flashlight in hand.

"Ted's body camera? He had it on?"

"Yeah, he did," Enrique said. "We've synced Ted's body cam video with the dispatch audiotape. Putting the two together, we've determined that Ted turned on his camera about eight seconds after he'd been shot. So with the automatic video rollback of thirty seconds, that gives us a pretty complete picture of what occurred. Of course, the first thirty seconds of the video is silent."

Travis was familiar with the recording system. As soon as a deputy turned on their body cam recorder, the internal workings automatically started the recording thirty seconds earlier, but without audio. If Ted turned his camera on just eight seconds after being shot, Travis could do the math. His stomach flipped over in his gut with the realization of what he was about to watch.

Enrique's voice was solemn. "Travis, we think it's important that you see this. You okay with that?"

Travis wasn't at all sure he wanted to sit and witness the murder of Ted Rosado, but he gave a nod and looked to the computer screen.

"Okay then," Enrique said. "We'll start the dispatch recording from when you and Deputy Peralta made your traffic stop on South Santa Fe. Ted called out his stop about fifteen seconds later. Then, a few seconds after that, we start the body cam recording. You ready?"

Enrique and Dannie looked serious. Murphy looked pissed. Uncertain, Travis knew he had no choice. "Yeah. Sure."

Enrique nodded. "Go ahead, Sean."

Murphy clicked on the audio file and the dispatch tape began with the voice of Ellie Peralta calling out the traffic stop. Again, there was the dispatcher read-back and the radio traffic went quiet. Ted's image remained frozen on the screen, but Murphy had his finger poised over the computer mouse, ready to activate the body cam recording at the correct moment.

The voice of Ted Rosado came over the dispatch record.

"*Station A, Unit Thirty-One Paul Fifty-Two, out on traffic, Civic Center and Pala.*"

At the sound of Ted's brief transmission, Travis closed his eyes and chastised his dead friend. Ted was a night watch rock star who logged felony arrests with the same gusto that a motor cop wrote speeding tickets. He took crooks off the street, and not just for a weekend. If he put the stink on somebody, he made it stick. Everybody knew that Ted's officer safety skills were top-notch. He took care of business like a cop who was always determined to make it home. But last night Ted had screwed up, and now he'd never be going home again.

Maybe Ted had thought the dispatchers were too busy and he didn't want to burden them with the details of another traffic stop. Could be the stop was for something minor and he planned on giving the driver a quick warning. No matter the reason, it was bad.

Like most cops would do a few dozen times in a career, Ted had radioed in that he was "out on traffic," giving nothing more than his location. No make or model of the vehicle. No plate. No mention of the number of occupants. Ted's complacency had put him down, and the cops now looking for his killer were flying blind.

There it is. That word. Complacency.

How many times, Ted? How many times did you drill that into my head? Don't get complacent. Complacency is the enemy. Complacency kills. How much grief did you give me about not getting sloppy on traffic stops?

Travis forced himself back into the moment. "I remember hearing Ted call out his stop. Peralta and I were out of the car. We were just getting ready for our approach."

Enrique jotted something in his notebook.

The dispatcher responded. *"Thirty-One Paul Fifty-Two, traffic, Civic Center and Pala."*

Two units radioed that they were out at the station. Another unit requested a tow truck. Enrique held up one finger. After several seconds, he brought it down. "Now."

Murphy hit the Play button and the screen came to life. Travis leaned in. For some reason, Ted had decided to turn on his body cam, but that reason was still thirty seconds away.

The first, silent images from the body cam video showed Deputy Rosado on his approach, already alongside the car. Travis's first thought was that it was too bad Ted hadn't turned it on just a few seconds earlier. Then the video might have captured the license plate, or at least the vehicle's make and model.

Ted passed by the rear window, shining his light directly into the glass. A bright reflection filled the computer screen and Travis saw movement in the light—a shadow that might be a backseat passenger. Ted lingered by the back window for a moment, then moved up to a position outside the driver's door. The video caught the raised window and, once again, the screen was flooded with reflected light from Ted's flashlight. Ted's knuckles appeared on the screen, rapping silently against the window. He twirled his fingers, motioning for the still invisible driver to roll it down.

Travis waited, the seconds ticking by in his head. Any moment now, and there was nothing he could do but sit and let it happen. His hands clenched and his pulse pounded. Travis watched Ted's reflected expression go from a casual smile to a grimace of terror. Ted had seen what was coming.

Exploding glass filled the soundless screen, and Travis half expected ten thousand shards to spray out across the office. The camera began to jump and tilt; the video jerked and heaved. The jumbled picture pixelated for several seconds, then refocused. Travis saw the flashlight drop from Ted's hand and the images on the screen turned darker. Still visible were Ted's arms, extended in front of him, flailing, as he tried to regain his balance.

The picture continued to bounce, then toppled and came into focus, brightened by an overhead streetlamp. Treetops and power lines rose and fell with what Travis knew was Ted's desperate, labored breathing as he lay on his back in the street. Ted's hand swept across the computer screen and the body cam recording beeped three times, the signal that the camera was going live with audio. Mortally wounded and near death, Ted had managed to turn on his body cam. For the first time, Travis heard Ted's agonizing screams, his panicked breathing.

"*Jesus, Mary, and Joseph. God no, no, no no. Not this, not this. Baby, baby, I'm sorry. Oh god, I'm sorry, girls. I love you guys.*"

In a matter of seconds Ted's voice turned to deadly choking. His last words were unintelligible. His arms jerked frantically across the screen and Travis knew Ted was struggling to key up his radio mic. He kept trying, even as the voice of Ellie Peralta hauntingly called out the sound of gunfire. Travis hoped Ted had taken comfort, knowing that he wasn't alone.

"*Station A, Thirty-One Paul X. We've got multiple eleven sixes, heard only, immediately north of our location.*"

Once again Ted's hand fumbled across the screen, markedly slower. His portable keyed up, and the pawing of his hand across the mic came over the audiotape. With both the body camera and dispatch audio in sync, everyone could hear the gruesome and lonely sounds of Teddy dying all over again, this time in stereo.

Seemingly unnerved, Enrique clicked off the dispatch audio. They continued to listen through the body cam, which picked up the dispatch transmissions coming from Ted's own portable radio. The video image went so still that, for a moment, Travis wondered if the computer had frozen or the camera had malfunctioned. Then he realized that both computer and camera were working fine, but Teddy was dead.

Sergeant Peña's voice came over the speaker, followed by the eruption of sirens in the background. Travis and Ellie were on their way from a mile away. Another sound came through, and just as Travis mentally identified the noise as movement coming from somewhere off camera, a new image filled the screen.

A face. A familiar one. Not much more than a boy.

He hovered for a moment, looking down at Ted, his heaving breath panicked and desperate. He turned as if to look down the street, then back. Ted's camera location made it so he was staring into the lens—directly at Travis—when he spoke.

"I'm sorry. God, I'm so sorry."

The audio captured more sirens, then what sounded like a jet engine, approaching the scene. The boy's eyes filled with a primal fear, and a moment later he was gone.

Travis felt transported back to the moment. Screeching brakes. The continuous piercing blast of a siren. Blue and red light flashing. Car doors. Then Ellie's anguished face, hunched down low and screaming.

"Teddy! Teddy! Don't you go! You hang on!"

"That's enough," Enrique said. "Turn it off."

But Murphy didn't turn it off. Instead, he reversed the image until the boy's face once again filled the screen, then froze it.

"Recognize him, Jackson?" It was the first time Murphy had spoken since Travis had entered the room.

"Of course I do." Travis thought he might throw up.

"Yeah. Thought you might."

Enrique took over. "According to Detective Murphy's field interview, his name is Omar Ortega. Eighteen years old. Frequent flyer with Eastside."

Travis shook his head. "I wouldn't know. I didn't talk to him."

"But," Enrique said, "you did see him? The call at Chito's Liquor?"

"Yeah. He was hanging out with a bunch of Eastsiders."

"Detective Murphy tells me a gun was recovered near where he was detained. A pretty nice gun."

"So what?" Travis said, not liking the tone of the question. "That gun was seized. It's in impound."

"So what?" Sean said. "I'll tell you *so what.* He got his hands on another one. Now a deputy is dead. Too bad he wasn't locked up."

Travis turned to face him. "What are you saying, Murphy?"

Sean ignored him and turned to the sergeant. "We've scouted the home address. My guys are on point and have the long eye on the apartment, front and back. SWAT is doing a chalked-out walk-through in the parking lot. They said they can be ready to blow the door at zero seven."

Enrique nodded to Sean, then turned to Travis. "That'll do it for now. Thanks for sticking around. At some point there will be an internal board of inquiry. Noncriminal, of course. Purely administrative."

Sean stood and mumbled, "Damn well oughta be criminal."

Travis stood as well. "Like I said, Murphy, you got something to say, just come out with it. Let's hear it."

"You want to hear it, Jackson? Fine." There was no more than a foot between them. "We coulda locked this little bastard up for the weekend at least. If you'd just done your job." He leaned in, cutting the distance by half. "You do that? Teddy ain't dead. That's on you."

Travis drove both hands into the man's chest, sending the bigger cop toppling backward over his chair. "Go to hell, Murphy."

Sean came back at him, enraged. "This didn't have to happen. You know it didn't."

Travis looked to Enrique, expecting some sort of intervention of support, but the sergeant only stared back. The voice came from the corner and startled all three cops.

"Both of you, stop it!" Travis turned to Dannie Gaines. She had a tissue in her hand and Travis could see she'd been crying. "Are you really going to do this? Start blaming each other?"

She stood and wedged herself between the two furious cops, who were both a foot taller than her. She pointed a shaky finger at the face still on the computer screen.

"Blame him." Her voice sounded dead. She looked at all three men. "*Bring. Me. Him.*"

29

"Damn it, Joaquin. Como pudiste?"

The familiar voice brought him awake. He'd been expecting the phone call and knew there'd be hell to pay. He sat up on the couch in his cramped living room and automatically reached for a phantom cigarette. Even after a year, the stale odor of a two-pack-a-day, forty-year habit remained embedded in the paint of the walls and fabric of the furniture. A constant reminder of an urge that would never go away and was worse at times like this.

"I tried to get hold of you, Anna. It went to voice mail four times. I texted you twice. Sorry, but there was no way I was leaving a detailed message."

Anna Ramirez was the community outreach and public information officer for the San Diego County Sheriff's Department. Having previously served as a sworn cop in Phoenix for twenty years, she knew more about crime scenes than press releases, but she turned out to be a quick study. When Sheriff Collier had brought her on three years ago, her marching orders had been to repair the tattered relationship that existed between the sheriff's department and the Latino community, particularly in the North County. Nowhere more than in Vista.

"Then you should've driven back out to the scene," she said, giving no ground. "You knew I'd be there. I can't believe you were involved in something like this. Do you even realize what you've done?"

"Believe me, it could've been worse."

"Worse? How? It's like watching a goddamn snuff flick, Joaquin. How could it be any worse?"

Yes, he'd caved. And yes, all because he was afraid of losing his job. But at least he'd talked Philip down from airing the images uncensored. He'd agreed to do both the English and Spanish voice-over if Philip would air only thirty seconds of the first deputies to reach the scene, without showing the face or bloody wounds of their slain comrade. The end product showed the tall white cop kneeling over the mostly hidden body, his arms covered in blood and his face spattered with red. His female partner stood over him, crying.

"Stop, Travis. Just stop. He's gone."

Even with the heavy edit, it was still the worst film production he'd ever been party to. Anna was right. It did feel like some kind of perverse snuff flick, and there he was at the end, with a microphone in his hand, like he was taking a bow. The bobblehead on the couch had summed it all up with her typical eloquence: "Damn, Boomer. Intense."

"I'm sorry, Anna. I am. I did all I could to keep it off the air."

She scoffed. "Really? Is the suspect standing off camera with a gun to your head?"

"I did what I could. I fought. I lost."

"You should know, the sheriff is beside himself. I've never seen him this angry. I mean, on top of everything else, he's got to deal with this? The murder of a deputy sheriff, broadcast practically live?" He'd never heard such emotion from her. "He wants me to blackball your station and anybody else that jumped on your . . . your demented *bloodwagon*. I can't believe you shared this. I can't believe anyone took you up on it."

When Anna had first hired on, she'd decided that the best way to reach out to the Latino community was through the Spanish-language media. She had come to the Univision studio, asked for Joaquin, and introduced herself as the new media liaison for the sheriff's department. They sat and talked in his cubicle for over an hour, then went to lunch and talked for two more.

They hardly agreed on anything. Both beat up the other person's organization. She talked of Univision's slanted news coverage of a recent series of shootings that involved Vista deputies. Joaquin responded that the "series" was up to six and that, in each case, the male suspect was Latino, unarmed, and ultimately dead.

In the end, they agreed to create a better way of communicating, a way for their organizations to work together. She promised Joaquin full access to local crime stories. He assured her, if he got that, the coverage would be fair and unbiased. They penciled out ideas for a half-dozen human interest stories aimed at improving trust between the deputies on the street and community members. They'd each held up their end of the bargain, and now, three years later, relations between the sheriff's department and the Latino community had never been better. Joaquin couldn't help but think all that progress was about to come undone.

"We're going to be making an arrest in a few hours," she said. "Whether I like it or not, I need your station to cover it."

"An arrest? On this case?"

"Yes, and it's going to hit the east side barrio pretty hard."

"I thought you said we were blackballed? Order of the sheriff?"

"No time for that now. This is probably going to get ugly and I need people, your audience particularly, to know what's really happening and why."

"And your boss?"

"He'll understand. But don't worry. Payback is coming." Her voice turned business. "I'll send out a group text at six fifty A.M. with the exact address. You'll want to be somewhere near the east side of Vista."

"What do you mean? Just give me the address," he said. Anna never treated him like one of the herd. He fumbled through papers and junk mail and found a pen on the coffee table.

"Like I said. You'll get the text."

The line went dead and she was gone. He looked at the time on his phone and saw it was after six. He should wake up Mannie, get him to swing by and pick him up. Call Philip and let him know an arrest was imminent. No doubt Philip would want to dovetail in the video and do another remote from the shooting location. They'd probably want to interrupt regular programming and show the arrest live. Then run it again as the lead for the evening news broadcast.

Forget all that. At this point, he figured it was best to just go it alone.

30

Travis walked out of the interview, fighting the urge to slam the door behind him. He lost. He'd gone from exhausted to wired, then wide awake, and now mad as hell. Quickstepping with his head down, he did his best to ignore the stares coming from the pockets of coworkers, both sworn and civilian, now dotting the hallways. Weekend employees were showing up for work to find out a deputy was dead. Huddled in small groups, they spoke in low voices. Others stood alone, dazed and confused by what they were hearing and seeing on television.

At his locker, Travis changed into workout gear, remembering his conversation with Molly. The fear in her voice still pulled at him, but he couldn't leave the substation—not yet. He wasn't ready to detach himself from what had happened, what he'd been a part of.

Once he pulled into that driveway, it would be like turning the page. Ted Rosado would be officially dead. Travis wasn't ready to let him go.

The weight room was empty but the television had been left on, and what he saw stopped him where he stood. On the screen, he was kneeling. His blood-covered hands were pawing at Ted's body. He bent down to give mouth-to-mouth. Ellie came up from behind him, trying to pull him away, and Travis flung her off. Both of them were shrieking like rockers at the end of some heavy metal song.

The last image had him looking directly into the camera, face spattered with Ted's blood, lips coated with it, eyes wild. Finally, the image cut away to a reporter who looked almost as stunned as Travis felt. He found the remote and stabbed it toward the TV, hitting the power button. The screen went black.

Molly saw that? Ted's wife? Goddamn media.

With the images still playing in his head, he lay back on the weight bench. The bar was already loaded, with a forty-five- and a thirty-five-pounder on each end. He shook out his arms, set his grip, and began a slow, methodical set. He pushed up evenly, blowing out air from deep in his lungs, giving the tension a release point. He let the bar come down and rest against his chest. Another long, steady push until his elbows locked. He continued to pump the weight and let his mind wander.

A deputy killed on his watch.

No. Not killed. Murdered.

Assassinated.

He'd been a mile away.

Less than thirty seconds.

How do I go back to work tonight?

How does anyone go back?

What if none of us did?

He pushed the bar up one last time and placed it on the rack, allowing headspace for the question he'd been avoiding. The question that would haunt him for the rest of his career. Maybe the rest of his life.

Was Murphy right? Is this on me?

He'd done his share of creative report writing over the years. Every cop had. Penned a few alternative facts here and there. A bit of embellishment, meant to tie up loose ends, fill in a few blanks. Cut out the loopholes. But in all his years of being a cop, Travis had never just made stuff up. He'd never written something in a police report that he couldn't defend as some strain of tortured truth.

He took the weight bar once again and went down low. *But what if I had?*

What if he'd just written that Chunks had been loitering near the dumpster? Or maybe that he observed this Ortega kid close the lid. Or, the hell with it. Man up and just do it. Write that he saw one of them throw a "dark object" into the dumpster. Even Ellie had said the gun belonged to one of them. If he had written anything close to that, the gangsters would have hit the pit, and there was a good chance Ted Rosado would be coming to work tonight. Instead, Ted was headed for the chrome table and a cool night in a lonely vault. Travis reracked the weight bar.

So, yeah. It is on me.

The door opened and Sergeant Peña walked in. "Hey, Jackson. Heard you were still around. You doing all right?"

"Hey, Sarge." Travis swung his leg over the bench and sat up. "Just trying to come down a bit. Decompress, I guess."

Peña nodded down the hall, toward the Investigation Bureau. "They done with you? How'd it go?"

"Went all right, I guess." Travis saw no reason to get into the ugly details.

"Yeah? Glad to hear it." Peña's tone said he knew better. No officer-involved-shooting interview ever went all right. They just sucked at different levels of intensity. "I think you're the last one still around from night shift. I wonder if you could do me a personal favor."

Travis said, "Name it, Sarge."

"I just got a call from the SWAT commander. They're out on an apartment on the east side. Got a guy in custody for Deputy Rosado's murder. Need a transport unit, just to run out there, bring him in, and throw him in a cell.

"I'd like one of our people to handle it. It's important to me. I think it would've been important to Rosado."

Travis stood, suddenly energized. "Done, Sarge. I'm on it."

"You sure?" The older man's face brightened. "Got enough left in the tank?"

"Absolutely," Travis said. "I'll suit back up. It's Saturday. The family won't even be awake for another couple of hours."

Travis wondered why he was willing to lie, knowing that Molly was no doubt awake and staring at the door.

"All right, then. I appreciate it. Log back on, get the address from dispatch. And listen." Peña pointed a finger to make his point. "Straight out.

Straight back. Track your mileage and make sure your body cam is on the whole time. This guy's a suspect in a cop killing. Everything by the numbers."

"Got it, sir."

"Great," Peña said. "I'll be here when you bring him in."

31

Travis negotiated the black and white up a steep hill, the road covered by cool morning shadows. He steered his way through the media vans double- and triple-parked on the narrow street, which was lined with building after building of run-down apartments. He rounded a bend in the road and saw the SWAT team's BearCat pulled up onto the hard-packed dirt lawn of a three-story building, the back end of the olive drab vehicle partially blocking the street. Two fully kitted team members stood guard to discourage the curious, M4s slung at the low ready, their faces covered by black balaclavas.

Onlookers from the neighborhood milled around in small groups, most still waking up, coffee cup in one hand, phone held up in the other. A half-dozen kids, no older than eight or nine, sat on top of a six-foot stucco wall, kicking their feet back and forth, mugging for the media cameras along with their own. Some reporters were doing person-on-the-street interviews, killing time until the real action began.

A Prius marked with the Univision logo was parked along the nearby curb. The reporter he had seen at the shooting—and on TV in the workout room—sat dozing in the driver's seat. For a moment, Travis thought about confronting the man. Millions of viewers would witness the death scene of Ted Rosado, and for what? Ratings? Advertising dollars? *How about a little follow-up video of me pulling you out the car window and beating your ass?*

Travis knew better, and shook it off. He parked behind the BearCat. He'd already read the call history on his computer terminal. The SWAT team had gone code 4 and announced that a suspect named Omar Ortega was in custody. The kid sitting on the ground by the liquor store. The one he could have locked up with a little creative writing. The one on Ted's body cam. Hindsight. It's a bitch.

He positioned his vehicle, popped the back door, and advised dispatch he was on scene, then waited. He was surprised at how alert he felt. Definitely on a second wind, maybe a third.

The reporters got it. Idling patrol car at the curb with the rear door open. Travis sensed their excitement building. Camera crews moved in, fighting to get the best angle for the money shot. A young man with surfer good looks, dressed in a shirt, tie, jacket, and tattered blue jeans, took up a position in front of a camera, microphone in hand. Travis watched as the swarm surged forward like flies to shit. The yard went thick with print media, television, and radio. The Univision reporter stepped from his car but held back, not joining the scrum. The spotlights came up. The cameras flashed. Showtime.

Murphy and another cop dressed in SWAT gear emerged from the blown-out doorway and started down the steps, leading a handcuffed suspect on a slow and obviously orchestrated perp walk. Sure enough, it was the same kid, still dressed in jeans and a Dodgers jersey. As he walked across the yard, he limped badly and his head lolled forward, his chin against his chest. Travis saw what looked like blood on the collar of his shirt. The kid heaved and vomit ran from the corners of his mouth.

A minute later, Murphy was pushing the prisoner into the backseat.

"Omar Ortega. He's eighteen, so no kiddie-jail bullshit. His ass goes to adult lockup. Straight to the station. Strip his property. An evidence tech is coming up from Ridgehaven to process him. After that, stick him in a cell. No visitors. No phone calls. No contact. You got all that?"

"Yeah. Got it."

The door slammed shut and Travis pulled away, staring at the prisoner in the backseat. He saw a look of dazed recognition on the boy's face.

Ortega's voice was barely audible. "Hey. You're that cop. The one from yesterday."

A boy. Travis saw he was just a boy. His voice was fearful. Hopeless. Even somehow harmless. But none of that mattered. This "boy" was the most wanted man in California, and Travis was consumed with a hatred he saw no reason to hide.

"Yeah, I am. And you're that *cop killer* from last night."

32

Travis pulled the squad car into the sally port that led directly to the station holding facility. He advised dispatch of his arrival and the mileage, evidence that he had driven directly from the scene of the arrest to the station, with no stops along the way. That, plus his body cam recording, would prevent any future insinuations of misconduct or mistreatment. Sergeant Peña stood in the entrance, beneath a sign that read, "No Weapons of Any Kind Beyond This Point," his face grim, arms crossed, feet at shoulder width.

After their initial exchange, Travis had intentionally avoided further eye contact with the prisoner and had said nothing on the ride into the station. Now he gave a quick look in the rearview and saw the kid's dark eyes looking back.

Travis got out of the car and went around to the trunk. Opening it, he stowed all his weapons and gear except for his body camera, which was still running. He slammed the trunk shut, then walked around and opened the car's rear door. He motioned with one hand.

"Get out."

The kid moved slowly. Travis resisted the temptation to reach down and grab his collar, hurry him along a bit. He knew that every second of the recording would someday be reviewed by teams of lawyers, prosecution and defense. The body cam might as well be a standing representative of the ACLU.

His prisoner maneuvered both feet out of the car and onto the cement floor. With his hands cuffed behind his back, he managed to shimmy his butt to the edge of the plastic seat. He rocked forward and tried to stand, then fell back. He looked up and spoke, his voice barely audible. "I don't think I can walk, sir."

Hearing what he took to be a plea for help, maybe even sympathy, Travis wanted the kid to know he'd have none of it. "Knock it off, Ortega. I saw you walk to the car. Now get up."

"Yeah," he said. "Because the cops were holding me up. Can you help me?"

Oh yeah, I'll fucking help you.

"What's going on?" Peña asked, coming near. Just in time, Travis thought. He turned to face Peña; from a position out of the camera's view, he pointed to his body cam, as both a reminder and a professional courtesy. Peña gave the slightest nod of acknowledgment.

"Says he can't walk, Sarge."

In a voice that was entirely reasonable, Peña looked at the prisoner in the backseat. "And why's that?"

"My ankle. It really hurts."

"Fine." Peña went to grab an arm, looking at Travis. "You get the other side."

Between the two of them, they half carried, half dragged Ortega inside the holding facility and seated him on the intake bench. Usually, at this time of day, there would be a few prisoners still left over from the previous night, but the jail had been cleared to accommodate the cop killer.

The facility had eight cells: six designated for men and two for women, a reflection of marketplace reality, gender equality be damned. This jail was the first stop for anyone arrested within the Vista city limits. Never populated by more than a handful of adult prisoners, and with no jail staff to speak of, the place was more a stopover than a real lockup. Most of the men and women brought here ended up signing a ticket and were then cut loose on a promise to appear in court. Others would be booked into the county jail, which was the next building over. From there, they might still be released within a day or two on their own recognizance.

But, for a select few, their arrival in this small, seemingly insignificant holding facility represented the first moments of what would be years, decades, or even a lifetime in custody. For these prisoners, their last taste of liberty was behind them. They'd never walk free again. Travis figured that was the likely fate of the Ortega kid.

"You got this?" Peña asked. "I need to let the watch commander know he's here."

"I'm good, Sarge. Do what you gotta do."

After Peña left, Travis forced himself to stay calm. Whatever anger, whatever hatred he was feeling, it would have to find another outlet. He placed a large wooden box on the bench next to Ortega. "Empty your pockets. Everything. Wallet. Money. Keys. Smokes. Coins. All of it. In the box."

Travis knew Ortega had no doubt been thoroughly searched at the scene of the arrest, so he wasn't likely to have any weapons or items that would be considered evidence, but all his property needed to be seized for safekeeping and inventoried.

There wasn't much: a thin leather wallet, a small set of keys. A folded piece of paper from the back pocket of his jeans. Ortega hesitated, looking at the paper before dropping it into the box. He shuffled on the bench, reaching into empty pockets, then looked up at Travis as if to signal he was finished.

Standing over him with his arms crossed, his voice deadpan, Travis said, "Take off your shoes. In the box. Socks too. You got a belt on?"

"Yes, sir."

Travis pointed to the box.

Ortega winced when he took off his shoe. Looking down, Travis saw the significant swelling, the angry purple skin around the ankle. Travis knew his body cam picked it up too. He reached down and pulled up on the boy's foot, causing him to wince in pain and pull away.

"Hold still, Ortega. Just let me see."

Travis pulled up the pants leg, and again the boy grimaced.

"The nurse at the county jail will look at it. How did you do it?"

"Jumped out of a car."

The question had been appropriate—he'd been inquiring as to the prisoner's health and safety. The answer had been unexpectedly intriguing. Travis knew better than to follow up, but he'd be sure to pass the information on to Detective Murphy.

"Any other injuries?"

"I cut my head, but I think it stopped bleeding."

Travis nodded toward the box. "Is that everything?"

"Yes, sir."

"Stand up."

Ortega got to his feet, favoring the injured leg. Travis searched him thoroughly, turning all his pockets inside out, even grabbing his crotch through his pants. There would be a more detailed search by the actual jailers.

He sat Ortega back on the bench and cuffed one of his wrists to the iron locking ring built into the cement, then carried the box to the booking counter. He began to remove each item and thoroughly check it for contraband. He looked in the wallet and found it contained only an ATM card. No cash. There was a James Madison High School ID behind clear plastic, bearing the picture of a smiling Omar Ortega with a full head of black hair. Handsome kid.

"You're still in high school?"

He nodded. "I graduate next week."

You were going to graduate, Travis thought.

Travis kept looking. A picture of a young teenage girl.

"Pretty," he said, holding up the picture. "Girlfriend?"

The boy shook his head, staring at the photograph. "She's my sister."

"Seriously?" Travis was surprised. "You carry a picture of your sister?"

The question got no response, but Travis didn't miss the look of dismay that sped across the teenager's face. He lifted the folded sheet of paper that Ortega had pulled from his back pocket. "What's this?"

The kid said nothing, making Travis all the more curious. He unfolded it and began to read.

"Is this for real?"

His voice was low. "It was."

"Wow." Travis kept reading. He was genuinely stunned. "Valedictorian? How is it that you—"

There was a *click*. The heavy metal door swung open and a portly woman pushed through with her butt, walking backward. She wore a white lab coat straight out of central casting and carried an orange Pelican case in one hand and a Nikon camera bag in the other. She looked at the prisoner, her gaze passing over him like he was a job. A task to be completed. She turned to Travis, her voice all business.

"Deputy Jackson?"

"Yeah. Travis Jackson."

The woman put the case and camera bag on the counter. "I'm from forensics. Is this Ortega?"

Travis looked back to the bench. "Yes, this is—"

"Fine." The woman faced the prisoner. "Mr. Ortega, my name is Judith McCarthy. I am a criminal forensic specialist with the San Diego County Sheriff's Department. You are in custody for a felony crime. Whether or not you committed the crime is immaterial to me. I will be processing your person for evidence collection. You *do not* have a right to refuse me, and any attempt to delay or interfere with the process will be futile. You *do not* have the right to consult with legal counsel prior to my collecting evidence."

McCarthy opened the orange Pelican case, retrieved a pair of blue latex gloves, and pulled one onto each hand. She put on a plastic face shield, leaving it in the up position.

"I will be taking all items of clothing and providing you a temporary replacement. If you are booked into county jail, and it is my understanding you will be, you will be provided more permanent attire. I will be photographing your body both clothed and nude. I will be collecting swabs for DNA analysis, as well as a blood sample and a hair sample."

She looked at his head. "Based on the length of your hair, I will make the collection from the pubic region. I'll also be taking fingernail scrapings from each hand. And I'll be completing a gunshot residue test."

She opened the camera bag and pulled out a Nikon D610. "My point in telling you all this, Mr. Ortega, is this will be a detailed and time-consuming process. I will be giving you instructions but I will not be asking you any questions. Please extend me the same courtesy."

Ortega spoke, his voice respectful. "I'm sorry, ma'am, but I don't understand. Why—"

She cut him off. "Don't ask, because I'm not answering."

McCarthy turned to Travis. "Deputy Jackson, I will need you to remain as a witness and for security purposes."

"Of course." The day just got even longer.

"All right, then," McCarthy said. "Deputy, remove the handcuff, please. Mr. Ortega, we'll start with photographs. Please stand against the wall and look straight ahead. And remember, you and I have nothing to talk about."

33

Joaquin had seen it so many times, he couldn't help but wonder how people kept buying this bread-and-circuses bullshit. Nothing more than public relations nonsense. Propaganda promulgated by American law enforcement, going all the way back to the days of J. Edgar Hoover. Then again, even he had to acknowledge that today's performance was exceptional. An eighteen-year-old kid named Omar Ortega, arrested for the cold-blooded murder of a deputy sheriff who was a loving husband and father of two. *Yeah, got to admit it. That's a hell of a perp walk.*

The squad car drove away with Ortega in the back. The SWAT truck was next to leave, their very specific mission already accomplished. Three reporters did live shots with the blown-up doorway in the background. Eventually, the last detective got into an unmarked vehicle and left the scene. The yellow tape was taken down and the patrol deputies assigned to perimeter duty opened the street. Other than the missing front door and a few newly broken windows, it looked like nothing had occurred. It was as if the neighborhood took a deep breath and decided it was already time to move on.

Joaquin watched it all from the front seat of his company-owned Prius, dozing off and on. He'd ignored eight calls from the studio and four from

Anna Ramirez. By now, Philip had undoubtedly figured out that Univision had been badly scooped. Every radio and television station in Southern California had broadcasted live from the scene of the most significant arrest and perp walk of the past several years. Every station, that is, except Univision.

Anna had probably come to realize that the only major Spanish-language newscast in San Diego County had not covered the event that everyone in the barrio was already talking about. Joaquin figured it would be a reminder to everyone of how to foster good working relationships: don't be a dick.

Now that he had appropriately snubbed Anna Ramirez and bitch-slapped Philip Cordova, Joaquin walked across the parking lot and up the short sidewalk. He couldn't deny the pull of the story. Inside, he knew exactly what he would find: confused and disoriented survivors with a look of actual shell shock, new veterans of a SWAT raid.

He climbed the steps, approached the shattered door, and called out in Spanish and English. When no one answered, he walked in, hit by the lingering, acrid smell of sulfur and gunpowder from the flashbangs. In addition to the obvious damage to the door, burn marks still smoldered in the carpet of the cramped living room. The holes punched through the walls seemed random and pointless. Every item of furniture, which didn't look to be much, had been piled in the middle of the room as if ready to be doused with gasoline and set on fire.

Joaquin called out again in Spanish. "No hay alguien aquí?"

A boy who looked to be around twelve or thirteen emerged from the hallway and stared vacantly at the stranger in his living room. He was barefoot, dressed in a T-shirt and shorts. He was clearly Latino, but his face was drained of color and had the look of a person in a significant state of shock.

Joaquin smiled and spoke softly. "Hola, mijo. Como te llamas?"

The boy stared for several seconds before answering. His tone told Joaquin not to expect a lot in the way of detail or cooperation. "Hector. I speak English. You're that guy on TV all the time."

"That's right, I am. My name is Joaquin. Are you here by yourself, Hector?"

The boy looked back over his shoulder, down a hallway that led to other rooms. When he spoke, Joaquin made him for a bad liar.

"Yeah. Why? What do you want?"

"I was hoping to talk to you about what just happened," Joaquin said, gesturing around the room. "With the deputies, I mean. That person they took away. Do you know him?"

His voice was steady, even defiant, but Joaquin saw the quiver of his chin. "He's my brother."

"Okay." Joaquin took a step closer. "I know that must have been really scary for you. You doing okay?"

Hector shrugged. "Those deps ain't nothing."

"Do you know why they took him away?" Joaquin asked.

"They didn't tell us."

"Us?"

"Me and my—" He stopped himself. "Just me, I mean. They didn't tell me nothing. What do you want anyways?"

"Hector, you said you know who I am, verdad? That I work for Univision?"

"Yeah. So?"

"Good. So you know, then, that our channel is broadcast in Spanish. Our news stories are generally about people like you and me. My family came from Peru. How about yours?"

"Mexico."

"Both your mom and your dad are from Mexico?"

The boy only nodded.

"And are they here now?"

Hector stared at him and said nothing.

"It's okay, Hector. I promise. I just want to find out what happened."

"Only my mom is here. I don't have— My dad isn't here."

A young girl came out into the hallway, her arm wrapped around the shoulder of a woman who looked unsteady on her feet. The girl wore a nightgown. The woman was tightly wrapped in a long robe. Joaquin nodded, acknowledging them, but he stayed focused on Hector.

"Is this your mom and sister?"

The boy looked over his shoulder. Turning back to Joaquin, he tried to speak with more authority, prepared to defend his family, but it was clear he was becoming overwhelmed. "Don't worry about who they are. We don't want you in here. Leave us alone."

"Hector, I think maybe I can help you. I mean, help find out what happened to your brother."

"Just get out. We don't need—"

"Hector," the girl said. "Listen to him. We need to know what's happening. Where they've taken Omar. Nobody else is going to help us."

"I got this, Sofia," Hector said. "Take Mama back in the room."

"Sofia?" Joaquin asked disarmingly and she nodded in reply. "That's a beautiful name."

Joaquin smiled at Sofia but spoke to Hector. "She's right. I can help you. Let me sit and talk with you and your family."

Hector dropped his eyes to the floor. "Why would you help us?"

"Because," Joaquin said, moving closer, "you have a right to know what happened to your brother. They should have told you where they were taking him, and if they didn't, I will make them tell you."

Sofia said, "You can do that?"

"I can do a lot of things. But you need to trust me. You need to talk to me."

Out of respect, Joaquin introduced himself in Spanish to the baffled-looking woman and repeated what he'd told her children. She turned to her daughter and spoke quietly enough that Joaquin couldn't overhear. In response, Sofia pulled her mother closer.

"Does anyone else live here?" Joaquin asked.

"Some guy," Hector said. "It's his apartment. We just have a room."

"And where's this guy?"

Hector shrugged. "Don't know, don't care. He drinks a lot."

"And he's not your dad?"

"I told you," Hector said, anger in his voice now, "my dad's not here. If he was, none of this would have happened to us."

To us, Joaquin thought. Not just to the brother but to all of them.

The mother whispered again in her daughter's ear. Sofia said, "We'll talk to you. We'll tell you what we know."

Studying the pile of furniture, Joaquin pulled out two kitchen chairs, then cleared items from the couch. He helped Sofia guide her mother to have a seat and coaxed Hector into one of the chairs. He took the other. They were sitting in a small, intimate circle. "Is this okay?"

Hector sat, arms crossed, staring at Joaquin, knowing that his attempt at being in charge was slipping away. Sofia hugged her mother against her body. Both women appeared grief-stricken and made no effort to hold back their tears.

Who was this young man to them? Accused of killing a cop. Someone vitally important, of that Joaquin was certain.

Joaquin turned to the mother. With the utmost respect, and speaking in Spanish, he made a single and straightforward request.

"Digame de su hijo."

She smiled tremulously and began to speak. Quietly and simply, Isadora talked about Omar, about the whole Ortega family, about their lives in America. Occasionally, one of the children would chime in. Sometimes there were smiles; at other times, all three wept. Joaquin held his notebook and pen in his lap. Once or twice he jotted something down, but mostly he listened, mesmerized by the family story. An hour passed and he didn't say a word.

34

Omar sat on the smooth pad of cement that jutted out from the wall that he figured was supposed to double as a bed and a bench. It sucked at both. The cell was the temperature of a meat locker, and sitting there in a baggy white jumpsuit made of some kind of thick paper, he shivered uncontrollably. Omar stared at the blinking red light in the corner of the ceiling—a camera. Of course he was being watched. He'd been alone in the jail cell for what seemed like hours, but he had no real way of knowing. He'd heard several people going in and out of the reception area where he had been stripped, photographed, poked, and prodded by the woman in the lab coat. He'd called out several times, but no one came through the solid metal door of his cell. No one, that is, until now.

The grinding sound of a motor kicking into gear startled him enough that he stood up quick. He heard the automated pull of a chain and the metal door began to slide across rails at the top and bottom. Detective Murphy stood in the now open doorway. He'd taken off his vest, revealing a black T-shirt that fit tightly over his muscular frame and featured a logo of rifle crosshairs surrounded by the words "This Is My Peace Symbol." The deputy's Yankees cap was pulled down low on his head. He carried a thin black folder stamped in gold with the image of a badge. In his other hand was a pair of handcuffs.

"Time for us to have a little chat." Murphy looked Omar directly in the eye and dangled the cuffs from one finger. "Do I need these?"

Omar thought to himself that this would be his third interaction with Detective Murphy in less than twenty-four hours and, so far, none had been good. But Omar did not want to pass up a chance to find out what was going on. To maybe tell Murphy what he knew. He'd be careful in his dealings with the man. The stakes couldn't be higher.

"No. You don't need to handcuff me."

Murphy stepped aside to allow Omar out of the cell. "Then come on. Let's go."

Omar walked out, hopping every other step to avoid putting weight on his ankle. He followed Murphy's directions to a doorway that led into a room just large enough for a chrome metal table and two metal chairs, all bolted to the floor. The room was cube-like in its dimensions and, other than the three items of furnishing, completely constructed of cement. A dark mirror took up most of one wall. Omar had seen enough episodes of *The First 48* to know that behind the glass was some sort of observation room. Murphy made sure Omar sat in the chair facing the glass; he took the other seat, careful not to sit directly across from Omar.

"Here's the deal, Seso, and for now I just want you to listen." His voice, although by no means friendly, lacked the aggression Omar had become accustomed to. Omar nodded and Murphy went on. "You already know this, but last night a deputy sheriff was shot and killed.

"We have probable cause to believe you were present at the time and played a role in the deputy's murder. Although you haven't been formally charged, you *are* under arrest. Do you understand?"

"I didn't kill anyone."

"I didn't ask you that." Omar saw that Murphy was barely able to contain his anger. "I asked if you understood why you're here."

"Yes."

"Good. Listen carefully." Murphy took a small card from his folder and began to read. "You have the right to remain silent. If you give up the right to remain silent, anything you say can and will be used against you in court. You have the right to consult with an attorney prior to any questioning. If you cannot afford an attorney, one will be appointed for you by the court prior to any questioning. The services are free."

Murphy looked up from his card. "Do you understand the rights I've explained to you?'

"Yes," Omar said, hearing his own desperation. "But I told you, I didn't kill anyone."

"You understand your rights, correct?"

"Yes."

"All right," Murphy said. "Since you understand your rights, are you willing to talk to me?"

Omar looked at the dark glass. He knew that no one behind the mirror cared about him. He saw the contempt in Murphy's eyes. The near hatred. But he also knew he needed to tell the cops what had happened. Explain how things had gone down. That was inevitable, but he didn't see how talking to this particular cop would help. The guy had never once shown any willingness to listen. Maybe talking to a lawyer was the way to go.

"Can we talk later? I mean, like, can I talk to a lawyer first?"

"That's not an answer," Murphy said. "You want to talk to me or not?"

"I do, it's just that . . ." Omar said, staring back, "I just think I should talk to a lawyer first. Then I can—"

"So, the answer is no?" Murphy practically folded his lips back in a sneer. "You won't talk to me?"

"I will, just not yet."

Murphy stared at Omar for several seconds. He shifted to take a quick look in the glass, then back at Omar.

"That's fine, Ortega. But I want to talk to you. All you have to do is listen. You don't have to say anything and you don't have to answer any questions. Fair enough?"

Murphy pulled a sheet of paper from his folder and laid it on the desk. It was a picture of Omar, one he'd never seen before. It had been taken at an odd angle, and so close that his face took up the entire frame. His eyes were wide and there was blood on his forehead.

"You have any idea where we got this picture of you, Ortega?" Murphy asked, then immediately put up his hand. "Don't answer that."

Omar stared at the picture as Murphy went on.

"I'll just tell you where we got it. It came from the body camera of Deputy Theodore Rosado, moments . . . *seconds* after he was shot to death."

Omar's stomach began to heave. "I know you don't want to talk to me, but I thought you should know, that picture, plus the video of you saying you're sorry . . ."

Surprised to hear the break in Murphy's voice, Omar looked up at him, seeing sadness overwhelm the man's anger, just for an instant. Murphy quickly covered his emotions and said, "You're heard saying I'm sorry to Deputy Rosado as he lay dying in the street, just before you ran away."

"Yeah, but—"

"Stop, Ortega." Murphy banged the table. "You don't want to talk to me, remember? You're just supposed to listen. So just sit there and keep your mouth shut."

Murphy pulled another sheet of paper from his folder. Omar saw that it was some kind of report from the San Diego County Sheriff's forensics laboratory: a graph, a table full of numbers, and a few lines of text.

"The picture is pretty strong evidence, but when you put it with this? Practically puts the needle in your arm. I know this nanny state hasn't actually executed any of you sons of bitches in twenty years, but the law is still on the books."

Nothing on the page made sense to Omar. Perhaps picking up on his confusion, Murphy explained.

"You remember when the lab tech dotted at your hand with a little sponge-like thing?" Murphy pointed at the web of his own hand, right between his forefinger and thumb. "Right around here? That's called a gun residue test. It tells us if someone has shot a gun recently.

"Your results show that you fired the gun that killed Deputy Rosado."

Omar remembered the trip into San Marcos, the way the gun had jumped in his hand.

"It wasn't like that. I—"

"Forget it." Murphy cut him off. "You said you don't want to talk. And I don't want you to." Disdain and frustration were clear in Murphy's voice. "I don't want to hear your bullshit, homeboy excuses about how you just barely got there."

"I didn't kill that deputy," Omar said, looking into the mirror. "You said his name was—"

Murphy stood halfway out of his chair and lunged across the desk, his face inches from Omar. "Don't you worry about his name. I don't even want to hear it cross your lips."

Omar shouted back, "I didn't kill anyone!"

"Then who did?" Murphy said. "Waive your rights. Talk to me. Tell me who did."

Omar looked at the enraged detective. He faced the glass, certain he was looking at someone else who probably hated him just as much. He realized these people really believed that he, Omar Ortega, had murdered a deputy sheriff. He couldn't really blame them.

But he hadn't done anything wrong. He needed people to understand that. He needed to talk, even if that meant he went to prison. He began to organize his thoughts, but Murphy interrupted him.

"So your old man got his ass deported, huh?" Murphy was looking at something else in his file folder. "How did that go down?"

Startled by the change in subject, Omar said, "What are you talking about?"

"Says here he got taken into federal custody a few years back. Got picked off by ICE?"

The memory of his father's disappearance always saddened Omar, but the fact that it was being thrown in his face by a deputy sheriff filled him with something closer to rage. Hatred even.

"He didn't do anything and he didn't get picked off by ICE," Omar said, his own personal troubles forgotten for the moment. It was his turn to be aggrieved over his loss. "He got *turned over* to ICE by one of you. A deputy sheriff."

"Whatever." Murphy shrugged. "But he got deported, right?"

"No. He voluntarily returned to Mexico."

"Jesus, Ortega." Murphy rolled his eyes. "ICE or deps, deported or whatever. I'm just saying your dad's not here anymore. He was illegal?"

"Why are we talking about this? I was born in Tri-City hospital, if that's what you want to know. I've got a birth certificate to prove it."

"Oh yeah, I know, Seso. I know where you were you born." Murphy smiled. "I'm more interested in where your mom was born. You think *she'll* be able to come up with a birth certificate?"

Omar paused, stunned by what he knew was being implied. "My mother has nothing to do with this."

"Sure, sure." Murphy nodded. "And believe me, I'd hate to see her get caught up in your criminal bullshit. So typical of you homies. Always dragging your family down with you."

"I already told you, when you busted the door in. Leave my family out of this."

"Or what, Ortega?"

Any sense that he should cooperate disappeared. Omar was done. "I'm not talking to you. I want a lawyer."

Murphy stood. "And a lawyer you shall have. But in the meantime? Happy birthday. Your ass is going to big boy jail. No juvie hall for you, and no bail for cop killers. You be sure to let me know if you change your mind and want to talk."

"When can I see my family?"

Murphy shook his head. "You got a warped view of how things really are."

"I just want to talk to them. I get a phone call, don't I?"

"I'll be the one making a call. To the feds, about your mom. If she can't come up with some documents, well . . . maybe she can 'voluntarily return,' like your old man."

Omar shouted, "Why would you do that? She hasn't done anything wrong."

"I know a lot of people who would disagree with that, Seso, seeing that she spawned a murderous fuck like you." Omar saw Murphy flinch as if he'd caught himself going too far, and probably on tape. "But it's really none of my business. That's between your mom and Uncle Sam."

"What about my sister? My brother?"

"Nothing I can do about them. I mean, they're anchor babies like you. But who knows? We might come up with something."

Omar's head was spinning. He needed to get back to his family. Whatever he had to do to get out of here, he would do. Say whatever he had to say.

"Chunks Gutierrez came to my house. He told me I had to come with him. He said I had to buy him beer."

Murphy looked at the dark glass and smiled. He took a sarcastic tone. "Oh, I'm sorry, Seso. Do you want to talk to me now?"

"Just promise me you'll leave my family alone. Then I'll talk to you."

"It don't work that way, homes." Murphy rapped his knuckles against the door, and within a few seconds it opened. "This is Detective Bennett. He's going to take you back to your cell."

"I want my phone call."

"Sorry, but I don't think so. Thanks for the tip on Chunks, but I can't have you calling him. Warning him. We'll let him know you said hello."

Murphy stood by the door. "I gotta tell ya, Seso. I figured you to step up eventually. You know, get in the game and all. But I was thinking you'd jack a car, maybe go along on a two eleven or some shit. But damn, man. You're all done. Your ass is fried."

35

Travis drove the twenty-year-old Toyota pickup northbound on the I-15 in the light Saturday morning traffic. He and Molly had bought the truck specifically for his work commute. Molly kept their newer car, the ten-year-old minivan they'd brought from Wisconsin. The truck's FM radio was cranked to max volume and the manual windows were rolled down so the wind coming through at seventy miles per hour would keep him awake, if not alert. Even with the music and hard breeze, he had to give his head a vigorous shake as he exited the highway at California Oaks Road. Almost home.

Ted Rosado lived—had lived—just a few miles farther up the road, in Murrieta. He and Ted had commuted together a few times, with Ted always picking Travis up and dropping him off. Early that morning, around dawn, Travis had seen the sheriff, along with the department chaplain, the station captain, and two deputies in dress uniform, leaving for the Rosados'. Since Travis had never been to Ted's home, he couldn't imagine the scene in any detail, but it was a type of comfort to know that department representatives would be posted at Mrs. Rosado's door until after the funeral.

Travis had no more than stopped in front of the house when Molly came through the door. He braced himself for the tirade he knew was coming. He should have been home hours earlier, and he hadn't called since waking her up. Even he had to admit that was pretty damn rude. He got out of the truck. As Molly drew near, he saw that her eyes were red and her face puffy. She fell against him and held him tightly around the neck.

"I'm so sorry, Travis. I'm so . . . I'm just glad you're home."

Three of his four kids had followed her out of the house; each found a place to grab hold. Brandon, the littlest, latched on to Travis's leg and exercised the typical demand of a two-year-old.

"Up, Daddy." Travis felt the slaps of tiny hands. "Up."

Travis hoisted him in the air and went back to hugging his wife and daughters. They stood in the driveway, knotted together the way a family should be. Eventually, Molly said, "Come inside. You must be exhausted."

"Where's Tyler?"

"In his room. He watched the news for a while." She shrugged. "I peeked in. He seems fine."

"Let me talk with him."

"Travis, you need to sleep. Really, he's fine. You two can talk later."

"It'll just take a few minutes," Travis said, as the group moved into the living room.

Molly kissed him on the cheek and took Brandon in her arms. "I'll get the bed ready. Don't be too long."

Tyler had to share his bedroom with his two-year-old brother. Travis knew it wasn't an ideal situation; it was a rare seventeen-year-old boy who would enjoy having his space occupied by a crib and changing table. But, after surviving the disappointment of two younger sisters, Tyler loved having a little brother. For all his acting out and fits of rebellion during the past couple of years, Tyler had never complained once about the living arrangements.

Travis knocked lightly on the door, then went in without waiting for a response. Tyler lay on his bed, his face turned to the wall, where a poster showed Aaron Rodgers rearing back for a pass. Travis sat on the edge of the bed.

"Hey, Ty. You doing okay?"

Tyler shrugged his shoulders without turning or looking at his father.

"Your mom says you watched some of the news this morning. Can we talk about it?"

"What's there to talk about?" He still didn't turn around. His voice was hollow of emotion. "A cop got killed. It happens a lot."

"Yeah," Travis said, trying not to react negatively to what he was pretty sure was false bravado. "But it's never happened quite like this. So close. It feels different to me this time."

The boy rolled over at last, and Travis was shocked to see the crusted tracks of recent tears, a major shift from the apathy and anger Tyler had displayed in the past few months.

"How? How is it different?" There was anguish in Tyler's words.

Over the years, as Tyler had matured, the two of them often talked about some of the situations around the country in which cops had been killed. Those conversations were serious and meaningful, but they never felt like this. This time it was intimately personal.

"Harder," Travis said. "A lot more painful, that's for sure."

Tyler nodded. The teenager sat up and settled against the headboard of his bed. "What about all that stuff on TV? You were the first one there? You found him?"

When things went wrong, when Tyler misbehaved or disappointed him, Travis didn't hesitate to remind his son that he was practically a "grown-ass man." That meant he had the right to be treated as a man. That had to go for times like this, too. He deserved to have his questions answered.

Carefully, Travis recounted the death of Ted Rosado, trying to avoid details that might be upsetting or frightening. He didn't want to scar his son, not in the way that Travis knew *he* was now scarred. When he was finished, he tried to explain to Tyler how it felt to have been a mile away from a cop gunned down in the street.

"A good man died, Ty. A good man doing his job. A friend. A really funny guy. He didn't deserve it, and I wish, more than anything I've ever wished for, that I could have helped him. But I couldn't."

"Who did it?"

"We arrested someone. A kid, really." As Travis said it, he suddenly realized that Omar Ortega was practically the same age as Tyler Jackson. "He's just a few months older than you."

"What will happen to him?"

"He's locked up. Later, he'll go to trial, I guess. Maybe some other people, too. The investigation is just getting started."

"Did you know him pretty good? The cop, I mean?"

"Yeah." Travis smiled, thinking of Ted. "He was one of my training officers, so we got pretty close. For the past few months, we've been on the same shift. Took a lot of calls together. Talked in the locker room and stuff. He was a good guy."

Tyler nodded. After a moment he asked, "You gotta work tonight?"

"Yeah, I do."

"Then you better get some sleep. I'll help Mom keep the kids quiet."

Travis smiled. This was the boy he knew. This was his son. "Thanks, Ty. I'm sure your mom will appreciate the help."

"Sorry about all that, Dad. Crying and stuff." Tyler swung his legs off the bed and sat up. He used the back of his arm to wipe more tears from his eyes. He looked embarrassed. "And I'm sorry about yesterday morning. I shouldn't have carried on like that."

"I'm glad you said that, Ty," Travis said. "I know the past couple of years have been tough for you, but we need to stick together. Right now, I really need that."

Tyler surprised his father again by pulling him in and hugging him close. Over the past couple of years, their hugs had become perfunctory. Light passes. Now he felt his son's strong arms around him, body tight against his chest. They sat there until there was a light knock on the open door. Travis looked up to see Molly standing in the doorway.

"Hey, Ty. Let's order Dad to bed, okay?"

Tyler gave his mom a half smile. "I just did." He let go of his father and Travis stood up.

"I'll come find you before I leave for work," he said, then crossed the hall to the master bedroom. Molly had hung a dark towel over the window and had a desk fan running on high in the corner of the room. The sheets were pulled back, and he wasted no time in stripping down to his underwear and collapsing onto the bed. Molly lay down next to him, barefoot, in capri pants and a sleeveless cotton blouse.

There were times—and this was one—that, when he looked at her, it was as though they were still juniors in high school. She was incredibly youthful for a woman who had four children, one still a toddler; was married to a cop; and was living two thousand miles from the only real home she'd ever known. Supporting herself on one elbow, she used the fingers of her other hand to lightly stroke his hair. It was a tactic she'd long used to help him fall asleep after hard shifts of police work.

"Rest, Travis. I'll wake you in time for work. Coffee will be ready." Her voice cracked with emotion. "Sleep."

Against his will, the face of Omar Ortega formed in his mind. As angry as he wanted to be, as much as he wanted to hate Ortega, he couldn't let go of one thought.

He's eighteen. Four months older than Tyler.

A kid, really. A kid who carried a picture of his sister in his wallet. Valedictorian of his high school class. *He's a brother. He's a son. And now, he's a cop killer.*

As he drifted off to sleep, Travis's last conscious thought was about not only the tragic loss that had been inflicted on the family of Teddy Rosado but also what might well be the equally tragic loss suffered by the loved ones of Omar Ortega.

36

Alone in the car, Joaquin was feeling refreshed after a few hours of sleep and a shower. His mind was sharp and going at full speed. He gave himself a lecture on the importance of putting personal feelings aside. Remaining objective and professional. He looked at himself in the rearview and talked out loud.

"You're a reporter, not an advocate. Just ask the questions. Stay on topic."

Joaquin had called in his notes and was surprised to be told he'd be given three minutes' airtime on the five o'clock broadcast. His segment would come immediately after the opening piece on the identity of the slain deputy, Theodore Jacob Rosado. That report would be a tribute; it would be about the Rosado family, about the deputy personally. There'd be plenty of tears and pain. Then would come Joaquin's shocking report— that Omar Ortega might be every bit as much a victim as Deputy Rosado.

Joaquin had a sickening feeling that law enforcement's famous rush to judgment was running at full throttle. After spending an hour talking to the Ortega family and then two more following up with people who knew Omar, Joaquin was sure of one thing: this young man, this kid, Omar Ortega, was not responsible for the death of the deputy sheriff. It just didn't fit. He didn't know what kind of evidence the deputies had, and he'd give

Anna a chance to defend the department's position and the arrest. But he had some tough questions to ask, and he would insist on straight answers.

He found an empty visitor's parking spot at the sheriff's headquarters on Ridgehaven Court and was soon pushing the buzzer at the main door. The lock clicked open and Joaquin entered the lobby of the building to find three uniformed deputies, one with sergeant's stripes, standing in front of the door that led to the administrative offices. All three men, well over six feet tall and solidly built, towered over Joaquin, who had a pretty good idea of what was coming.

"Good afternoon, deputies. I'm Joaquin Fonseca of Univision. I'm here to see the PIO, Anna Ramirez."

"We know who you are, Fonseca," the sergeant said. His name tag read "Olivares." "We saw your broadcast this morning. And on behalf of the entire San Diego County Sheriff's Department, we want to let you know what a low-life, scum-sucking piece of shit you are. No debate. No equivocation. And that's on the record, by the way. Feel free to air it."

Nothing in the sergeant's voice indicated the man wanted an explanation, so Joaquin didn't offer one.

"Believe me, Sergeant. I can understand your feeling that way," Joaquin said. "Like I said, I need to meet with Ms. Ramirez."

One of the other deputies spoke up. "She's unavailable."

"Could you find out when she will be available? It's important. I have information I think she'll be interested in."

"Really?" Olivares said. "Tell me. Maybe *I'll* find it interesting."

"Look, guys, I know everyone is feeling—"

Olivares took another step toward Joaquin. "Shut the fuck up, Fonseca. You don't know what anyone is feeling. If you did, you wouldn't haven't had the balls to walk through that door. Because right now, what we're feeling is that we'd like to take you out back and—"

"I got this, Jaime."

Anna took the sergeant lightly by the arm and turned him so that they stood face-to-face. She spoke softly. "You're all helping coordinate Ted's funeral arrangements, aren't you? That's more important. Let me deal with Mr. Fonseca."

None of the deputies seemed to be in a hurry to leave, but eventually they drifted off, muttering under their breath and shooting dark glances at Joaquin. When they were gone, he turned to Anna.

"Nerves are a bit fraught, I guess."

"Why are you here?" Anna's voice was only slightly less hostile than the sergeant's.

"I just met with the Ortega family. I've got some questions about the arrest."

"That's funny," she said, like it was anything but funny. "Because I just met with the family of Deputy Rosado. They have questions too. Some of them were addressed to you and your station."

"Knock it off, Anna. I'm serious. I wonder how much the sheriff's department knows about this kid and—"

"Stop right there. I will not have you portray this man as a kid. If you're going to do that, we're done. He is an adult and he will be held to answer as such."

"He turned eighteen two months ago and he graduates from high school next week. Valedictorian of his class, by the way. Say what you want, but he's a kid."

The valedictorian comment had caught her off guard. He didn't want to let up. "He's got a pretty long list of admirers at James Madison High. At the armed forces recruiting office, too. Apparently, when he walked in six months ago to ask about enlisting, the recruiters practically fought over him. He picked the army. He was due to leave for basic training next week."

Anna stammered a bit but held firm. "Good. So you won't be chasing the 'woe is me' angle. Sounds like Mr. Ortega had plenty of opportunity to make something of himself."

"From what I've been told, I wouldn't so much call it opportunity as I would overcoming adversity. He's quite a young man, Anna." Joaquin softened his tone. "Really, I just want to be sure you hear who this kid is. He doesn't seem to fit the profile—"

Anna laughed. "Really? You're going to tell us we should pay attention to his 'profile'? Jesus, Joaquin. Talk about wanting to have it both ways."

Joaquin ignored the jab. "Do you know why he was out last night? Do you know about the knock at his door?"

She blew out a long breath. "No, I don't. And I also didn't know about his wonderful scholastic achievement or patriotism. Do you want to know why? Because, believe it or not, the detectives are still investigating. As much as I know you'd love to play the tunnel-vision card, I think you should know we have very solid evidence against Ortega and we are continuing to build a case. In fact, we've identified a second suspect, who we believe acted in concert with Mr. Ortega."

Joaquin tried to get in a question, but now it was Anna's turn to step in close. Although she wasn't the physical threat the deputies had been, she had the cop thing down pretty well—and why not, after two decades on the force? She could be intimidating when she wanted to.

"There is *no doubt* that Ortega was present at the time of Deputy Rosado's murder, and there's ample evidence he's a principal in the crime," she said. "If you spin this any other way, you're going to end up looking foolish."

"He was practically accosted in his home," Joaquin said. "You could argue he was kidnapped. That was witnessed by two other persons. Is the sheriff's department investigating that? The threat to his family?"

She raised a hand to cut him off. "You know what, Joaquin, let's do this: You've got an evening broadcast coming up. Why don't we just clear the air—I mean between your station and the sheriff's department. How does that sound?"

Joaquin was suspicious. "You mean live? One-on-one? You'll answer questions? No reading from a press release?"

"Exactly. We'll do it at the Vista substation. I'm assuming it'll be the lead story, so we can meet a couple of minutes before five."

"Do you want to go over some parameters? Let me know what areas you want to cover?"

"The only restriction I'd insist on is you not tie our interview into the video from the shooting scene. We don't want to be associated with that footage. Otherwise, we'll answer any questions you might have." Shifting her attention to her phone, she typed out a message. "Sound good?"

Too good, but Joaquin figured he could handle whatever she was planning. "I'll get ahold of Mannie. We'll set up in Vista before five."

"That's fine," she said. "I'd appreciate it if you'd use the flag at half-staff as a backdrop. That whole area of the lawn is covered with flowers and cards. A kind of spontaneous memorial to Deputy Rosado. I'd like that to register with the public."

"I can agree to that."

"See you at five." She spun and walked away.

37

He lied, Hector thought. *Just like everyone else.*

Hector clutched the reporter's business card in his hand, ready to wad it up and throw it away. The man had said he'd help and, for that, they'd agreed to tell him everything. All about their family. Their troubles. About how Omar had been trying to protect them from Chunks and E-Boy. He said he would tell people the truth about Omar. But he was a liar.

Hector had spent most of the day sitting on the old man's couch, flipping through the channels. It was the same thing over and over. Omar being led down the sidewalk to the curb and pushed into the back of a police car. Reporters saying he had killed a deputy sheriff. Most of the reports showed pictures of the deputy right after he was shot. There was blood everywhere. Blood all over another deputy who was screaming. Hector even recognized the street, just a few blocks away. It seemed like something from a movie, not the news.

More yelling came from the kitchen and he heard his mother crying. He jammed the card in his pocket, stood up, then sat back down, overloaded with raw emotions that, these days, seemed to fester inside him all the time. People just figured he was always angry. Angry at his family. At his teachers. At his life.

The smash of glass made him jump. What could anyone expect him to do? He heard Omar's voice in his head.

Well, do something.

But what Omar didn't know was that the anger everyone thought flowed through Hector wasn't really anger at all. It was fear, and right now it was fear mixed with shame.

Renteria shouted again. He was drunk. When he'd come back to the apartment, he'd cornered Hector's mom in the kitchen and started screaming at her. Yelling about the door and all the damage. About who was going to pay for his furniture. Omar would never let Renteria talk to their mother that way. His brother would walk right up to Renteria and tell him to shut the hell up. To leave his mother alone. The old man would listen, too. Sofia came down the hall, walking slowly toward the kitchen.

"No, Sofia," Hector said. "Don't go in there."

More yelling and a banging against the wall. He sent Sofia to the bedroom and told her not to come out, no matter what she heard. He looked around for something heavy. Something he could use if Renteria didn't listen. He picked up the glass ashtray, dumping the butts and ashes on the carpet, and knocked it against his hand a time or two. He imagined himself throwing it at Renteria's head, seeing the big man topple over like something from a video game. Struggling to take a full breath, he headed for the kitchen just as a new voice called out from what used to be the front door.

"Federal officers. Anyone here?"

The yelling stopped. Renteria walked out of the kitchen and stood with his large body blocking the entryway.

"Who are you?" Renteria asked. "What do you want?"

Hector moved to get a clear view. Two men. Both white and both wearing black uniforms. Both had guns on their belts. He didn't know what a federal officer was, but he figured they must have come because of all the yelling. For sure they would take the old man away. Hector listened closely as one of the men spoke to Renteria.

"I'm Agent Paulson. This is Agent Greenberg. Who are you, sir?"

When Renteria answered, Hector could tell the man was all kinds of shook up. He was scared as hell even though he was going for tough. "My name is Renteria. This is my apartment. I came home and found out the cops raided the place looking for that chollo fucker Ortega. They call him Seso."

He pointed toward Hector like an accuser. "You can ask him. He's an Ortega. There's another one in the kitchen. They're the ones who caused all the trouble. Not me."

The man who called himself Paulson spoke up. "All right, Mr. Renteria. I'll need to see some identification."

"No problem sir. It's in my room." Hector hardly recognized Renteria's voice, as the old man tried to sound all smooth. Whoever these guys were, they had the asshole's attention.

Paulson nodded to his partner. "Go with Mr. Renteria and have a look at his docs."

Renteria walked to his bedroom with the man following behind. The other one, Paulson, looked at Hector, then at some papers attached to a clipboard. "Let me see. You must be Hector Elias Ortega. Age thirteen. Is that right?"

"Yeah. How'd you know that?"

"And my understanding is you were born in the United States?"

"Uh, yeah. I was born in Oceanside. Why are you—"

Again, his eyes went to the clipboard. "And your sister, Sofia Isabella Ortega. Where is she?"

Hector was starting to get a bad feeling. He thought about lying but remembered that Omar had told him that lying to a cop was illegal. Hector wasn't even sure this guy was a cop, but he had a gun and a uniform. Hector pointed toward the hallway. "She's back there. I told her not to come out."

"Why did you tell her that?"

Hector nodded his head in the direction of Renteria's bedroom. "Because he was yelling at my mom. I didn't want Sofia to get yelled at too. Is that why you're here? Because of all the yelling?"

For a brief moment, Hector thought Paulson looked sad, but the expression went away quick.

"So, your mom is here?" Paulson nodded toward the kitchen. "In there, I'm guessing? What is her name?"

"Why?" Hector didn't like all these questions about his family. The man should just worry about Renteria. His chest started to feel tight again. "Why are you even here? Who are you?"

"Like I said, we're federal officers. We're with Immigration and Customs Enforcement."

Hector cocked his head a bit. He'd never heard of a federal officer. He knew about immigration stuff. Hell, everybody did. But customs? He wasn't so sure. But then the man cleared it up.

"You know. *ICE*."

Hector heard the word and the air ran out of him. Now he knew who they were and what they wanted. They didn't care about Renteria. Once again, he tried to think of what Omar would do.

"You need to go away," he said through gritted teeth. He gripped the ashtray tighter. "Just go away and leave us alone."

Paulson looked at Hector's hand and moved his own hand closer to the pistol on his hip. "Put that down, young man. Do it now."

Energy surged through Hector as he stared at the ICE agent, who looked back, hand now resting on his pistol. He thought of his father. Gone. He thought of Omar. Gone. Hector began to raise the ashtray. He was angry now, as angry as he'd ever been. Seeing Paulson close his hand around his weapon didn't frighten him. Nothing frightened him. For once, he wasn't afraid.

Then she stood in front of him.

"No, hijo. No. Calmate." His mother gently took the ashtray with one hand and laid her other hand on his cheek. She smiled at him, her eyes wet, but as always filled with love. She turned and faced the man.

"Buenos dias, señor." Hector watched as his mother bowed slightly, then straightened. "Yo soy Isadora Monique Solis-Ortega."

Agent Paulson spoke passable Spanish. He and Isadora communicated well enough that Paulson took notes as she answered his questions. He stepped into the kitchen to make a call on his phone—Hector could not hear anything he said. The other agent returned with Renteria, whom he directed to sit on the couch. Paulson came back to stand by the front door.

"Señora Ortega, I have no record of your being legally admitted into the United States. In that you can provide no such documentation and you have freely admitted to being born outside the country, at this time I am taking you into federal custody for violation of Title Eight of the U.S. code, section thirteen twenty-five. You will be held in a detention facility, awaiting an appearance before immigration judicial authorities."

Hector could only think of one thing to do. He threw all his weight against the man and screamed, "Leave her alone!"

Paulson easily knocked him to the ground. "I'm going to let that go. Once. Do it again and I will take you into custody for assault on a federal officer. You *will* go to jail. Do you understand?"

Sofia ran down the hall, calling for her mother. Hector was certain she'd heard everything. The children both threw themselves onto their mother, nearly knocking her over.

"Please, don't do this," Sofia begged. "Don't take her away. She hasn't done anything wrong. She would never hurt anyone."

"It is a criminal violation for any foreign national to enter the United States without proper authorization and documentation," Paulson said. "Your mother will be provided legal counsel and due process of law. But right now, she's under arrest."

Hector thought the man talked like he had said all this before. He could be talking about anybody. But right now, he was talking about Hector's mom, and that made him hold her tighter.

Sofia fell to her knees, now hugging her mother around her legs. Isadora prayed quietly, shaking, her hands on her children. The men looked on, clearly annoyed and ready to get on with it.

"You can't take her," Hector shouted. "You can't."

Anger simmering in his voice, Paulson said, "All right, that's enough. Say your good-byes and back away."

None of them moved. The two ICE agents had to pry them off their mother. Hector held tight, but slowly his grip began to slip and his arms came open. Renteria got up off the couch, grabbed him hard around the waist, and pulled him away, the stink of the man's breath hot against the back of Hector's neck. It was easy for the two federal officers to break Sofia's grip; Renteria grabbed her, too. Isadora offered no resistance as the agents led her away.

Renteria held both Hector and Sofia aloft like sacks of beans. Hector could feel Sofia fighting hard. She kept kicking and screaming for her mother in a voice that Hector did not recognize. Renteria needed both of his hands to control her, allowing Hector to break free.

He reached the curb just as the agents were getting into a large black car. Isadora was nowhere in sight. The men looked back at him, their ex-pressions bland and bored, the emotional scene already forgotten. As the car pulled away, Hector caught a glimpse of his mother in the backseat. She smiled weakly at him and laid her palm flat against the wire mesh as the car pulled away.

"Mom-my!" Hector screamed, falling to his knees. He flung himself facedown in the dirt of the yard and wept. He lay there for several minutes, hearing the whispers and snickers of others around him. At last, knowing Sofia was alone with Renteria, he got up. He had few options. He pulled the newsman's now crumpled card from his pocket and went inside.

38

Even as Travis hustled out of the locker room, he wondered where his energy was coming from. He figured that, in the last forty-eight hours, he'd gotten a total of seven hours' sleep. Molly had begged him to stay home. She knew enough about police work to know that he could have easily called in and gotten the night off. The bosses wouldn't have hesitated to accommodate a time off request under the circumstances; it wouldn't even be charged against Travis's vacation or sick time.

What Molly didn't understand was that Travis didn't care what the bosses thought. He didn't care about sleep. He cared about Ted, about Ellie, and about all the other deputies who worked the shift. He wasn't going to let them down, and apparently he wasn't the only one who felt that way. He opened the door and stood to take in the power of the scene.

The briefing room overflowed with uniformed deputies as well as officers from agencies all over San Diego County. Most had sorted themselves by shoulder patch. Detectives from several substations—men and women who usually worked burglary, car theft, forgery, and sex crimes—had donned ill-fitting uniforms. A few, who had been out of patrol for so long they no longer had a complete uniform, wore jeans and polo shirts, with external vests that adequately, if not very professionally, identified them as deputies. Everyone wanted to be on the street.

Travis wasn't surprised to see GSU standing shoulder to shoulder with gang enforcement teams from three other agencies. A plastic dish full of black elastic bands had been left by the door, and pieces of black tape were stuck to the wall for the cops who wore tactical BDUs with cloth badges. Travis took one of the bands and slipped it over his metal badge as he looked for an open chair.

At the front of the room, Sergeant Peña stood flanked by the sheriff and the station captain. Travis finally spotted Ellie Peralta, in an area of the room that was normally empty, though not today. Travis saw an open seat in a corner and made his way over, sitting down just as the sergeant took charge.

"All right, everyone, pipe down." His commanding presence worked even on the outsiders and the room went quiet.

Peña scanned the crowd. "This is a hell of a thing. To come to work the day a fellow cop is killed on the job. Gunned down. Murdered."

When Peña paused, it seemed to Travis that time stopped. After several seconds, he went on, "I've done this more times than I care to count, as a marine and as a cop. But every time I've done it, it reminds me of the three rules of combat."

Peña held up a single finger, making eye contact with as many cops as he could. "Rule number one: good people will die."

He held up a second finger. "Rule number two: you don't get to change rule number one."

Once again he scanned the room. He added a third finger. "And rule number three: somebody has to walk point. Last night, Teddy Rosado was walking point. Tonight, everyone here will do the same, and we'll do it together. And, God willing, we'll all go home safe."

Sergeant Peña looked at his boss; his fondness for the man was obvious and unmistakable. "Sheriff Collier would like to say a few words. Sir?"

Sheriff Alexander Collier stepped to the podium in his dress green uniform and badge covered with a black band. He had recently won his third term in office, meaning he was probably as good a politician as he was a cop. He'd originally run for sheriff when he was nothing more than a lowly patrol sergeant, working out of the Lemon Grove substation. Most people said he didn't have a chance, but Collier had the support of the men and women working at the troop level.

When the race tightened, the sitting sheriff had offered Collier an immediate promotion to lieutenant and his choice of any assignment he desired. Collier had refused, even when threatened with being permanently assigned to day shift patrol in the high desert heat of East County. He'd started tossing squeeze tubes of 100 SPF sunscreen to the audience at his political rallies, and he won the election by twelve points.

"Good afternoon." Collier's normally loud voice was dialed back. "I want to thank all our brothers and sisters from the allied agencies, not only for their support last night, in our greatest hour of need, but also for tonight, as we head back out to do just as Sergeant Peña said: walk the point."

The rest of the sheriff's speech was essentially a eulogy for Teddy Rosado. His comments were personal and specific enough that it was clear he had known the man well. He ended by telling his listeners about time he'd spent that day with Ted's widow and children, and about the funeral arrangements and the motorcade that would escort the body to its final resting place. When he was finished, there were few in the room with dry eyes. Travis looked at Ellie; her head was bowed but her eyes were clear.

"I'm going to leave now." The sheriff's tone changed to something less intimate, bordering on grave. "Got a date with the media."

There were a few comments, none positive, but Collier didn't object. He looked back to the podium.

"Just as well. I know Sergeant Peña works best without the brass looking over his shoulder." There were polite chuckles in the room. The sheriff and the sergeant exchanged a knowing glance. "Orlando, the floor is yours, sir. Thank you for allowing me to participate."

The sheriff and captain headed out amid a smattering of applause. He shook a few hands, and some of the senior deputies who knew him best hugged him close. When the sheriff was gone, Sergeant Peña stared at the door for ten or twelve seconds before he looked back to the audience.

"I believe the sheriff spoke for all of us when he talked about Deputy Rosado. A good man. A good deputy. A good cop. Dedicated husband and father. Next week, we'll send him off in style.

"But tonight, I have two words for you." Peña reconsidered. "Make that three."

Peña looked around the room. "*Zero. Fucking. Tolerance.*"

His voice grew in intensity with each word. "And 'zero' means just that.

Let there be no mistake: that policy is in full force tonight and it shall be directed at any and all members, associates, or shitheel friends of those murderous bastards the Eastside street gang. If any of those pumpkin head sons of bitches so much as puts a toe on the sidewalk, or if any of their skanky women shake their ass on the street, I want them swallowed up in green, hooked and fucking booked. You figure out what for, but you will fill my jail. *Is that understood?*"

Travis was stunned by the visceral delivery, but even more so by the response. The room erupted like Lambeau Field on a Sunday in January. The noise didn't die down until Sergeant Peña raised a fist to signal for quiet.

"Detective Murphy has some intelligence updates on the murder of Teddy Rosado."

Murphy spoke from where he stood, along the back wall.

"This case is moving very quickly. As I'm sure you've all heard, this morning, at zero seven hundred hours, SWAT hit the apartment of a known Eastside associate, Omar 'Seso' Ortega. We have very strong evidence that Ortega was not only at the scene but also the shooter. Ortega is in custody."

Cheers and shouts came from the crowd.

"But Ortega did not act alone. For those of you familiar with Eastside, I'm sure it won't come as any surprise to hear that we're putting out a PC pickup for Alonzo 'Chunks' Gutierrez. He's been ID'ed as the likely driver of the vehicle. He's good for arrest right now, and we'll have a signed warrant first thing Monday morning."

Travis took one of the sheets being passed out. It was the standard PC pickup, which amounted to a sworn statement from a cop that there was probable cause to arrest Gutierrez, until a warrant could be obtained from a judge.

"The weapon used to kill Deputy Rosado was a three eighty, so we could be talking revolver or maybe semiauto. The lab guys recovered several rounds, but the ones that hit Ted's vest are pretty flattened out."

Murphy paused as if what he had to say next was difficult. "The fatal shot was a through and through—in through the throat, out the back of his neck. We've scoured the area, but no luck finding the bullet. So, bottom line, ballistics is going to be tough, but we still want that gun.

"GSU will be hitting several known locations frequented by Gutierrez. We'll also be conducting parole and probation checks on just about every Eastsider currently on the roster. We'll be making a lot of hard knock house calls, so be ready to roll if we need cover."

His voice took on a command quality. "Let's keep the air clear as much as we can. High-profile stops only. Joe and Jane Citizen get a free pass tonight. If there aren't at least two shaved heads in the car, let it slide."

Murphy's hands rested on his gun belt. "Any questions?"

There were a few, about known gang associates and target locations. After that, he turned the floor back over to Sergeant Peña.

"We've got a lot of out-of-towners and we're damn glad to have you," Peña said. "Tonight is all about sending a message, and that message is, If you come at one of us, you'd better be ready to deal with all of us."

Another cheer went up, not quite as boisterous as the first.

"All units out tonight will be two-persons," Peña said. "To avoid any issues of geographical familiarity, I've paired station deputies with officers from outside agencies. The roster is posted by the door. Get your assignments, find your partner, and go ten eight. Be sure you discuss takedown cues, backup gun locations, and all that sort of tactical intelligence. The team that doesn't bring me at least one shaved-head prisoner by twenty-one hundred hours will spend the rest of the shift making jail checks and booking property.

"Any questions? I didn't think so. Let's get out there."

Travis had started to make his way to the roster when a strong hand clamped down on his elbow.

"Hey, Jackson," Sean Murphy said. "Listen, in the interview this morning, I acted like an asshole. I said some stupid shit and I was way out of line."

Travis was happy that the man let it go at that. Apologies always came across weird between cops.

"I appreciate that, Sean, but you weren't completely wrong. I wish I could go back, change a couple of things." Travis looked around the room. "Then none of this would be necessary and Teddy would be going ten eight."

Sean moved his hand up to Travis's shoulder and squeezed even harder. Travis was shocked by the intensity on the man's face. "Don't even go there. If you do, sure as hell you'll be out of work and living on antidepressants and Jack Daniel's inside a year. We've both seen it happen. Dannie was right. This is on the gangsters. Not us."

"I appreciate it. And that was a hell of a job, getting Ortega into custody that quick."

"I didn't do anything," Sean said. "Ted caught him. Can you believe it? Shot to shit and bleeding out and he thinks to turn on his camera. But now, let's go find Chunks."

The men shook hands, then parted. Travis headed for the bulletin board to see who he was riding with.

"Hey there, hayseed." Ellie was just turning away from the roster.

"Hey, Ellie. Did you get some sleep?"

"More than you, I'll bet." Her voice was low, and nothing like that of the ballsy woman he'd gotten to know so well just the night before. "I hear you booked Ortega. If I'd known you were going to volunteer for that, I would've stuck around and come along."

"Didn't volunteer. Peña was in a jam and I wanted to help him out. No big deal. I was home before noon. Got a few hours." Travis nodded toward the board. "Who you with?"

"Cop out of Esco." Ellie looked around the crowded room. "You ever done this?"

"Done what?"

"Come to work the day after we lost one?"

"Nope. Hope I never have to do it again."

"I hear you," Ellie said. "My goal? Get through the night. Get off on time and go home safe. If you ask me, Peña needs to chill a bit."

Travis was surprised. He had every intention of doing exactly what Peña had ordered and he had no problem with it. He was about to challenge his partner of one day, but she changed the subject.

"By the way," Ellie said, "Rob and I were supposed to host a political event tomorrow afternoon. Something about drug prevention, kids, I don't know. We canceled, of course, but we've got a ton of food and no plans for the whole day. How about you come over with the family? Hang out. Give us a chance to talk. Or maybe better yet, not talk. Just decompress."

"I don't know, Ellie. Probably ought to just hang out at home. But thanks. Maybe another time."

"Did I mention we bought enough beer, wine, and booze to loosen the wallets of about a hundred fat-cat donors?"

"Tempting. But really, tomorrow isn't—"

"Now or never, hayseed." She poked him in the chest. "And if you don't say yes . . . Next time I'm servicing my husband? I'm going to tell him to give you some shit-ass assignment in court services."

"Does he listen?"

"Putty in my hands, baby," Ellie said. "Come on. The kids can swim in the pool. Maybe walk on the beach."

"The pool? Walk on the beach? Jesus, Ellie. Where do you live?"

"I'll text you the address. Be there by noon or I swear you're going to be working the search line for family court in La Mesa. That'd be, what: sixty miles one way from your little slice of paradise?"

"All right. Enough." He smiled. "We'll be there."

"You Jackson?"

The newcomer, a female cop, was a good six feet tall, with the sculpted body of a marine. Her uniform was tailored to form fit and her highly polished black basket weave belt was a nearly perfect match for the tone of her skin. She didn't look to be a day over twenty-five. Her patch showed she was Oceanside PD.

"Yeah. Travis."

"Great. Shelia Matthews. Looks like I'm riding with you." She turned to Ellie. "Sorry. Didn't mean to interrupt."

"No worries." Ellie stuck out a hand. "Ellie Peralta."

"I checked out a squad already," Travis said. "It's all geared up. We're good to go."

"Sounds great. Let's do it." Shelia turned back to Ellie. "Nice meeting you."

Ellie looked back at Travis, and he wondered if she felt it too. After what they'd been through the night before, it seemed odd heading out with someone else. Almost like disloyalty. He didn't doubt it was a connection they'd feel for a long time to come.

"Okay, then," Ellie said, not looking away. "You guys be careful out there."

Yeah. She felt it. He was sure she did. He watched as she waded into the crowd to look for her new partner.

"Yo, Travis," Shelia said. "You ready?"

"Yeah. Sorry," Travis answered. "Come on. Car's this way."

39

Late-afternoon shadows blanketed the crowd that gathered in front of the Vista substation. In the twenty minutes since Joaquin and Mannie had pulled up in the Univision van, the crowd had doubled in size, to well over a hundred people. Many brought flowers that they laid beneath the poster-size portrait of a smiling Deputy Theodore Rosado, displayed reverently on an easel beneath an American flag flying at half-staff. A few children had brought stuffed animals that they propped up in the carpet of green grass. Mannie stood back and quietly filmed the scene. Joaquin couldn't help but notice that the crowd was almost entirely white.

Some in the gathering were carrying homemade signs. Joaquin nudged Mannie on the shoulder and pointed to one:

EYE FOR AN EYE
DEATH TO ORTEGA

"Make sure you get that one," Joaquin said, pointing to the man with the sign in one hand and an American flag in the other. "And get a close-up of his face."

Joaquin had promised himself he would maintain objectivity. To report the news. But the phone call he'd received from Hector Ortega a little more than an hour ago had changed everything. He felt as if battle lines were being drawn. Looking at the crowd, with their flowers, flags, and signs, he knew that the scene playing out in front of him represented one side of a story. No doubt, it was the side of superior strength and affluence. But there was another side, and by god, Joaquin was going to tell it.

He'd spent the day digging deeper into the life of Omar Ortega. The five o'clock broadcast would open with on-camera interviews he had edited himself, beginning with the high school principal, who spoke of Omar's excellent academic record, maturity, and personal integrity. Added to this were some heartfelt comments from Carol Hillman, a teacher who happened to be married to a San Diego Police sergeant.

The military recruiter Omar had signed up with had given Joaquin a positive quote, but later called and tried to recant, saying, "The United States Army has no official position on the arrest of Omar Ortega, who is not currently and never has been a member of the armed services."

Reluctantly, Joaquin had agreed to not air the footage of the man in uniform, but he'd told the recruiter he'd still be using his original words: Omar Ortega had the potential to be one of the most outstanding soldiers to ever come out of Vista. An army attorney had called not long after that, threatening legal action. It wasn't the first time Joaquin had run into that attitude, and he figured it would not be the last on this particular story.

Once the broadcast went live, with Anna on camera, Joaquin would drop his bomb. This case already had a stink on it, and Joaquin suspected there was more to come.

As promised, Anna walked out of the station just a few minutes before five o'clock, accompanied by the area captain and none other than Sheriff Alexander Collier himself. Both men were dressed in full uniform, badges banded in black. As the two men moved through the crowd, they paused to shake hands and accept hugs. Anna gazed in Joaquin's direction, and even though they were still some distance apart, Joaquin could see her look of satisfaction. Right then, he knew. Like him, she saw what was happening. And like him, she had picked a side.

The three officials moved slowly through the adoring crowd. The man with the death sign moved in to pat the sheriff on the back while leaning in to whisper in his ear. Joaquin turned to Mannie, who didn't need any prompting. With his camera pointed directly at the two men, he spoke to Joaquin without looking away.

"Don't worry, jefe. I got it."

Joaquin's earpiece came to life; a voice told him the news broadcast had begun with the recorded interviews. They would be going live in two minutes. As he'd promised, Joaquin moved to a position that ensured the picture of Ted Rosado, the flag, and some of the memorial would be picked up by the camera and seen by viewers. He reminded himself that was the only promise he had made. Anna walked over, the sheriff by her side and the captain trailing behind.

"Good afternoon, Joaquin," Anna said, shaking his hand. "I think you've met Sheriff Collier a time or two. He's decided to handle this interview himself. We'd like to do it in English. We trust your team will use an accurate voice-over translation."

"Word for word, of course," Joaquin said. He extended his hand to Collier. "Good to see you again, sir. My condolences to you and the men and women of the sheriff's department. This is a tragic situation. Thank you for agreeing to come on camera."

"I hope you mean that, Mr. Fonseca," the sheriff said, accepting Joaquin's hand like he was meeting an enemy combatant during a temporary truce. "So far, the coverage by the media has been less than I would have hoped for. A bit sleazy, even."

Joaquin had grown fond of the sheriff. In his time in office, the sheriff had done a great deal to legitimize the buzzwords "community policing." Joaquin could remember a time, not so long ago, when the department was led by a man who'd had the patrol cars painted green and white to celebrate his Irish heritage. That was as close as the old guard had ever come to cultural diversity. Collier was a definite improvement.

"I'm sorry you feel that way, sir," Joaquin said, even as the news director squawked the thirty-second warning into his ear. "Perhaps we can clear all that up right now."

"That's exactly what I plan on doing." The sheriff's voice held a note of challenge. Joaquin would have liked a few more seconds to connect, but the final countdown started in his ear.

Joaquin began the broadcast in Spanish, the camera focused on the portrait of Deputy Rosado. Mannie slowly pulled away, giving viewers a panoramic view of the crowd and the display of flowers and mementos as

Joaquin commented on the outpouring of public emotion and the quick arrest of an alleged suspect.

After introducing the sheriff and switching to English, Joaquin threw a softball. "This must all be quite heartwarming, sir. I mean, the response of the community to this human tragedy."

The sheriff turned so the camera caught his profile as he stared directly at Joaquin. "Yes. The response of the community to the murder of Deputy Rosado has been humbling and incredibly gratifying. Unfortunately, I can't say the same about the media in general and you and your station in particular, Mr. Fonseca. The images you showed, of my deputies under such terrible circumstances, were nothing short of appalling."

Looking now at the camera, Collier went on, "It reminded me of an incident about twenty years ago. A newspaper up in Riverside made a similar decision, to put a picture of two slain deputies on the front page. The *Press Enterprise* lost about half its readership inside of three weeks. Perhaps that sort of impact on the bottom line is what it takes for the media to get the message."

Joaquin waited, allowing the live translator—whom he could hear in his earpiece—time to catch up. Catching sight of Anna's grim smile from where she stood, off camera, he knew immediately he'd been set up. The sheriff had no intention of clearing the air. This was going to be a sermon that amounted to a public ass chewing. As much as Joaquin wanted to respond directly, he knew that the seconds were ticking by, and he had a point of his own to make.

"I know there's been some controversy over the initial reporting, sir, but since that time, much has come to light about the young man who has been arrested, Omar Ortega. Perhaps that is what we should discuss."

"Fine, let's discuss Mr. Ortega." The sheriff looked off camera and reached out his hand. "Captain?"

The captain handed Collier an eight-by-ten photograph. "My understanding is that you've expressed some concern about the evidence against Mr. Ortega. This photograph was taken by the body camera of Deputy Rosado as he lay dying on the street. It shows the face of Omar Ortega."

The sheriff held the picture straight out at arm's length in a way that made Joaquin sure it took up the entire screen. The photo showed the face of a young man, contorted in fear and desperation, bleeding from an unseen wound.

"Typically, I would not allow the public release of evidence during an ongoing investigation," the sheriff said. "But candidly, Mr. Fonseca, I do not have faith that your newsroom will get the facts straight. So I'll do it for you."

It was a compelling piece of evidence, and Joaquin wanted to question the sheriff further about the photograph. "Sir, if I could just ask—"

"I'm not finished." The sheriff took a second document from the captain and held it high. "We also have scientific proof that Mr. Ortega had fired a handgun shortly before his arrest. A handgun killed Deputy Rosado."

"But, Sheriff—"

"I also believe it's important to let the public know that, as recently as yesterday afternoon, Mr. Ortega was observed, by my deputies, in the company of several members of the Eastside street gang. A firearm was recovered from that scene. So, as you can see, Mr. Fonseca, the evidence against Ortega is very strong. The investigation is continuing. We're certain other members of the gang were involved. As information becomes available, we will share it with the public."

Damn right, others are involved, Joaquin thought. Hector had told him of the late-night visit by Chunks Gutierrez and another man named E-Boy. But Joaquin knew he could not discuss what had happened in the Ortegas' apartment. If he did, not only would Omar's life be in danger, but so would the lives of his family. Still, he wasn't going to let Collier go unchallenged. His earpiece buzzed again: one minute to commercial.

"That may very well be, Sheriff, but isn't it also true that this young man, the valedictorian of his graduating class, has a great deal of support within the community? Can you tell us, sir, does Mr. Ortega have a criminal record of any sort?"

The sheriff shook his head as if annoyed. "I don't care what kind of grades he got or if he's ever been arrested. That doesn't change the fact that—"

Thirty seconds to commercial. Joaquin cut the sheriff off, knowing that he was about to officially surrender his objectivity.

"Then perhaps, sir, you might care to comment on the treatment of the Ortega family since Omar was arrested?"

"I don't know what you are insinuating, but the family has been treated with courtesy and professionalism."

"I'm referring to the arrest of Mrs. Ortega, sir. A twenty-year resident of Vista who, like her son, has never run afoul of the law."

From the sheriff's hesitation, Joaquin knew he had caught the man unaware. "I don't know anything about that."

"Mrs. Ortega was arrested this afternoon by ICE for alleged immigration violations. Her two minor children, who are both American citizens, are now alone."

When the sheriff only stared at him, Joaquin went on, "Is it typical for the sheriff's department to punish family members of persons arrested, or is this some sort of investigative tactic? An attempt to gain the cooperation of Mr. Ortega?"

It was the sheriff's turn to be on the defensive. He aimed a lasered stare at Anna, who shook her head in confusion. The sheriff recovered quickly. "Any enforcement activity performed by federal authorities was independent of this investigation."

"Sir, with all due respect, I find it hard to believe—"

The sheriff faced Joaquin directly, his professional veneer badly cracked, and he nearly shouted in response. "I don't care what you believe, Mr. Fonseca. My deputy is dead and Omar Ortega and the entire Eastside street gang will be held to answer for it."

Surprised at the raw emotion, Joaquin drew back a bit. A raucous cheer erupted from the crowd, catching both Joaquin and the sheriff off guard. Mannie quickly panned the crowd, which had continued to grow in numbers and volatility throughout the interview. Joaquin shifted position to put the mob behind him and keep them on camera. With the lens pointed their way, many people gave vent to an even more explosive rage.

Looking at the sheriff, who had gone pale, Joaquin said, "Thank you, Sheriff Collier." He raised his voice to be heard over the shouts and chants. "*Joaquin Fonseca, en vivo desde Vista, California.*"

40

"Damn, Travis." Shelia leaned toward the open window. "You all need a damn ocean up around here. Cool things off a bit."

"Yeah, I know it's hot." Travis smiled. "But it's a dry heat."

"I got some sweat running down places that would disagree with you. I'm about moist as shit."

Travis and the Oceanside cop had settled in and got familiar with each other. Shelia wanted to know more about his transfer out from the Midwest. He asked if she liked working in a town that doubled in population every weekend and for most of the summer.

"I like the tax base, that's for sure. Those hotel occupancy fees add up." She gave him a wink. "There's a reason we're highest paid in the county."

About halfway through their surprisingly uneventful shift, Shelia said, "I thought it would be a little more active. Pretty quiet so far."

"My guess is they're laying low. Smart enough to stay off the street. I got no problem with that. I'm good with quiet."

"After last night? I'll bet you are," she said. "That was a hell of a thing you went through. I mean, from what I saw online. You doing okay with it?" Her concern seemed genuine, not like she was looking for fodder for gossip.

"Which part?" he asked, then thought better of it. "Actually, it doesn't matter which part. To be honest, it sucks from every possible angle."

"I can believe it. We lost an officer the year I got hired. Same kind of bullshit. Gangsters and a gun. I was working that night. Nothing like what you went through, but it was crazy, no doubt about it."

Travis didn't want to be rude, but he wasn't ready to compare war stories of dead cop friends. He didn't know if he ever would be. Fortunately, the radio steered them in a different direction.

"Station A, GSU, we're out on seven, at the Seventy-Eight underpass, on Smilax." Travis recognized the voice of Sean Murphy. "Roll us a couple of cover units."

"Let's take that," Travis said, already pulling up the street map in his head. Shelia acknowledged the call and Travis drove. They arrived at the two-lane road underneath Highway 78 within two minutes, only to find that three other units had jumped the call and were already out on cover. Counting GSU, their car was fifth on the scene, and Travis had to smile. Teddy Rosado had always believed that a five-car response was a warning sign of an impending clusterfuck.

"Looks like they got this," Shelia said, reaching for the mic. "I'll put us ten eight."

"Let's hang out for a minute. See what's going on."

She shrugged and unbuckled. "It's your rodeo."

The parked patrol cars were fanned out and aimed toward the group, high beams and spotlights on, as if the young men lined up along the curb were on a stage. Traffic surged above them, a constant California urban night sound that Travis was finally growing accustomed to. He stepped from the patrol car just as a big rig passed overhead, setting off a clap of concrete thunder that rippled the ground under his boots.

Six young men sat on the curb with their backs toward the wall of the underpass, heavily tagged with what looked to be fresh Eastside graffiti. The entire lineup sat with their legs straight out, ankles crossed. Four of them, who Travis figured had already been searched, sat on their hands; the one on the end still had his hands laced behind his head, waiting to be patted down by the GSU detective, who was in the process of frisking number five.

The detainees were all dressed out in different combinations of Easton hats, Dodgers jerseys, and blue hoodies. Travis couldn't help but remember

Murphy's comments. They did look particularly arrogant tonight, but why not? One of their own had taken out a dep and it was time to strut their shit.

Sean Murphy had his field interview pad out and was working his way down the line while his partner conducted the pat-downs. Two deps, responsible for close-in security, stood alongside Murphy, one with his Taser unholstered and tucked behind his back. Four other cops stood just outside the lighted area. By their shadows, Travis could see that two faced inboard while the others watched the road. Sean glanced up, acknowledged Travis with a nod, and held up four fingers.

Code 4, no further assistance needed.

Travis looked at Shelia. "You're right; they got this."

He headed for the car just as one of the gangsters spoke up.

"Yo, yo, man. You be that dep on TV." Travis turned to the voice and saw the kid was the smallest in the lineup. He looked at Travis with glassy eyes and spoke with a lazy tone. "You okay, man? You looked pretty messed up."

The one next to him, who looked several years older, sniggered. "Damn, L'tl Beast. Don't be starting any shit."

"Little Beast" went on talking, and it was clear that starting shit was exactly what he wanted to do. He looked Travis's way and began making exaggerated gestures with his hands.

"I mean, like, damn, ese. You be howlin' like one of them hyenas when they get busy killing their dinner and shit."

The whole lineup let out a good laugh and Sean pointed a finger. "Sit on your hands and shut your pie hole, Montoya."

"No, I mean seriously." The kid lifted up one cheek at a time and slipped his hands back under his butt, still running his mouth. "Y'all see that? Homes be on his knees, all covered in blood. Carrying on like a crazy motherfucker."

The kid pulled his hands out again and kicked his head back. Cupping his hands around his mouth, he gave a loud howl. A couple of others joined in, the sounds echoing off the cement walls. Sean moved in. "I told you to shut your—"

Travis closed the distance before Sean could finish. From straight on, he kicked Montoya deliberately, so that every square inch of the bottom of his size eleven boot slammed evenly against the boy's chest. The howl became an *oof* of escaping air. If there had been a radar gun, Montoya would've clocked double digits as he flew backward, landing flat in the hard dirt. Every cop and gangster on scene fell silent. Traffic droned on overhead.

Walking over to the youngster, Travis leaned down to make sure he would be heard. His voice echoed off the cement walls. He matched the boy's own cocky belligerence. "You go right on and howl, *L'tl Beast.*"

Gasping for air, the teen had gone from badass gangster to sniveling kid. Beginning to whimper, he rolled onto his side and covered his face with one arm to hide his tears.

Travis was still looking down at the boy when he felt two hands on his back, firmly pushing him from behind and guiding him away. It was Sean Murphy.

"Damn, Jackson. What the fuck?"

As the reality of what he'd done set in, Travis ran a hand through his hair, shocked by his own actions. "I . . . I don't know. I mean, I just . . . shit."

"That there was some fucked up shit, homes." One of the older gangsters looked like he might decide to stand, but the dep with the Taser quietly convinced him to stay put. More bitching followed, but apparently nobody felt strongly enough about their fellow gangster to take a five-second ride of the lightning.

"Goddamn center punched him is what you did," Sean said, just loud enough for Travis to hear. He turned and spoke up. "Bennett, check on him. The rest of you finish up the FIs and cut these guys loose."

Bennett protested, saying, "What about Peña? He said—"

"I'll worry about Peña," Sean said. "Just get them outta here."

Travis watched Bennett pull the kid up off the ground. He had tears streaming down his face and was breathing ragged gulps of air, and Travis now saw that he was probably eleven or twelve years old.

"You and your partner, go," Sean said. "I'll take care of things here. I'll get with you later."

"I'm sorry, man," Travis said, still dazed. "I don't know what I was thinking."

"Just go. I'll deal with this."

Travis headed for his patrol car, walking past the line of mumbling, pissed-off Eastsiders, who stared him down, and silent cops, who all looked away. Ellie stepped from the shadow into the light, her thumbs hooked on her gun belt, her mouth hanging open in disbelief. Her eyes followed him as he brushed by. Her voice was low but terse. "What the hell was that about?"

He ignored her and looked to his riding partner. He tried to keep the tremor out of his voice. "You coming?"

She stood still long enough that he started to think she wasn't, then she moved toward him, shaking her head like she was regretting their partnership. When she got to the passenger side, she addressed Travis over the roof. "You need to find a spot where we can talk. Somewhere we won't be interrupted."

"Fair enough."

In his own head noise, he heard the familiar voice of Teddy Rosado. *"Told ya, brother. Five cars means you're headed for a clusterfuck."*

41

"Hey, Ortega. Your lawyer's here. Get up." The jailer stood outside the solid metal door and spoke through a small opening, heavy keys already rattling.

"What lawyer?" Feeling confused, Omar pulled himself up and sat on the edge of the metal bunk in the cell of the Vista Detention Facility, or, like he'd heard it called around the neighborhood, VDF.

When he'd arrived at intake, they gave him fifteen minutes in a cell with a half-dozen phones mounted on the wall. Problem was, there were twelve other guys lined up to use them. Two phones appeared to be the permanent property of a couple of homies no one was going to argue with, so Omar waited. When he finally got to a phone, he dialed his mother's cell. It went straight to voice mail. He called his own number, thinking Hector or Sofia might pick up, but the same thing happened. It made sense that the deps would have seized his phone when they searched the apartment. Did they take his mom's phone too? Wouldn't she be waiting for his call?

He was trying to think of someone else to call when the next guy in line pulled the phone away. He had a flat, ruddy face and a thin head of hair buzzed short on the top and straggling down his back. "Two-call limit, rice and beans. Back of the line."

It didn't matter. Other than his family, Omar had no one else to call. He sure hadn't called any lawyer.

"Are you sure they're here for me?"

"Omar Ortega." The deputy stood blocking the now open door. "The cop killer, right?"

"I'm Ortega, but I didn't—"

"Shut the fuck up. Just get your ass out here."

After the interview with Murphy, Omar had been taken back to the cell in the substation. After what seemed like several hours, two deputies he hadn't seen before came in, shackled him around the waist, and hand-cuffed him. He limped, unassisted, to a van parked in the same garage he'd arrived in, no telling how long ago.

Without the benefit of any sort of window, Omar could only use the lurching movement of the van to figure out where they might be. He was pretty sure they went westbound on the 78 and exited within a few miles of Vista. Sure enough, when the van stopped and the hatch opened, they were at the emergency room of the Tri-City hospital. He'd been born there, a little over eighteen years ago, and hadn't been back since.

He spent hours lying shackled and handcuffed to a gurney in the hall-way of the ER before being wheeled into a room where a woman in green scrubs, with the physique of a heavyweight cage fighter, came at him with a staple gun that looked right off the shelf at Home Depot. She said it would hurt, and she was as good as her word as she snapped it against his scalp a half-dozen times. She wrapped his foot, ankle, and lower leg in a black walking boot, again being none too careful. It all took less than five minutes.

"He's all yours and absolutely cleared for custody." She gave both of the deputies a long hug and whispered in the ear of each one of them. She looked back toward Omar, her eyes narrow and hateful. "Get him the hell out of here."

Back in the van for another short drive. Once again the rear hatch opened and Omar was ordered out. The two deputies escorted him through a doorway marked "Intake." After his pointless time in the phone tank, he limped along with the other prisoners through a number of hallways and locked gates. The walking boot helped, and Omar was able to stand when they came to a tomb-like room where they were lined up and ordered to strip naked. Omar was trying to figure out how to take off the paper jumpsuit when a deputy came to stand in front of him, a large pair of scissors in his hand. The deputy moved the scissors to his throat and Omar froze in fear. The deputy began to cut away at the paper suit, and within a minute Omar stood naked, wearing nothing but the walking boot.

Another deputy conducted a humiliating search that included him sticking out his tongue, lifting his nut sack, and spreading his ass cheeks.

A white dude in a blue jumpsuit with the word "Trustee" stenciled on the back threw him a pair of black slip-ons, gray chonies, and his own blue jumpsuit, which was marked with the letters UW. The trustee, who Omar figured had to be pushing fifty years old, saw Omar's confusion and cleared it up.

"Upper West," he whispered. "Best be ready, son. That's where the big dogs run."

At last he'd been taken to an empty cell with bunk beds similar to the ones he shared with Hector and Sofia, except they were constructed of heavy metal and bolted to the cement floor. A mattress that looked like the floor mat of a car was permanently attached to the metal of the bed. The metal toilet didn't contain any water, but the guard said it would flush automatically every six hours. "Best you get yourself on a schedule."

The only other thing in the cell was a metal sink built into the wall. There was a window no more than a foot square with heavy wire mesh buried in the thick frosted glass. Apparently, this was home.

Now they tell him he's got a lawyer.

Omar pulled himself off the bunk and limped to the open door where the deputy stood, holding the already too familiar leather cuff-belt. The deputy cinched the belt around Omar's waist, then cuffed his hands to the front.

The deputy pointed. "Let's go."

Outside the cell was an empty room about the size of one of his classrooms at school. Two of the walls were lined with doors—probably cells like the one he'd been placed in, Omar thought. Five-sided metal tables, with five attached chairs, were spread throughout the room and bolted to the floor. An ancient-looking television set hung from a wall. The TV was off. The lights were dim, but not completely out. The room was empty.

"What time it is?"

The deputy gave it some thought, like he was deciding whether he wanted to be that accommodating. He kept it short. "Almost midnight."

The guard escorted Omar down a dark hallway. They rode silently in an elevator, then down another hall, until they came to a door marked "Legal Visits Only." The guard led Omar inside a room that was similar to the one where he'd sat with Murphy, though there was no glass mirror, just the same sort of table and two chairs.

Waiting inside was a tall, slender man with gray hair cut close to his scalp. His face was lean and tan and his dark suit fit him well, giving him an athletic appearance. When Omar walked in, he smiled kindly. He saw the boot on Omar's leg and his expression changed to one of concern. He quickly stepped forward, offering Omar his support.

"Here, let me help you." Accusation filled his voice when he spoke to the guard. "I assume Mr. Ortega's injuries have been thoroughly documented?"

"*Mr. Ortega* came in like that," the guard said. "He's already tapped us for a couple of grand in medical bills. People like you and me foot the bill for that, no pun intended."

The older man helped Omar take a seat at the table, then rested his hand on Omar's shoulder. "Thank you, Deputy. I'd like to speak to my client in private. I assume any and all recording devices in the room have been disabled."

The guard was already halfway through the door. "We didn't beat your client, and this is a legal consult room. It's not wired for sound. Take all the time you want. You're damn sure going to need it."

The deputy left, pulling the door shut. Omar heard the bolt slide home.

"Omar, how are they treating you?" the man said.

Ignoring the question, Omar asked, "Who are you? You're a lawyer?"

The man took a seat, pulled a business card from his jacket, and slid it across the desk. "Ransom Shaw, attorney at law. They have to let you keep that. I wrote my cell number on the back. Once I was informed of your arrest and other related matters, I wanted to meet with you as soon as possible."

"Informed by who? What do you mean, 'related matters'?" Omar asked, still working to orient himself to another completely foreign experience.

"You have friends, Omar. People who are concerned about you. I was contacted by Joaquin Fonseca. Perhaps you've heard of him? He's a rather prominent television reporter."

Though Omar rarely watched the news, Renteria did. A dim mental image of a man came to mind. "Yeah, I think so, but I don't know him. Why would he call you?"

"He's covering the circumstances of your arrest. He's concerned about you," Ransom said. "We've known each other for many years."

"So what, then?" Omar asked, reviewing what little he knew about the legal system. "You're, like, one of those public defenders?"

"No, although I was a public defender for many years. Those men and women are very fine attorneys. I'm sure if one of them is assigned your case, they'll work diligently on your behalf." He placed his forearms flat against the wood of the tabletop and leaned forward, speaking slowly and with confidence. "But I work for an organization called Justice for All. We offer pro bono legal representation to persons accused of capital crimes but who don't have financial resources to mount an adequate defense."

Omar couldn't believe what he was hearing. He wanted to be sure he understood. "So what, then? You work for free for people who might get the death penalty?"

Ransom smiled, but his face remained grim. "Joaquin said you were a very bright young man. You're right. That is precisely what we do."

"And that's why you're here?" Omar enunciated each word carefully. "To represent me? Because you're saying I might get executed?"

"The situation is this, Omar. On Monday morning, you'll be formally charged with the murder of an on-duty deputy sheriff. This—"

"I didn't kill that deputy."

"Just let me explain, Omar. This case is a potential capital offense that has already captured a great deal of media and public attention. Now, even though the governor has placed a moratorium—" Ransom paused. "Do you know what that means? A moratorium?"

"Yeah," Omar said. "To stop doing something."

"Exactly, Omar. The governor has ordered all executions to be stopped. But the penalty will remain on the books, and I anticipate, with a crime of this magnitude, the district attorney may well decide to pursue a penalty of capital punishment. You need to mount a very vigorous defense. I'd like your permission to act as your legal representative. And as I said, neither you nor your family will need to worry about any legal expenses."

Capital case. Vigorous defense. His exhaustion made it difficult to sort through what was an impossible situation. How had it come to this? In a jail cell, talking to a lawyer about killing a cop? Maybe this Shaw guy would help, but Omar needed to make him understand.

"I got no problem with you being my lawyer, at least for now, I guess. But, like I said, I didn't kill anyone. I graduate from high school next week. I'm joining the army. Maybe I should just talk to the police? Tell them I didn't do it? My family needs me. I need to go home."

"Omar, I'm sorry to tell you this, but you won't be going home anytime soon. As for talking with the police, I'd advise against that. At least for now."

"Why?" Omar didn't understand. "I haven't done anything. If I don't tell them what happened, how will I ever get out of here?"

"We will tell the truth, Omar, I promise. But first we have to see what evidence they have against you. Why they arrested you." Ransom took a breath. "Now, tell me. I'm sure they tried to question you, didn't they?"

"Yes. A detective named Murphy. I told him I didn't want to talk to him." Omar saw the man's face brighten. "I said I wanted to talk to a lawyer first."

"That's great, Omar. That was very smart. When you told him you wanted to speak to an attorney, what did he do?"

Omar thought back. "He showed me a picture."

"A picture of what?"

Omar's gaze dropped to the floor. "They got this picture of me. Said it came from the body camera of the deputy. The deputy who was killed."

He saw a shocked look register on the lawyer's face.

"When was this picture taken?"

Recounting the moment with Murphy caused a feeling of hopelessness that Omar could hear reflected in his words. "They said it was from right after he was shot. They said on the tape they can hear me saying I'm sorry."

"Did they tell you anything else?" Ransom spoke with less confidence than he had just a moment before.

"They said I shot a gun. They tested my hands."

"A residue test?"

"Yeah," Omar said. "That was it. A gunshot test."

Ransom stared at the table for several seconds. Omar didn't miss the look of deep concern on his face. "All right. We'll deal with all of that. Anything else? Anything at all you can think of that you said to the detective or he said to you?"

"He threatened my family."

"He what?"

"He said he would call immigration. Tell them to go after my mom."

Shaw was quick to move on. "You'll be arraigned in court on Monday morning. If you accept my offer of help, I will be right there with you. That's when we learn exactly what the charges are. I can tell you right now, there will be no opportunity for pretrial release, but I will make a case for it anyway. There will be a great deal of media present and I want them to hear what an outstanding young man you are.

"Now, listen to me, Omar." Ransom spoke slowly and deliberately. As he made each point, he firmly tapped one finger against the wooden desktop. "You talk to no one. Not the police. Not a detective. Not a nurse, doctor, or another inmate. You don't talk on the phone. You don't talk in your sleep. You talk only to me. Do you understand?"

Omar nodded. "Yeah, I got it."

Ransom leaned forward with his forearms flat on the table. "All right then, Omar. About that night. Start wherever you want and tell me what happened."

42

The automated directions coming from the GPS app on Molly's phone had led them to the coastal community of Solana Beach, where the temperature was twenty-five degrees cooler than their home in Temecula. An hour drive, Travis thought, but a world away.

Molly had reluctantly agreed to the day trip. She was always hesitant to show up at someone's house with four kids in tow unless she'd already warned the host and hostess personally. She had spent the first twenty minutes of the drive lecturing the two girls, Nicki and Hannah, about remembering to use *please* and *thank you*.

"Dad says there's a pool, Tyler. So keep a good eye on Brandon."

"You already told me, Mom. Like thirty times." Tyler was always the wiseguy, but at least this time his voice was playful. He sat way in the back, next to his little brother's car seat. Travis had thought the teen would resist the idea of a social call, but Tyler had actually put on a T-shirt without any holes, board shorts, and a clean pair of Vans. It felt like his recent conversation with his son had made a difference, giving them both a chance to reset their relationship.

They turned onto a wide street shaded by tall eucalyptus trees. A cool breeze that smelled of salt and sea kicked in as they pulled up to a single-story adobe set back from the road and surrounded on all sides by a deep green lawn. The tires of the minivan crunched over the pebbled shells of the long driveway.

"Oh, Travis," Molly said. "I think I'm going to hate this woman."

"You're right. I'm turning around. Kids, duck down."

Molly slapped him lightly on the arm as the massive wooden door opened and Ellie walked out onto the Spanish tile porch. She waved at the van and Molly smiled and waved back. "Yep. I hate her," she said quietly out of one corner of her mouth.

Travis parked behind a late model Lexus coupe. There was a sheriff staff car parked on the other side of the driveway. "Okay, guys, remember. Best behavior."

As the Jacksons climbed out of the van, Ellie walked over, carrying what looked to be a margarita. She wore shorts that showed off strong, tan legs. Her top was sleeveless and she was barefoot.

"Hi, Travis. Glad you guys could make it." Gone was the sarcastic, wise-cracking cop, replaced by smooth politeness. "Hello, Molly. It's great to meet you. I'm Ellie Peralta."

"You have a beautiful home, Ellie." Molly's voice was gracious and sincere. "Thanks so much for inviting us over."

"Thanks for coming," Ellie said, smiling at the children, who were looking around as though they'd just pulled up to Disneyland.

Looking at the red tile roof, adobe walls, and plants in bright painted pots, Travis thought the place looked like something out of one of those home and garden magazines Molly was always drooling over.

"Damn, Ellie." Travis took it all in. He could already see it was way more home than most cops could manage to afford, and they hadn't even been inside yet.

Ellie seemed almost embarrassed by her obvious good fortune. "Advantage of being a California native. Plenty of time to grow into the craziness of the real estate market. But I tell you, it's like playing craps. We got lucky on this place."

Just as Travis finished introducing the kids, the front door opened and a boy who looked to be about ten—and the spitting image of his father—came out. Ellie introduced her son, Jeffrey, and asked him to show Nicki and Hannah where they could change into their bathing suits. The girls skipped off, excited to have another kid to hang around with, even if they did have to settle for a boy.

Before the rest of the group could move toward the house, the door opened again and a teenage girl stepped out. Ellie glanced at her and said, "Hey, hon," before turning back to her guests.

"Everyone, this is our daughter, Rainey."

Rainey had her mother's dark skin and eyes but her father's tall, slender build. Her dark hair was pulled back in a braid that ran to the small of her back. Travis guessed she was probably fifteen or sixteen years old. He snuck a look at his own teenager, who looked like a cartoon character, his mouth practically hanging open and his eyes bugging out.

"Hey, you." Rainey's faced brightened as she walked toward the Jacksons. "Oh, Mom, he's so cute." She dropped to one knee and stretched out her arms toward a smiling Brandon, who was hiding behind his big brother's leg.

Tyler smiled at his dad and waggled his eyebrows. Travis couldn't remember the last time he'd seen a happier expression on the face of his sullen teenage son.

"Who's this little guy?" Rainey asked, tilting her head up.

"Who? Me?" Tyler pointed at himself. It took all of Travis's willpower not to laugh out loud. Recovering quickly, Tyler said, "Oh, you mean him? Uh, Brandon."

Rainey laughed. "Okay, and what about you?"

Travis was glad to see his son was able to laugh at himself and get his act together.

"Tyler. Nice to meet you."

Rainey offered to show the boys the path down to the beach, and Tyler promised his mom he'd keep a close eye on Brandon. Ellie took Molly lightly by the arm, leading her into the home. Travis followed. Inside, Commander Peralta insisted everyone call him Rob. He led Molly onto the back patio, where Travis could hear his girls already splashing in the pool. Through the window, Travis could see the house was situated on a high bluff overlooking the Pacific Ocean.

Ellie turned to him with a serious expression. "I wasn't sure you'd show. You doing okay?"

"Sure," Travis said, trying for nonchalant. He and Ellie hadn't spoken since his meltdown in the field. But this was only last night, after which they went their separate ways. So it sounds strange for him to have gone out of his way to avoid her. "It's all good."

"I saw the door closed," Ellie said. "You and Peña in the office. You were in there awhile."

She wasn't going to let it go.

"Yeah. He heard GSU go out on seven and then go ten eight with nothing. I figured it was on me to tell him why."

"How'd he take it?" Ellie sipped her margarita.

"Fine." He shrugged. "It's all in how you tell it."

Ellie cocked her head. "Not sure how you sell that one, Travis."

"Hey, the boy was told to sit on his hands and keep his mouth shut. He didn't do either."

"And that's why—"

"Furtive movement, Ellie."

She laughed out loud and he heard her familiar cynicism reemerge. "You're gonna go with that, huh? Anybody get video? Body cam, I mean."

"None. And, yeah. I'm gonna go with that."

"So, no formal complaint yet? Kid looked pretty young. Must have some parents out there."

"Sean did some checking for me. Dad's locked up for murder in Pelican Bay, eligible for parole in about eight years. Mom's a frequent flyer but currently out of custody. We haven't heard anything from her. Not yet, at least. But hey, I think I'll be okay. No pics. My word against his. And you know, it all comes down to what was in my head."

"Wow," Ellie said. "This is like a whole new side of you, hayseed."

"Look, Ellie, I'm not proud of it. I screwed up. But believe me, I already got my ass chewed—by Matthews, the Oceanside cop, and by Murphy, if you can believe that. But he dusted the kid off, sweet-talked him a bit. So, if I can ride it out, that's what I'm going to do. If it turns into something formal, I'm not asking anyone to lie for me. If you get called in, just say what you saw."

She took a longer drink, looking over the top of the glass. She swallowed in a way that told him she liked her margaritas with a kick. "I'm glad to hear you're not proud of it. And you'd better hope they don't call me in."

Travis got the message. He'd been out of line, and she wouldn't lie for him. He wasn't going to judge her for it. They'd already talked about it more than he wanted to. He nodded toward the glass in her hand. "Fair enough. Now, can I get one of those?"

Two people Travis didn't know walked in from the patio. Ellie smiled and motioned them over with her hand.

"I thought you said it was canceled," Travis said in a low voice. "The party, I mean."

"Relax," Ellie said, as the couple approached. "Just friends. Cop family."

"Hey, guys." Again the hostess, Ellie said, "This is Travis Jackson. We work together. Travis, Jim and Carol Hillman. Jim's a sergeant for SDPD."

"Nice to meet you, Sarge," Travis said, shaking hands, immediately at ease with another cop.

"Jim," he said. "Likewise, Travis. Sorry about your friend. Ellie tells me you two were first on scene."

Travis nodded. "Yeah. We were. It's was tough, but thanks. Teddy was a great guy."

"Carol and I used to teach together," Ellie said. "A lifetime ago. She still teaches at James Madison High in Vista."

Travis nodded. "Nice to meet you, Carol."

Ellie looked directly at Travis. "Carol just told me that Omar Ortega was in her Latin American History class."

An awkward silence fell over the group and hung there until Travis finally broke it. "Really? History, huh?"

"Yes," Carol said. "I've known Omar since he was a freshman. One of the brightest students I've ever had. He's our . . . well, he *was* our valedictorian."

"Yeah, I saw the letter." Travis looked at Ellie, sure he'd been set up. "Hard to figure. What went wrong, I mean."

"Yes, it is," Carol said. "I just can't understand how—"

"Travis," Molly called from the sliding glass door that led outside. "You've got to see this view."

Travis smiled at the Hillmans. "Excuse me. I'd better go. Nice meeting you."

Walking away, Travis saw the pained look on Carol's face, but the last thing in the world he wanted to talk about today was Omar Ortega.

They stayed at the house most of the afternoon. Travis had a couple of drinks before switching to ice water, thinking about the long drive home. He told one or two stories about Ted from their training days, making

Jim and Rob laugh. Mostly, the men wanted to hear about working in a small department in the Midwest. After listening to a few of his stories, They wondered out loud why he'd left. He didn't tell them he sometimes wondered the same thing.

The sun was beginning to set over the ocean. Travis sat alone in a teak-wood lawn chair, taking in the view. He couldn't help but think the Peral-tas had probably spent more on their outdoor patio than he and Molly had in furnishing their entire home.

His daughters and the Peraltas' son, Jeffrey, were playing some kind of video game. Tyler and Rainey, back from a walk on the beach, were talking on the couch, with Brandon between them. Molly and Ellie had made themselves comfortable at the kitchen table, chatting like they were sisters. Travis figured he was about as content as a man could be nearly two days after his fellow deputy and friend was shot to death.

"Beautiful place, isn't it?" Carol Hillman said, taking a seat in the empty chair next to his.

"Sure is. When people back home think about living in California, this is what they imagine."

She nodded. "And to think, when I met Rob and Ellie, they were living in a little studio apartment in Ocean Beach. I had walked over to ask them to please keep it down. Italians are noisy people. Especially when . . . well, you know."

Travis laughed. "Really? How long ago was that?"

"Let's see. I was still single. They were newlyweds. So about sixteen years, give or take."

Travis went back to looking at the ocean. Carol kept talking. "I just don't think I could do your job, Travis."

He knew right away it was a preamble, and he hoped to steer the conver-sation in a different direction. "Likewise. I mean, all day with a classroom full of teenagers? That's got to be tough."

"It can be, but I like it because every once in a while one comes along who makes it all worth it."

She wasn't going to let it go. Might as well get it over with.

"Let me guess. Ones like Ortega."

"Why do you say it like that?" She sat up straighter, and her voice stayed friendly even though she mocked him. "Ones like Ortega."

"Look, it's obvious you really care about him. I get it. But if there is one thing I've learned as a cop? Sometimes you just don't know someone as well as you thought you did. I know it's hard for you to believe he did this."

"You're right. I do care about him." She looked straight at him and he held her gaze. "And I do know him. I know him very well and I know he certainly didn't kill a deputy sheriff."

Travis didn't want to argue with her, but he did think she needed to take the blinders off. See the truth.

"Have you seen the news coverage about the evidence? The picture of Ortega taken by the body cam? The gun residue found on his hand?"

"Yes, and so what? Has anyone asked him what happened? Let him explain it?"

"He's clammed up. Decided to do the whole *remain silent* thing. Let his lawyer do the talking."

"Well, I'm glad to hear that, at least," she said.

Now she was getting under his skin. "You sure don't talk like a cop's wife."

"How should I talk?" Her voice grew more serious. "I'm telling you, I've known Omar Ortega since he was thirteen years old. He didn't kill anyone."

Travis didn't respond. He'd run through what little sympathy he had, and now he was getting annoyed, but this woman just wouldn't let it go.

"Do you know what Omar was going to do after graduation?" Travis shook his head. "He was going to join the army. He'd already signed up. Our principal has been trying to talk him out of it for months. Wanted him to apply for college scholarships, but Omar was determined. You know why?"

"No idea, Carol." He really wished she'd pick up on the cues that he was done talking about it. He shrugged his shoulders and did his best to sound flippant. "To see the world?"

"Perhaps," she said, like she knew she was being taken lightly. "But mainly so he could take care of his family. He was moving them to San Marcos with money he'd saved. He was going to use his army pay to help his mom with the rent."

"Impressive. It really is," Travis said flatly, not hiding the fact that he didn't mean a word.

"The papers were all signed. He was ready to leave. He was so excited, but he told me I couldn't tell anyone about the move. He didn't want any problems from the kids in the neighborhood. The 'homies.'"

"Yep," he said, still doing his best to leave no illusion about how he felt about her star pupil. "That's how they talk. *Homie* this, *homie* that. I met him the afternoon Ted was killed, hanging out with a bunch of gangster buddies behind a liquor store. We recovered a gun out of a dumpster right next to where he was standing."

She looked offended. "It sounds like your mind is pretty much made up. I mean, why bother with a trial?"

"Because they make us go through the motions." Travis stood. The gloves came off. "He'll get his day in court, Carol. He'll get a chance to tell everybody why he killed a man who had a family, a wife and two little girls. I'm sure he had his reasons—I mean, being the great kid he is and all."

Carol put a hand to her mouth and looked as if she might cry. Too bad. A cop's wife? Pushing buttons like that? She sure as hell should know better. He got to his feet and turned toward the house, to see Molly, Ellie, Rob, and Jim all staring back.

"Time to get going," Travis said, looking at his wife. Molly spoke quickly to Ellie, then gave her a hug. The kids gathered at the door, carrying wet bathing suits wrapped in towels. Tyler picked up Brandon and said an awkward good-bye to Rainey.

Travis opened the tall mahogany door and let the kids file out. He and Molly hung back to say good-bye to their hosts.

"Thanks, Ellie. And thank you, Commander. We had a great time, but we need to be going."

"See you tomorrow at the courthouse," Ellie said. "I'm sorry if—"

Travis put up a hand. "No. Really. Let's not. See you in the morning." Beyond Ellie, he saw Carol's husband sitting down next to his crying wife.

The hour ride home was quiet.

43

The voices drifted into his cell, loud and profane. Conversations that had the sort of back-and-forth rhythm Omar had spent the last two years trying to avoid. The kind of talk he identified as friendly for the moment but that could go hostile with a single word. He sat on his bunk, elbows on his knees, staring at the open door, remembering what his attorney had told him about keeping quiet.

He'd spent an hour with Ransom Shaw before the guard escorted him back to his cell. The solid metal door slammed shut behind him and he heard the bolt engage. He was locked in and that was fine with him, because that meant everyone else was locked out. But at exactly 7:30 A.M., the cell door—like the doors of all the other cells on the block—opened automatically. Omar heard men begin to congregate in the large, square room. The voices of guards could be heard, announcing breakfast and showers in thirty minutes. Omar didn't so much as take a peek.

Sounds of card playing, checkers, and dice rattling in a cup began to mix with the voices. The television came on and he heard the familiar theme song to the show *Cops*. None of it interested him. He wanted nothing to do with the social side of jail life.

"Yo, Seso, what up? I heard you'd be coming in."

Omar looked up to see Miguel Fuentes sauntering into the cell, wearing a navy blue jumpsuit identical to the one Omar had been given the night before.

"Hey, Migs." Omar felt a mix of relief and apprehension at seeing his old childhood friend. "What're you doing here?"

"Shit, man." Miguel helped himself to a seat on the bunk. "You know what's up. I got rolled up for that tagging bullshit. Plus assault on a deputy. Then I get here, find out they put everybody through an X-ray machine. Chunks and his bullshit ideas. I'm looking at a couple felonies, plus all that gang enhancement nonsense they always be tacking on. I'm fucked, homes." Migs stopped himself up short, as if he'd just remembered who he was talking to.

"Well, not like you or nothing. I mean, damn, Seso. What the hell?"

Shaw's voice echoed in his head. *You talk to no one.* When he said nothing, Miguel threw up his hands. "Come on, tell me. How you get all wrapped up in that shit?"

He wasn't going to be able to just play stupid. That wasn't going to work. But he had to be very careful.

"I got a lawyer. He's going to handle everything."

"Yeah, right." Miguel laughed and leaned into him with his shoulder, friendly like. "Sure he is. I got me some public defender. Already talking about how he can get me five to seven. Like I'm supposed to be good with that? But he says if I go to trial, I'll get twice as long. Kinda hard to beat a possession rap when they pull the shit out your ass."

Omar changed the subject. "So what goes on? They just leave the doors open?"

Miguel stood. "It's the dayroom. Come on, I'll show you what's up."

"Nah, I'm good here."

"No, you ain't," Miguel said. "You sit in here all the time, homies gonna be thinking you be some kinda bitch. A little punk ass. Besides, man. You best check in."

"Check in?"

Miguel leaned over, keeping his voice low. "Look, Seso. You gotta go along if you wanna get along, all right? We all do, but it's good, man. No street drama. Nothin' but a bunch of homies up in here, and we got each other's backs. But you gotta listen and you got to know your place. So come on. You need to pay your respects and shit."

"Nah." Omar leaned back against the wall, crossing his arms on his chest. "Like I said, I'm good."

"Motherfucker, you be thinking this shit is optional?" Miguel turned all hostile. In the real world, Omar would walk away and not think twice about a threat from a guy like Miguel. He liked to play hard, but he and Omar had some good history beyond the gangster bullshit. But in here, Omar could already see, things were going to be different. He didn't have a choice.

As if to drive the point home even further, Miguel grabbed him by the arm. "Get your ass up."

Omar let Migs drag him to his feet without much resistance. "All right, Migs, but seriously, I just want to lay low until I figure out what's going on. I got court tomorrow morning."

"Shit, Seso. Court ain't gonna matter. You smoked a dep, homie. You in the game now. You might as well jump in. Come on."

Out in the dayroom, every table had at least three or four occupants, most of them eating out of a clamshell Styrofoam box. Sure enough, every man in the room was Latino. Every head turned his way as Miguel walked him out and began to fill him in.

"We be in Upper West, which is what they call high control. This is C-mod. The brothers be in B-mod. The white boys is in D, at least the badass ones. The paisas and white boys who ain't players, they be in A-mod. Then they got the jotos and desviados, off on their own somewhere."

There was a tall metal bread rack that held a few more clamshells, but it was close to empty. Omar didn't care. He couldn't remember when he ate last but he wasn't a bit hungry. Murmured voices saying "Cop killer" and "The dead dep on TV" followed him across the open floor. Some of the stares carried respect, but in most of the hard looks, Omar knew he was already being sized up. They were testing him even as he walked by.

"From seven thirty to four is dayroom," Miguel explained. "As long as nobody fucks up, we can hang. Play cards, watch TV, kick it in our cells. But anybody throws down or talks smack to a guard? They'll lock us down for twenty-four hours a day. I mean, like, they be sliding food under the door. And it be nasty shit. Gets old quick." He looked back over his shoulder. "But I know you, man. No worries, right?"

Miguel didn't wait for an answer. He held his hand up to signal they had arrived. "All right, Seso. Remember. Be cool."

They stood in the open doorway of another cell. Migs posted up and said, "Yo, Psycho. Here he is."

Omar had only met Luis Valdez on two prior occasions. Valdez had been with Chunks the day Omar had been brought in to decipher the finer points of the gang injunction. The very next day, Valdez had hit him up on the street, asking Omar where he was from and who he claimed. He had checked Omar hard with a chest bump and Omar reminded him they'd met the day before. That Chunks had already given Omar a pass. Valdez had stared back, his dry, cracked lips finally breaking out in the demented smile that had earned him his name. "I just be fucking with you, homes."

It was later that same day that Valdez pulled the armed robbery. When Omar saw him on TV, getting dragged off by the deps, Psycho had that same crazed grin plastered on his face.

Now, Psycho Valdez sat on the bottom bunk with his back against the wall. Two men Omar didn't know sat on the top bunk, their legs hanging over the side. They both looked to be in their thirties, their thick arms tatted out in green ink. Both of them were leaning forward, with their hands flat on the bunk as if ready to jump. Considering the way they were staring at him, Omar knew just where they'd land.

"What up, Seso?" Psycho looked him up and down, his eyes practically buzzing in their sockets. Once again, Omar figured the street name was well earned. "Welcome to Sureños High Control, killer. You settled in?"

"Hey man," Omar said, trying for cool. "Yeah, I guess. They got me in a cell."

"Well, no shit they got you in a cell, boy," Valdez said. "You gonna be in a cell for the rest of your fuckin' days." Valdez looked at Omar's foot, then tapped his head in the same spot where Omar had staples in his scalp. "Let me guess. You got all that jumping out the car?"

The words were like a vise closing tight around Omar's throat.

Valdez pulled out a phone that had been tucked under the mattress and held it up where Omar could see. "Straight up, word from the man. Your ass be stupid enough to be bailing out like that? Then you get to carry this shit. You hear what I'm sayin', homes?"

Omar didn't answer, but he was pretty sure Valdez could see his pulse beating in his neck. He tried to calm down.

"Right now, you probably thinking that order comes from that fat bastard we all know, but it ain't like that. He be out the picture now. Feel me on this, Ortega. This shit comes from way up top, ese."

"Look, man," Omar said. "I'm just—"

"Look, my ass," Valdez said. "Here's how it is. You gonna do the time for the killing. It ain't complicated, homie. You start talkin' and your family starts payin', and that ain't no bullshit."

Valdez stood up and got in Omar's face. "Any part of that you don't understand?"

Again with the threats from an Eastsider, and just like before, Omar was badly outnumbered and powerless to act. Standing here, right now, could he take Valdez? Oh, hell yeah. On one good foot. He might even put some pretty good knocks on the thugs who would be coming down from the top bunk. But then what? Omar barely recognized his own voice.

"I hear ya."

"So I can let the man know you got the message, right? We good?"

Omar nodded, mute.

Valdez clapped his hands hard over both of Omar's shoulders. "Look at it this way, Seso. You and me, we both gonna be doing a lot of time. But no worries. I'm gonna take care of you. I mean, you're my homeboy."

"I got it all worked out for ya. Toon here? He's gonna be your cellie. He's got your back. You won't have any problems from nobody. I mean, damn, ese. You put down a dep. Your shit be tight for life, homes."

Psycho went back to his bunk and stretched out. "Now go on and get yourself some breakfast. Eat the eggs, but stay away from that nasty gray shit. It'll clog you like a motherfucker."

"Come on." Miguel pulled Omar away by the arm. They walked into the dayroom, Omar trying desperately to kick his brain into gear. Take the rap for a murder? A cop killing? How could he defend himself and still protect his family? There were always solutions; he just needed to think it through. Roadblock, go around. Locked door, kick it in.

In the background, *Cops* had given way to a local Sunday morning news broadcast, and despite the haze in his mind, Omar heard his own name. Looking at the screen, he saw the familiar face of that reporter. Joaquin something. The one Ransom had talked about. The reporter was standing in Brengle Terrace Park, where Omar had spent many a Sunday kicking a soccer ball with Sofia and Hector. The banner across the bottom of the screen read "Immigration Protest in Vista."

A crowd was gathered behind the reporter, many holding signs with his name. Others had the word ICE, circled, with a line through it. As he listened to the Spanish broadcast, blood rushed to his head and he wavered, unsteady on his feet. His body swayed and he sat on the bench of an empty table, listening closely as the reporter went on.

44

Joaquin counted only three Mexican flags being displayed by protesters at one end of the courthouse steps, versus seven American flags at the other, but the pro-Ortega crowd was definitely larger. Then again, most of them were younger folks, Facebook and Twitter having really driven the turnout. The arraignment of Omar Ortega was scheduled to begin 8:00 A.M., and most of the media outlets had already moved inside to take up positions in the courtroom. But even with no cameras to play to, both sides kept going at it. Still, he thought, it's nothing like yesterday.

The demonstrations had started up in earnest Sunday morning, the day after Univision aired Sheriff Collier's interview and reported on the arrest of Isadora Ortega. Minutes after the broadcast, the North County Immigration Task Force began to mobilize. Known throughout the region for their hard-line stance against ICE and federal immigration policies, the community activists called for a Sunday morning protest at Brengle Terrace Park. Within an hour of the rally being announced on social media, hundreds of people from throughout San Diego County converged on the park. Organizers led a march through the streets of Vista to the sheriff's substation three miles away.

Joaquin and Mannie had broadcast live from the park during Univision's Sunday morning show. The crowd was surprisingly diverse in ethnicity, age, and apparent income, and Joaquin conducted a number of live interviews in both Spanish and English. The arrest of Isadora Ortega had definitely touched a nerve with a cross section of the population, and the sheriff's tough guy approach hadn't gone over with everyone.

Reporter and cameraman followed the march through the streets, and by the time the demonstrators arrived at the station, the crowd had doubled in size. They were met by a full contingent of deputies and officers from allied agencies, all in riot gear. Joaquin liked to think the restraint demonstrated by the deputies was due to their professionalism and department leadership, but he was pretty certain the dozen news crews, from every media outlet in San Diego, might have had something to do with it.

Today's demonstrations at the courthouse were much smaller—not surprising, since, for most people, Monday morning meant time to go back to work. Still, there was a good turnout, especially of people Omar's age. Joaquin's phone buzzed in his pocket with a text message from Mannie. Time to get inside.

"Looks like you got your wish," Anna Ramirez said, walking toward him.

"How's that, Anna?" Joaquin asked, already knowing where she was going.

"All this," she said, gesturing at the crowd. "It's like a media wet dream. Where's Mannie? Don't you want some film for tonight at five? Or are you guys going live?"

"He's inside, setting up for the arraignment. I was just heading in myself." Not looking for an argument, Joaquin turned away, but Anna wasn't finished.

"You know, I didn't think the sheriff could get any more pissed at you, but by god, you got it done."

"What do you mean?"

"Oh, come on, Joaquin. Don't be coy. You sandbagged him with that ICE angle. Well played. Got the whole county whipped into a frenzy."

"Are you saying the sheriff's department didn't coordinate with ICE to arrest Mrs. Ortega?" After a beat, Joaquin decided to take it a step further. "You're okay with it?"

Joaquin knew that Anna had been born in Mesa, Arizona. He also knew, from off-the-record conversations, how she spent the first ten years of her life living in the shadows with her parents, who were both undocumented. It wasn't until Reagan's immigration reform of the 1980s that she and her family began to enjoy all the rewards of life in the United States.

"Off the record?" she said.

"Sure," Joaquin replied.

"It's a big department, Joaquin, and tempers are running pretty hot right now. The call to ICE probably did come from inside, but it could've been anyone. Sheriff Collier did not authorize it."

Anna paused and her expression softened. "But to be honest, I'm glad it's out there."

"Really? And why is that?"

"Going after mom? That was classless. People should know about it."

"Fair enough," Joaquin said, hearing the honesty in her voice. "I need to get inside. Since I missed your perp walk, if I blow it again, I'll be back to chasing ambulances for sure."

He headed for the courthouse and saw a familiar couple walking up the steps. He hurried to catch up.

45

Trawling the courthouse lot, Travis beat out a stringy-haired, twenty-something tweaker chick in a primer-covered Vega for a shady spot close to the main entrance. The bitch flipped him off and he was quick to return the favor, throwing in a two-word lesson in lipreading. Dressed in a coat and tie, with his SIG Sauer 9 millimeter concealed on his belt, he wasn't technically on duty until he got his subpoena time-stamped. He figured he might as well enjoy his freedom of expression.

He had gotten his first full night of sleep in a week, aided by a few late-night beers. After getting the kids settled down, he and Molly sat on the back patio of their house, a slab of cement that overlooked the slab of cement patio of an identical house. They'd held hands and sipped Leinenkugel's, neither of them saying much.

She didn't bring up the end of the afternoon at the Peraltas'. In fact, she didn't mention the visit at all. He was sure Molly would love a pool with a vanishing edge and an ocean view, not to mention a Lexus, but he was also pretty sure she loved him more than all those things. They went to bed and he'd held her close all night and slept soundly.

"Hayseed. Wait up." Ellie Peralta was quickstepping her way through the parking lot, wearing a knee-length navy blue dress and black heels. She wore her hair up, same as at work. She carried a small purse, and he didn't doubt it was deadly. They were both off that day, but Dannie Gaines had subpoenaed them to appear, a highly unusual move.

The arraignment would be simple. Ortega would be informed of the charges against him and allowed to enter a plea. Not guilty, no doubt; nobody's guilty. There'd be the legally required but totally symbolic discussion of bail. Considering the charges, a pretrial release was out of the question. A date would be set for the preliminary hearing. No witness testimony would be presented by either side. Yet Dannie wanted both Ellie and Travis on hand as the first deputies to have arrived on scene.

"I'm glad I caught you," Ellie said, a little out of breath. "Sorry about yesterday. The thing with Carol, I mean."

Travis stared back and let her talk.

"She called last night. She felt awful. Said she ambushed you. I've never heard her like that. So distraught, I mean. She wanted me to tell you she's sorry."

"What about you?"

Ellie cocked her head. "What about me, what?"

"Carol says *she* ambushed me?" Travis said. "Felt like she had some help. Kind of like a tag team."

"Are you serious? I invited you over so we could *not* talk about it. I had no idea Carol had this kid as a student. I didn't have anything to do with her hitting you up. And I'm not sure why you think I did."

"Fine." Travis felt a slow burn smoldering right up close to the surface. Was it Ellie? Carol? The girl in the Vega? Maybe all of them. Or maybe it was just his friend was dead and a part of him felt responsible. It was all that shit.

"Let's go," Travis said, turning to the courthouse.

"Hey." He felt her hand on his arm. "You doing okay? I know this is all completely nuts, but I mean in your head. You all right?"

"Let's just get inside."

The steps of the courthouse were covered with dual protests that looked like a couple of nonmatching bookends, separated by a skirmish line of uniformed deputies. On one end of the steps were a few dozen people holding signs supporting the police, many waving American flags. Several held up pictures of Ted.

The other group was larger, younger, and a hell of a lot rowdier. Some

of their signs slammed the sheriff's office, but ICE was the favorite target. One man had a bullhorn and was leading chants. As he and Ellie approached, Travis told himself that if the guy broke into the "No justice, no
peace" mantra, he was going to have to walk over and punch the son of a
bitch in the face.

"Can you believe these dumbasses?" Travis said, not really caring if
anyone heard him. He gestured toward people who waved Mexican flags—
and other flags that he didn't recognize but was pretty damn sure came
from somewhere south of the border. "Like flying a foreign flag is going to
get you any sympathy."

He and Ellie badged their way through the turnstile, had their subpoenas stamped by the clerk, and headed for the courtroom. They were halfway down the long corridor when Travis heard someone call his name. He
turned and saw the reporter, Fonseca, cutting through the crowd toward
him. Ellie stopped too. As he got closer, the man slowed to a walk, took a
deep breath, and produced a nervous smile. He stood in front of them, still
panting a bit, and his first words were labored.

"Sorry to bother you, Deputy, but I was hoping to talk to you for a moment." He turned his head to Ellie. "Both of you, actually."

The slow burn torched up about a hundred degrees. He and Molly had
watched some of the coverage of the demonstrations at the substation,
which had been instigated by Fonseca's bullshit reporting. "I'm pretty sure
we've got nothing to talk about. You want an interview, go find the PIO."

Fonseca put his hands in front of him, showing they were empty. "No
cameras. No microphones. Strictly off the record."

Travis glanced at Ellie, who gave him a shrug of indifference.

"What is it?" Travis said.

"I want to apologize for what my station aired," Joaquin said. "Of both
of you with your comrade. It was inexcusable."

"Really?" Travis smirked. "It's made you into quite a celebrity. Isn't that
what you media guys are about these days? Star power and all that sort of
thing?"

"I know that's probably how you see it, and I don't blame you. But just
so you know, I believe it was wrong to air it."

"All right," Travis said. "You got to say your piece. Can we go now?" He
turned away, not waiting for an answer.

"There is one other thing, Deputy Jackson," the reporter said quietly.

"There always is," Travis said with an ill-concealed sigh.

"I haven't reported this on the air, but I have it on good authority that two ex-cons went to Omar Ortega's house the night Deputy Rosado was killed. Just hours before, in fact. One was a man I'm sure you're familiar with, Alonzo Gutierrez. They call him Chunks."

Impatient, Travis said, "We know who he is."

"The other man was called E-Boy. They wanted money, and when Omar tried to talk his way out of it, they threatened his sister and little brother." Fonseca's voice was emotional but controlled. "They all but forced him to leave with them."

Ellie asked, "Has your source told this to the detectives?"

Fonseca looked up and down the hallway and lowered his voice. "My source is the kids. No one from your department has talked to them, but I'm not sure they would tell you anything. They're both scared to death, and now that their mother has been arrested, they're on their own."

A muscle jumped in Ellie's jaw and Travis knew the man was getting to her. He took over. "Look, Fonseca. I'll tell the detectives what you had to say. But the kids are going to have to talk to the investigators. You don't get to play go-between. Like I said, I know this is all about airtime for you, but—"

Fonseca paused, blowing out a deep breath. "It's Travis, isn't it?"

"I'm partial to Deputy Jackson."

"Fine." Fonseca nodded. "*Deputy* Jackson, you can think whatever you want about me. You can blame the media all you want for what's going on outside. But know this: you've got the wrong guy behind bars. I've talked to his family. I've talked to his teachers, his principal. And I know what happened in their apartment that night. This kid didn't kill your friend."

"We've got a picture and gunshot residue test that says otherwise," Travis said, with no hint of uncertainty. "But I don't doubt some other gangsters were involved. Best your boy is going to do? Start talking and cut himself a deal. He better hurry up, though. Last thing he wants is for this case to get in front of a Vista jury."

Ellie said, "We're going to be late for court, sir. Thanks for the info. We'll pass it along."

They headed for the courtroom, leaving the reporter behind.

"I talked with Dannie," Ellie said. "The schedule has been arranged so that the Ortega arraignment will come up first. Everything else is on hold until we're finished."

"Good. The quicker the better. Maybe this could still feel like a day off at some point."

Travis pulled the door open. They stepped inside, and then stopped.

"Oh my god," Ellie said.

46

Every seat was occupied by a deputy sheriff dressed in tan and green with a black-banded badge. In the front row, immediately behind the railing separating the spectators from the well of the courtroom, Sheriff Collier sat in his full dress greens, next to a young woman wearing a dark dress, her hands knotted nervously in her lap—Ted's widow, Travis assumed. The assistant sheriff was also in the front row, along with the rest of the command staff, including Commander Peralta, all in full dress uniform. Deputies, detectives, and cops from agencies throughout the county took up all the standing room.

Dannie Gaines waived Travis and Ellie forward, holding the swinging gate open for them. Detective Murphy, dressed in courtroom attire, sat at the prosecution table. He'd even shaved. As case agent and lead investigator, he was a formal member of the prosecution team.

Working their way through the crowd, the new arrivals were directed to two chairs set back a bit from the prosecutor's desk. The jury box had been surrendered to the media, and it looked as though most stations from San Diego and Los Angeles had dispatched a camera crew. Travis saw Joaquin Fonseca slip in and join his colleagues. Every lens was already trained on the Plexiglas cage, which currently stood empty.

A tall man with close-cropped hair emerged from the doorway that led to the area where prisoners were held and walked over to Dannie Gaines. He wore a well-tailored suit that, in this environment, marked him as a lawyer. The two shook hands and stepped away from the onlookers before beginning what looked like a spirited exchange, leading Travis to conclude that he was the defense attorney.

"All rise," the bailiff called out. The judge entered from a door behind the raised bench. The bailiff went on, "This court is now in session, the Honorable Judge Michael Washington presiding."

"Take your seats." Judge Washington was all business. "Clerk, call the first case."

"The People of the State of California versus Omar Ortega, Case 20-A44391, murder in the first degree with special circumstances, to wit: murder of an on-duty peace officer engaged in the lawful performance of their duty."

Dannie Gaines returned to the prosecution table, shooting Travis and Ellie an excited look before turning to the judge.

The tall man in the suit spoke first. "Ransom Shaw for Mr. Ortega. We're ready to proceed, Your Honor."

"Danielle Gaines for the people. We're ready."

Judge Washington scanned the audience as every media camera turned his way. Looking directly at the grieving woman seated in the front row, he said, "Before we go any further, I would first like to extend my professional, personal, and deepest condolences to Mrs. Rosado. And to every member of the San Diego County Sheriff's Department and all men and women in the law enforcement community. You have suffered a terrible loss."

His voice grew less personal as he continued, "With that said, today begins what will no doubt be a very emotional and difficult legal proceeding. I expect order to be maintained within the courtroom. Members of the media will follow the guidelines that I know have been distributed."

Judge Washington scanned the crowd a final time and took a deep breath. "Bailiff, please bring in the accused."

All the cameras and every head swung to study the doorway behind the Plexiglas enclosure. A sense of anticipation filled the room. As if for dramatic effect, the first indication that someone was approaching was the sound of rattling chains.

A boy appeared in the doorway and stopped. At first, Travis didn't recognize him. Dressed in a baggy blue jumpsuit, he looked smaller than before. His dark eyes darted over the crowd. Scanning. Searching. Travis figured he was looking for some sign of support, a familiar face. When he found none, his head dropped and he stared at the ground. Two guards pushed him along. Beside Travis, Ellie sighed, and without thinking, he reached over and squeezed her hand.

Ortega's hands were shackled in front of him and attached to a leather belt around his waist. He limped into the enclosure. Ortega's lawyer took a position between him and the audience, as if to shield his client from the hostile stares of a hundred cops.

Judge Washington read the charges into the record. When the moment arrived for the submission of a plea, the judge spoke directly to the defendant.

"Mr. Ortega, you've heard the charges against you. How do you plead?"

"I didn't kill anyone." Travis was impressed that, even under these circumstances, the boy was able to put some confidence in his response.

An angry murmur rolled through the crowd of cops, stopping the moment Judge Washington looked their way. He turned to the defense counsel. "Mr. Shaw, would you please instruct your client to enter a plea."

Ransom stepped closer to the Plexiglas box, and Ortega shifted to put an ear up to the opening. After listening briefly to his attorney, he spoke again.

"I'm not guilty." The lawyer looked at his client, and Ortega said, "Not guilty, *Your Honor.*" This time Travis heard a hint of anger, or maybe resentment, in the boy's voice.

The judge was stoic. "The record will reflect a plea of 'Not guilty.' Let me hear from both parties on the issue of bail."

Dannie stood. "If it please the court, Your Honor."

Washington nodded and said, "Ms. Gaines."

"Your Honor, the victim in this case is San Diego Deputy Sheriff Theodore Jacob Rosado, a thirty-four-year-old man who leaves behind a wife of eight years and twin girls who are not yet four years old."

Moving out from behind the prosecution table, Dannie walked toward the holding pen. "Mr. Rosado grew up right here in North County, San Diego. After high school, he enlisted in the marines and did three combat tours in Afghanistan. He was a decorated veteran and the recipient of the

Navy Achievement Medal with a Combat V. He was a nine-year veteran of the San Diego County Sheriff's Department. He was active in his home community of Murrieta, where he coached youth sports."

Staring through the clear Plexiglas, the ADA spoke as if she were talking only to the person directly in front of her, though her words rang through the otherwise silent courtroom. "Two days ago, while on duty as a deputy sheriff, serving the people of San Diego County, Theodore Rosado, Teddy to his friends, was gunned down. Though he was shot several times in the chest, he likely would have survived those injuries because of his bullet-resistant vest. But Deputy Rosado was also shot in the throat. He bled to death on the road. Compelling photographic and scientific evidence has identified the defendant as the person responsible for the murder of Deputy Rosado."

Travis heard the muffled cry of Mrs. Rosado and he had to wonder, was Dannie that calculating? Was it all somehow part of the plan? He listened as she went on.

"Your Honor, the district attorney is well aware of the reluctance many prosecutors may feel in seeking the death penalty against an accused who is just eighteen years of age. The reason I was chosen to prosecute this case is because I suffer from no such reluctance."

Dannie moved closer, until she was practically speaking into the cutout in the side of the holding pen. She stared straight into the eyes of Omar Ortega. "Upon conviction, the district attorney's office will be seeking the only punishment that is commensurate with this heinous and brutal crime: a penalty of death by lethal injection."

"*You go, Dannie.*"

The low whisper came from somewhere in the audience of cops.

"Who said that?" the judge snapped.

He actually seemed to be waiting for someone to raise their hand. Travis could only assume the man was not up on the code of silence. After a moment, he said, "Fine. Bailiff. Face the seating area."

The bailiff turned and Judge Washington went on, "I want you to watch very closely. I will not have these proceedings disrespected in that manner. Any further outbursts and I will have the offending party charged with contempt and I will clear this courtroom. Am I making myself clear?"

Travis figured even this group of hardened and currently very pissed off members of law enforcement would now be on their best behavior.

Dannie returned to her position at the prosecution table and continued her argument. "Based on these facts, Your Honor, the people believe bail is out of the question. We respectfully request that the defendant be remanded in custody and that bail be denied."

"Mr. Shaw," Judge Washington said. The lawyer remained seated, leaning back in his chair, looking at the room's high ceiling. Several seconds passed before the judge spoke again.

"Mr. Shaw, please let me hear your argument for bail."

"I'm sorry, Your Honor. That was all a bit overwhelming." Getting to his feet, Shaw faced Mrs. Rosado. His voice sincere, he said, "Deputy Rosado was clearly an incredible man and his loss is indeed tragic.

"Your Honor, if it please the court," the attorney said, moving closer to the holding pen and facing the judge, "I will make a similar argument. Mr. Ortega is also a fine young man, one who is devoted to his family and a credit to his community. Mr. Ortega has never been arrested. He was preparing to not only graduate from James Madison High this week; he was preparing to give the valedictory address.

"Mr. Ortega was then to be sworn into the United States Army. Just like Deputy Rosado, Mr. Ortega intended to serve his country. Your Honor, I could line up dozens of character witnesses who would speak to the outstanding personal qualities of this young man."

Travis looked toward Ortega. The kid was looking at Mrs. Rosado, and his face held as much pain and suffering as hers.

"Mr. Ortega is the primary source of financial support for his mother, younger sister, and brother. The family's financial reality is such that even the most reasonable bail would be beyond their ability to pay. Therefore, I ask that Mr. Ortega be granted pretrial release on his own recognizance."

Travis couldn't believe what he had heard, and apparently Dannie couldn't either. She jumped from her chair, genuine anger in her voice. "Your Honor, that is nothing short of disrespect—"

"That's enough, Ms. Gaines. I've heard your argument."

The judge turned to the defense counsel. "Mr. Shaw, are you seriously arguing for an OR release?"

"Yes, sir, I am. We intend to prove that Omar Ortega is factually innocent of this crime, and I believe he deserves the opportunity to participate in a vigorous defense while receiving the support of his family and community. There is nothing in my client's history or character that would indicate he would not stand tall and defend himself against these charges. He is in no way a flight risk."

"I must say, Mr. Shaw, I find that a bit outrageous. This is a capital murder case. Of a peace officer."

"And I would remind Your Honor that this defendant is presumed to be innocent of those charges, heinous as they may be. To sit here and discuss the execution of an eighteen-year-old boy before so much as a single word of testimony? Does Your Honor find that equally outrageous?"

Judge Washington's response was dismissive and immediate. "Bail is denied. The accused will be remanded into custody. Mr. Shaw, will you be filing any motions prior to the preliminary hearing?"

"Oh, indeed I will, sir."

The defense counsel and Judge Washington began to confer. Dannie pushed her chair back and whispered to Ellie and Travis, "Just before we got started, defense threw us a curveball. Or a gift, I'm not sure which. You two available right after the arraignment?"

They both nodded.

"Your office?" Travis asked.

Judge Washington began to wrap things up and Dannie spoke quickly.

"No. The interrogation room in Upper West. We can take the tunnel. I'll walk with you and explain on the way."

47

"This is bullshit, Dannie. He doesn't get to dictate how we work this case."

Sean Murphy's anger was apparent in his voice and posture. Sitting next to Ellie in the small interview room, Travis watched the deputy and the prosecutor going at it across the table.

"You're right, Sean," Dannie said. "It is bullshit, but we already talked about it. What you got out of Ortega in that first interview was sketchy at best. A denial and the name of Gutierrez. That's it. That's all we got. Not to mention, most of it came after an unequivocal invocation. That motion is going to be rough."

"Bring it, Dannie. I did it on purpose. I know this kid. He and I got history. He's a smart little shit. I wanted him to know what we've got on him. I knew he'd come around and want to talk. And now that he is, he should be talking to *me*."

"He says he won't talk if you're in the room," Dannie said. "So we're going to—"

Sean cut her off. "Kiss his ass, that's what we're going to do. He's a cop killer, Dannie. The hell with him. We don't need his bullshit statement."

Dannie turned to Ellie and Travis. "The defendant has approached us about a free talk. But he'll only talk to the two of you. Don't ask me why, but that's where we're at. Of course, his lawyer insists on sitting in. I'll stay in the observation room. Sean, I want you in there with me."

"I should be at the table." The words practically came out as steam.

Dannie was having none of it. "I'm not passing on this chance, Sean. If you're really that bent about it, next time you're interviewing a murder suspect, try not to come off as such a prick. And his mother, Sean? Really?"

Murphy shot to his feet. "He killed a deputy, Dannie. Not a lawyer, a deputy. If he got his feelings hurt, he's lucky that's all it was."

The two of them stared each other down. It was Dannie who finally bowed her head.

"I'm sorry, Sean. I know how important this is to you, but we really need this. There's a lot we don't know. He's offering a free talk under the one condition that you're not in the room. I'm taking it."

"The hell with this." Sean headed for the door, glaring at the other two cops. "He's all yours, Peralta. Make sure you hold the little bastard's hand. Wipe his nose, like you did with that other ass-bag."

"Jesus," Ellie said, when the door had slammed shut behind him. "Like we asked for this?"

Dannie looked to the door and shook her head. "He'll just have to get over it. I'm not letting this get away from us. Ortega wants a free talk—off the record, of course. Afterward, hopefully the lawyers can work out some kind of agreement. Get him to testify under oath and on the record."

Travis didn't like the sound of that. "What kind of agreement?"

"Don't worry. The best he'll get is we take the death penalty off the table. When he's found guilty, he gets life without parole."

"Fuck that," Travis said. "I'd take the needle."

"Shaw said he's not even looking for a deal. Just wants to tell his side of it. But he said he'll only talk to 'the lady cop and her partner from the alley.' Apparently that's you two?"

Ellie nodded. Travis shrugged.

"Could be he's screwing with us," Dannie said. "Don't let him get over on you. But, then again, if all he wants to do is sling a bunch of bullshit, we can use that to impeach him at trial. Just get him talking. Hopefully he'll hang himself."

There was a knock on the door, then Sean opened it and walked in, holding up one hand.

"I was out of line, Dannie. I'm sorry. This is all getting to me." Sean turned to Ellie, and Travis couldn't help but think to himself the guy sure seemed to apologize a lot. "The hard approach didn't work on this little turd. Maybe if you reason with him, he'll open up. Like I said, I've known him for a while. He's no dummy."

"Thanks, Sean," Ellie said. "We'll try that."

He turned back to Dannie. "I'll see you in the observation room."

He walked away, and Dannie had the final word as she followed him out. "There's a lot riding on this. Good luck."

"Any ideas, hayseed?" Ellie asked.

"Only that I'd probably come across as an even bigger prick than Murphy. How about I just keep my mouth shut and stay out of your way?"

48

With four people at the table, the room was cramped. This was, what? The third time in two days? In the first eighteen years of his life, Omar had never set foot in a police station, not to mention an interrogation room, and now here he was again. But this time Omar was determined to call the shots. He looked at the glass, knowing Murphy was on the other side. That's the way he wanted it. The way he'd planned it. He wanted the man to see he wasn't afraid. That he wasn't going to let any more cops talk shit to him or about him. It was Murphy's turn to sit down and shut up.

Ransom Shaw sat on his right, and Omar could feel the tension and anxiety spilling out of the man. When Omar had told Ransom what he intended to do, the lawyer tried to talk him out of it. Said it was too early. That it was bad strategy. Omar shook him off. Good guy, yeah. Smart, and probably a great lawyer. But at this point Omar was sure of only one thing: He didn't need anyone telling him what to do or say. He needed to speak for himself. It was time to step up.

The one called Jackson sat across the table, giving him a hard look, the same as when they had locked eyes in the rearview. Now Omar stared right back, with a hard look of his own.

The female deputy sat next to her partner and directly across from

Omar. Her expression was so different from Jackson's that Omar wondered how they were able to work together. Her face didn't have that same look of judgment. Her head was tilted slightly, and when she looked at Omar, he felt like she was searching for an opening. A connection of some sort. Some place where they could start a conversation about a murdered cop. In some ways, Omar was more comfortable with the hostility coming off Jackson. Probably, Omar thought, because he was feeling it too.

Ransom spoke up first. He placed his phone on the table, the running timer of the recorder clearly visible on the screen.

"Good morning, deputies. Mr. Ortega has agreed to waive his Fifth Amendment right for the limited purposes of a free talk. It's important for you to know that the reason Mr. Ortega has done this is because he is factually innocent of the crime for which he stands accused. He believes he has information that will assist you in bringing the guilty parties to justice.

"He has specifically requested to speak with the two of you. I will remain in the room and be an active participant in this interview. And, like you, I will be recording every word. And just so we're clear, I would like to—"

Omar couldn't wait any longer. He took aim at Jackson. "Who arrested my mother? Where are my brother and sister?"

Both cops kept their hands casually folded on the table and said nothing. Omar, with his hands still cuffed and in his lap, nodded toward the mirror. "It was Murphy, wasn't it? He called out ICE, didn't he?" Omar was surprised when it was the woman cop who spoke first.

"Omar, my name is Deputy Eleanor Peralta. I know you've already met Deputy Travis Jackson. We were told you wanted to speak to us."

Fine, he thought. Talk to her.

"I saw it on television. My mother's been arrested. ICE has her. Who did that?"

"We don't know any of the details. ICE is a federal agency. We—the sheriff's department, I mean—we don't arrest people for immigration laws."

"Bullshit." Omar saw Jackson flinch. "You guys work together. Where is she?"

Jackson leaned in. "Watch the attitude, Ortega."

"Watch *my* attitude? You called me a cop killer." Omar knew they weren't used to being shouted at, but he didn't care. "It's not true. I didn't kill anyone. Now, where's my family?"

Jackson turned away. Omar knew it was meant as a show of disrespect, but he also knew he was getting under the man's skin.

"I think you need to tell your client how a free talk works, Counselor," Peralta said, looking to the lawyer. "He talks. We listen."

Ransom laid his hand on Omar's shoulder. "Let's all try to calm down. I think we need to—"

Once again Omar cut him off. "I didn't kill that deputy. I would never have done that."

"But you were there," Peralta said. "We know that for sure."

"Yeah," Omar said. He felt Ransom cringe beside him. "I was there."

"Can you tell us how that happened?" Peralta asked. "How you happened to be present when a deputy sheriff was murdered?"

"We've got your picture, Ortega." Jackson's eyes still smoldered. "And we know you fired a gun."

Omar realized he was on the edge. He was angry, lashing out. In a way, it felt good, but he needed to slow down. To stop playing the part of a killer, the part they were trying to hang on him. He needed to be Omar Ortega. He took a deep breath and looked at Peralta.

"Was he your friend?"

Her eyebrows knotted a bit. "My friend? You mean Deputy Rosado?"

"Yes, ma'am. Was Deputy Rosado your friend?"

"Yes," she said. "Ted was my friend. He was a good man. A good cop."

"I'm sorry for what happened to him," Omar said. "I'd never met him before. I know some of the deputies who work in the barrio, but I didn't know him."

Omar stared across the table, letting his eyes shift to Jackson, then back to the woman. "But I didn't kill him. I want people to know that."

"Can you tell us who did?" Peralta asked. "Can you tell us what happened?"

"I just need to know about my family. Where's my mother? Are my brother and sister safe?"

Jackson blew out a long breath and leaned back in his chair. "Once again, Counselor. Your client needs to be educated. He's in no position to make demands. Maybe you two need to take a minute."

There was movement under the table; Omar was pretty sure it was the woman smacking her partner. When she spoke, he could sense the honesty in her voice. At least, he wanted to believe it was honesty.

"Omar, you're in a terrible position. We have strong evidence that indicates you were involved in the murder of a deputy sheriff. If you weren't and you know who was, you need to tell us. For your own sake and the sake of your family. And if you tell us what happened to Deputy Rosado, I promise—" Her gaze shifted briefly to her partner. "*We* promise to do everything we can to look out for your family. To keep them safe."

Omar stared across the table, knowing that everything was stacked against him. These cops? They got to decide the rules as they went along. They could practically make shit up. The lawyers and the judges and juries, they'd all line up behind them. All Omar had on his side was the truth. And what good did that do? The deputies wanted the truth so they could lock him up for the rest of his life. So they could mess with his family. It was the same truth that more than a few gangsters would be willing to kill him over. The truth just weighed him down. It was like a burden he carried, and no matter what he did, that burden came with one hell of a high price.

He folded his hands on the table and began to tell his story, starting with the end of the school day and how Hector had gone to the wall. He told them how he'd come to be in the alleyway when the deputies arrived, about the late-night visit by Chunks and E-Boy. He told them about getting money out of the ATM, then how Chunks drove to Chito's and bought beer.

"I hoped that would be the end of it, but Chunks, he just kept driving."

Jackson butted in. "Back up, Ortega. You skipped something."

"What do you mean?"

"The gun in the dumpster. Who'd it belong to?"

Omar knew the question was a test, to see how forthright he was going to be. Ransom placed his hand on the back of Omar's arm and looked directly at Jackson.

"That incident has no relationship to the shooting death of Deputy Rosado."

"But I want to know." Jackson never took his eyes off Omar. "I'll ask you again, who dumped the gun?"

Ransom leaned in, his voice louder. Indignant. He pointed a finger toward Jackson. "And I'll say again, it's immaterial to the case and beyond the scope of this interview. We did not agree to—"

"It belonged to Chunks," Omar said abruptly. His attorney's wince was accompanied by an audible sigh. "He tossed it just before Murphy showed up with his crew."

"Why didn't you tell us?" Jackson said. Omar heard the seething anger in his voice. No. More than anger—revulsion. He shook his head. Like Murphy, this one just didn't get it.

"It doesn't work that way. That's not how you get by. That's not how you survive."

Deputy Jackson gave him a dismissive look that said he wasn't buying it. The woman got them back on track. "All right, so you gave them money for beer. What happened after that?"

Omar told them about the drive through San Marcos and how they ended up in a house still under construction. Remembering the gunfire, Omar couldn't keep the anger out of his voice, but this time it was anger directed at himself.

"I shot it too. They said we couldn't leave unless I did. E-Boy even pointed the gun at me. Threatened me with it."

"What kind of gun was it?" Jackson asked, his skepticism clear.

"One that has the bullet thing in the bottom. A clip, right? I think E-Boy called it a three eighty."

The two cops exchanged a look. He guessed he'd given them something of value.

Deputy Peralta commented, "So you're saying that's why you had gun residue on your hand."

Omar nodded. "Had to be. It's the only time in my life I've ever fired a gun."

Jackson leaned in. "So let me see if I got this. Earlier that day, you helped a gangster avoid getting arrested. That night you go out with that same gangster and some other guy you conveniently don't know. You buy beer, you smoke pot, you shoot a gun, but you don't have anything to do with the murder of Deputy Rosado, is that it?"

"I didn't smoke pot, but I did drink beer," Omar said.

"Tell us about getting pulled over," Peralta said.

This part was hard to talk about, and he knew it wasn't going to be easy for them to hear. But he had to tell it all. And he did, the shots still ringing in his head. Sure enough, Omar could see the story hit both cops hard, and he was surprised when he felt sorry for them. He went on, his voice low.

"I tried to warn him. I banged on the window and yelled, but it was too late. E-Boy started shooting. The deputy never had a chance.

"Chunks started to drive away. I opened the back door and jumped. I hit the street pretty hard. Not really sure how long I laid there. Just a few seconds, I think. But when I got to the deputy . . . when I crawled over to him . . . he was dead."

"Why did you jump out of the car?" she asked.

Omar looked steadily at her, ignoring both his lawyer and Jackson. This was between him and this woman. "I couldn't leave him there. I wanted to help him."

"What did you do after that?" she asked.

"I ran home. I was sleeping on the bathroom floor when you guys showed up—the SWAT guys, I mean. I was going to turn myself in in the morning, but . . ." Omar stopped talking and Ransom took over.

The lawyer looked down at the scribbled notes on his tablet and began to read back all the major points of Omar's statement. He didn't miss a thing. When he finished, he looked to Omar, his voice solemn. "Is that an accurate recounting of your statement, Omar?"

Omar looked at the deputies. "Basically, yeah. That's everything."

"Where's Chunks now?" Jackson was quick to ask, and it was obvious he expected an answer.

"I don't know. I don't even know where he lives. But he's never too far from the east side."

"And this other man, E-Boy," Peralta said. "What can you tell us about him?"

Omar provided a physical description as best he could remember. "Chunks said they met in prison. E-Boy got out a couple of months ago."

Jackson gave Omar another hard look. "So riddle me this, Ortega. Why did you run?"

"Are you serious?" Omar was shocked by the question. It was nothing short of idiotic.

"Damn right, I'm serious. If you're so innocent, why did you run?"

Omar leaned across the table and spoke the obvious. "People be getting shot by deps in Vista a lot lately. Most of them look like me."

"But if you hadn't done anything wrong, if you were trying to help Deputy Rosado, why run?"

"It doesn't matter if you did anything wrong or not," Omar said, beginning to realize that no answer was going to satisfy this cop. "When the deps show up, you run."

"That doesn't make any sense." Jackson seemed irritated.

"Not to you, maybe," Omar said, looking away, his own anger beginning to surface once again.

"Not to me, either, Omar," Peralta said. "If what you're saying is true and you hadn't run away? You'd be home right now, with your family."

Omar was trying hard to control his emotions, but these clueless white cops were never going to get it. Of course he ran, and he'd run right now if he could. But these two? He was done talking to them. "Neither of you understand. You never will."

"Then tell me." For the first time, she sounded angry. She sounded like a cop. "What is it we don't understand?"

Fuck it. That's it.

Omar shouted, "My dad didn't do anything wrong, so he didn't run. And where's he?"

"Oh, yeah, here it comes." Jackson spouted out his words. "'It's my daddy's fault. Nobody loved me. It's my *environment*.' That's such bullshit, Ortega. Show some pride, man."

"I don't blame *him*," Omar spat right back. "I blame *you*."

The woman deputy put a hand on Jackson's arm as the man leaned toward Omar. The two men glared at each other. Omar's heartbeat pounded in his head. After a long pause, the woman said, "I think you need to explain what you mean, Omar."

As if I could, he thought. He hated thinking of that day. He hated everything about it, and that included the deputies sitting in front of him. He hated them for asking, for making him remember.

She leaned in across the table. "Please, Omar. Try."

And he did. He breathed deep and dove in.

"The same month I started at James Madison, my dad got— No, wait. That's not it."

Omar stopped. That wasn't the beginning. If he was going to make them understand, he needed to start at the beginning. He shook his head, thinking about what his life had once been.

"A while back, most of my life even, we lived in a nice house. Me. My parents, Hector and Sofia. We didn't own it or anything, but we lived there for ten years. Good neighborhood. Mostly families. My dad pretty much owned his own business. Worked for himself pouring concrete, and man, he stayed plenty busy. No problem finding work."

For a moment Omar felt himself leave the compact room filled with cops and lawyers. More watching from close by, he was sure. He ignored them all. He hadn't let himself think about this for a while, and instead of being angry and resentful, he felt warmed by the memories.

"Dad played in a soccer league. Him and the other guys from his team, they won a big game against some hotshot club out of San Diego. It was a big deal to them, so my dad invited everyone over to celebrate. They all sat in the front yard, drinking a few beers. Listening to music. My mom and all the wives were cooking in the kitchen. It was fun. Nobody was, like, drunk or anything. Just hanging out. Still in their jerseys. I was there too. Fifteen years old. Just listening to them talk about the game."

The picture in his mind changed, and the memory of that day darkened. But he went on. He had to tell it. "A deputy drove by and stopped. When he got out of his car, everybody just dropped their beer and ran away. Except my dad. He sat there. I was scared, but he said there was nothing to be afraid of. That we hadn't done anything wrong."

Omar saw his father's tall, lean figure. His skin weathered but still youthful. Always with the easy smile.

"The deputy, he was all kinds of pissed off. Asked my dad why everyone ran. Dad said he didn't know. So, the deputy? He said my dad was drunk in public. That his music was disturbing the peace. Dad tried to talk to him. He wasn't drunk. Told him he'd turn down the music. Dep didn't care. Just up and arrested him."

Omar came back to the room. He leaned his chest against the wooden table. "Dad called from jail. Told my mom the dep put an immigration hold on him and they were going to keep him until he had a hearing. They said it could be months. They were going to ship him off to a federal lockup in Texas."

Ransom and the two deputies sat in silence, staring back. Omar wasn't sure if he could go on. It wasn't a story he liked to tell or share with anyone.

"He told my mom that if he agreed to voluntarily return to Mexico, they'd let him go. So he did. They put him on a bus and drove him to Tijuana. He called right away. Said not to worry. He'd be home soon.

"He called a few days later. Said he was crossing that night and he'd call to let us know where to pick him up." Omar smiled at the memory. "Said the first thing he wanted to do was go to In-N-Out."

Omar looked up at Jackson, the man's eyes still angry, but maybe with just a bit of doubt. "Last thing he said? He laughed and said, 'Next time, hijo, I'll just run!'"

It was Omar's turn to feel embittered by loss. "He didn't call. Not that night. Not the next. He never called."

Omar stared at the tabletop. He didn't want to look up. He didn't want to see any of them.

"Everything changed after that. We lost our house and had to move. We've moved a lot since then. Last time was just a couple months ago. We got a room we all share. We've sold everything. My dad's truck. His tools. Everything. My mom, she works keeping house during the day. Then a few nights a week she cleans offices."

He finally looked up. "So you want to know why I ran, Jackson? Because a deputy arrested my dad for drinking a beer in his own yard and that was the last time I ever saw him. You really think I'm going to stick around? Wait for you guys to show up and find me with a deputy who's dead?"

Ransom was shaking his head. Omar guessed he'd heard plenty of similar stories. The cops just looked stunned.

"Everybody I know has a story like that," Omar said. "Maybe not exactly, but something like it. That's why we run. That's why we all run. If you don't get it? If that isn't good enough for you? I guess I can't do anything about that, can I?"

The woman shifted in her seat and Omar could see what he thought might be some sort of sorrow in her eyes. Maybe even pity.

"Why us?" Deputy Peralta asked. "Why did you agree to talk to us?"

"I saw you with Toon. You were, like, nice to him. Talked to him and stuff. I've never seen a cop act like that. I thought maybe you'd listen.

"You?" Omar looked at Jackson and shrugged one shoulder. "I just figured it would piss off Murphy."

The woman smiled. Jackson rolled his eyes. Omar went on, "And there's one other reason."

"What's that?" she asked.

"From what my attorney told me, everything I just said? Unless I say it under oath, it doesn't mean anything."

When both cops just stared back, Omar kept talking. "I know you want me to testify in court. And I'll do it. As soon as I know my family is safe and all together. Otherwise? I'm not saying anything and you can charge me with whatever you want."

"We aren't authorized to make any deals," Peralta said. "That will be something for the attorneys to work out."

"You're not hearing me," Omar said. "I don't want a deal. Not for me, at least. Just leave my family alone and I'll testify. You can do whatever you want with me."

He turned to his lawyer. "That's all I'm saying for now."

Ransom looked thoughtful as he turned to the deputies. "You've heard my client's statement. If it's true, and I would point out that neither of you has any reason to believe it's not, then Mr. Ortega is factually innocent of the murder of Deputy Rosado. It is my expectation that this exculpatory statement will be fully investigated. I hope both of you recognize the trust he's placed in you."

Ransom stood and placed his hand on Omar's shoulder. "We're done here."

49

"I suppose it's plausible," Enrique said. "But pretty damn convenient."

Travis and Ellie, along with Sean Murphy, Dannie Gaines, and Enrique Soledad, were on the fifth floor of the Vista courthouse, in the law library that doubled as a conference room. Enrique went on, sharing his opinion about the free-talk interview of Omar Ortega.

"I don't want to say you got played, but . . . Nobody ever said this kid wasn't smart, and he's painted himself as having zero culpability in the whole scenario. Nice and neat. A victim of homeboy circumstance. And this whole mystery man thing? What's his name? E-Boy? I'm not buying it."

Ellie spoke up. "You should know, just before the arraignment, we got chased down by that reporter from Univision. Fonseca."

"Oh yeah?" Sean looked to Travis. "What hospital did they take him to?"

Travis smiled and said, "Yeah, guilty. That was my first thought."

Ellie ignored them both and went on, "He reached out to the Ortega family. From what Fonseca told us, sounds like the brother and sister gave him the same story Omar gave us. The kid, Hector, even remembered the name E-Boy." She eyed Enrique. "Fonseca said no detective has even interviewed them."

Enrique shrugged. "We've had our hands full. They're on the list."

"True or not, it doesn't matter," Dannie said. "It's the story he's stuck with from this point forward. So our job is either to confirm it or punch some holes in it."

Sean said, "I'll tell you one hole we can punch in it right now and sink his ass."

"What are you talking about?" Dannie asked.

Sean gave a nod to Travis. "Jackson nailed him on the most important point. Ortega now admits that he saw Chunks dump the gun. From the way I see it, that makes his original denial an act in furtherance."

Dannie narrowed her eyes, obviously intrigued. "Go on."

Sean put his elbows on the polished wood of the conference table and clasped his hands under his chin, all his ink on proud display. "Here's what I'm thinking. Ortega sees Chunks, a known Eastsider, not to mention a convicted felon, in possession of a firearm. He sees Chunks dump the gun. When he's questioned by law enforcement, Ortega lies so Chunks won't go to jail. So a shot caller for Eastside stays on the street."

Sean let his logic sink in, then kept going, "We declare that as an act in furtherance of the gang. Stack on his known gangster associates, and his street name. Hell, I'll throw in what he was wearing. With all that, we finally get to document Ortega. We go retroactive on him, so from that time forward, he's Eastside."

"And since he's admitted to being present at the shooting," Enrique said, nodding with approval, "with the right jury instructions, that pretty much gives us an ironclad murder conviction."

Sean smiled. "Boy howdy."

"Hang on a second," Ellie said. "What if he's telling us the truth?"

"Doesn't change the facts," Sean said. "The law's clear. If one gangster does a shooting, all the other gangsters who back his play are just as guilty. They all pulled the trigger."

"That might be what the law says, but come on," Ellie insisted. "If the kid is telling the truth, what choice did he really have?"

"What choice?" Sean said. "Oh, I don't know. Maybe one that doesn't involve leaving a cop to die in the street? That's a deal breaker. I say he goes for murder one. Stick a needle in 'im."

"Is that why you called ICE?" Ellie asked. "Just another way to stick a needle in him?"

"Really, Peralta?" Sean said. "You're gonna give me shit when the twist I put on the kid worked exactly as planned?"

"What's that supposed to mean?" Ellie asked.

"It loosened his tongue, didn't it? Mexican boys are all the same. Mama's always their weak spot."

"Jesus, Murphy." She made no effort to hide her disgust. "You really are something else."

Travis had to agree with Ellie on that one. Bringing ICE down on the mom was pretty bush league, but then again, Murphy might be on to something. If Ortega was documentable as a gang member at the time of the incident at Chito's, then later that night, when he was rolling around in the car, he was, in the legal sense, an Eastsider. That meant just by being present at the scene of Rosado's murder, he became a principal in the crime. Ortega was bought and paid for.

Enrique moved things along. "What do we know about this E-Boy? Is this Ortega's phantom fall guy or is he for real?"

"I'm working on it, Sarge," Sean said, "but there are over a hundred entries in the statewide database with the moniker E-Boy. You can thank El Cerrito, El Centro, El Monte, Elk Grove, Eureka, and Escondido for that. It might take a day or two. We need to cross-reference some different prison records. But if Gutierrez has a known associate with that moniker, we'll find him. If not? Big surprise. Ortega's full of shit."

"Well, Dannie," Enrique said. "Is the DA's office still ready to go forward? Prosecute this gangster for a cop killing?"

Dannie nodded. "For now? Yeah, we're still moving forward on Ortega as our S-1, but we've got a lot of work to do. But most importantly, I don't want him to lose his sudden spirit of cooperation."

"Meaning?" Ellie asked.

"Meaning, let's do what he asked. I'll talk to the feds about his mom. We'll see if deporting a mother of three with no criminal history is really that vital to national security."

Sean quickly chimed in, sounding flippant, "You happy now, Peralta?"

Ellie wasn't amused. "Fuck you, Murphy."

Dannie ignored the banter and kept going. She pointed to Travis and Ellie. "You guys do a welfare check on the sibs. Until I can see about mom's release, it's probably best we take them into protective custody."

Dannie turned to Sean. "And, I want Gutierrez in custody. I know he didn't go far."

"My team will find him," Sean said.

Ellie spoke up. "What about looking into the gunplay at the construction site?"

"Horseshit story," Sean said. "My bet is he made it up on the fly to explain away his positive GSR. Let the defense chase it down."

Enrique cut in. "Nah, Peralta's right. We've got to pursue all the angles." Looking at Travis and Ellie, he continued, "I'll talk to Sergeant Peña and get you both cleared for a special detail. First, find the brother and sister. Get both their statements and get them settled into protective custody with CPS. Then, start trying to run down the construction site. Get ahold of the original reporting parties who called in the gunfire. You can check a car out of the detective motor pool. I'll authorize whatever overtime you need."

"I'm good if you are," Ellie said to Travis. He nodded, already dreading the pile of paperwork that came along with getting a kid through intake at Child Protective Services.

"Great," Dannie said. "I'll touch base with defense counsel. Let him know we're doing our due diligence. I want to brief again tomorrow morning at zero nine. Since you guys are doing all the legwork, I'll come to you. We'll meet at Ridgehaven."

Enrique stood and dismissed the cops. "Plenty of work to do, so let's get to it."

As Travis headed out, Sean threw an elbow, hitting him on the arm. "Nice job on Ortega. You got just what we needed."

Ellie stopped alongside them, giving the GSU detective a cold stare.

Sean kept talking. "And about that kid the other night. I got it covered. You can relax."

Ellie gave a loud exhale of disgust and walked away. Both men watched her leave.

"Thanks, Sean. But I'm going to get with Peña and fill him in. I don't want him getting blindsided with a call from an attorney. Or the media, if the kid's family goes that route. Peña deserves a heads-up."

"No worries, man. I'm telling you, I got this. It's gonna go away."

"I gotta run. We'll check in with you later." Travis hustled down the hall and caught up to Ellie just as the doors on the elevator started to close.

Ellie ignored him and pushed the button for the first floor. Sharing the space with a couple of senior citizens with juror tags, they rode down in silence. Outside, the cool morning had evaporated and the day was starting to heat up. The protests had fizzled, and even the media vans had packed up and left.

She didn't say a word until they were into the parking lot. When she did speak, it was to give him an out, and he knew she was hoping he'd take it. "You okay with this? I mean, it's just a bunch of busywork. Couple of statements. Check the kids into Polinsky. Probably call a few construction companies. I can handle it, if you'd rather get home."

"What are you saying? You'd rather work alone than worry about me drop-kicking some well-deserving youth across a parking lot? Get you mixed up in my rage issues?"

He'd meant it as a joke, but judging by the expression on her face, she was taking him seriously. "Is that something I need to worry about?"

"No," Travis said, all kidding aside. "You don't, Ellie. Not a bit."

"Then the only thing I'll worry about is Molly. Talking to her yesterday, she struck me as one of those rare women who actually loves her husband. I'm sure she'd rather have you at home."

"Molly gets it. Until this case is over, any chance I get to work on it? Hell, I'd do it for free." They reached his truck. "Are you buying it? Ortega's story, I mean?"

Ellie stared ahead. "Do I want to believe him? Sure. What's wrong with that? I want to believe he's a good kid. But more than anything, I want to know the whole truth."

"So what are you thinking?" he asked. "What's the whole truth?"

"I don't know, but we need to find his brother and sister. Dannie's right. The better he feels about his family, the more cooperative he'll be. Start with Hector?"

Travis gave a thumbs-up and unlocked the pickup. Ellie had parked her Lexus a few spots over. He waited for what he knew was coming.

"Nice truck. Between that and the minivan, what's next? A pre-owned Kia?"

They were back on the same wavelength, and there was no denying it felt good. He gave her the middle finger. "See you at the motor pool, partner."

50

The assistant principal of Cesar Chavez Middle School, a pleasant woman who insisted they call her Sonya, returned to her office with a sullen young Latino boy in tow. For a middle schooler, he was on the smallish size, but he bore a striking resemblance to his brother. Hector looked at Travis and Ellie with smoldering brown eyes that were now very familiar.

Sonya rested her hand protectively on Hector's shoulders. "Hector, these people are with the San Diego County Sheriff's Department. They'd like to talk with you for a few minutes. Is that okay with you?"

Hector shrugged and looked away. His tone was all homeboy. But unlike the confidence of Omar, Travis knew, with Hector, it was a front. The boy was scared.

"What if I don't want to?"

Ellie broke in without moving from her chair.

"Hector, my name is Ellie Peralta. I'm a deputy." She nodded to Travis. "This is my partner, Deputy Travis Jackson. Your brother, Omar, asked us to come and check on you."

Hector's head jerked back around. Travis knew they had the boy's attention, but his mistrust remained. "You talked to him?"

"Yes, we did. We had a long talk after he was in court this morning."

"He was on TV all day yesterday." Hector's defiant tone began to weaken. "This morning, too."

"He says he didn't kill the deputy," Ellie said. "He talked to us because he wants people to know that. Hector, do you think Omar is telling the truth? That he didn't kill Deputy Rosado?"

"I know he is. He would never have done that." Hector's eyes went glassy; his chin quivered. Ellie handled it well. Getting out of her chair, she kneeled in front of Hector and took his hands in hers.

"Do you want to help him?"

"What can I do? How can I help him? And what about my mom? She's gone too."

"You can help both of them by answering our questions," Ellie said. "By telling us everything you know. Will you do that?"

Without warning, the act came to an abrupt end. Hector sobbed aloud and let his body fall against Ellie, collapsing into her arms. "It's all my fault. All of it."

Ellie rocked Hector back and forth, lightly stroking his back. He told his story in stuttering gasps and sobs. Hector talked about the after-school trip to the wall and the late-night visit from Chunks and a man named E-Boy. He told them about the ICE agents coming to the apartment and taking his mother away.

He buried his head in Ellie's shoulder. "If I had just listened to Omar, none of this would've happened."

"It's not your fault, Hector. It's not."

"Will you tell Omar I'm sorry?" Hector asked, swiping his sleeve across his face. "Tell him he was right."

"Right about what?"

"About everything." Hector gave the deputies a brief first smile. "He's always right about everything."

51

Ellie drove the unmarked Crown Vic to the high school, four blocks from where they had interviewed Hector. Travis rode shotgun. He glanced her way and spoke the truth.

"Hell of an interview, Ellie. Great job."

"How is that even possible?"

Travis waited, but nothing. Finally, he asked, "How is *what* possible?"

"That people . . . that kids get . . . screwed over like that. Right out in the open. The system just . . . just bends them over and *fucks* them."

Travis, shocked at the graphics, followed up. "What are you getting at?"

Ellie's eyes were on the road, but Travis could feel her intensity building. "I mean, think about it. Some patrol dep gets a hard-on for a guy drinking a beer in his front yard. Hooks him up for what you and I both know is a completely bogus charge. Gets him a one-way ticket to TJ on a voluntary return; his family never sees him again."

Ellie gripped the steering wheel until her knuckles went white. "Then, when his son tries to step up, he ends up getting dragged into a cop killing that he's probably got nothing to do with. And, just for good measure, we decide to reach out and bitch-slap the family one last time and send ICE to hook up mom. Leave two kids to pretty much fend for themselves. How does all that happen without anyone so much as . . . hell, I don't know. It just seems like, at some point, someone would've stepped in and said enough already."

Travis had listened while Ellie interviewed Hector. The boy's story followed Omar's, chapter and verse. If it was true? Sure. It would make a pretty good defense. But Travis couldn't help but wonder if that's all it was. A good story, concocted to get Omar out from under a cop killing. If there was one thing they knew about Omar Ortega, it was that he was nobody's fool. Could be Hector was just as cagey. Apparently, Ellie was a mind reader.

"I know what you're thinking, but he's telling the truth, Travis. I'm sure of it."

"You mean Hector?"

"I mean both of them." Her mind was made up. "Omar didn't kill Teddy. He didn't have a thing to do with it."

Travis wasn't there yet. Not even close. "You heard what Murphy laid out. Ortega? He's bought and paid for."

"The hell with Murphy. I mean, I know he's your new best bro and all, but personally I've about had my fill of his tatted-out warrior-cop bullshit. And by the way, his name is Omar. Don't talk like he's some kind of gangster."

"Uh, okay," Travis said. "But he *is* a gangster."

She turned and gave him a look so cold the skin on his arms bumped up. He tried to change the subject.

"Let's just talk to Sofia," Travis said. "See if she's got her story straight. Then—"

Ellie smacked his arm. Hard. "Damn it, Jackson, listen to yourself. 'Got her story straight.' What are you thinking? Omar comes home at two o'clock in the morning, wakes up his brother and sister, and says, 'Hey guys. I killed a cop. We need to get our story straight'? Were you even listening to that boy? Did that sound like a kid making shit up?"

"Jesus, Ellie." Travis was careful not to admit that was exactly what he was thinking. "Poor choice of words. I agree. If Sofia gives a similar statement, there are real problems with this case. But let's talk to her first, okay?"

"I swear, some of you guys," Ellie said. "Believe it or not, sometimes we arrest the wrong people."

Travis was starting to think that a female partner wasn't all that different from a wife. Need to watch every word you say. For Travis, the facts were pretty clear. Ortega was, as of now, a legally documented gang member; his brother sure had the look of a wannabe. By their own admission, Hector willingly went to the wall that afternoon, and later that night, Omar willingly got in the car. Checkmate. But, like in any good marriage, Travis knew that sometimes unspoken thoughts were the best kind to have. Sure enough, he felt the stare.

"What are you thinking?"

"Oh, nothing," Travis said. "Nothing at all."

They parked the car and walked into the administrative offices of James Madison High School. Travis let Ellie take the lead, and he hung back while she talked to the man behind the attendance counter. Ellie pulled out her badge and spoke to the clerk in a low voice. After a brief conversation, she gave the man her card, shook his hand, then walked away.

Travis waited until Ellie got up close. "Got a room number or are they bringing her to us?"

"Neither," Ellie said, and Travis heard the concern in her voice. "She's not here. Clerk said they figured, with Omar getting arrested and all, she didn't want to come to school."

"But Hector said they rode the bus. They got on together. Did they make a call to confirm? You know, to a parent or . . ."

Ellie glared back and Travis knew he had walked right into that one.

"Let's check the apartment," he said. "Good chance she changed her mind about school and went home. Can't blame her for wanting to avoid the drama. Hell, my kid stays home for a stomachache."

Ellie wasn't listening, because she was already quickstepping for the car. Travis could tell her mind was racing with possibilities, none of them good.

A few hurried minutes and a short drive later, they climbed the steps to the apartment and found a sheet of plywood hanging awkwardly in the doorway. The broken windows had been boarded over.

Travis pushed on the plywood and called, "Sheriff's department. Anybody around?"

When there was no response, Ellie yelled out a second announcement. A heavyset man with bushy, unkempt hair and a thick mustache came to the door. "Now what?"

Ellie was only interested in one thing. "Sir, I'm Deputy Peralta. This is Deputy Jackson. Is Sofia Ortega here?"

"You see this shit?" The man slapped the plywood with his open hand. "I called the manager all day yesterday and still I got no door. He says I gotta pay. Why should I pay? It was the goddamn SWAT—"

"Sir," Travis cut him off. "We need to know if Sofia Ortega is here. It's very important that we speak with her."

The man—Travis assumed this was Renteria—threw up a hand in disgust and cursed in Spanish. "She went to school. Her and that little chollo brother."

"Yes, we know that, but did she happen to come back?" Travis asked.

"No, and she better not. You can tell both of those little hyenas to find somewhere else to sleep tonight. I don't need them around here. Look at this place. Tell them to stay away. Them and their mother. Now, are you going to call somebody about my door or what?"

Travis's phone rang with a call from Sergeant Soledad. "I'd better take this." He walked down the steps for privacy. What the sergeant had to say changed everything.

After the quick conversation, he returned to find Ellie listening to Renteria express his deepest affections for the sheriff's office, the Ortega clan, and the manager of his apartment complex.

"We need to go," Travis said, interrupting without remorse. "Good luck with your door." Taking Ellie by the arm and pulling her toward the steps, Renteria continued his rant behind them.

"What did Soledad want? Did you tell him Sofia is missing?"

"I didn't get a chance. He wants us in Oceanside. They found Gutierrez. Maybe the car."

"Let me guess. Chunks will only talk to the nice lady cop and her partner?"

"Gutierrez won't be talking to anybody," Travis said, looking at Ellie. "Ever."

"Get the hell . . ." Her voice trailed off. "O'side capped him?"

"Worse, at least for Chunks. Somebody torched him and the lowrider his fat ass was sitting in. Soledad says it sounds like the car Ortega was describing."

"I'll drive," Ellie said, picking up the pace to the car. "You need to get on the phone with dispatch. Put out an at-risk missing person bulletin on

Sofia. It should rate an AMBER alert. Get them to send a patrol car to the middle school. Take Hector into protective custody right away."

"Agreed," Travis said, getting in on the passenger side. "What about Orte— I mean, what about Omar? What do we tell him?"

"Nothing yet," she said. "He doesn't need to know."

Ellie began to pull into traffic, then stopped for a minivan blocking the road. Travis reached over and banged on the horn.

"Damn, Peralta. It's a police car. Quit driving like a pussy."

52

They made the drive to Oceanside in less than fifteen minutes and pulled up on a section of North Pacific Street that was taped off at either end. A still-smoldering boat of a car took center stage. Travis made it for a midsixties Chevy. A Biscayne, or maybe an Impala. Hard to be certain because the distinctive rear lights were melted into misshapen chunks of red plastic. Travis saw the crowd of self-appointed tapeworms had arrived and taken their place along the yellow line of demarcation. Cops on one side, worms on the other. Most of them were dressed for the beach, but a few looked like they should be getting back to work, not standing around a police barricade craning for a better look at the carnage.

Sergeant Soledad and Detective Murphy stood inside the tape, along with a couple of suits Travis figured belonged to Oceanside PD. The OPD crime scene van, a repurposed ten-year-old ambulance, was parked just outside the barrier. It hadn't rained in a month, but the pavement around the car was wet and dotted with shoe-soaking puddles. Even the grass along the road was soggy. The crew responsible sat parked in a lot across the street, a half-dozen men stripped down to short-sleeve blue T-shirts and yellow rubber pants held up by fire engine–red suspenders. Their work complete, they hung around the dripping fire truck in various positions of repose, like they were preparing for a calendar shoot.

The Pacific Ocean at high tide served as a dramatic backdrop, dotted with surfers and boogie boarders oblivious to anything other than the next wave. The sweet, putrid odor of burned meat had what any cop would identify as the unmistakable aroma of human flesh, even when diluted by the salty ocean breeze. Ellie called out to Sergeant Soledad. He motioned them in and they slipped under the tape.

"Came out as a car fire," Enrique said. "Somebody definitely helped it along. Burned-up gas can in the backseat. OFD showed up and found it fully engulfed. They put ten thousand gallons on it before they saw the body in the front seat. They called out their cops. OPD called us."

"How bad?" Ellie asked.

"Not so bad that we can't make an ID. It's definitely Gutierrez. OPD's lab guy has already found an entrance wound in the side of his head. Says the angle looks like the round came from the passenger side at close contact. Hard to say, of course, but it's a tight hole. A three eighty is definitely a possibility."

"You're thinking this is the car, then?" Travis asked. "From Ted's stop?"

"Good bet. See the broken glass sprayed on the street? All the windows blew out from the heat. Except for the driver's window."

Travis nodded, his mind clicking back to Ted's body cam and the image of shattering glass. "Because it was already gone."

"Exactly," Enrique said.

"RO?" Ellie asked, inquiring after the registered owner of the vehicle.

"Address out of Fallbrook. Reported stolen a week ago. It's cold-plated, rear only. Plate comes back to a similar make and model out of Encinitas. No theft report on that yet."

Travis recognized the standard gang auto rip. Steal a car, then find a similar car and steal one plate. The theft of the car would be reported right away, but sometimes it took days, if not weeks, for a person to notice they were missing a license plate. In the meantime, if a cop ran the plate, it would come back to a similar make and model with no wants.

Enrique led them closer to the Chevy. Sean Murphy walked over and gave a nod of acknowledgment. "Heard the missing person go out on Sofia Ortega. Any chance she's a runaway?"

Ellie shook her head and looked at the detective in a way that said he'd better not argue the point. "Doesn't look that way. She got on the bus for school but never showed."

Travis leaned into the burned car and the odor intensified. It was off-putting, but he'd been around enough decomposing bodies in the Mid-western heat and humidity to know how much worse human remains could smell. This was more like a devil's barbecue.

The body had been pretty much cooked to a medium well, its large head and face mostly consumed. The ears were down to burned nubs, and the bony skull was flaked with a dusting of ash and skin. Both arms were still hefty, but charred as hell, and pulled up tight against the torso in a classic pugilistic pose. One eye bulged outward, round and black, like an eight ball had been wedged into the socket. Travis figured that was consistent with the close contact gunshot followed by the fire. The lips were gone, making visible the distinctive, gapped teeth. That and the girth confirmed it. Chunks Gutierrez had suffered a well-deserved and miserable death.

Rest in peace, motherfucker.

"Any sign of the gun?" Travis asked. "The three eighty?"

Enrique looked toward the pier lined with fishermen and a few hundred tourists. "No, but if it weren't for what I owe my two ex-wives, I'd bet a paycheck it's about fifty feet below the waterline. I'm guessing this E-Boy fella takes care of business with Chunks, walks out on the pier, tosses the piece, then goes and has himself a nice breakfast at Ruby's."

Ellie looked at the blackened corpse. "Maybe, maybe not. Gangsters like to hang on to their gats. I still want to run down the construction sites. Look for the shooting scene."

"Is that really priority one right now?" Travis asked. "Maybe we ought to just concentrate on finding Sofia. ID'ing this guy E-Boy."

"I'd love to find Sofia, but where do we even start? Patrol has been told to be on the lookout. And as far as E-Boy goes, if we find the shooting scene, that might give us the intel we need to find him."

Travis started to ask Ellie what she meant, but Sean spoke up.

"You need any help? I mean, now that the search for fatman is officially over."

"That'd be great," Ellie said, exchanging a look of surprise with Travis.

"My team will stick around here and help out until OPD finishes up," Sean said. "Send us our assignments and we'll get on it."

Travis and Ellie headed back to the car.

"San Marcos is a hot area in North County," Travis said. "Gotta figure there are a couple hundred houses going up. We can get up with city hall and get a list of active construction projects. Dispatch will have the address of whoever called in the gunshots. We can use that as a starting point. Move out from there."

When she didn't answer, he looked her way and saw her staring toward the water. "Yo. Earth to Peralta."

"What? Oh, sorry." She looked at him but then turned back toward the ocean dotted with surfers riding the eight-foot waves. "Did you know that Teddy loved to surf? He was actually pretty good."

"Didn't know."

They were quiet getting back to the car. Travis drove. Five minutes later, they were eastbound on the 78. Ellie got on the phone with dispatch. After that she called San Marcos City Hall, Planning Division.

53

It was after four o'clock when Travis and Ellie finished the last site on their list. Thirteen different residential construction projects were currently under way within San Marcos city limits, ranging from six to seventy-six units. They had started with the projects closest to the gunshots-heard-only call and moved out from there. Based on Omar's description, they ruled out all single-story structures. Given Omar telling them that E-Boy and Chunks had kicked holes on the first floor, they'd decided to thoroughly check all two-story structures for damage, or for drywall damage that had already been repaired.

Murphy's team handled the projects to the west. Travis and Ellie had taken the east. In all, 275 partially constructed two-story homes had been searched. None showed indications of vandalism by way of gunfire. The day had been long, hot, and entirely unproductive.

"That turned out to be a monumental waste of time," Ellie said. Her hair had frizzed up in the heat and her face was red from the sun. Both of them were covered in dust and sweat. She leaned back against the front of the unmarked Crown Vic, arms crossed with a look that said she felt like she'd taken them on a fool's errand.

Not really, Travis thought. It showed Ortega's story was bullshit. It'll play great in court. But he kept that to himself.

"What if we got more people?" Ellie asked. "Maybe the academy could help out. Get a bunch of the cadets out here. Divide them into teams. Hell, we went house to house. Let's go wall to damn wall."

Travis let it go, but he really hoped she was just spouting off in her desperation. Ellie motioned toward the nearby construction crew. "What about these people?"

Travis looked out over the street, where a dozen homes were taking shape. A hundred men and a handful of women populated a scene that buzzed with the sound of power tools, hammers, and chattering voices.

"What if," Ellie asked, "we question workers on the site? See if any of them saw anything."

"We did, Ellie." Travis tried to be patient. He knew she wanted a different outcome, but then again, it was time to face facts. "I mean, we didn't formally interview anybody, but we talked to, what? Maybe fifty construction workers. Nobody said anything about vandalism by gunfire."

"Seems like someone would notice, right?" Ellie said, maybe coming around. "A three eighty doesn't leave a huge hole, but from what Omar said, they capped off a bunch of rounds. You figure anyone working in a house with that kind of damage would have said something to a boss."

Then again, Travis thought, what if no one was working on the house? What if no one was working on the project at all?

"Hey, Ellie," Travis asked, "every site we went to today, there were people working, right?"

"Yeah. So what?"

"Aren't there always a few projects that kind of fold up? You know, just don't get finished." He looked at her and saw she was already dialed in to where he was going. "Building code problems. Finance issues. Whatever."

Ellie pulled out her phone and hit Redial. "It's not five yet. There should still be—Hello," she said. "This is Deputy Peralta again, with the sheriff's office."

Travis listened to Ellie's conversation with someone at San Marcos City Hall. Two minutes later, she was giving her email address.

Ending the call, Ellie walked over and shoved Travis hard in the chest with the flat palms of her hands. "Son of a bitch, hayseed. You think maybe you could've thought of that four hours ago?"

"What did they tell you?"

"Dormant projects are kept in a separate database. Fricking egghead at city hall said we asked for current housing construction." She shrugged and cocked her head. "Which, to be fair, we did." She opened her email, looking for new messages.

Ellie grinned at Travis. "There are four dormant projects. I've got the addresses."

54

It was after six and the summer sun was just starting to head for the horizon. They'd completed searching a dilapidated project of sixteen homes that hadn't been worked on in six months. There were plenty of indications of vandalism, all of the transient variety: sleeping bags, fast-food wrappers, empty bottles of cheap wine, blown-out condoms, burned-up tins of Sterno, and no shortage of human shit. But no bullet-riddled walls.

Travis turned down the unpaved cul-de-sac of their second new search site, about a mile and a half from the home of the citizen who called in the gunfire. He figured they had an hour of good light left. After that, it would be impossible to see well enough inside the unlit homes. The development was made up of twenty-four units on four streets, all framed, but it looked like only about half had been hung with drywall before the project dried up.

Travis parked at the curb. "We probably ought to split up. We need to cover more ground before we lose the light."

"Okay," Ellie said, looking out the window at the massive homes with three-car garages. "But let's do this street together. Looks like they have five or six bedrooms."

They entered the first house through the door from the garage and stopped in their tracks when they saw two boot-size holes in the drywall in front of them.

"Oh shit," Ellie said, picking up the pace and heading for the wood-framed steps, with Travis right behind her.

Upstairs, they came to a room with a large picture window facing west. The sun was low enough in the sky that it shone directly through the window, making the brass bullet casings sparkle against the wooden floor. Their heads turned in unison to face a wall full of tight, uniform holes, and their cheers went up simultaneously. Travis was surprised when she gave him a long hug.

"We found it, Travis. This is it."

Travis counted eleven holes in the wall and three more in the ceiling. "Man, they really did shoot the place up. Just like Omar said."

Together, Ellie and Travis traced the eleven horizontally fired rounds through ten sheets of drywall, but there were no holes in the exterior wall.

"Looks like the rounds are buried in the wood and stucco," Travis said. "Need to get the crime scene guys out here, dig these out nice and careful. With any luck, E-Boy will hang on to the gun. We can do a comparison."

Ellie led him back to the room with the picture window. "I don't care so much about the rounds. It's the casings I want."

She kneeled down carefully among the dozen nuggets of brass. "Not even dusty yet. These are perfect."

"What are you thinking?" Travis asked.

Ellie nodded toward his waist. "The bullets you have in your forty cal right now. When did you load them?"

Travis thought it over. "About a week ago, at the range. Why?"

"And when you loaded up, where did you get the ammo?"

"From the range master," Travis said. "What are you getting at?"

"No, I mean specifically. Where was your ammo before you put it in the magazine?"

"In a box, Ellie. What's your point?"

"Right, put there by a machine." Travis had never really thought about it like that before, but he knew where she was going.

"Then you come along and take it out."

Travis smiled. "Yeah. Right out of the box."

"And that's pretty much how everybody does. From the box to the gun," Ellie said. "And here's the real beauty of it. With a semiauto, you don't just pick up a round and slip it into a cylinder or drop it into a breech. No, you have to fit each one into a spring-loaded, tight-fitting magazine. And to do that, you push your thumb firmly against the smooth metal jacket of the round. Just you. Nobody else."

"I'll be damned."

"Yeah." Ellie pulled rubber-tipped tweezers and a small ziplock bag from her pocket. Travis figured she'd been carrying the tool all day, hoping for a chance to put it to use. "Back in the day, a semiauto casing was a great place for a talented fingerprint expert to collect a latent. But these days, you give a DNA examiner a recently discharged shell casing from a semiauto? Now you're talking home field advantage."

She picked up a casing with her tweezers and dropped it into the plastic bag. "And we got fourteen cracks at it."

"And," Travis said, "Chunks and E-Boy met in prison. That means he's in CODIS."

"You got it." She looked at the brass casing through the plastic. "Call Murphy. Tell him we found the site. I'll get hold of the crime lab. Let 'em know we've got a priority job."

Ellie reached for her phone and paused. She must have seen the grin on Travis's face. Looking confused, she said, "What?"

"I'm just thinking about Ted. How proud he'd be of you."

She smiled back. "Maybe. But he'd also say we aren't there yet. Lot of police work left to do."

She was right about that. Travis pulled out his phone and dialed Sean Murphy.

55

The emergency room at Paradise Valley Hospital in National City was a busy place even at 12:45 on a Tuesday morning. Mothers comforting feverish infants, seniors on walkers and canes, and more than a few of the homeless brigade just looking for a place to crash. In the past thirty minutes, no fewer than a dozen people had stumbled up to the ER reception desk. Except for a guy with a knife sticking from his gut, every one of them had been told by the staff nurse to have a seat. There were a few empty chairs, but Travis stood in the farthest corner of the room with his back to the wall and his arm draped over his concealed gun. Still, he was pretty sure he could feel a host of airborne diseases attacking his nasal passages. Typically, it was the kind of scene that would irritate the hell out of him, but not tonight.

Unlike the waiting patients, Travis had no complaints. A cop killer was off the street. The life of an innocent young man might be returned to its promising path. And, most important, the death of Ted Rosado had been avenged.

DNA belonging to Emiliano "E-Boy" Cisneros had been found on nine of the fourteen casings Ellie and Travis had recovered from the vandalized house. As anticipated, his profile was found in CODIS, the Combined DNA Index System. Cisneros was a documented member of the East San

Diego Santos street gang who had been floating in and out of group homes and juvenile correctional facilities since the age of ten. The initial beefs had been for graffiti and shoplifting. His first documented act of violence was when he was twelve; he punched a store clerk who'd caught him shoplifting. At thirteen, Cisneros was arrested for assault with a deadly weapon with a great bodily injury enhancement—he'd stabbed a kid in gym class. According to the sentencing report, Cisneros went at his classmate with a butterfly knife, inflicting ten stab wounds. If the teacher hadn't been trained as an EMT, the victim would have bled to death at the scene. Since the law required that he be tried as a juvenile, Cisneros was remanded to the California Division of Juvenile Justice until his twenty-fifth birthday.

Three months after getting out, Cisneros was arrested on a homicide charge. A late recant by the lone witness kept the case from going to trial, but Cisneros ended up with a three-year prison sentence for an assault he committed while in pretrial confinement. While serving that time, Cisneros not only became a soldier for La Eme but also shared a cell with Chunks Gutierrez.

Cisneros had been released on parole eleven days before the death of Ted Rosado. A warrantless emergency entry into the last known address of Cisneros by patrol officers of the National City PD had resulted in his arrest. Sofia Ortega had been found in a bedroom closet.

In a National City PD interview room, Sean Murphy and an NCPD gang detective took a run at Cisneros, but he refused to even acknowledge his name. The only information he provided was that the teenage girl had been a willing participant and that she had told him she was eighteen.

"Just ask her," he said. "She knows what to say."

Cisneros was booked into the central jail in downtown San Diego. Due to his Le Eme pedigree, he was tucked away in administrative segregation and kept under constant surveillance. Cisneros was a major shot caller whose influence moved like a fluid river throughout the California prison system, even into the tributaries of local jails. Travis was certain the gangster's next stop would be death row at San Quentin. Or maybe the supermax at Pelican Bay, where he could spend the rest of his years buried alive in an eight-by-eight concrete tomb.

So far, Sofia had not said a word. Even when, after much persuasion by Ellie, she'd agreed to come to the hospital for a medical exam, she'd only nodded silently. When they arrived, Sofia had clutched Ellie's hand, drawing her into the examination room with her. They had been there for the past two hours.

It was almost three o'clock when the two women emerged from the treatment rooms. Travis escorted them to the unmarked car. Ellie rode with Sofia in the backseat while they drove to the Polinsky Children's Center. Ellie had called ahead and asked that, under the circumstances, an exception be made to the center's rules regarding the housing of juveniles by gender. The director had agreed. When they pulled up to the entrance, Hector was standing outside, waiting for his sister.

After the Ortega siblings were settled, Travis called Molly to let her know he was safe and that they had arrested the gunman who killed Ted Rosado. He was going to attend the 9:00 A.M. meeting with Dannie Gaines, and after that he planned to come home and sleep for a week.

They pulled into the Vista Detention Facility parking lot at 4:00 A.M. Travis asked the night watch to wake Omar Ortega and bring him to the legal consult interview room. Omar walked into the small room cuffed and still limping. When he saw the deputies sitting at the table, he froze.

"Why are you here? What's happened?"

"E-Boy is Emiliano Cisneros," Travis said. "He's in custody. We made him off DNA from shell casings we collected at the construction site you told us about. Your brother and sister are now in protective custody. Together."

Travis did not mention what Ellie had told him about Sofia. The medical examination had been completed by a doctor assigned to the sexual assault response team. There had been signs of significant trauma and rough sexual activity. The doctor had concluded that Sofia had been the victim of violent rape, most likely multiple times.

"And my mother?"

"The prosecutor on this case, Danielle Gaines, has contacted the chief legal counsel for Immigration and Customs Enforcement," Ellie said. "No action is going to be taken against your mother. Ms. Gaines will petition the court for a special U visa that will allow your mom to stay in the country for the foreseeable future. Out of custody, of course. She should be released first thing in the morning."

Omar sat down at the table, visibly stunned. "Everyone is safe?"

"Yes, Omar," Ellie said. "Everyone is safe."

"What about me? What happens to me now?"

"Right now, nothing changes," Travis said, not wanting to get Omar's hopes up too high. "We're meeting with the prosecutor in a few hours. I'm sure your attorney will be in touch with her, too."

"I told you I would testify," Omar said without hesitation. "I'll do it. Chunks. This Cisneros guy. Let's get on with it."

"Let's talk about that later," Travis said, offering up no details on the death of Gutierrez.

Ellie told Omar she had gotten to talk with both his brother and his sister. She talked about what fine young people they were. How certain she was that his father would be proud of the job Omar was doing. She told him what Hector said: *"Omar is always right."*

"You guys worked all night for me?" Omar looked like he still couldn't believe what was happening.

"Yeah, we did," Travis said. "For you. For Deputy Rosado. So did half a dozen detectives, a SWAT team, and a bunch of lab geeks."

"I never would've . . ." He looked down at the table, then up at each of the deputies in turn. "Thank you." The boy swallowed hard, and at the moment, Travis saw him as exactly that. A boy. Who was quickly becoming a man.

Omar stood up and headed for the door.

"Hey, Omar," Travis called. "About what you said, why you ran and all."

Omar looked back. Travis stood and approached him. "I don't agree with you. You don't have to run from cops. But I get it. I understand why you did. I think Deputy Rosado would have understood too."

Travis put his hand out. At first Omar hesitated, then he nodded. He brought both his cuffed hands forward and shook Travis's hand firmly. "Thank you. And I am sorry about your friend. I wish I could've helped him."

Travis held on. "I know you do, Omar. And you did. You helped him a lot."

Once they were alone, Ellie asked, "Should we have told him? It seems like he has a right to know."

"You mean about Sofia?"

"All of it," Ellie said. "Sofia. His own troubles. He's still a long way from getting clear of this."

"Later. Let him have the moment."

"You're not driving home, are you?" she asked, looking concerned, as they left the consultation room.

"Nah, I'd never make it. I'll hit the crash cave. Set the alarm. I'll be at the meeting on time."

"I'm heading down to Ridgehaven now. Catch a couple of hours in Rob's office. If you're interested, he's got two couches. One's even a pullout. Remember what Teddy said. I need to beef up my rep a bit."

"Very funny, but I'm pretty sure after all this, your rep will be just fine."

56

Omar lay in his bunk, wide awake. Miguel was asleep below, turned to the wall, snoring in a steady rumble that Omar had timed out as once every nine seconds. Omar had been listening to Miguel for the past two hours, but it didn't matter. After being returned to his cell, he knew he wouldn't be going back to sleep.

For the first time since he had gotten into the car with Chunks and E-Boy, Omar started to breathe normally. As he'd listened to the deputies, little by little, almost word by word, the crushing burden he'd been carrying began to ease. It wasn't like everything was going to spring back to normal. He knew he wasn't going to be joining the army. Attending graduation was out too. He didn't get to turn the clock back on anything. But compared to twenty-four hours ago? Man, at least now he could breathe. It was as if he were floating. He remembered the sensation and thought back. How old had he been? Seven? Maybe eight? With his father. Bobbing. Swaying. Just breathing.

It had been a Sunday when the family had spent the day at Bonita Cove, near Mission Bay. Sofia and Hector were splashing in the shallow water under his mother's watchful eye. Mateo took Omar out on the water in a rented rowboat just big enough for the two of them. Omar had never been on the water before, and when the boat began to bob up and down and rock side to side, he'd grabbed hold, trying to steady it, but he only made it worse.

In a near panic, he'd told his dad to turn back. Mateo just laughed, stretched out on the bottom of the boat, then pulled Omar down next to him and held him tight. Soon the boat was gently swaying, like it was part of the water. They lay there, watching clouds pass overhead, calling out the shapes as they floated on the sea.

That's what he felt like now, like he was on some mystic body of water. Sofia and Hector were safe. His mom was being given special consideration. He could start to think ahead, maybe see some chance for a normal life. He could almost feel his father's strong arms around him and see the clouds passing overhead.

The lights came on and the door clicked open. Miguel came off his bunk like he was shot from a gun. He stood in the middle of the cell and rubbed his face, then reached out and slapped Omar on the hip. His morning voice was a low mumble.

"Wake up, homes."

"Already awake, Migs," Omar said, masking his regret that the moment was gone.

"Hey man, Chorizo Tuesday. I mean, it ain't great, but it ain't gray. Come on."

Omar wondered if it was Chorizo Tuesday for the all the mods or just the homeboys. "I'll be out in a minute. You go on."

"Shit won't last. You're gonna miss out." Miguel left to join the already growing crowd in the dayroom.

Wanting to find that peaceful place again, Omar closed his eyes, but the chorus of voices and the sound of the television told him that wasn't going to happen. He sat up and dropped to the floor, landing on his good foot.

Jailhouse chorizo? Pass. He rolled out his shoulders and assumed his push-up position. He stacked his bum leg on top of his good one, lifted his head, and stared at the wall. He was going to see this through. One way or another, he was going to come out okay. He just knew it. He felt a surge of strength. He started in.

One, two, three, four . . .

Maybe Ransom would come soon with good news.

Eleven, twelve, thirteen . . .

The deputies had definitely come around. Had he even won over that Jackson guy?

Twenty-five, twenty-six, twenty-seven . . .

He'd gotten an email from Ms. Hillman. It had been printed out and slipped under his door. She wrote that she knew he was innocent, that when he was released she'd help him sign up for classes at community college. He still had a bright future in front of him.

Forty-three, forty-four, forty-five . . .

When Omar had first read the letter, he'd wanted to tear it up. All had looked hopeless. But maybe she was right. He imagined someday, many years from now, pulling that same letter from a drawer. In a house. Where he lived with a family of his own.

Fifty-five, fifty-six, fifty-seven . . .

Maybe, once he got all this behind him, he could find a part-time job. One good enough that they could still move to a new place. Yeah. Community college could be a good start.

Sixty-four, sixty-five, sixty-six . . .

Miguel returned, carrying his breakfast clamshell. He put his foot on Omar's back and pushed down, laughing, his mouth full of tortilla. "Now do a push-up, soldier boy."

Omar turned his head and smiled, pushing up off the floor hard enough that Miguel almost lost his balance.

"Damn, ese." Miguel shoved in another mouthful. "You like the Hulk or some shit."

Seventy-two, seventy-three, seventy-four . . .

Omar kept his head up, watching to see if Miguel would try again, but the boy was looking out the window. "Oh shit, Seso," he said, almost choking on his food. "Check her out. Oh my god, look at this girl."

"Hang on, man."

Eighty-one, eighty-two, eighty-three . . .

"No, serious. Come look. She's going in the courthouse." Miguel was looking out the window, pointing frantically, a tortilla still in his hand. "Damn, you gotta see."

"In a sec."

"Man, if I wasn't locked up and I could hit that every day? I'd never go back to bangin'. I'd be stayin' home and never going out. I swear, they want me to go straight? That shit right there would do it."

Ninety-eight, ninety-ninety, one hundred.

Omar jumped up from the floor, careful to favor his busted foot. He looked at Miguel, still staring out the window like he'd found love or something. There were times Migs still seemed like an eight-year-old. Getting all excited about some girl a hundred yards away, barely visible through a fogged-over, wire-meshed window. Dumb as it might be, Omar liked that about him.

Shaking out his arms, Omar walked over to stand next to Miguel and look out the window. He draped an arm around his friend's shoulders. "All, right, Migs, let me see this—"

A violent shove from behind pressed him up against the cement block wall. His face hit the window. Whoever was behind him was strong, but Omar's energy was still surging. He used his good foot to push back off the wall and slammed his attacker against the metal bunk.

Omar turned with his fists already up, ready to go on the offensive. Five sets of eyes stared back, their faces wrapped up and covered with T-shirts. Migs was cowering in a corner of the cell, still clutching his clamshell. His mouth hung open, full of tortilla and chorizo. He looked at Omar with helplessness and sorrow etched into his expression.

Hands blurred through the air. Omar felt a dozen quick thrusts into his stomach and chest. Even after he fell to the floor, the hands and cuts kept coming. He heard an alarm, doors slamming. Guards shouting. Migs screaming. His attackers fled in a rush. It was chaos.

He pulled his legs up to his chest and lay balled up on the cold cell floor, filled with a loneliness like none he'd ever known.

He wondered if his mother would still be allowed to stay. He hoped so. If she did leave, if she went back to her village in Coahuila, Hector and Sofia would go too. It would be hard on them at first, but they'd be together. They could be happy there. He hoped that someday Sofia would meet a man who made her feel safe. Loved. Who made her smile. Maybe Hector had finally figured things out and would get his act together. Omar felt sure he would. He gave a final thought to all that might have been, were it not for . . . No. Not now.

The noises faded away and Omar found himself once again in the bottom of a small boat, staring into a brilliant blue sky. From somewhere beyond the water, he heard his father's voice, strong and filled with love.

Omar emptied his mind of all the things that had somehow led to this moment and called out.

It's me, Apa. Omar. Ya voy.

As the sea bobbed and swayed beneath him, Omar Ortega took a last breath, closed his eyes, and sank slowly into the warmth of the mystic waters.

57

0830 HOURS

Travis slept soundly for almost three hours. When he woke up in the crash cave, he splashed water on his face, then threw on a pair of jeans, a T-shirt, and a windbreaker. The I-15 was a parking lot, so he cheated, taking the HOV lane and getting the old pickup to do eighty. It was almost nine by the time he pulled up to Ridgehaven. The elevator looked to be stuck on the third floor, so he took the stairs, hoping the proceedings hadn't started yet.

He was eager to fill Dannie in on the arrest of E-Boy. On top of that, he'd decided he was going to make a hard argument that Omar be released. Sure, a case could be made that the kid was a participant in Ted's murder, but that would be a cruel interpretation of the law. He was pretty sure that Sean Murphy would argue that they needed to hold the threat of charges over Omar's head to ensure his cooperation. But Travis was confident that Omar's status could be changed from suspect to witness and that Omar would do the right thing.

Getting him into the army might be a stretch, but Travis figured that, with a little help from Carol Hillman, Omar might still be able to give the valedictory address. If not, he could at least walk across the stage to get his high school diploma. Travis had every intention of being there to see it.

He took the steps two at a time, then jogged to the conference room. He walked in and Dannie Gaines stopped talking. She turned, her face somber. "Hey, Travis, grab a chair. Sorry, we just went ahead and got started."

Travis looked at the end of the table, where Sheriff Collier was staring out the window that overlooked the I-15, his lips pressed into a thin, straight line. Enrique Soledad sat beside Ellie; both were expressionless. Murphy was conspicuously absent. Travis took a seat and Dannie picked up where she had left off.

"As I was saying, the case against Cisneros . . . there really isn't one. The DNA lifted off the casings allows us to charge him with misdemeanor vandalism. There's no way that ties him to the scene where Deputy Rosado was murdered. We got nothing from the car. We've got no gun. The only real tie-in was Omar's testimony, and even then, honestly, it wasn't going to be a slam dunk. But now?" Dannie threw her pen down on the legal pad in front of her. "We got nothing, guys."

Confused, Travis asked, "What happened? Omar seemed ready to go when we talked to him. What changed his mind?"

He'd thought Ellie's eyes were red-rimmed from exhaustion; now he realized she had been crying. "Don't you know, Travis?" she asked, her voice barely above a whisper.

He scanned the room. He seemed to be the only one who was lost. "Don't I know what?"

"Oh, Travis, you don't know?" Dannie turned her chair to face him. "I'm sorry. I would've thought you heard."

"Heard what?"

"Omar is dead."

The room was silent except for Ellie's sniffling and the sheriff's knuckles rapping lightly against the wooden table.

"Tell me that again?"

"He was attacked in his cell this morning. Stabbed. It was some kind of orchestrated hit. Looks like five or six involved. Murphy's there now. He called just before you walked in. Said, from what he's got so far, word got out that Cisneros was in custody at Central. The plan all along was that if Cisneros got booked, the green light was on."

"How could they know?" Travis asked. "I mean, we just arrested Cisneros. He didn't even hit Central booking until six o'clock."

"Murphy seized a cell phone off a player named Luis Valdez. Goes by Psycho," Dannie said. "Looks like the hit got phoned in."

Travis felt a wave of nausea, just like when he had watched the film of Ted's murder. There was nothing he could say. Nothing he could do.

Turning to the sheriff, Dannie said, "I'm sorry, sir. He was literally *five minutes* from being moved into protective custody. I'd already signed the authorization. I was going to petition the court for his release this morning, but in the meantime, I wanted him to be safe."

"It's not your fault, Dannie," Collier said. "Maybe we were all moving too fast. Maybe we should've . . ." Travis was startled when his boss's voice broke. "My god, how did I let this happen?"

An uncomfortable silence hung over the room until the sheriff spoke again. "Does his family know? His mother?"

"Not yet, sir," Enrique said.

"I'm sure I'm the last person they want to see," Collier said, "but I can't put it on anyone else."

He turned to face Ellie. "Deputy Peralta, could you come along? You and Deputy Jackson?"

"I've never met her, sir," Ellie said. "I don't know how much help I could be."

"But you met her son," Sheriff Collier said, looking at her and Travis in turn. "Both of you worked hard for him. I'd like her to hear it from you. That we know her boy didn't kill Deputy Rosado. I want her to know we'll do everything we can to make people understand that."

It was Ellie's turn to look out at the morning traffic on the I-15. Travis filled the silence.

"We'll come, sir."

"They should be together," Ellie said, still staring out the window. "The Ortegas. We should tell them all together."

Sheriff Collier nodded in agreement. "Yes, you're right. Dannie, can you make it happen?"

"I'll see what I can do. In the meantime, we need to figure out a way to hold on to Cisneros." Dannie looked at Ellie. "I hate to ask, but can you talk to Sofia?"

"She'll do it," Ellie said. "I'm sure she will."

EPILOGUE

ONE WEEK LATER

Travis reached out and touched the black marble, cool and smooth against his palm. He allowed his fingers to drift down and trace the ornate engravings: The inlaid shape of a badge and the brightly colored image of a smiling face. Words and dates.

THEODORE JACOB ROSADO
TEDDY TO HIS FRIENDS
LOVING FATHER AND HUSBAND TO HIS FAMILY
DEDICATED DEPUTY SHERIFF TO THE PEOPLE

Travis gripped the headstone and tried to shake it, knowing it wouldn't budge. He wanted to feel the strength of it. The permanence. He stepped back and, in his dress greens, took a position of attention at the foot of the grave and offered a salute.

Two days ago, Ted's funeral had been attended by more than three thousand deputy sheriffs, police officers, state and federal agents, and other law enforcement professionals from around the world. Every state in the country had been represented. The Royal Canadian Mounted Police had dispatched a color guard. Mayors and other elected officials from throughout San Diego County, plus the lieutenant governor of California, had put their political differences aside to pay their respects to Deputy Theodore Jacob Rosado.

The motorcade from the church in Murrieta to the Oak Hill cemetery in Escondido had stretched for miles on the I-15, with more than a thousand police vehicles in the procession. On the one hand, Travis had been proud of the homage paid to his fellow deputy. On the other, he couldn't help but see that the widow and her children were completely overwhelmed by the enormity of it all. Travis knew the family had just wanted to say good-bye.

Molly walked up from behind him and took his hand in both of hers, leaning her head against his shoulder. She looked at the polished head-stone, which was surrounded by dozens of floral arrangements that still looked fresh.

"You think Teddy would have liked all that? I mean, the cameras, news stations? Half a dozen helicopters? All the people?"

"Causing a traffic jam from Fallbrook to Escondido?" Travis allowed himself a smile. "I think he would've gotten a kick out of that. The rest of it? I don't know. He was really a pretty down-to-earth guy."

Molly looked at the comparatively small group that had gathered nearby. "Different feeling today, huh?"

"No doubt about that," Travis said.

"You ready?"

"Yeah," Travis said, his gaze still focused on the black stone. "Let's go."

He kept hold of her hand and let her lead him down the grassy hill.

Joaquin stood alongside Sheriff Collier, some distance away from the small gathering of people who were waiting for the ceremony to begin. Joaquin was certain the sheriff had been advised by his legal team not to do this interview. He was sure that Collier had been told to avoid accepting any sort of responsibility or making any apologies. He'd always heard that cops were terrible at taking legal advice.

Sheriff Collier had asked Anna Ramirez to translate what he was saying, so she was standing next to him. He wanted people to hear as directly from him as possible. Although he began by defending the initial arrest of Omar Ortega by his deputies, he credited those same deputies with eventually proving Omar's innocence. He accepted full responsibility for the public unrest and even for the death of Omar Ortega. He said that for any person to die while in the custody of law enforcement was a significant failure, but when the person was innocent of any crime, it was a travesty and required accountability.

"The fault is mine." Much as he had done just a few days prior, Sheriff Collier looked directly into the camera as he spoke, but his fighting spirit was gone, replaced by sorrow and humility. "It's clear I was mistaken in my initial assessment of Mr. Ortega.

"Omar Ortega was indeed a fine young man and played no role in the murder of Deputy Rosado. In fact, it was Mr. Ortega who identified the killers responsible for Deputy Rosado's death. The loss of these men, Omar and Ted, is doubly tragic. If I made any statement to the contrary, I was wrong, and I deeply regret my personal rush to judgment in this case."

Anna translated perfectly, though her voice broke several times. When she was done, and with the cameras still running, Joaquin shook the sheriff's hand. "You're a man of great honor, sir. I know I can speak for the community when I say thank you for your heartfelt comments."

Joaquin signed off. When the camera's light went out, the sheriff's shoulders slumped and his face fell. Without another word, Collier walked to a waiting staff car.

"He thought it would be disrespectful to stay," Anna said, to Joaquin's look of surprise. "I mean, after all that's happened."

Joaquin watched as the staff car drove slowly through the peaceful crowd that had gathered at the entrance to the cemetery. The sheriff's department had asked that all demonstrators respect the family's privacy, and they had, keeping their distance. There no longer seemed to be a division between the two sides; signs and flags had been replaced by lit candles. Everyone stood together outside the iron gates, a few praying aloud.

"How about you?" Joaquin asked. "Are you staying?"

She nodded. "I'd like to. Is it okay if I stand back here with you? I don't want to intrude."

"Of course," Joaquin said. "I'd like that."

Hector stared at the long wooden box and thought, There's no way Omar's inside. That box could never hold his brother. He would fight his way out. He'd punch through those boards. Or better yet, he'd talk his way out.

Yeah, Hector thought, smiling inside. No way that box can hold him. Hector didn't see how Omar could be gone. It just didn't make any sense.

He sat beside his mother, who rocked gently back and forth in her chair, eyes closed. Sofia sat on Isadora's other side. Hector felt foolish in his too-large suit, but his mother had really wanted him to wear it. It had been Omar's until he outgrew it. Now it was Hector's.

He used his fingers to count all the things that, had he done them differently, would have led to Omar still being alive. If he hadn't gone to the wall. If he hadn't opened the door. If he had listened to Sofia and called the police. Then, today, instead of sitting here, they would be living in a new house. Omar would be heading off to the army. Their lives would be almost like before.

He kept ticking off all the ways he'd let his brother down. He counted until both his hands turned to fists. His mother reached over and wrapped her hands around his.

"No mas, hijo. No mas."

Hector looked up from the knotted coffin and saw a deputy coming down the hillside, holding hands with a white woman. It was the same deputy who had come to Hector's school to talk to him. The one who brought Sofia to that place where they slept in bunk beds. He'd seemed kind of mean at school, but Sofia said he'd been nice to her.

The last time Hector had seen the deputy was when he came to tell them that Omar was dead. He'd been different that time, like a big kid who had just gotten beat up really bad. Why was he here?

Hector saw the deputy looking back at him. He didn't know what to do, so he just turned away and looked at the box. His hands turned into fists again.

Omar wasn't in there. No way.

Travis and Molly walked toward the small crowd. Travis spotted Omar's brother, Hector, but when he tried to make eye contact, the boy quickly looked away. Ellie and Rob Peralta stood at the back, with the Hillmans beside them. Travis steered Molly to join them. Ellie hugged Molly first, then squeezed Travis's arm. Unsmiling, she wore dark glasses and kept her arms crossed tightly as if to fight against the cold, though the morning had already begun to warm.

There were a few teenagers on hand. Most looked to be about the same age as Omar and seemed entirely uncomfortable with their surroundings, not sure how to behave at the funeral of a peer. One girl was crying openly. She stood with her hands to her face, shoulders hunched as she sobbed. A man and a woman—Travis figured them to be the girl's parents—stood on either side of her. Other adults clustered around the edges. Travis had heard that a number of Omar's teachers, some from elementary school, would be attending. Omar's defense attorney, Ransom Shaw, stood alone, away from the others. He made brief eye contact with Travis, then turned away without acknowledgment.

Travis turned at the sound of a closing car door. Sean Murphy and Dannie Gaines walked down the grassy slope toward the gravesite. Dannie was wearing a dark dress, Murphy was in pressed denim jeans and a navy blue blazer. Travis nodded toward his fellow cop and got a single grim nod back. Dannie forced a smile. He wondered if she felt it too . . . anger, despair, and shame at what they all had allowed to transpire.

The plain wooden casket was positioned above the freshly dug grave, a single bouquet of flowers on the closed lid. There was no headstone; instead, a single cement-brick marker had been set flush into the ground. The five-digit number that designated the grave location was chiseled into the brick, along with the year and the name: *Ortega*.

The ceremony was short and mostly in Spanish. A few of Omar's teachers spoke, and Travis saw Sofia whispering into her mother's ear, probably translating. When Travis had met Isadora, he'd been shocked at her youth and moved to tears by her grief and by the grace that she'd maintained in front of the strangers who'd brought the news of her son's death. Now, looking tiny, dressed entirely in black, she sat with her eyes closed, swaying gently in her chair, like a mother comforting a frightened child whom she held in her arms.

A few days earlier, Sofia had spent three hours with Dannie and Ellie, telling them how two men had grabbed her after she'd gotten off the bus at school. They'd forced her into a car and driven her to the apartment where she had later been found. Setting aside her shame—a shame Travis couldn't entirely understand, though he knew it was very real to the entire Ortega family—Sofia provided painful details that corroborated the medical evidence already collected.

At the end of the interview, she'd identified a photograph of one of the men who had kidnapped her and repeatedly raped her. She said she would tell her story to anyone who needed to hear it and she would identify the rapist in open court. Emiliano Cisneros had been rebooked, once again for charges that carried penalties far exceeding his life expectancy.

Even with Cisneros locked away, the family needed protection. La Eme would be eager to silence them.

Remembering Omar's story of how his mother grew up in the mountains of Mexico, where snow fell in the winter, Travis made a few phone calls. He and Anna Ramirez had gone to meet with Isadora and he explained his idea. They would be far away and safe. His friend spoke fluent Spanish and had a clean, comfortable trailer the family could live in. She would help Isadora find work. The kids would be able to go to school. Isadora had been grateful but uncertain. Travis hoped she would eventually accept the offer.

Prayers were said and the service concluded. Travis stood at a distance while the casket was lowered into the ground. One by one, the friends and family of Omar Ortega stood over the grave. Each one said a final good-bye, and many appeared to pray, as they tossed down a single handful of dirt. The hollow *thud* against the wooden box and the thought of the boy being buried in the ground nearly drove Travis to his knees. Isadora, who until that moment had been quiet in her grief, was finally overwhelmed, and her woeful sobs could be heard over the wind that blew through the oak trees.

The priest led the Ortegas to a waiting car. Travis turned to look for Ellie and saw that the Peraltas were getting into their own car. She didn't look back. Dannie and Sean were nowhere to be seen. The last of the attendees drifted away. Two men in black suits used shovels to finish filling in the grave, and then they too were gone.

Molly kissed him lightly on his cheek.

"Take all the time you want. I'll be in the car."

Finally alone, Travis moved in close and stood over the mound of freshly turned earth. Reaching into his pocket, he pulled out a single sheet of paper. It was just a copy. He'd taken the original from evidence and given it to Isadora. He'd sat with her and watched as she read the words written in Spanish, moving her finger across the page. Her smile grew with each glowing compliment. When she finished, she clutched the paper to her heart.

"Gracias, Señor Jackson. Gracias."

Travis went down on one knee and placed the letter on the grave, weighing it down with a smooth stone the size of a fist. He silently read the last paragraph, the words staying with him as he stood and walked away.

> *So again, Mr. and Mrs. Ortega, from all of us at James Madison High School, congratulations on your son's extraordinary academic achievement and his selection as class valedictorian. His spirit, drive, and can-do attitude are an inspiration to us all. Omar is a wonderful representative of our country's best and brightest. We are all very proud of him and we know he is destined to accomplish great things.*

ACKNOWLEDGMENTS

Thanks as always to the amazing team at Forge Books, particularly my editor, Melissa Ann Singer. Melissa was supportive from the start, pushing me to write a story that she recognized was deeply personal. Her early and continued encouragement kept me going.

Thanks to my agent, Jill Marr, and everyone at the Sandra Dijkstra Literary Agency. *Family* is not too strong a word to describe our bond.

Thanks to Ruben Navarrette, Jr., for his counsel, feedback, and friendship.

And to my wife, Olga Diaz, a woman who has personally experienced the world of Omar Ortega in a way that I, as a cop, never could. I've seen the heartache it has caused, but also the resilience, courage, and compassion it has forged within her. She has committed her life to providing equal opportunity to the marginalized young people of our country, who are so often overlooked. She inspires me every day.

A NOTE FROM THE AUTHOR

I'd like to tell you why it was important for me to write the story of Omar Ortega.

Omar is a fictional character, but I've met dozens of men just like him.

Omar represents people who travel the hazardous middle lane of barrio street justice, a virtual no-man's-land between two opposing forces. On one side are the cops, whose only real connections to the community are a badge and paycheck. They don't buy homes in that neighborhood. They don't send their kids to those local schools, coach soccer, or shop at the corner market. Four or five days a week, they vector in from some outlying suburb, occupy the streets for a required shift, dole out their personal standard of law and order, and leave.

In the lexicon of law enforcement, the other lane is occupied by *the bad guys,* and that description is not inaccurate. In almost any urban community, a small but impactful percentage of brutish men engage in low-level organized crime. We could and should debate the sociological causes of this dead-end choice, but no matter the cause, the reality remains. These are the street gangsters: men prone to violence, who extort, harass, and rob local businesses. Those who intimidate and threaten innocent families, and aggressively recruit new members, all in the furtherance of their clique.

It's no exaggeration to say these two sides are at war. The police, armed and equipped to a level of military readiness, routinely sweep in with overwhelming force. They ramrod and bulldoze their way into every alley, parking lot, and living room occupied by their enemy. As in any combat operation, the collateral damage inflicted on families and civilians is considered a regrettable but unavoidable part of the equation.

Street gangs may not have sophisticated equipment or training, but they have the real estate. They move with brazen fluidity. They hide in plain view and communicate in code. Like any committed insurgency, they are worthy opponents.

In the middle of all this, you find countless men like Omar Ortega.

When the cops see Omar, they see a gangster. So that is how they treat him.

When the gangsters see Omar, they see someone who should jump in, put in the work, and pay the tax. Too often, as in Omar's case, they threaten those dearest to him, creating a literal life or death dilemma of *go along to get along.*

This is Omar's reality, every day.

As I said, I've met dozens of men and boys like Omar. In a best-case scenario, I've met them under circumstances where I could be a positive force. Police officers have direct access to programs that can minimize the daily risks to people's lives, such as after-school activities that offer a safe haven from violence, not to mention air conditioning and a slice or two of pizza. The Police Athletic League, also known as PAL, should be part of every law enforcement agency in the country and funded with SWAT-like enthusiasm.

I had the good fortune to run a Police Explorer Post for ten years. Many of the young men and women who participated are currently working in law enforcement or other public service careers. Their stories represent my greatest professional victories.

But sometimes I met men like Omar when they were sitting across the table from me in an interrogation room, desperate to explain how they came to be in that car or on that corner. How in their mind, they had no choice. They would tell their stories; I'd sit and listen. Being fine young men, they'd tell the truth, and for that, they'd go to jail. Then to state prison. Some are still there. I think of them often and wonder what the outcome might have been if our paths had crossed earlier.

Omar's story as I have told it is not a stretch. It is, in fact, unsettling in its authenticity. I have come to understand this reality not only from my professional viewpoint but also in ways much more personal. My wife is the daughter of Mexican immigrants who came to this country a little more than forty years ago. When our son was born, my wife and I were proud to blend our two family heritages.

As the years have gone by, I've come to realize that the only thing that separated my son's life from the life of Omar and those like him is that my son was gifted with his grandparents' bravery and grit; his mother's intelligence, discipline and gumption; and my fair skin. If not for those thin slices of privilege, Omar's life could have been his. When something hits that close to home, you can't help but take notice of it.

That's why I conjured up the story of Omar. And that's why I wrote this book.

—Neal Griffin
San Diego, California
September 2019